Rude Awakening

His hand was now resting on her inner thigh, his forefinger almost absently brushing her sex. It wasn't as expedient as his more obvious caresses of a moment before, but it was still enough. Enough to make her orgasm continue to mount, gathering in her lower belly ready to burst through the dam. She focused all her attention on it. Fought to keep her thighs from trembling as her body strained in reach of it. Held her breath, her nostrils flaring in the agony of keeping herself silent. Waited. Just another few seconds would be all it would take. Another few seconds of that casually brushing finger. Just . . . one . . . more . . .

And McClusky withdrew his hand. Right at the last possible moment.

Rude Awakening
Pamela Kyle

BLACK LACE

Black Lace books contain sexual fantasies.
In real life, always practise safe sex.

This edition published in 2006 by
Black Lace
Thames Wharf Studios
Rainville Road
London W6 9HA

Originally published 1995

Typeset by SetSystems Ltd, Saffron Walden, Essex
Printed in Great Britain by CPI Bookmarque, Croydon, CR0 4TD

ISBN 0 352 33036 8
ISBN 9 780352 330369

The Random House Group Limited supports The Forest Stewardship
Council (FSC), the leading international forest certification organisation.
All our titles that are printed on Greenpeace approved FSC certified
paper carry the FSC logo. Our paper procurement policy can be found
at: www.rbooks.co.uk/environment

Mixed Sources
Product group from well-managed
forests and other controlled sources
www.fsc.org Cert no. TT-COC-2139
© 1996 Forest Stewardship Council

Chapter One

*B*elinda smoothed the skirt of her slinky black dress and lounged back in her chair in decadent comfort, a glass of champagne in her hand; the side-split of her skirt fell open to reveal a large expanse of naked white thigh.

She loved to dress up, to look the part, for a session of sexual domination; it always put her in the perfect mood. Not that this was ever difficult to do, and tonight was no exception. She was wearing a long, black, satiny number that clung to her figure in all the right places, accentuating her already voluptuous curves and tight enough to delineate every nuance of a naturally sexy body; even to the casual eye it was obvious she was wearing nothing beneath it. Black was her colour, matching as it did the jet of her hair and highlighting her stunning green eyes. She knew she was looking terrific and she felt just as she looked: dominant, and very, very sexy.

She turned to Alison, who was looking equally ravishing in a basque and nothing else. Her hair was as blonde as Belinda's was black and tumbling to her naked shoulders in a chaos of gentle curls. 'When do you think he'll be ready?' she asked.

Alison chuckled. 'Oh, he's ready right now. I mean,

have you ever known Robert not be ready for one of our little sessions?' She was dangling a leather strap between finger and thumb, and let it slap meaningfully onto the open palm of her hand. 'But seriously, yes, he's in there now' – she flicked her eyes towards an oak-panelled wall, where only a discreet handle betrayed the existence of a well-disguised door – 'naked and waiting.'

Belinda's eyebrows rose in surprise: she hadn't realised he was already *in situ*, awaiting the start of the session. And naked too! 'So what are we doing out here, then?' she protested, the thought of Robert's muscular body already teasing her loins. 'Why don't we go in and get started?'

Alison held up her hand. 'Whoa,' she chided gently. 'Patience, Bel, patience. We're in no hurry. And it never does any harm to make a masochist wait; to let him sweat a bit in nervous anticipation. It's all part of his torment. It's like the old chestnut, isn't it, where the masochist says, "Please whip me," and the sadist says. "No!"'

Belinda groaned good-humouredly, and Alison went on: 'So, let him stew for a while. I told him to stand facing the door with his legs apart and his hands on his head, so right now his heart will be thumping while he waits for the door to open, knowing two women will be walking in to find him like that ... but not knowing when. Gradually he'll become a nervous wreck.' She reached for the bottle of champagne, refilled her glass and raised it in toast. 'Enjoy your bubbly and relax for a while; Robert can wait. Cheers.'

Belinda grinned. 'Maybe Robert can, I just wonder can I? Cheers.' She raised her glass, champagne bubbles tickling her nose as she sipped from the crystal flute; she hoped Alison wouldn't be too long in getting the scene under way, whatever her motive, and looked around to help pass the time.

The upstairs sitting room in the Corsair mansion might easily have featured in *Country Living*. Reached via the back stairs of the magnificent old house – the narrow, angular stairway that would once have been access to the servants' quarters – it was furnished in a way that reeked of old money. The walls were panelled in light oak throughout, and were abundantly hung with original paintings of typical country scenes: dapper, red-jacketed huntsmen were everywhere, enjoying a stirrup cup with their hounds baying impatiently; or else leaping ditches in spectacular fashion, the nostrils of their noble mounts flaring, equine muscles rippling with effort as they enjoyed the thrill of the chase. Belinda had a passion for horses and had many such pictures, though not original, in her own tiny flat; they were as close as she'd ever come to having a horse of her own.

The room boasted a huge, old-fashioned fireplace, which in winter would blaze with logs cut from the mansion's estate but which now, in midsummer, featured instead a splendid filigree screen. Beside this, continuing the equestrian theme, was an ornate bootjack in which were standing a dozen or more leather crops – which, no doubt, were sometimes used for riding!

Above the fireplace, a pair of antique shotguns held pride of place on the breast, and a leaded-glass cabinet off to the side displayed an impressive and expensive collection of guns both antique and modern. The carpet was Axminster, with a pile so deep it was almost like walking on air.

Not just old money, Belinda decided as she dug her toes into the luxurious pile, almost inhaling the room's heady opulence; money, full stop. It took wealth, and a great deal of it, to live this sort of life-style.

She sipped chilled Krug; still, one would get bored with living like this ... given twenty or thirty years!

Finally, however, her eyes came back to the discreet door to the playroom, a *frisson* of excitement teasing her loins as she imagined Robert behind it, his naked body beading with sweat, perhaps beginning to tremble in anticipation of the women's entrance.

She slipped a hand into the split of her skirt, and pressed fingertips to her inner thigh' savouring the image.

Alison interrupted her thoughts. 'You know,' she said, 'I often wonder what those stuffed-shirt city associates of his would think if they could see him as he is now: not in one of his Savile Row suits waving his Filofax in control of his empire, but bollock-naked and with nothing to wave but his dick as he awaits a session of pain and depravity at the hands of two women.' She dipped a finger in champagne, ran it thoughtfully over her nipple, which was peeping enticingly over the top of her basque, and shivered in dreamy ecstasy. 'Mmmm, don't you just love champagne?'

She picked up her thread of thought and went on: 'Yes, one of these days I must take a photo of him standing like that. Threaten to send it to his secretary or something.'

Belinda was shocked. 'You wouldn't!'

'Send it, no,' Alison said with a chuckle, her blue eyes sparkling sapphires of mischief. 'But it'd be fun to threaten it, eh? Robert would be utterly mortified.'

Belinda chuckled with her, slowly shaking her head. 'You're a cruel bitch, and that's a fact.'

'I know. It's why Robert loves me, the dear.' She swigged the last of her drink, set the glass on the arm of the chair and pushed herself to her feet. 'So, are we going to get started, then?'

Belinda was up before she had finished.

'Oh crikey, yeah.'

Chapter Two

Robert's buttocks were smooth and taut, a creamy white against the year-round tan of the rest of his athletic body, and were unblemished but for the two angry red stripes striating them.

Alison was regarding her handiwork with a critical eye, and Belinda licked her lips wondering how far, tonight, Alison would permit her to go. The stirring heat between her legs, which had been growing steadily since the session began, was now a forest fire out of control; after almost two hours of constant arousal, she would have to come soon or burst with desire. The question was, how would her friend allow her that pleasure?

Alison's strap fell for a third time, making a resounding *thwack* as hard leather met yielding flesh, and the heat in Belinda's loins flared anew as Robert's buttocks clenched in sudden spasm and a third red stripe grew across them, glowing and burning.

Alison watched for a moment as Robert's buttocks gradually relaxed, then took a step closer. She reached between his tied-apart legs and was gratified to feel his penis hugely erect, throbbing hotly in her palm. She stroked it softly, thrilling to feel it pulse as she deliberately aroused it further, then let her hand come slowly back. She paused a while to massage his testicles, the fragile orbs restrained in their tight leather strap, then turned her hand over to let the back of a long middle finger glide up between his buttocks; she tickled the stretched skin of his perineum before sliding her finger right into the opened crevice. There, her fingernail scratched lightly across the puckered ring of his anus, lingering there to threaten his most dreaded intrusion.

Belinda watched, spellbound, as Robert's bottom twitched, his buttocks tightening in the desperate but vain attempt to close the crevice between them and so save himself the humiliation he feared as Alison's finger began to prod, its tip worrying the delicate petals of his anal opening. The tension mounted, and Belinda pressed her thighs together, savouring the thrill of it as she watched Robert wait, helpless and tense.

But then Alison stepped back, withdrawing the threat of her finger, and the tension eased as if the room itself had suddenly sighed with relief; Robert, for now, was reprieved.

'So tell me,' Alison said, weighing the strap in her hand and addressing Belinda, 'have you got any further with David, then?'

Belinda forced her eyes away to look up, and shook her head with a wistful sigh.

'No. And it's beginning to look as if I never will,' she muttered, envying Alison her better fortune.

Alison and Belinda were lifelong friends.

They had discovered their mutual proclivity for sexual sadism in their final year at boarding school, when they and a group of other girls learned that a local lad had taken to spying on them in the showers. The girls had laid a trap and captured him – a rugged but simple farm-boy – and had stripped him naked before tying his hands to a showerhead. As the boy howled, they had set about his buttocks with plimsoles to teach him a lesson he wouldn't forget. They had kept it up for some while,

6

too, beating him mercilessly until, eventually tiring of the sport, one by one they had wandered away.

All, that is, but Belinda and Alison. Alone with the lad, a look had passed between the two girls, and they had both known, then, that each was getting far more from the lad's punishment than a mere sense of justice or a bit of fun at the boy's expense, as had seemed to be the extent of the other girls' interest. With a little embarrassment at first, they had realised it was giving them a sexual thrill.

And so, with the boy at their mercy, they had turned his punishment overtly sexual, keen to experiment ...

Stripping themselves – Alison naked, Belinda down to her panties – they had begun by teasing the boy, flaunting their bodies before him and watching in mute fascination as his penis thickened and grew. Male genitalia, aroused and expectant, were new to them – the copies of *Health And Efficiency* that were occasionally smuggled into the dorm never showed men erect – and they had taken it in turns to toy with him, enthralled by the bobbing and twitching of his penis as it grew to full erection, the various sighs and grunts they could bring to his throat with a touch here, and squeeze there. Gripping his balls, both were astonished and delighted to discover the extreme tenderness of a boy's testicles: with even moderate pressure they found they could have the lad writhing in utter agony ... and had squeezed them again and again for the thrill of so easily making him scream!

Their excitement growing, they once again picked up their gym shoes and aimed their rubber soles at the lad's reddened buttocks.

They had made him beg them to stop. And stop they had, eventually, but only to grow still crueller; making him beg them, then, for sexual relief – to implore them to 'please, finish me off', as their inexperienced but avid hands had excited him to the brink of orgasm. But inexperienced or not, they had known intuitively when

7

climax was imminent and had not the least intention of 'finishing him off'; instead they would deny his penis at the very last moment to leave it bucking and twitching as it strained for a climax it couldn't, alone, achieve, the boy's face contorting in sexual agony as a drop of clear fluid, but nothing more, appeared at the glistening eye at the tip of his tortured cock.

The girls themselves were no strangers to sexual sensations, to the warm glow of sexual arousal that would stir and moisten between their young thighs – masturbation, even mutual masturbation, in the dorm was common – but never had either girl experienced such sexual thrills as she did that afternoon. The sense of power it gave them to have the lad at their mercy – the fact they could pleasure or hurt him at will – was intoxicating, enough to dizzy them as it took them to unknown heights of erotic desire.

And only reluctantly had they finally freed the boy, though in a last act of wickedness had refused him his clothes, to laugh at him as he'd scampered away, naked and red-faced, his penis, erect and ungratified, jiggling obscenely before him. Laughing, maybe, but they, too, were in more urgent need of sexual release than either of them had ever recalled. And so was awakened in the two young women the need for sadism, and for domination in general, that would come to be at the core of their adult sexual beings.

However, Alison had fared by far the better of the two in terms of gratifying these dark and thrilling desires. From leaving school, and throughout her twenties, Alison had found a string of suitable partners – men who, if not actually masochistic, were sufficiently submissive to indulge her in her unusual sexual tastes so long as her games remained mild. It had been enough to keep her reasonably fulfilled until, at thirty-one, she had met and married Robert Corsair, wealthy heir to the Wondermart chain, when her fantasies were suddenly realised beyond even her wildest dreams.

Ruggedly good-looking, Robert Corsair was a tall, athletic man, who played tennis and squash like a pro; a real jock. He ran his business empire with an iron fist, and, to most who knew him, he was the epitome of machismo: the dominant, Alpha male. It all belied, however, his sexual nature. For Robert Corsair was not just sexually submissive, but a dyed-in-the-wool masochist with an amazing tolerance for pain. Pain, and for most other imaginable aspects of sado-masochistic activity: Alison's boat had come in. And today, at thirty-three, she lived in fabulous style in the Corsair mansion, spending much of her time exploring and exploiting those tolerances to their absolute limits.

Belinda had not had Alison's luck. Despite having had many lovers in a life largely devoted to hedonistic pursuit – at least, as far as the limited budget of a struggling writer allowed – she had yet to find her sexual counterpart. And the only fulfilment of her sadistic needs, apart from in fantasy, had come in recent months, when Alison had taken to occasionally allowing her to participate in her sessions with Robert.

Even then, such participation was slightly bitter-sweet and frustrating. Bitter-sweet since, Belinda knew, the main reason she was invited to take part at all was in order that Alison would have more to control. Alison was a control freak and had been for as long as Belinda had known her. As children it was always Alison who would say what game they would play and she wouldn't play at all unless she was in charge, calling the shots. And she hadn't changed: Alison got off on control. Having an additional person there for one of her sessions with Robert gave her more to manipulate, was all. Belinda was under no illusions regarding her friend's motivation, and couldn't deny that it rankled her slightly: she was essentially a pawn in Alison's game, as she had been for most of her life.

And her frustration, in part, was a spin-off of this. For although Alison had twice allowed Robert to fuck her –

9

his penis was large and enticing, and after a session of exciting SM she would be longing to have it inside her – this wasn't usually on offer: Robert was Alison's man, not for sharing unless Alison was directly to benefit in some way, and the only sexual contact he was more usually permitted with Belinda was oral, when he would be made to lick her to climax. This was as much for the purpose of Robert's humiliation – the presence of another woman giving Alison this further option for her husband's subjugation – as any act of altruism on Alison's part, for Belinda's pleasure *per se*.

Still, Belinda wasn't complaining: Robert was good with his tongue, and whatever the principal reason for his having to use it on her, he always brought her to good, fulfilling orgasms. And having the opportunity to indulge in dominant sex, slight dampers or not, well, it was certainly better than nothing at all.

Belinda gazed, now, at the glowing stripes on Robert's bottom, thrilling to the sight of them, knowing the pain they had caused; breathless in anticipation of the next stroke as Alison's arm poised, about to deliver it.

And deliver it she suddenly did: the strap fell with an abrupt *thwack*, brought down with force to draw a fourth parallel stripe across Robert's buttocks and bringing a muffled grunt from his throat. Belinda pressed her fingertips through the thin satin at the front of her skirt, applying a gentle pressure to her pubic mound in order to contain the volcano bubbling within; that, and the better to savour it as she watched Robert's buttocks clench in pain and a fresh wave of excitement surged through her loins.

Alison's arm dropped to her side, allowing Robert a moment's needed respite, and she turned to Belinda, picking up the conversation from where she'd left off: 'But I thought you had high hopes of David being submissive?' she said, exertion and her own growing arousal quickening her breathing.

She was referring to David McFarlane, a stockbroker by profession, whom Belinda had met at a party some six months before. They had become occasional lovers, and Belinda had for a while harboured hopes that he might be masochistically inclined; once, she had squeezed his balls a little too hard during foreplay, and though he had yelped and complained in no uncertain terms, there was no doubt that his cock had responded, hardening further into her palm; excited in spite of – because of? – the pain. Another time she had inadvertently walked into the bathroom while he was in there using the toilet. He had blustered and blushed, and yelled at her to get out. But when she hadn't, and had lingered a while to watch, she was sure she had seen a dark excitement glittering in his eyes. Had the humiliation of a woman watching him urinate, like it or not, turned him on?

But since, sadly, there had been no further sign that David was at all masochistic, and any attempt Belinda had made to steer him in a submissive direction had been met with resolute dissent. Her hopes, gradually, had faded and were now all but gone.

She said so with a sigh, just as Alison laid a fifth stroke directly over the fourth, and Robert's tethered body snapped rigid before it began to shake.

'Just see he's all right, will you, Bel,' said Alison. 'That one was pretty severe.'

Belinda forgot about David and moved to the front of the padded leather trestle over which Robert was bound. His ankles were tied to the trestle's feet, keeping his legs spread wide, and his arms had been pulled forward and down to where his wrists had been cuffed, so keeping his chest pressed hard to the bench and the flesh of his buttocks stretched taut. He couldn't move his body at all, though his head was left free.

Belinda crouched in front of him, and lifted his chin to look into his face. There was a penis-shaped gag in his mouth, and he was making mewling noises around it;

11

he was sweating profusely, and his brow was knotted with pain. Seeing his agony, Belinda felt a *frisson* of excitement tingle her spine.

But his eyes were heavy-lidded and she saw ecstasy in them as well as pain. She knew that in his own, different way, Robert was enduring his anguish with as much gratification as it was giving her, Belinda, to see it. How awful to be a masochist, she thought.

'Yes, he's fine,' she announced. 'He can take plenty more yet, I'm sure.'

'Good,' said Alison.

And struck, hard, with the strap.

Robert's head snapped up with a jerk and his face contorted with sudden new agony. Belinda smiled, and moved back to where Alison was stroking burning buttocks with tender fingertips, smoothing away pain with a sensual caress.

'Yes, he can take quite a bit,' said Alison, with what might have been pride. 'Such a frightful masochist, aren't you, dear?'

Robert grunted, the gag suppressing an obedient 'yes', and Alison grinned and turned to Belinda.

'But not so with David then, after all,' she said. 'What a terrible shame. Here,' she handed Belinda the strap as her palm slid tenderly over Robert's buttocks to reach between his legs, 'just give me a minute, then you can vent your frustration on Robert: give him a half dozen yourself.'

Robert's buttocks were on fire: the last two strokes, especially, had been wicked. But, agony that it was, it was as nothing compared with the almost unbearable ache in his balls. An ache, partly, that was due to the cruel tightness of the cock-strap fitted around them; Alison had strapped it onto him at the start of the session – how long ago now? An hour? Two? In his suffering it was difficult to tell.

But an ache, mainly, that was the ache of sexual

frustration. For Alison had kept him aroused for most of the day in preparation for the evening's sessions. She had kept him naked for a start, itself perversely exciting, not least with Alison's pretty young maid in the house, coming and going about her duties, her young eyes witness to his nakedness, to his abject submission. Her young eyes seemed almost to mock, and the humiliation of that was profound (serving only to further excite him; sometimes he cursed his masochism).

And then had come the session itself, and all the two women had done to him, had been making him do for their pleasure. All of it further arousing him. All of it further frustrating him.

And now, on top of all else, a hand – whose hand he couldn't be sure – had snaked between his spread thighs and was casually handling his penis; a wrist brushing his testicles with each stroke as it fondled his straining shaft; running up and down the length of it and wanking him with delicate fingers. But fingers that were a little too delicate, that were cleverly cruel, doing just enough to torment, not quite enough to bring him to climax. They were driving him out of his mind.

He wanted, desperately, to come. But was being, he knew, deliberately thwarted; the hand kept him right on the edge, but careful to deny him the relief it was so wickedly making him crave.

He tried to focus his mind: to picture the two beautiful women at whose mercy he was, in the hope the imagery would provide the additional stimulus necessary to trigger his climax. He knew there would be a price to pay if he did manage to come, so cheating that hand of its cruel intent, but he strained to anyway. He was desperate enough not to care as he made the images appear in his mind:

Both women were very attractive, and the way they were dressed, tonight, made them especially so. Alison was wearing a basque, and apart from her shoes nothing else; her nipples, with their dark areolae, peeping enticingly over the bodice, her golden bush exposed below. Belinda, less brazen but no less ravishing, was wearing a long figure-clinging dress in shiny black satin, cut low to reveal the deep cleavage between her voluptuous breasts and with a side-split up to the waist. She too, Robert knew, was wearing no panties – earlier, her skirt had wafted open and he'd been treated to a rare and fleeting glimpse of her long, naked thighs and the neat V of curly black hair nestled between them.

Exciting indeed. But, maddeningly, mental imagery alone, even such delightful imagery, was proving not enough. For one thing the fire in his buttocks was a constant distraction; it kept disturbing the images, shattering them with white flashes of searing pain that shot spasmodically up to his brain, making concentration impossible. It was a cruel irony, he had often mused, that whilst pain sexually excited him, making him want to come, that same pain impeded his ability actually to do so!

If only just one of the women would come round in front, he thought, where he could actually see her. The visual stimulus might just be sufficient to allow him to blot out the pain and, together with that seductively teasing hand, trigger the release he was so desperately close to. As it was, there was nothing to see but the women's feet between the legs of the trestle as the anonymous hand worked on, driving him crazy. He was utterly helpless, and could only suffer the exquisite agony of unrelieved arousal and await the women's mercy.

Though a mercy, he feared, that would be long in coming tonight. For Alison never allowed him relief until right at the end of a session, when she herself was fully and finally satisfied, and the sessions seemed always to be long when Belinda was there; long, and severe – Alison seemed to be especially sadistic when entertaining her friend, as if she were trying to impress

14

the other woman with his capacity to endure her cruellest excesses.

But none could be crueller than that merciless hand! Even the pain of a whipping was more easily borne than that wicked teasing, and if it didn't stop soon he feared he would pass out with the surfeit of sensation tormenting his loins.

At last, however, just as he felt he could stand it no longer, his senses swimming on the verge of oblivion, the hand began to withdraw; soft fingertips giving his swollen glans a final stroke before brushing back along the shaft's sensitive underside. He let out a juddering groan of relief as the sensations torturing his straining cock were allowed to subside to a more bearable level.

But relief was short-lived, and turned quickly to chagrin as he sensed the hand turn over and felt a fingernail scratch lightly across his exposed perineum and come to rest, as it had before, against the puckered skin of his anus. He knew now whose hand it had been, whose finger it was, and he held his breath in apprehension and dread as Alison teased aside the delicate petals of his anal opening, the tip of her finger softly probing a fraction inside the meatus.

He tensed, waited, blood pounding through his temples as Alison's finger made tiny circles and he prayed for a second reprieve. But this time there was none, and a moment later, in a single sudden movement, the finger darted inside him; twisted, and reached high in quest of his prostate. Reflexively, his sphincter clenched on the sudden intrusion, released, and clenched again. He couldn't help it, and could do nothing to stop it, even though the muscular spasms transferred to the root of his cock, causing his penis to leap and jerk with each contraction and forcing a mewling gasp from his throat.

The finger allowed him no respite: it began to move, then. To slide back and forth, to rotate inside his rectum, stimulating the rectal wall and causing his aching cock to buck and twitch in agonising convulsions.

But the physical sensations were as nothing compared with the psychological angst, the utter humiliation of being digitally buggered while the women looked on. Beads of sweat sprang out on his brow as he imagined what they could see, and he was only thankful the young maid wasn't present, as she had been the last time Alison had subjected him to this particular indignity.

And that was when he groaned. For as if on perfect cue came the sound of the door opening and closing behind him, and the maid's voice said, 'You said to serve champagne at ten, madam.'

Belinda tore her eyes away from Alison's probing finger, and turned to look at the maid. She was carrying a tray, on which there was an ice-bucket containing a bottle of champagne, and two glasses.

'Ah, Tina,' said Alison. 'Yes, set it down on the table, please, I'll open it shortly. And, ah, fetch the Polaroid camera from the drawer there, would you?' Her eye caught Belinda's, and she winked mischievously. 'You remember we were talking about taking a photo, Bel, to send to Robert's office? Well, wouldn't this make an excellent shot?'

Robert grunted, and pulled frantically, if futilely, at his bonds.

'And what's wrong with you, might I ask?' said Alison, jamming her finger firmly into his bottom. 'I think Miss Fearnley, your prim little secretary, would get quite a buzz from a picture like this, don't you?'

Tina returned with the camera.

'Good. Now if you crouch down just there, Tina,' Alison told her, 'you'll be able to get the perfect shot. Make sure you get the master's face in the frame, beneath the trestle, so there can be no mistaking who it is.'

At that, Robert's head jerked up to keep his face out of camera. But Alison rapped his testicles sharply with her free hand, and he dropped his head back down with a grunt.

Tina went down on one knee, aiming the camera.

'Do you have his face in the picture, Tina?'

'Yes, madam.'

'And my finger here?' she asked, splaying her other fingers over Robert's buttocks while driving her middle finger high up his rectum. 'Do you have a clear view?'

'Oh yes, madam. Perfect.'

Robert flinched, and Alison said, 'Good. Then snap away.'

There was a flash as the camera clicked, then the whirr of the motor as it spewed out the rapidly developing film. Alison withdrew her finger to take it from Tina.

'Oh, yes,' she purred delightedly as the picture gradually formed, the colours brightening and sharpening. 'Perfect indeed. Look, Robert,' – she briefly held it where Robert could see it – 'look how your face is in perfect focus: no mistaking it's you, is there? And no mistaking what my finger's doing either, stuck up your bottom like that.' She chuckled and showed the snap to Belinda, then handed it back to Tina.

'Take good care of it, Tina,' she said. 'After all, we wouldn't want the master finding it and destroying it, now would we? OK, that'll be all.'

Dismissing the maid, Alison turned to Belinda.

'And now,' she said, 'after that little diversion, I think it's time for those six strokes I promised you. Are you ready?'

Belinda was. She was more than ready, her loins tingling in anticipation as she raised a trembling arm.

The playroom on the top floor was fully equipped for pleasure and pain. Furnished throughout in polished leather, its walls were bedecked with paddles and whips, with items of bondage and instruments of torture, toys for pleasure and trivia for fun. Along one of the four walls was a large double bed, manacles attached to its corners, and against two others sat comfortable leather safas. It was soundproofed and there were no windows:

an important consideration in the days before old Mrs B had retired, when the Corsairs had needed privacy for their bizarre sexual games. Though since the appointment of Tina, carefully chosen by Alison, such was no longer the case.

The centre of the room was dominated by the trestle over which Robert was bound. As Belinda stood behind him and delivered the last of the six strokes Alison had ordered, the thrill of it almost – almost, but not quite – precipitated her climax.

Her legs were shaking as Alison took the strap from her hand.

'I think that's enough whipping for now,' she said, running her fingertips over the raised weals on Robert's trembling nates. 'Time to move on to other things. You unfasten his wrists, Bel, while I take care of his ankles.'

The women bent to the task, and a moment later Robert groaned as he slowly straightened his back; reached behind him to rub the fire from his glowing buttocks.

But Alison allowed him no such relief.

'Hands on your head, slave,' she commanded. 'And get those legs wide apart, while we decide what to do with you next.'

Robert's penis was iron-hard, standing almost flat to his belly as he adopted the required position. It was beginning to purple in colour, and knotted veins stood out on its shaft, both the result of the cock-strap fastened tightly around it. The strap comprised of a rubber ring which fitted snugly around the base of the penis. From this, leather straps ran down to the testicles, passing around and between them, pushing them out from the body and separating them into two delicate – and extremely vulnerable – orbs, before press-studding together at the back of the scrotum. It was a device Alison considered almost essential for a session of domination, since the constriction of the rubber ring made it all but impossible for the wearer, once having achieved an erection, to lose it again. It kept him hard and excited while at the same time impeded ejaculation, so making it very difficult for the wearer to come – it called for less vigilance when physically teasing, since the risk of triggering an inadvertent release was greatly reduced. The penis became, therefore, a much more interesting plaything: so much more in the teaser's control!

'So then, what do you think, Bel?' Alison asked. 'What shall we do with him now?'

Belinda was eyeing Robert's cock lasciviously, almost hungrily.

'You could make him fuck me,' she suggested hopefully. 'Fuck me to climax – without him coming himself,' she added quickly, hoping the innate cruelty of this would appeal to Alison and so seduce her agreement.

'Mmm.' Alison rubbed her chin reflectively. 'It's an interesting idea all right ...' She stepped up close to Robert and slid his penis into her hand, giving it a gentle, teasing squeeze. 'What do you think, slave? Mmm? Having to fuck Belinda to climax, her hot pussy clenching in orgasm around your cock as she comes' – her hand worked as she spoke, in simulation of a pulsating vagina – 'but not allowed to let yourself come? Now wouldn't that be cruel of us, eh?'

Robert's penis twitched, and he let out an audible groan; the thought of it evidently filling him with horror.

Alison smiled, then frowned. She slid her hand down the length of his cock to take hold of his testicles, and suddenly lifted. Robert came up on his toes, grunting in agony through the gag in his mouth.

'You didn't answer me, slave. I said, wouldn't that be cruel of us, eh?'

Robert nodded his head vigorously.

'But I like to do cruel things to you, don't I, slave?' she went on with a little-girl pout. 'It turns me on, doesn't it?'

Again Robert nodded, sweat beginning to bead on his brow.

19

'So maybe that's just what I'll have you do, mmmm? After all, you wouldn't want to deny me my little pleasures now, would you? What, just to save yourself a bit of exquisite torment?'

Robert shook his head, his eyes pleading. And at last Alison relented, releasing her grip on his balls and letting him back down on his heels. Relief showed in his eyes. But his look of horror at what was being proposed remained, and Belinda crossed mental fingers; *had she found the key to getting Alison to let Robert screw her?*

She felt a twinge of dismay, however, when Alison then shook her head and said, 'But no, I don't think so. Not this time. I think your tongue can satisfy Belinda tonight. I take it you're ready for an orgasm, Bel?'

Belinda pushed disappointment aside to exclaim, 'God, am I!' with an enthusiasm that refused to be dampened. She had been ready for an orgasm for a very long time!

As Alison had said, Robert had been naked, facing the door with his hands on his head, when the two had walked into the playroom, a cock-strap maintaining a partial erection and promising an exciting evening in prospect. And they'd begun by having him stand before them, his legs apart, and to masturbate for them while they had sat and watched. Not enough to make himself come: Alison had warned he would lick it up if he did – a potent threat to judge by his involuntary shudder – but enough to bring himself fully erect within the tight constraint of the strap; his large penis had become hard and tempting as, on Alison's orders, he had brought himself right to the brink and enough to crimson his face with the humiliation of it as his hand had worked, wanking himself in front of the two smirking women. Seeing that humiliation in his eyes, sensing his mental anguish as he abased himself for their pleasure, had immediately set Belinda's sexual juices a-flow, kindling the fire of arousal deep in her belly.

They had gone on to humiliate and sexually degrade

him in a variety of ways, each new perversity fanning the flames ever hotter, until the thrill of the whipping had turned her loins into a seething cauldron of burning desire. Oh yes, she was ready for an orgasm all right. And if it was to be on Robert's tongue, and not on his glorious cock, well, the disappointment of that she could live with!

'Go and sit on the sofa, Bel,' Alison suggested, 'while I get rid of his gag. He wouldn't be much use to you with that in his mouth.'

Belinda went over to one of the two sofas, and raising her skirt she sat down on the edge of the seat. The leather was cool to her naked buttocks and the sensation was, she mused, in itself quite erotic. And as she lay back and parted her thighs, so too was the swirl of cool air against the moist heat of her sex: it seemed to caress her with ethereal fingers, and her thighs began to quiver in anticipation of the actual caresses to come.

Alison had by now unfastened the strap that was holding Robert's gag in place, and Belinda watched as he pushed the squat rubber penis out with his tongue; grimacing, clearly disgusted by the thing and glad to get it out of his mouth.

Alison chuckled dirtily. 'It's only a bit of rubber, for God's sake,' she said, discarding the phallic gag. 'One day I'm going to bring a man along, and have you suck on a real cock. See how you'll like that.'

Robert visibly quailed, and his mouth came open as if to protest. He thought better of it, perhaps deciding it was a spurious threat it would be wiser to make little of – at least, willing himself to believe that's what it was – and instead shut his mouth and said nothing.

Alison chuckled again, an enigmatic chuckle which gave nothing away as to whether or not she was serious, deliberately letting him wonder, and reached a hand for his penis. She took a firm grip on it and used it to lead him to where Belinda eagerly awaited his tongue, her

21

thighs already apart and her skirt rucked up until it barely covered her crotch.

'Kneel,' Alison ordered, pushing Robert in front of the sofa.

Robert dropped to his knees.

Alison knelt down beside him, and patted the seat of the sofa.

'Here, Bel,' she said. 'Bring your feet up on here; it'll give him better access.'

Yes, thought Belinda, hesitating, *and a better view too*, knowing the position would show more of herself than she really wanted Robert to see. Actually, she liked it best when Robert was made to service her blindfold, when the pleasure was exclusively hers and he wasn't even rewarded beforehand with the sight of where he must lick. It always faintly embarrassed her to have a man's eyes on her sex, especially at such close proximity. And the thought of Robert having so close a view of her pussy, not to mention the even more intimate place the position was sure to reveal, was enough to bring a blush to her cheeks.

Nevertheless, she decided argument – which, against Alison, she was unlikely anyway to win – wasn't worth the delay it would mean, her need too urgent to let coyness postpone her fulfilment. As Alison reached forward to push her skirt higher up, revealing her bush, she lifted her feet up onto the seat of the sofa to reveal all, hyperconscious of Robert's eyes settling upon her as she opened herself to his view. Her vulva, she knew, would be swollen with need, pouting open to expose pink inner flesh that would be glistening with her sexual juices. She knew Robert could see right inside her, while lower down he had an unimpeded view of that secret part of her which she had seldom let any man see. And yes, it was embarrassing. Acutely so.

Her blushes, however, were mercifully short-lived, for a moment later Alison said, 'Lick, slave, don't look,' and pushed Robert's head between her spread thighs, too

22

close for him to see anything but for her trembling belly as he began to lap from her feminine font.

The first touch of his tongue on her expectant flesh was like a small electric shock, so thrilling was it, and as its tip parted her throbbing vulva to delve inside her vagina, then rose to swirl around the aching stem of her clitoris, Belinda felt her orgasm instantly beginning to gather, like a spring coiling deep in her belly, tightening as if ready to snap. She tensed, ready, waiting for Robert's tongue to burst open the straining flood-gates of erotic sensation. But before it could, bare moments before, Alison suddenly stopped it, pulling Robert's head away by his hair.

Belinda almost screamed with frustration: what the hell was Alison doing? Didn't she know how very close she was? How very near to the relief for which she was aching so much?

But when Alison spoke, addressing Robert, Belinda at once forgave her.

'No, slave,' Alison told him. 'Not her pussy yet ... First lick lower down; her bottom.'

The wonderful perversity of it sent an abrupt new thrill to flood through Belinda's loins: *he was to be made to lick her bottom! How delightfully kinky.* And as Robert's tongue, hesitantly at first, did Alison's bidding, sliding lower until he was actually licking her anus, though it took her no nearer to the climax she had all but reached, the sheer depravity of it was ample compensation for her having to wait for a while.

And there was even better to come ...

'Now you must tell me, Bel,' said Alison, 'if he isn't pleasuring you properly. Because if he doesn't, he's going to be sorry.'

And at that, two things happened at once: one, there was a grunt of sudden pain from Robert, the outrush of air from his gasp like a tiny explosion between Belinda's buttocks, and two, the tip of his tongue darted all the way into her; breaching the petals of her anal opening to

23

push right inside her virgin passage. Belinda squealed in delight, guessing Alison had given Robert's balls an abrupt squeeze by way of a warning. (And was tempted to lie so she'd do it again, but didn't.)

'Oh, no, he's doing fine, Ali,' she gasped truthfully. 'Just fine.'

It was more than just fine, she thought as the thrilling sensation went on; it was exquisite – the intrinsically pleasant feel of a warm tongue on her bottom made all the sweeter by the sadistic delight in knowing how utterly degrading it must be for poor Robert to be having to do it.

Alison made him go on for some time, too, no doubt retaining her grip on his testicles to dissuade him from slacking, until, finally, she told him to stop; to return his attention to Belinda's pussy.

And the moment he did, his tongue leaving her anus to glide up to her labia, parting the lips in search of her hungry vagina, the rise of her orgasm instantly began from where it had left off. This time, she knew, there would be no interruption, and she once again tensed, the muscles of her abdomen taut, ready for the internal release that would transport her to heaven. Lifting her hands to her breasts, she kneaded the now trembling mounds through the satin of her dress, to let sensation merge with sensation and bringing herself closer and closer.

As the zenith approached, however, she found herself wrestling with a familiar dilemma: on the one hand she could barely wait for her climax to trigger, for the spring to snap and send her exploding on the head-spinning rush to relief; but on the other, she wished the agony-ecstasy of being right on the brink could go on for ever. And even as she continued to stimulate her lust-swollen breasts, Robert's tongue industrious between her quivering thighs, she was struggling hard not to come; fighting to hold herself back, to keep herself there on the nerve-jangling edge and so savour it for as long as she could.

But when Alison reached a hand to her pubis, and applied the pressure of gentle fingertips to the sides of her clitoris, so forcing the little nub from the protection of its fleshy hood, and told Robert to now lick her there, it was finally too much. She could resist no longer, and as Robert sucked her clitoris into his mouth and flicked it rapidly with the tip of his tongue, the dam of pent-up need was finally breached and she was sent soaring to a shattering climax; her world dissolving into myriad sensations of sparkling pleasure as the orgasm merged into a second, and a third after that; a long multiple climax that went on and on.

For Belinda, it was the culmination of an all-too-rare session of thrilling SM. For Robert, though he wasn't yet to know to quite what extent, it was only the beginning of a long and arduous night . . .

Chapter Three

*T*he morning sun shone brightly through the breakfast-room's leaded windows, lighting up Alison's
blonde curls and warming her body, making her feel
even hornier than she already was. She was wearing a
silk kimono, beneath which she was naked, and after her
morning's bath the touch of sun-warmed silk against her
freshly scrubbed skin was deliciously sensual. Not, however, that this was by any means all that was turning her
on.

She pushed away the remains of a light breakfast and
turned her eyes to the ceiling, picturing the scene which
at that very moment would be playing in Robert's
bedroom. Her instructions to Tina had been quite
specific, and a *frisson* of excitement teased her loins as
she imagined the girl carrying them out, Robert regretting, as he no doubt had been all night, his outburst of
the previous evening – an outburst which had brought
the session to an abrupt and, for him, very premature
end.

He would be regretting it especially, since, Alison
knew, Robert genuinely hated it when she involved Tina
in his sexual domination, or even to have the young girl
witness to his submission, which she frequently was.

The trouble was, for Robert, it also turned him on. For this was the one criterion Alison would apply – given, of course, that it was something she herself would enjoy – in deciding what she would or wouldn't do with Robert as her slave: not whether he would like it or not, which was irrelevant, but whether or not it would turn him on. Unfortunately for him, the two – liking something and finding it sexually exciting – were by no means one and the same. It was a cruel irony, but such is the cross the masochist must bear!

And by now, Alison mused, it was a cross he would be bearing with considerable unease: she imagined him blushing furiously, worms of humiliation crawling in the pit of his stomach as the young maid followed her orders. Though perversely, that same humiliation would at least help prevent it from being prolonged: it would do much to facilitate the task the maid had been given and her job would quickly be done. He would soon be ready for what Alison had in mind.

It was a thrilling thought, and as she let herself think it she slid a lazy hand inside her kimono and cupped a breast in a kneading palm the better to relish the sexual imagery that was teasing her loins with growing desire. Pinching firmly, she made her nipple erect between finger and thumb and felt her sexual juices beginning to flow, readying her for the pleasures to come.

Tina smoothed down the skirt of her uniform as she stood at the door to the master's bedroom: the skirt was micro-short and barely covered her crotch; rucked up as it was from climbing the stairs, it didn't even do that. The wearing of panties was strictly forbidden – in order, so the mistress had told her during a job interview that no longer seemed as bizarre as it had at the time, that she would remain aware of her posture and so be sure to carry herself with the straight-backed deportment befitting that of a maid. And if Tina thought this a somewhat spurious reason for her not being allowed to wear panties, she couldn't deny that it did serve this purpose remarkably well.

Satisfied she was as decent as her skirt would allow, she pushed open the bedroom door.

She was not at all surprised by the strange scene which greeted her upon entering the darkened room – the mistress's instructions had been perfectly clear, and she had known already what to expect. And anyway, nothing surprised her in this weird house any longer: in the three months she had been the Corsairs' resident maid she had seen it all: up in the playroom, where she had seen the master subjected to all manner of sexual abuse and where she was sometimes required to assist with his bondage or to release him afterwards; or merely to be present to watch – this, she presumed, to intensify the master's humiliation at whatever it was being done to him. She could certainly see how it would.

And it wasn't just in the playroom, either: entering any room in the house she might well find her employers engaged in some form of sexual or sado-masochistic activity in the throes of one of their sessions. Or even outside in the grounds. On the tennis court, for example, where only the other day she had watched them playing the best of three sets; the mistress wearing smart designer tennis-whites, the master nothing at all – stark naked, and with heavy weights suspended from his testicles. Well, whatever else, it would at least have evened the contest!

Oh yes, in the past three months she had seen it all.

And certainly wasn't complaining: apart from anything else, the job paid her three times the going rate for more conventional domestic employment, and if keeping it meant her witnessing bizarre scenes from time to time, even performing some very peculiar duties, then so be it: the interview had been perfectly clear as to what the position entailed, and she had taken the job with her eyes wide open. For that money, she would have happily taken it with her legs wide open!

28

And didn't she almost wish! For the master was an absolute hunk, with an incredibly sexy body – a body that turned her on, and that she frequently made love to in the secret world of masturbatory fantasy. Living under the Corsairs' roof she tended to masturbate often. It was difficult not to. For if in the beginning she had accepted their bizarre sexual life-style on purely mercenary grounds, she had come to regard her salary as only the icing on a very exciting cake: regularly seeing the master naked, that gorgeous body as God had made it, was almost reward enough in itself. And seeing the kinky things the mistress did to him opened up whole new areas of sexual fantasy, which kept her vibrator consistently busy. Life in the Corsair household might well be bizarre, but it was certainly never dull!

And now, as she entered the master's bedroom, it was to find the master tied to his bed, just as the mistress had told her; his wrists and ankles bound to the four corners, and just a single sheet draped over him. The sheet was tented where the shape of his widespread legs came together beneath it, and even in the room's dim light it was obvious he had an erection. There was a pair of knickers taped over his face, arranged so their gusset was held to his nose, and a further piece of sticky tape covered his mouth. Tina knew he had spent the night like this, following the session in the playroom, and apart from the thrum of arousal that it stirred in her belly, making her thighs feel heavy and full, she took it all in her stride.

'Good morning, sir,' she said breezily, crossing the room to throw back the curtains. She said it as brightly as the sunlight that suddenly streamed in through the windows and quite matter-of-factly, just as any maid might upon entering her employer's bedroom, perhaps with his breakfast tray in the morning; as though everything were perfectly normal.

Well, for the Corsair mansion, wasn't it normal enough? Just the start of another day!

* * *

Robert rolled his head on the pillow, squinting his eyes against the harsh morning sun that had woken him from restless sleep, and swallowed into a dry throat on seeing the young maid in his room. Groaned inwardly as he watched her turn from the windows, her gaze taking in his debasing condition, and felt his cock twitch with a treacherous life of its own.

Tina was a pretty nineteen-year-old with sparkling blue eyes and a fresh complexion. She had long, shapely legs – the skirt of her uniform cut short enough to reveal an enticing courtesy-gap between the tops of her thighs – and breasts which were small but delectably pert, with tiny up-turned nipples that poked cheekily at the front of her blouse. Enough to make any man lust, let alone a masochist tied up and degraded, helpless before her!

She performed her duties – all her duties – with a zestful enthusiasm, and there was a jaunty bounce to her stride as she came to the foot of the bed. *And just what*, Robert wondered with some trepidation, *were her duties to be that morning?*

He was about to find out.

'Madam says I'm to uncover you, sir,' said the girl. 'And to see that you're, ah, fully awake.'

Robert could only groan as the pretty teenager drew down the sheet, exposing him to her smiling young eyes.

The master's organ was hugely distended; never had Tina seen it so big. It was quite purplish in colour, and its bulbous head was an enormous plum impaled on a vein-knobbled shaft: the rubber ring around its base, which looked, after so long, to be biting quite uncomfortably now into the swollen flesh around it, kept the foreskin stretched tight and back, giving it the appearance of one circumcised, the flange of the fleshy plum flaring wide of the shaft to make it appear still bigger. His testicles, too, seemed larger than normal and the leather straps around and dividing them were stretching the skin translucent over the two swollen orbs, to show delicate blue veins beneath. They looked like a pair of overripe grapes, fit to be plucked from their fleshy vine.

The whole organ bobbed and twitched as Tina regarded it, as if her gaze had substance somehow, and was physically stroking it with gossamer fingers. Watching its involuntary twitching, its helpless response to these phantom caresses, Tina felt herself flood with her juices and was more conscious than ever of her lack of panties; she could only pray that she wouldn't leak!

Her thrill, however, at seeing the master so highly aroused was tempered somewhat by a sense of dispirit; a sense, almost, of having been cheated. It was exciting, yes, to see that magnificent cock hard and quivering, straining with masculine need; to imagine it throbbing inside her as it drove her to climax – it would provide the perfect focus for fantasy later. The only trouble was, he was aroused too soon. For her instructions had been to strip off the sheet and to tease him fully erect, ready for the mistress's pleasure. She had been looking forward to that, to actually getting her hands on that gorgeous hunk of a body: touching him in a directly sexual way was a delight she had seldom had, save in fantasy, and the prospect of it had thrilled her. Yet, now, here he was already erect, and she doubted she could make him any the more so.

Still, she thought, stretching sophistry right to the limit, she could always try, couldn't she? And kneeling on the foot of the bed between the master's widespread thighs, she refused to let a little thing like lack of necessity spoil a rare treat, and reached a hand to his penis.

He gave a muffled, nasal grunt as her fingers closed on his tumescent shaft, groaned as she began slowly to wank him – perhaps, it occurred to Tina, it was a groan of dismay, for fear that her orders were to bring him to climax. For although the relief would surely be welcome, the ignominy of it, of having her watch him spurting over his belly, most certainly would not. (Tina was learning fast the subtleties of the male sexual psyche, and knew that, to the master, this would be humiliating in the extreme.) He needn't, though, be worried: making him come was the last thing she must do. And when, after just a few seconds, she felt his cock beginning to pulse, saw a dribble of clear fluid leak from the cleft at its tip, she knew she had better stop.

Reluctantly letting his penis slip from her hand, she climbed down off the bed and resmoothed her skirt. She crossed to the telephone on the bedside table and punched out the number that would make its duplicate ring in the breakfast-room.

She let it ring three times, the pre-arranged signal that the master was ready, and replaced the receiver. And, her instructions complete, she hurriedly left the room, keen to get back to her own where her vibrator would do for her what the master could not.

Alison walked into Robert's bedroom, and thrilled to see him just as she'd left him the previous night; his penis hard and huge, prepared for her pleasure. Tina had done her job well.

As she moved closer though, she noted that his eyes, unlike his manhood, looked weary and tired; he had clearly spent an uncomfortable night.

'Oh, you poor dear,' she pouted, feigning sympathy. 'Did we not sleep very well?'

His eyes said 'No', as if that were the understatement of the year, and Alison chuckled.

'Perhaps that'll teach you, then, not to go calling me names.'

Last night, once Belinda had recovered from the orgasm Robert had given her, they had tied him up, much as he was now, and had set about teasing his penis; taking him right to the brink again and again, but never, quite, allowing him over it. It had made for great sport as they took it in turns to torment him: watching him writhe in his bonds as he grew ever more desperate for the relief he was being denied; his hips jerking up from the bed in a parody of intercourse as his cock searched frantically for further friction against their omnipotent hands; but hands that were careful to allow it no more than would serve only to deepen his torment. They had thrilled to his anguished moans each time they withheld a final caress that would have taken him over the top, to leave him instead in an agony of frustrated desire. Great sport indeed. But after almost half an hour of relentless tantalisation, it had finally proved too much – in his frustration Robert had called Alison a bitch. That had been a mistake. A mistake he had spent the night regretting.

'Are you ready to apologise, slave?' Alison continued. 'Or shall I leave you here for the rest of the day? Have Tina come in from time to time to, ah, keep up your interest?'

Robert shook his head vigorously, his eyes pleading even as they widened in horror.

'Oh,' Alison said mischievously. 'I see you're shaking your head. So you're telling me you're not prepared to apologise, then?'

Robert's head shook wildly. Stopped. Almost nodded, but didn't; dithered between nodding and shaking. For the phrasing of the question had made it cruelly ambiguous, impossible for him to do either without Alison contriving, if so she chose, to misread it. In the event he did neither, his eyes imploring helplessly and knowing his fate was entirely at Alison's whim. Alison chuckled, knowing it too, and let him sweat for a while, denying him the chance to apologise; letting him worry that unless he did, she would make good on her threat to leave him there, tied up and frustrated, for the whole of the day. It wouldn't have been the first time!

'It's lucky for you, slave,' she said, at last relenting, 'that I'm in serious need of this' – she gave his erection a sharp slap, making it sway in a bobbing arc – 'or you really would have been here for the rest of the day. Swearing at me indeed!'

She leant over and tore the sticky tape from his mouth. 'Well?'

Both relief and gratitude showed on Robert's face as he blurted anxiously, 'Yes, yes, mistress, I'm sorry. Really I am. It just slipped out; I couldn't help it.'

'Then perhaps your punishment will help you keep better control in the future, huh?'

'Yes, mistress,' Robert muttered contritely. Chewing on his lower lip as he added, 'It was just with, well, you know, with what you did . . .'

It was true that Alison had been especially cruel. Her turn to tease him, she had been stroking his penis with delicate, brushing caresses; enough to keep him yearning, at a peak of desire, but just insufficient to trigger his climax. But she had said that if Robert were actually to beg her to, then she would wank him more firmly, and that this time she wouldn't stop as his orgasm mounted, but would go on to give him relief.

Robert had begged – clearly discomfited at having to do so in front of Belinda, but, by then, desperate enough not to care – and, as promised, Alison had quickened her stroke; making it firmer and more deliberate, allowing his climax to gather. Robert had tensed in expectancy, orgasm fast approaching as her skilful hand worked on, his abdominal muscles taut and rippling, his face contorting in the agony-ecstasy of near-relief after so many hours of unabated arousal.

'Are you ready, slave?' Alison had said, watching him carefully, shortening her stroke to concentrate on the sensitive frenum.

And clearly he had been. His breath was held, his eyes hooded, every sinew knotted with sexual tension; rigid thighs were beginning to to quiver as orgasm gathered and rose; his long-held seed collecting, building up behind the tight rubber ring and set finally to erupt in climactic release; about, at last, to come . . .

And then Alison had let go of his cock.

Right at the very last moment, the very split-second

before it began. She had laughed as she watched his penis twitch and jerk in mid-air, straining to finish itself off, the cock-strap helping to stop it, and straining uselessly, left on a brink it was helpless to breach. And that was when Robert had cracked.

'You ... you bitch!' he'd gasped, incredulous at what she had done.

It had been capricious of her, she knew, to have deliberately built up his hopes so, only to dash them at the very last moment. But, still, he shouldn't have called her a name. That was a big mistake.

Because that was when she'd decided, by way of punishment, that he wasn't to come that night at all.

Straddling his face, she had ended the session by having him lick her to climax – after all, there was no reason for her to be left unsatisfied too. Then, deaf to his pleas, she and Belinda had taken him through to his bedroom where they had tied him as he was now, spreadeagled and helpless. And with no way of relieving himself during the night.

The panties had been Belinda's wicked idea, and they had giggled their way through Alison's laundry, searching for the most obviously used pair they could find, before carefully positioning their crotch to his nose and using sticky tape to hold them in place. They had taped his mouth shut, too, so forcing him to breathe through his nose. This was how they had left him.

Alison now reached over; she lifted the panties from Robert's face and brought them up to her own. She felt a moment of sympathy for their intimate scent was still quite pungent, her feminine fragrance lingering even now on their crotch, and this, she knew, would have added greatly to Robert's nocturnal discomfort. To Robert, a woman's sexy scent was an irresistible turn-on, and having to breathe it in all through the night, with no way to avoid it, would doubtless have kept him extremely aroused, his cock hard and throbbing for much of the time, and sleep very difficult indeed.

35

The thought gave Alison an exhilarating thrill, the pang of sympathy instantly gone as a flood of excitement surged in its place. She loved the thought of a man aching with sexual need. It was what made teasing the delight that it was: it gave her a heady sensation of power to know that she, and she alone, could permit a lover to come; to save him the agony, or to make it go on for as long as she chose. It was the ultimate in sexual control.

There was an obvious drawback, of course, to her limiting Robert's relief for the high of feeling that power: as it had last night, it meant her denying herself the use of his cock. And though last night she had been satisfied well enough by his tongue, she had woken that morning with a throbbing longing between her legs, yearning for his penis inside her. Her thoughts of his suffering such cruel deprivation, as she lay in bed coming slowly awake, served only to deepen that longing.

But a longing, now, that would soon be assuaged.

Climbing onto the bed between Robert's spread thighs, she reached for his swollen penis. She leant forward and took it into her mouth; not to fellate him *per se* – her need too urgent for the luxury of foreplay – but just to coat it with warm saliva the more easily to slide it inside her. Her vagina was wanting it badly.

Swirling her tongue around the bulbous head, she wet it thoroughly, then let it slip from her lips; she dropped her kimono and, naked, she at last went to straddle his thighs. She reached down to prise his iron member away from his belly, and held it upright while she carefully positioned it to her. And slowly, very slowly, savouring each thrilling inch of it as his penis slid into her, she gradually sank herself down. Down and down, swallowing more and more of the maleness she craved, sheathing it in feminine warmth, until she had taken its entire length, its velvet head nudging softly at the neck of her womb, and with a deep shuddering sigh of pleasure, she flattened her palms on Robert's chest to let it bear some of her weight, ready to ride him to a much-needed come.

Robert moaned, and his eyes began to glaze and grow distant.

Alison saw it, and was quick to respond. 'Don't dare come, slave,' she warned. 'Not yet. Not until I'm ready for you. Come now, and you'll have to satisfy me with your tongue. And with my pussy full of your come, I don't think you'd enjoy that one bit.'

Robert shuddered. But there was more than revulsion contorting his face as his hips began to move, stimulating his organ inside her. And he suddenly gasped, 'I ... I don't think I can hold – '

'Stop!' Alison cried, a stab of panic tightening her gut as she watched pre-orgasmic tension deaden his eyes. 'Don't dare move a muscle.'

His long ordeal of sexual torment had left him too excited, she realised, to hold himself back, and even the tight constraint of the cock-strap would not be sufficient to keep him contained: if she tried, now, to ride him to orgasm, regardless of any threats she might make (or even precisely because of them!), he wouldn't be able to help himself and would come before she could.

But at least, thank God, he hadn't come yet. She had made him stop moving his hips – if, to judge by his face, with a monumental effort of will – and the crisis was held in abeyance. A fragile abeyance at best, however, and while he was still inside her he might come at any moment: a problem she would have to address with care.

'Don't dare move a muscle,' she repeated, breathless with tension: if he came now she would die with frustration.

And slowly, even more slowly than she had taken him into her, careful not to let her vaginal muscles contract, or to allow the movement of its slippery walls against his sensitive glans to precipitate his climax, she began to lift herself from him. Inch by careful inch. Until at last there was a wet smack as his penis finally sprang from her to slap at his belly, and as Robert groaned in frustration, Alison breathed a long, low sigh of relief. He was close. Very close. But he hadn't come.

Feeling tension ease from her shoulders like a physical weight lifting from her, she swung her leg over Robert's thighs and climbed off the bed; she reached for the telephone on the bedside table, her course of action decided. If Robert's cock was to bring her to climax, he would need the distraction of pain to help dampen his ardour.

Picking up the phone, she dialled Tina's room and waited for the maid to answer.

At last there was a click. Then: 'Yes?'

She sounded oddly breathless, Alison thought.

'Ah, Tina. Go along to the playroom, will you, and fetch me a riding crop. Bring it to the master's bedroom.'

'Yes, madam.'

Alison put down the receiver, reflecting on the breathlessness she had perceived in Tina's voice: *was it*, she wondered, *the breathlessness of sexual excitement?* It had certainly sounded like it; her voice had been unusually husky as if laden with sexual tension. Had Tina been masturbating, then been interrupted by having to answer the phone? Turned on by her morning's duties, and relieving herself with the aid of Robert's photo, the Polaroid they had taken last night? (The very reason, though only Alison knew it, it had been left in the girl's care.)

It was an interesting thought. But for now Alison put it to the back of her mind, with more pressing things to consider. Like, anticipating Robert's reaction to what she was about to tell him.

'I'm going to have Tina thrash you while you fuck me,' she said, dropping the bombshell.

Robert's reaction did not disappoint her, his eyes making sudden saucers of shock, his cheeks puffing as he spluttered: 'No. Oh no, Alison, you . . . you wouldn't!'

'*Mistress*,' Alison snapped. 'When you're Slave, there is no Alison; only Mistress Alison.'

'Yes, mistress; s-sorry, mistress,' Robert muttered, knowing the penalty for this oversight was usually severe. Nevertheless, evidently emboldened by the outrageousness of what Alison proposed, it didn't stop him protesting. 'But, mistress, you wouldn't ... I mean, you couldn't!'

'Why ever not?' said Alison innocently, knowing perfectly well why she shouldn't.

Robert had been horrified when, on the retirement of old Mrs Beatty three months ago, Alison had announced her intention to take on a young maid to replace her. A young girl who, among her other duties, could assist her in his domination. He had flatly forbidden it; had refused, absolutely, to allow her to do any such thing.

Tina had been hired the following week.

But, thus far, her role had largely been limited to that just of onlooker; the mere presence of the pretty young girl, watching as Robert was made to submit, enough. Enough to make whatever was done to him doubly humiliating, and so doubly exciting for Alison.

The girl would occasionally help out in the playroom, with buckles and straps and such. But only a couple of times, as they had that morning, had her duties extended to anything more.

And she had certainly never been let loose with a whip!

To have to submit to Tina, a young chit of a girl – not to mention a maid, a paid employee – whipping his backside, would be dreadfully humiliating for Robert. But in the circumstances Alison could see no alternative. At least, it was as good an excuse as any.

'I can't see how else,' she said, giving voice to her thoughts, 'you'd be able to satisfy me before coming yourself. In your state, without the pain of a thrashing to hold you back, you'd be bound to come before I could.

And that would hardly be fair, now would it, so it's no use complaining – it's not my fault, it's yours.'

It was enough. Robert looked defeated, and though his cheeks continued to puff in silent disgruntlement, he didn't argue it further: when Alison had set her mind on something she could seldom be swayed, and he seemed resigned to his fate. Besides, his penis was twitching beyond his control, betraying his secret excitement – the thought of it thrilling him whether he liked it or not.

Alison smiled to herself: oh, how she loved masochistic men, helpless slaves to their cocks!

She set about untying Robert's bonds, and was busy with the last of them when Tina arrived with the crop. Robert tried instinctively to cover himself with a hand, but Alison slapped it away, her expression telling him he should know better, and made him lie as he was, his genitalia on open display.

She looked up as the maid came in. 'Ah, Tina, good.'

The girl's face was flushed, her cheeks pinked by the unmistakable glow of sexual arousal. It all but confirmed Alison's earlier conjecture: *so she had, then, been masturbating when the phone had rung.* Alison would have bet Robert's fortune on it, and it was an encouraging thought: her plan was coming together. Over the past few weeks she had been secretly toying with the idea of extending the girl's duties in all sorts of ways; beyond, even, having her whip Robert. For if she was turning on to their kind of scene, as Alison had sensed and as this new evidence now seemed to confirm, then maybe she could be persuaded to take a full and active part in their sessions.

Not for the first time an exciting image formed in Alison's mind: Robert was lying on his back, and so too was Tina – lying face up, naked, on top of him. Robert's penis was lodged in her bottom, buggering her, and her legs were spread wide, her pussy open and glistening and awaiting the kiss of the whip. Alison had never whipped a pussy, but it had a definite appeal. Especially

40

since, in that position, the soft leather strands of a sauna-whip could hardly fail, too, to connect with Robert's balls: a double delight.

She let the image stay for a moment, then shook her head to dislodge it. Perhaps it could, one day, become an exciting reality. But not today. Today, she had other pleasures in mind . . .

'In a moment,' she announced to Tina (whose eyes were locked on Robert's straining organ), 'the master's going to make love to me. And while he does, I want you to whip his bottom.'

If Tina was shocked, it didn't show. There might even have been a gleam of delight in her sparkling blue eyes. Alison smiled within: how well she had chosen in Tina – the girl was a minx and no mistake!

Alison sat down in an armchair, shifted her buttocks to the front of the seat and lay back. She turned to Robert, still prone on the bed.

'Right, slave, I'm ready; you can come to me now.'

The armchair was squat and low, and as Robert came to kneel between her spread thighs, her hungry sex was presented to him at the perfect height.

'You won't need to lay the whip on terribly hard,' Alison told Tina. 'His bottom will still be tender from the whipping we gave him last night. The important thing is to keep up a steady rhythm. And whatever you do, don't stop till I say. I don't want him coming before I do, and the whip will see that he doesn't.' She looked to Robert. 'Well, what are you waiting for, slave? Begin.'

Robert looked nervous and tense as he shuffled himself forward, conscious of Tina behind him. Kneeling up, he took hold of his penis in a trembling hand and guided it to Alison's sex; he ran its bulbous head along the slippery channel between her swollen inner lips, bathing it in her sexual juices, then positioned it to her vagina.

And Alison told Tina: 'Now!'

Tina swung with the crop. There was an abrupt, staccato *crack* as its leather tongue snapped against the still-tender skin of Robert's buttocks. And Robert's hips jerked forward, driving his penis hard into Alison's body and filling her with male tumescence. Alison gasped in delight: this, she was going to enjoy!

After a moment, Robert began to withdraw. Slowly, and tentatively: knowing he must, but knowing too that the whip would be raised behind him, in wait of his buttocks; to withdraw was to present them for a second cut. And, indeed, no sooner had he reached the end of his stroke than the crop struck again, sending him forward in a second pain-driven lunge.

And so the pattern was set: the long, slow, hesitant withdrawal, with Robert cringing in anticipation of the whip's next stroke, then, when it came, his grunt of sudden agony and the violent thrust forward which buried his penis deep into Alison's sex, she thrilling, watching Robert's face twist in the agony of each sharp *crack*; watching his eyes. Eyes which one moment would be filled with pain, the next would hood over with rapture as pain diffused, transmuting to sexual pleasure, though never quite reaching the zenith of ecstasy, always driven back by the next searing cut.

Alison watched the montage with growing arousal; turned on by his rapture; letting his pain wash over her in great surging waves that took her up towards climax even as it kept Robert from his.

If this was Tina's first time with a whip, it was almost hard to believe: she was timing her stroke like an expert, and, to judge by Robert's reaction, gauging its strength to perfection; striking not so hard as to break Robert's rhythm, but rather dictating his rhythm with a level of pain just sufficient to serve its purpose.

Robert was clearly suffering, nevertheless, and was only fortunate that the combined affect on Alison, of seeing that suffering and the feel of his large penis thrusting inside her, soon had her close to the edge; the familiar coil tightened deep in her belly as her orgasm rapidly gathered.

And during those exquisite moments of uncertainty before climax becomes inevitable, Alison brought her hands to her lust-swollen breasts to complete the *mélange* of sensation. Taking her erect nipples between fingers and thumbs, she squeezed. She squeezed hard, deliberately making them hurt; shared Robert's pain in a devil's pact as she edged herself nearer and nearer to ecstatic release: her eyes locked on Robert's eyes as Robert thrust on, taking her closer, and closer still.

Until at last she was poised at the precipice, looking over into the heady chasm of carnal fulfilment into which she was about to be plunged. And finding only the breath for a single word, she exhorted Tina to stop — wanting Robert to come, now. To come with her, when the throb of his climax would prolong her own.

And the instant Tina stepped back and the sound of the last *crack* died away, she sensed Robert's climax beginning, his eyes misting with ecstasy as, no longer distracted by pain, his long-denied orgasm swiftly approached.

Control, she thought. What a wonderful thing was control.

It was her last conscious thought before Robert threw back his head and thrust himself into her in a final desperate lunge, a long, guttural groan escaping his lungs as the throbbing inside her began. And her senses were sent spinning in a giddying vortex, unable consciously to think anything at all as the thrill of her climax engulfed her: all just a blur as they came together in a violent surge of mutual release.

How long it was before Alison recovered she had no idea, lost in a timeless oblivion of erotic sensation; her mind floating on puff-ball clouds of physical content in a sky of insouciant bliss.

But, gradually, her body calmed and conscious awareness began at last to return.

Robert was still kneeling between her thighs, his penis

still inside her. When they were Mistress and Slave, he wasn't allowed to withdraw after intercourse until Alison gave him permission; it was a standing order. And not his most favourite, either: like most men, the moment he came his sexual interest instantly vanished, and he would want only for the session to end. Right then, to be on his knees with his cock in her pussy would be the last thing he'd want. But, remain he would for a while: Alison liked the feel of a penis inside her in those moments following climax, and if it was uncomfortable for Robert, if the head of his cock was raw with sensation, sensitive nerve-endings screaming, then so much to the good – it was the price he could pay for his pleasures.

Indeed, she would often clench her vaginal muscles around his softening shaft, gripping and releasing him just for the amusement of watching him wince. But not today. Today, she was too exhausted: her muscles had done enough clenching and unclenching during her orgasm, and wanted now to relax.

Nevertheless, only when she had fully recovered, and in her own good time, did she finally let Robert withdraw. Let him sit back on his haunches to relieve the strain on his thighs.

'And now,' she said, deciding on a wicked little finale as an amusing end to the session, 'I think you should thank Tina for the whipping she gave you.'

Robert's cheeks instantly crimsoned, and Alison chuckled within. How he would hate having to do it, she mused; to have been whipped by the maid in the first place, but now to suffer the further humiliation of having to thank her for doing it! Especially just then, immediately following orgasm when, sexually drained, he was always at his least masochistic. But have to do it he would. For even though he had come, that in itself meant nothing: he was still Slave, and until Alison released him the rules of the session pertained – like it or not, he must do whatever she said.

'Well?' she prompted.

Robert swallowed hard and muttered, 'Thank you,' under his breath.

'Thank you for what?' Alison pressed. And deciding to up the ante, added slyly, 'And look at her while you say it.'

Robert gulped again, but turned slowly to face the young maid.

'Thank you for . . . for whipping me.' It was still barely a whisper.

'Now say it properly, Robert,' Alison told him sharply. 'Or I'll have you kiss her pussy to thank her more nicely.'

Tina blushed coyly. (Though gave no sign she'd have minded!) And Robert flinched, his eyes narrowing as he spun to face Alison again; as if to say, 'You wouldn't.'

But when Alison's expression said yes, she would, he quickly turned back to Tina. 'Thank you, Tina, for whipping me.'

Tina's blush deepened. But there was a definite look of amusement in her twinkling eyes, the touch of a smirk on her lips. And watching Robert cringe, Alison thought: yes, a minx indeed.

She chuckled. 'All right then, Tina, thank you,' she said, dismissing the girl.

When Tina had gone, Alison sat forward in her chair and reached down to Robert's genitals. She unclasped the strap behind his scrotum, and made Robert wince despite the care with which she slid the ring from his still-swollen penis.

'There,' she said, giving his member a gentle pat, 'you're free. And you're Free too.'

Free was the release word: the word that meant they were no longer Mistress and Slave, but Alison and Robert Corsair once again; a normal married couple – well, as normal as their vast wealth allowed – who would now resume their normal married lives. Until the next time Alison said the word Slave.

Robert sighed, relieved.

'You really are a bitch, you know. And especially when you have Belinda here. Jesus, teasing me like you did, on top of all else, and then leaving me aching all night.'

'Shouldn't have sworn at me then, should you?'

'All bloody night though!'

Alison pouted her little-girl pout. 'Oh, don't be such an old stick, Bobbums. Anyway, you know you love it really.'

'Yes, but I sometimes think you go too far. And having Tina whip me, well, that's really too much.'

'But I have to keep testing your limits, Robert,' Alison said seriously. 'For you and for me. I have to keep thinking up new things to do to you, to keep it thrilling for us both. And actually, talking of Tina, I'm thinking of involving her more.' She saw Robert was about to protest, and added quickly: 'But we'll see about that.' Now wasn't the time to be talking of stretching his limits. When he was sexually excited was best; she could get away with just about anything then.

Robert's protest died unborn, her rider enough to appease him. But then he frowned. 'And that bloody photo you had Tina take: you'd better be sure and get that back.'

Alison chuckled. 'Oh, yes, I'd almost forgotten about that. But don't worry, it'll be safe. I'll let her use it as a masturbatory aid for a day or two, then – '

'A what?' spluttered Robert.

'Oh, come on, Bobbums, it can't have escaped you that Tina has the hots for you. Jesus, the way she was eyeing your cock just now: she was looking at it as hungrily as Belinda was last night. And by the way, she's another one who's dying to fuck you again. Lucky boy, eh?'

'Yeah, well, with you dictating the play that remains to be seen. But what's that got to do with the photo?'

'Well, that's why I let Tina have it, wasn't it – let her wank to it for a couple of days, as a treat.'

'Jesus, you – '

'Anyway, come and give me a cuddle,' Alison said quickly, changing the subject. She was not about to mention that turning Tina on to him was at the root of her plan to inveigle the girl more fully into their scene. 'I think I deserve one, don't you?'

'What, after what you've just put me through?' pouted Robert.

'*Because* of what I've just put you through, you gorgeous masochist, you. Not to mention a gorgeous hunk of a man. Now, c'mere with that cuddle.'

Robert chuckled as he knelt upright and folded her into his arms, and Alison sighed contentedly, nuzzling his naked chest. It had been a terrific session; a terrific, fulfilling climax to it. And as for her ideas for Tina, well, Robert would come around in the end. He always did.

It was a happy thought: Alison liked to get her own way.

Chapter Four

*I*t was a warm, sunny day, the last day of July, and the scent of horses clung to the still air as Alison strode across the cobbled courtyard towards the stables adjoining the house.

Robert was away at a business meeting and it was Tina's day off, and Alison was home alone, pottering about and wrestling her conscience. She had a dilemma.

It had just been announced on the local news that a sex shop specialising in fetish-wear had opened that morning in Braybridge, as improbable as that seemed, and she was keen to check it out: see what it had to offer before the residents of that prudish backward community had time to shut the place down. Braybridge was a small rural town with a village-like mentality, and it was unlikely to tolerate such an unsavoury business for any longer than it took to rally the local gestapo; the twin-set-and-pearl brigade whose moral high-ground was an Everest of Victorian values.

A browse round that shop might, Alison was thinking, spark her imagination; give her new ideas for her sessions with Robert. It was never easy, even given her considerable capacity for sexual inventiveness, to keep coming up with ideas; new things to do with her 'slave' that would keep the sex between them vibrant and fresh. Indeed, she sometimes wondered if it wasn't Robert who had the easier role. He might be the one to suffer, yes; to endure the pain and humiliation on which they both thrived. But there must be a certain insouciance in sexual submission: to have nothing to do but to lie back and enjoy; to revel in erotic sensation, and leave all the decisions to somebody else. Still, she wouldn't have wanted their roles reversed – it wasn't *that* difficult to come up with ideas!

A visit to a sex-shop, though, wouldn't hurt: she might pick up a sexy new outfit – erotic play-wear was always inspiring – or find a new toy that would prompt ideas. It would, anyway, be fun.

The trouble was, Belinda was due round and Alison had promised her faithfully that they would go riding that afternoon. And therein lay the dilemma. For Belinda had a passion for all things equestrian that bordered on obsession. Not at all like Alison, for whom horses were just a trapping of upper-class living – something to put in the stables. Oh, the animals themselves she liked well enough. But apart from enjoying an occasional ride in very fine weather, that was as horsey as Alison got: putting on green wellies to trample about in hay and horseshit wasn't her idea of having a good time. Belinda, on the other hand, would have happily mucked out stables all day for the loan of a horse for an hour. And that was the problem: she might, herself, quite fancy a browse round a sex-shop – but in preference to riding? Alison doubted it: she would be terribly disappointed if the ride was called off. And anyway, Alison had promised her now.

Alison reached the first of the stable doors, and Samson, her handsome gelding, came over to greet her.

She rubbed his nose affectionately. 'And you'd be glad of the exercise, wouldn't you, boy?'

Samson snorted *Yes*. And there was an accompanying

49

whinny from the stable next door: Lady, the small bay whom Belinda would ride, added her voice in support.

Alison chuckled. 'I know,' she called through the stable wall. 'And you would too.'

She rubbed Samson's ears, thinking. The draw of town was strong; it would be a fun afternoon. And the shop might be gone by tomorrow, shut down by the good folk of Braybridge. But she had promised now: Belinda would have set her heart on a ride. To go back on her word and do anything other would be terribly selfish of her.

When Belinda arrived, they went into town.

Chapter Five

'Hey, now look at this, Bel,' said Alison with sudden excitement.

Belinda looked up from the catalogue of leather corsetry through which she was half-heartedly browsing, and Alison showed her a white plastic tube she had taken from out of its packaging: it was about four inches long, and its diameter was large enough, just, to accommodate an average-sized penis. Its surface was perforated, and as she spoke she pushed what looked like a pop-rivet through one of the little holes; a blunt metal spike came through to the inside of the tube.

'Imagine that,' she said, picturing the bulbous head of Robert's cock protruding from the top of the sheath, its shaft swelling inside it. 'There're about twenty or so of these little metal spikes that push through to the inside. Then this leather collar laces up around the whole thing to keep them from pressing back out. Ouch! Can you imagine Robert's cock, hard and throbbing, in that?'

'But you'd never get it on him, Alison,' Belinda argued dismissively, for once not sharing her friend's enthusiasm. 'Not the size of Robert, you wouldn't. The tube itself, maybe – though even then at a pinch – but with the spikes sticking through, the inside diameter would be way too small; he'd simply never fit.'

'No, silly, not with a hard-on he wouldn't. But you wouldn't try to get it on him when he's already erect: you'd put it on while he's soft – '

'Then turn him on,' Belinda finished for her, seeing the point. And suddenly animated, a gleam of excitement finally brightened her green eyes.

Earlier, Belinda had been bitterly disappointed that they weren't to go riding as planned, and as Alison had driven them to town she had sat in the passenger seat in a sullen silence, not saying a word throughout. Unfortunately, her mood had not been improved when, on arriving at the shop, they had been greeted by a picket line of irate protesters – a turn-out of mumsy local parishioners, waving their banners in moral outrage that such a disgusting business should have come to their precious town. Seeing them, Belinda had suggested they give it a miss even then; there was still time to go back for a ride.

But Alison's resolve had been firmer than ever. 'Listen, Bel, this lot will have shut the place down by tomorrow, then the nearest sex-shop's in London again. I'll be damned if I'll let a bunch of fuddy-duddies stop me enjoying it while the place is still here, right on our doorstep.'

Dragging Belinda behind her, she had pushed a path through the gathered protesters and they had entered the shop to find themselves in an Aladdin's cave of erotic delights.

Even so, Belinda, not usually given to sulking, had continued to pout, as if determined not to be impressed by the array of erotica that on another day would have thrilled her.

Now, however, eyeing the spiked tube, such a simple yet ingenious device for sexual torture – no doubt imagining its use on Robert – the pout had finally gone. She appeared at last to have forgotten about riding, and, her pheremones finally doing what pheremones do, actually to be glad they had come.

'How delightfully wicked,' she said, as Alison pushed in more of the spikes.

'Isn't it just,' Alison agreed. 'The spikes aren't too sharp, not enough to be dangerous; I mean, they wouldn't actually break skin or whatever. But they'd be damned painful, nevertheless, to a teased cock throbbing against them, helpless to stop itself.' She turned to the balding assistant behind the counter, who was pretending not to be listening. 'Wouldn't you say so?' she said.

'Erm, pardon me?' the man blustered, his cheeks glowing pink.

Alison chuckled. 'Never mind. I'll take this, please.'

The Tack-tube, as the device was labelled, was only the first of many items Alison purchased that afternoon – she was tempted to buy the entire shop – and as they drove home there was a large bag laden with assorted paraphernalia resting on the back seat of the car.

Back at the mansion, Alison parked the Range Rover in the garage next to the stables, killed the ignition and climbed down from the car. She reached back in for the plastic bag and caught up with Belinda who was waiting by the garage door.

The two chattered like excited schoolgirls as they made their way to the house, engrossed in thrilling discussion: Alison was planning on a session with Robert for later that week, to which Belinda was already invited, and they were discussing the use they would make on him of the various new toys they had bought, absorbed in sexual imagery. So absorbed that not even Lady's whinny caught their attention, and they saw nothing of the men who'd disturbed the mare: two men, who stepped from the stable door as they passed.

Men who wore balaclavas, and who poured a clear liquid onto thick linen pads.

Neither woman saw anything before hands reached from behind to press wet rags to their faces, filling their nostrils with a chemical stench, and by then it was already too late.

Chapter Six

A lison awoke with a throbbing head and a sweet taste cloying at the back of her throat that didn't go away when she swallowed.

It wasn't her only concern: she came up only slowly from a narcotic oblivion, and at first didn't understand why she couldn't move – to her still-fuddled brain, it didn't make any sense. Then she realised that her wrists and ankles were tied, bound to the corners of a large double bed. And that brought her fully awake; the throb of her head forgotten as she struggled to make herself think. *What the hell was happening? Why was she tied to a bed?*

For a moment a claw of terror clutched at her gut, like a vicious unseen talon reaching inside her to tear at her innards. But fear was quickly dispelled by anger. And anger, in its turn, changed to absolute outrage. Whoever was responsible for this monstrous affront would pay, would pay dearly, for what they had done.

And just what had they done? She was suddenly struck by a disquieting thought: had she been touched? Sexually molested?

She made a hurried mental check of herself. She didn't feel as though she'd been hurt: apart from the slight pull on her arms and legs she was in no physical discomfort.

And straining her neck to bring her head off the pillow, she could see she was still fully clothed; dressed in the same summer blouse, the same cotton skirt she'd been wearing when she returned home. She hadn't worn a bra, and with her arms stretched above her, her breasts felt vulnerable, their nipples poking at the front of her blouse as if positively inviting attention. But her blouse was still buttoned, and there was nothing to suggest that her breasts had been touched. Lower down, she could feel the elastic of her panties tight on her thighs, so they had not been removed. Her shoes were gone, but that was of minor concern. No, she didn't think she'd been assaulted in any sexual way.

Which was something, at least. But not much; she had still been attacked – physically if not sexually assaulted, drugged into oblivion, and brought . . . *where?*

It occurred to her that she had no idea where she was, unnerving enough in itself, and her eyes swept the room for possible give-away clues. There were no windows in the small square chamber, and she had the distinct impression it was below ground level. It was warm, though, certainly not damp or dank, and had none of the feel of a cellar. Yet a basement of some sort it undoubtedly was, and that was some information at least. It was about all there was, however, for its ceiling was white and featureless, giving nothing away; its walls plain but for a bank of cupboards built into the one opposite: the one which housed the door.

This she stared at. Beyond it, what?

She decided it was time to find out. Drawing on outrage to lend her the courage, it outweighing peripheral dread, she suddenly screamed, 'Whoever is out there, get in here. Now!' her voice a piercing stab in the room's still air.

She strained her ears to listen. But as the sound of her scream died away, there was nothing to hear but silence.

Until the door began to open.

* * *

The man was huge, a giant of a man, and had skin as dark as polished ebony. His features, though, were European, with a narrow nose and full lips. His eyes were a deep gravy-brown, and if he were not so intrinsically menacing he might have been handsome.

Seeing Alison, he grinned, showing a flash of brilliant teeth, which did nothing to make Alison feel any the easier.

She swallowed hard to collect herself. Fear had returned, but this she fought back; wanting anger, not fear, to be her predominant emotion. Timidity was not in her nature and she felt the need to attack: for that, the angrier she was the better.

'What the hell is going on?' she demanded, as if in a position to demand anything at all.

The man didn't answer, his grin not wavering as he came to stand by the bed.

What was he, deaf? A moron? Both? 'I said,' Alison persisted, 'what the hell is going on. Where am I? And who the hell are you?'

The man still didn't answer. And his grin only broadened as he cast a lascivious eye over Alison's slim body, his gaze removing her clothing and coming to settle, she saw, where her groin felt suddenly naked.

She was sharply reminded of her opened legs, and tried, instinctively, to close them. But she felt only the tug of the ropes on her ankles, bringing fully home to her just how helpless she actually was; how unnervingly vulnerable – this man could do with her just as he pleased, she realised. And sensing she had just read his thoughts, a new fear suddenly reared.

'Don't you dare touch me,' she warned.

As if acting on cue, the man reached down; took hold of her skirt and casually flipped it over to expose the white of her panties, his gaze lewd as he feasted his eyes on her crotch.

Alison flinched, the humiliation of it burning her cheeks.

'How dare you!' she choked, indignation constricting her throat. She was about to demand that he cover her that very instant, when she saw something flash in his eyes. She knew lust when she saw it and instead repeated her warning, this time with venom. 'Don't even think it, you bastard!'

But he did more than just think it, and her stomach lurched when the very next moment he slid his hand between her spread thighs, cupping her crotch in his palm; a long middle finger pressed to her sex and it felt hot through the silk of her panties.

Sudden bile rose in her throat and she almost balked; she swallowed it back but still couldn't speak, too shocked to react. And as his finger began to move, tracing an upward path along the silk-covered groove, she could do nothing but lie there and let it. Never had she felt so utterly impotent.

'You'll regret this,' she spat vehemently, finding her voice at last and resorting to threats – her only possible recourse. 'Do you know who I am? My husband is a rich and powerful man –'

'Precisely,' the man said. The one word saying so much.

It said, no, he was not deaf. And no, he wasn't a moron. But of much more significance, it told Alison precisely what this was about.

'You ... you intend to hold me for ransom,' she said quietly; thinking aloud as the truth of it dawned.

The man chuckled. 'You catch on real quick, lady.'

'You'll never get away with it,' Alison snorted, putting a deliberate sneer in her voice in an attempt to sound confident; hoped it might faze him into thinking again. She squirmed at the demeaning caress of his finger, but did her best to ignore it: she would need her wits about her if she were to convincingly argue her case. 'I mean, there's the police. And my husband's resources: not just money, you know, but people. People in high places. Together, they'll track you down. They'll ... they'll ...'

Her words petered out, enervated by the man's arrogant chuckle.

'The boss has been getting away with it these past twenty years,' he said vaingloriously. 'Knows what he's doing, see ... You see this house?' He waved his free hand in an expansive arc. 'Cost him two mil, this house, paid for in cash. All donated by the grateful relatives of people exactly like you; all with the influence their money buys, their friends in high places. But none of that crap cuts any ice with the boss: he's turned kidnap into an art-form, has Martin McClusky. Oh yes, we'll get away with it all right. No worries on that.'

His finger was all the while sliding between Alison's thighs, pressing her panties into the groove of her sex and making it difficult to think. Thoughts were tumbling through her brain like autumn leaves in a squall, but they refused to cohere, to fuse into words and sentences that would make for salient argument. Distracted, she could think of no rebuff to her kidnapper's cocky assertions; nothing to say that might shake his arrogant air.

And nothing to say that would make him remove his hand; she could do nothing but lie there, in passive acceptance of his intimate caress and let it go on. It was humiliating in the extreme.

The man's free hand moved again, then, its movement drawing Alison's eyes as it went to the front of his trousers. And her heart fell further as she saw he was growing aroused, was beginning to bulge massively where he rubbed himself with a palm. She groaned inwardly: what he was doing to her – his finger now on her clitoris, its tip making tiny circles through the thin veil of silk – was clearly exciting him, turning him on. It was a disturbing thought.

Worse – it shocked her to suddenly realise – despite all, and quite impossibly, it had begun to arouse her too! At least in terms of a physical response. It was the last thing she expected – expected or wanted – but she couldn't help herself: unable to escape the persistent stimulus of the cleverly teasing finger, her pussy had begun to respond; in its treachery it was sending tendrils of lust to worm through her loins. And a hot flush reddened her cheeks as she felt her juices beginning to flow; she knew it would soon be moistening the crotch of her panties, where this liquid proof of her growing arousal would convey an insidious message to her grinning tormentor.

She wanted to shut her eyes; to think about something, anything but the unwelcome sensations racking her body; she wished to blot them out and so stem the embarrassing flood. But she couldn't; she was mesmerised by the man's frotting hand as he rubbed at the front of his trousers, and was forced to watch. Rubbing himself more fervently now, the bulge at his crotch was still growing, perhaps having sensed already the moist heat of her sexual response and further excited by that. She feared that at any moment he would reach for his zip, free that massiveness from the restraint of his pants in search of a greater pleasure. She imagined his black cock rearing up at her, a tumescent pole of polished ebony springing rigidly up from his groin, perhaps him forcing it into her mouth, making her suck it fully erect to prepare it for her own violation.

Well, if that was his plan, then let him: she would bite the fucking thing off!

But it didn't come to that. For just then the door swung open, and the man snatched his hand from Alison's crotch as if something had bitten his finger.

A young man, not much more than a boy, with a fresh complexion and an almost pretty face, came into the room. His hair was honey-blond, cropped short at the top and sides but left long at the back.

The first man seemed to relax. 'Oh, it's you, Steve,' he muttered.

'Only me,' said the youth.

His eyes fell on Alison's crotch, where the white of her panties was still exposed, and he grinned a crooked grin.

Alison cringed, a new wave of humiliation crimsoning her cheeks, relief at her timely reprieve from the big man's attentions tempered by having this boy feasting his eyes on her splayed-open thighs.

The lad looked faintly embarrassed, but kept his grin to add, 'But they'll be here any second, B.J. I think you'd best cover – '

He didn't finish. The door once again swung open, and both men turned towards it as yet another man entered, accompanied by a woman.

The man was tall and dark, the woman petite and fair. Physical opposites. But they shared an air of authority that made it immediately obvious that they were in charge. *What had B.J. said his boss's name was?* Alison tried to remember. Something McClusky, wasn't it? This must be he.

The woman had an attractive, if hard face, with glittering diamonds for eyes, and was probably in her mid-twenties. But it was not to her, but to McClusky himself that Alison's eyes were drawn; something about him causing a breath to catch in her throat. He wasn't as handsome as B.J., and certainly had none of the prettiness of the boy, Steve. But he had an unfathomable quality all of his own – an aura of power, somehow, that was extremely appealing. About forty, Alison guessed, he was a man who obviously kept himself fit – even a cursory glance was enough to see he had a hard, lean body beneath the stylish cut of his suit. His hair was black, beginning to fleck at the temples. And his eyes were remarkable: dark and grey, the texture of wet slate, they seemed to hold a myriad secrets his lips would never disclose. They were extraordinary. And very, very erotic.

Aroused as she already was – unbidden, unwelcome arousal, maybe, but aroused none the less – Alison felt a *frisson* of excitement shiver the length of her spine, arousing her further.

But this is crazy, she thought, catching herself in mid-tingle; *utterly bizarre*. Here she was in a dire situation – the victim of kidnap, having been abducted and tied to a bed; with perhaps, who knew, even her very life in danger – and she was experiencing a sexual thrill. It hardly seemed possible.

Nevertheless, as those compelling eyes went to her, she was achingly conscious of her sexual being; of the spread of her legs, of her naked thighs above the tops of her stockings, of the exposed crotch of her panties – a crotch she had dampened with her sexual juices – and she could do nothing to resist the erotic thoughts that suddenly flooded her mind. This strangely exciting, all-powerful man could take her, she knew. Had only to shift aside the leg of her panties to ravish her right then and there, in front of that audience, his sexy eyes holding hers while he pleasured himself in her body. And the thought of it, somehow, was perversely thrilling.

'Have you made contact, boss?'

It was B.J. who had spoken, his words cutting through Alison's thoughts like a knife through warm butter. *Had they made contact?* He obviously meant with Robert, and she forced erotic imagery to the back of her mind to make herself listen: the next few moments might be critical to her very existence. The ransom: would Robert agree to pay it?

A second question rode on the back of it; the answer to which she was far less sure: *would the authorities allow him to pay?*

McClusky shifted his eyes from her to look up. 'Yeah. Sweet as a nut, B.J.' There was just the hint of an accent in his deep, gravelly voice. An Irish accent, the soft brogue of the south. 'He's keeping the police well out of it – if anyone asks, his wife's gone on holiday, is all. And he's agreed to the million we've asked for, to be paid over in the usual way.'

Hearing this, Alison felt a sweep of relief loosen some of the knots in her stomach. So, Robert had agreed to their terms without any fuss. Outrageous affront that it might be, it could have been a lot worse – at least they wouldn't have to resort to cutting off bits of her body to send him by way of persuasion. And the authorities, far from interfering, would not even know: he would simply pay these people the money – a million pounds, it would hardly ruin him – and they would let her go. Thank God!

But her heart sank abruptly as the woman spoke. The accent was also Irish, but hers was the harsher sound of the North. 'Says he needs a month to raise the cash. Bit of a sod, that, but it'll have to be lived with.'

'A fucking month!' B.J. complained.

A month! thought Alison in horror. But they couldn't keep her there for a month. A month spent tied to this bed? Well, surely not that. But, still a month of imprisonment. A month of indignity. A month of God only knew what, with that B.J. around with his pawing hands. They couldn't. They just couldn't!

McClusky gave a small shrug of his big shoulders. 'The man's a canny businessman. Hasn't got stacks of cash lying around, doing nothing; it's all invested. He's got it all right, just needs the time to get it together.'

By the look of B.J., he wasn't appeased; for a moment his face was a dark thundercloud brawling in off an angry sea. But then his eyes suddenly flashed; the sullenness in them displaced by something not sullen at all. Something Alison had seen there before, and it chilled her to see there again . . . Lust.

'Well, if we're gonna have to babysit for a month,' he said, 'can we at least have us some fun with the goods?'

A knife twisted in Alison's gut: *have some fun with the goods?* It took no imagination to think what that meant.

McClusky looked to where Alison's skirt was rucked up, then back to B.J. There was, for Alison, an encouraging hint of reproof in his voice as he said: 'It looks like you already were.'

B.J. grinned sheepishly. 'Some.'

McClusky exchanged a glance with the woman, then said, 'Well, I don't see why not.'

'But no intercourse,' the woman said quickly, something dark and secret momentarily ageing her young face. 'Tell 'em, McClusky.'

'You heard her,' said McClusky, his eyes flicking in warning between the two men. 'And, ah, not this one; she's not to be touched. Have the fun you want with her friend.'

Her friend? thought Alison. Then they had Belinda as well. And not only had her, but were about to use her as their sexual plaything; do as they wished with her. Alison's heart went out to her.

But at least she, Alison, was to be spared the indignity – or worse – of being put at the sexual disposal of these two men; presumably so Robert's 'goods' could be returned unspoiled. That was some comfort. But poor Bel!

Disappointment showed in B.J.'s eyes as they roved hungrily over Alison's blonde hair and slim body. But then he shrugged, grinning. 'OK, boss, you got it,' he said. Then to the boy: 'C'mon, Steve, let's go have us a good time.'

The two henchmen left, and Martin McClusky turned to Alison.

'If you behave, you'll come to no harm,' he told her. 'Your husband will pay us the ransom, and you'll be sent back to him all in one piece. Meantime, so long as you don't make yourself a nuisance, you'll find a small button close to your right hand. Press it if there's anything you need.'

With that, he adjusted Alison's skirt, covering her panties, and he and the woman left.

Leaving Alison alone with her thoughts.

And a nagging longing between her legs. A longing she could do nothing to ease.

Chapter Seven

*B*elinda was awakened from dreary, deep sleep by a persistently slapping hand. Not slapping her hard, but over and over, and enough to make consciousness begin to return, a return, however, she was not at all sure that she wanted. She had a dim recollection of a hand reaching from behind her to press something malodorous over her face, her nostrils filling with a sweet, chemical stench, then a spinning something to nowhere; a meaningless black void.

A limbo, maybe, but she had the uneasy notion that an empty void was the safer place to remain.

But the slapping palm was forcing her from it.

Reluctantly, she slowly opened her eyes. They wouldn't focus at first – she was still disoriented, and she squinted up into a blurry face wondering drunkenly why it was there.

'Ah, you're awake.'

There was a flash of something white. Teeth. Yes, the sound had come from the disembodied face, a row of brilliant white teeth flickering in time to the words.

The face moved back an inch or two and she managed to bring it in focus. It was a handsome face, she saw, but that didn't explain its presence there, hovering above

65

her. Or why it was ogling her with a lecherous expression. Or why – *Oh God* – her hands and feet were tied!

Oh God, Oh God, Oh God: she was tied to a bed! With this stranger looming above her, a salacious gleam in his eye.

Oh God.

Dread realisation at last cleared her head, and she thought, with all certainty, that she was about to be raped. For why else, if not for a sexual motive, had she been abducted? Why else would she be tied to this bed; was this man regarding her with lascivious intent?

She swallowed hard, and from somewhere inside her she found a small voice; a voice that tremored with fear. 'Oh, please,' she implored. 'Please don't hurt me. Do whatever you want, but please don't hurt me.'

The man chuckled.

'There, now what did I tell you, Steve?' he said.

Only then was Belinda aware of a second man in the room. A man whose boyish face now appeared from behind the other's massive shoulder.

'I dunno, B.J.,' said the younger man, looking uneasy. 'I'm still not sure about this.'

'Oh, shut up,' retorted B.J. 'You heard the woman yourself: do what we want, she said.' He looked down at Belinda, taking in her voluptuous body and long legs. 'Ain't that right, now, honey? We can do whatever we like?'

Belinda was frozen with fear, but managed a small nod of her head, her eyes beseeching as she looked from one man to the other. 'Just don't hurt me, please.'

Steve came to sit on the side of the bed. 'Don't worry,' he said gently, 'we don't want to hurt you ... do we, B.J.?'

B.J.'s lack of reply was less reassuring. But the younger man pressed him, his expression concerned: 'Tell her, B.J. Tell her we don't mean to hurt her.'

For a moment B.J.'s eyes were unreadable. Terrifyingly

unreadable, and dread crawled through Belinda's belly like a hundred malignant spiders. But the moment passed, and he suddenly grinned.

'Nah. We just want us some fun, is all . . . This kinda fun.'

With that, and with no other warning, he suddenly reached forward and clamped his enormous hands onto Belinda's breasts, his fingers tightening around them.

Belinda gasped, and choked back a sob. Not a sob of pain, for he wasn't squeezing so hard as to hurt, but in shock. Shock, and humiliation. For as he released his grip and squeezed again he was handling her breasts as if he were kneading dough, or else testing melons for ripeness in a market stall, and it was degrading in the extreme.

'Nice firm tits,' he observed, reddening her cheeks still further.

She wasn't wearing a bra – it had been a warm, sunny day, that carefree day she recalled a million years ago now, and a bra had seemed a stifling encumbrance. She regretted that now. She was wearing only a thin cotton top through which she could feel the heat of the man's palms on her skin, seeming to scald her flesh with his demeaning caress. It was awful. And this, she knew, was only the start.

'With rock-hard little nipples,' B.J. went on, trapping them between fingers and thumbs.

He pinched them firmly, drawing a tiny gasp from Belinda's throat as he twisted them in his powerful grip.

'Hey, steady on, B.J.,' exhorted Steve.

Nah, it's OK,' B.J. assured him. 'Like rock-hard little acorns, they are, just dying to be pinched. They're loving it. But not too much pleasure too soon, eh?'

So saying he abruptly released the tender buds, causing Belinda to wince as the blood rushed suddenly back into them, making them burn. She wished she could rub them, to soothe the fire away, but could only endure it until the searing heat gradually suffused, absorbed into the surrounding flesh.

'Look how they're standing up,' said B.J., flicking the jutting points with the tips of his fingers. 'Prodding at the front of her top and begging for more. Here, let's have a proper look . . .'

Belinda quailed. And B.J. must have seen it, but only chuckled as he pushed up her top, summarily exposing her breasts.

'What do you reckon, Steve? A nice pair or what?'

Steve's manner was still uncomfortable. But he didn't look away; his eyes riveted on Belinda's full breasts while he chewed on his lower lip.

'Go on, Steve,' B.J. urged. 'Have a feel. She said to do what we liked, remember; wouldn't want to disappoint her now, eh?'

Steve hesitated, as if wrestling his conscience, but then slowly reached out a hand; stroked the underswell of Belinda's breast with light and sensitive fingers.

'Oooh, softly, softly,' B.J. scoffed, watching him. 'Give her a proper feel. Like this . . .'

Reaching again for her nipple, he gripped it between finger and thumb; squeezed, and at the same time lifted, stretching Belinda's breast before releasing it to regain its shape with a jiggle. Belinda let out a whimper, but as pain diffused she felt her breast expand with the beginnings of physical arousal. She blushed as she heard B.J.'s chuckle.

'There, you see,' he said smugly to Steve. 'Look how her tit's firming up; swelling with lust. That's how they like to be touched; none o' that softly, softly malarky. Here, let's get rid of this top so we can play with 'em properly.'

His left hand was still on Belinda's T-shirt, keeping it rucked up to her throat, and it was now joined by his right. And when he tugged on the thin material he might have been shredding tissue so easily did it rend in his powerful grip; leaving her breasts naked and heaving as he threw the ruined garment aside.

'There, that's better,' he said, his grin lewd. 'Now we can have a proper feel.'

Then both men's hands were upon her; squeezing, pinching, moulding – handling her breasts with outrageous licence.

And Belinda dealt with it in the only way she was able: she left reality to seek refuge in fantasy – *these men were her slaves*, she told herself desperately; *there for her pleasure, not theirs. They were caressing her breasts upon her command, obediently pleasuring their mistress.*

It was a psychological ploy, mental trickery, but a ploy in which Belinda had faith. After all, she reasoned, what these men were doing to her physically was no more than others, many others, had done before: there was nothing new about her breasts being fondled. What had to be dealt with, then, was not so much the physical assault, but the inherent humiliation of it; the fact that she could do nothing to stop it. And fantasy would allow her to discount this element, for in adopting the dominant role, if only in her mind, humiliation was no longer a factor.

It was a fantasy, fortunately, which Belinda found it easy to conjure, since it was a self-delusion she frequently practised: never having found a submissive partner in the real world, all her lovers were slaves in that other world in her head. If a man was licking her, he would be doing so upon her command; servicing her for hours on end – didn't she wish! – until his tongue was aching with effort. When she was fellating a man it would be, in her mind, a torment for him; he would be struggling desperately not to come while she expertly milked him of his masculine seed. It brought a thrilling new dimension to very ordinary sex.

And would be equally valid in this situation, she reasoned: as long as these men wanted no more from her than ordinary, straightforward sex – and as long as they didn't hurt her! – then she could let the familiar fantasy play out in her mind; delude herself that she was in charge, and so escape the humiliation of it being forced upon her.

Both men were good-looking at least, in their own different ways (perfect as slaves), and if she could believe in the fantasy strongly enough, perhaps she might actually enjoy what they did: what was going to happen would happen anyway, so she might just as well try to!

And as the two men continued to fondle her breasts – *upon her command* – it slowly, but surely, began turning her on.

In the next room, Alison might have slept; she wasn't sure. It was all so disorienting: in the windowless room she had no way of telling if it was night or day, if it was dark or light beyond the four walls of her small bedroom prison. Relief, that she was not to be sexually used as Belinda was, swam through her senses only to drown in the whirlpool of dread that wouldn't quite go away; the silence was deafening and the indignity of her spread-eagled position profound. Yet why was she feeling so horny?

She remembered reading somewhere of a psychological phenomenon known as the Stockholm Syndrome, so named when a bank raid in that city went badly wrong and led to a five-day hostage ordeal for some of the bank's staff. Such was their instinct for survival that the hostages grew close to their captors, coming to form with them deep emotional bonds, empathising with them to such a degree that a female teller actually fell in love with, and later married, one of the men who had terrorised her. Was her own response, Alison wondered – feeling horny, her undoubted sexual attraction to the man McClusky: a man, after all, upon whom her very existence depended – something vaguely akin? Her instinct for self-preservation subconsciously preparing her for sexual humiliations that might yet be on the agenda?

70

She didn't know. She knew only that the sanctuary of oblivion was preferable to lying awake, confused and disoriented, and feeling sexual longings she could do nothing about, and she had tried to drop off to sleep.

Maybe she had managed to; she wasn't sure. But she was awake now. Wide awake. Brought to full consciousness by the sound of the door being opened.

She strained her neck to see who it was. It was Martin McClusky.

Her initial response was one of relief: at least it wasn't B.J. come to demean her again with his pawing hands. But relief was tempered by a sense of disquiet, once again horribly conscious of the spread of her legs as McClusky came into the room.

And just what did he want? she wondered, as she waited for him to speak.

But he didn't speak. Without a word he came to the side of the bed, reached down, and to her horror he pushed up her skirt to re-expose the naked thighs he had earlier covered up for her. She was about to cry out in protest, when she suddenly froze; saw what he held in his hand. A knife! *What the hell did he want with a knife?*

Her protest unvoiced on breath held in terror, she watched the blade glint malevolently in the light from the overhead bulb. Too terrified to speak as McClusky lowered it to her: lowered it down to her crotch, and she jumped as she felt cold steel against the warm skin of her groin.

Then, *snick!*

The elastic of her panties went suddenly slack and she felt them snap aside; knew her blonde bush was now on show at the crux of her widespread thighs, and shuddered as her sense of vulnerability soared to a new peak. She gulped, swallowing into a dry throat – was McClusky about to ravish her then? Despite his warning to the other two men that there must be no enforced sex, was this precisely what he now had in mind?

Snick! The knife cut a second time, severing her panties

71

at her other thigh, and McClusky pulled the flimsy garment out from under her buttocks, exposing her fully as he threw them aside.

If he intended to take her, there was nothing, now, to prevent him. Nothing Alison could physically do to stop him. And she wouldn't beg; she would not give him that satisfaction. To beg would be to surrender psychological, as well as physical control, and she wasn't prepared to cede him so much. No, if he was going to ravish her, then so be it. Let him. And she would endure it in stoic silence, in control of her inner self if not of anything else. She steeled herself, ready.

But what McClusky did then could not have shocked her more.

He carefully arranged her skirt to form a neat hem an inch above her bikini line, leaving her pussy exposed . . . and left.

He had not said a word throughout.

Belinda was meantime enjoying herself . . . *with her slaves obedient to her every whim*.

Indeed, thus far, maintaining the fantasy could not have been easier. After their initial assault, and a frenzy of grabbing and tugging, the men had settled to caressing her breasts in a way, as Mistress, she might well have ordered herself – stroking them sensuously, sensitively, tender fingertips encircling her nipples and keeping them fully erect; palms warm on her skin as they rolled the delicate buds between fingers and thumbs, making them spark with lambent desire. B.J.'s massive hands had turned out to be surprisingly sensual, and the boy's, whilst clearly inexperienced, were soft and gentle; thrilling in a way of their own. And, so far, they couldn't have been pleasuring her more if they were in reality her slaves, working at her command.

And now, having secured her promise not to resist, the men had begun to untie her – Steve loosening the cords at her wrists, B.J. freeing her ankles – and she was positively looking forward to what was to come.

When her legs were free B.J. told her to bring them together, and she winced as her groin protested, the muscles of her inner thighs flexing after being held apart for so long. But the discomfort was fleeting and had already passed when B.J. climbed onto the foot of the bed and came forward.

Planting a knee on either side of her feet, he put his huge hands on her knees and began sliding them upwards, reaching under her skirt. They moved slowly, sensuously, along the outsides of her thighs, until finally reaching her hips. Came inwards then, over her pubis, and Belinda held her breath as his fingertips gradually neared the naked softness between the tops of her thighs. Slipping both hands between her legs, his fingers pressed them a little apart, then began stroking her there; first caressing the hollows on either side of her mound, then making her jump as they brushed directly over her labia, only the thin veil of her panties between them and her lust-heated sex. She moaned softly as a knot of desire tightened in her trembling belly and the beginnings of orgasm stirred.

B.J.'s hands worked on: flattening his fingers he pressed them to her crotch, applying a firm but gentle pressure while moving his hand in a circular motion. As wet as she was, it caused her vulva to slide together lubriciously, stimulating her clitoris between them and tightening the knot of desire still further. Her thighs began to tremble, and her pulse quickened; a throbbing began in her lower belly and her knees felt suddenly weak.

Before her nearing climax could trigger, however, B.J.'s hands moved on; sliding upwards, now, to the waist of her panties. Hooking his fingers beneath the elastic, he began taking them down, drawing them from her in a whisper of nylon as they slid over her stocking-clad legs. The air felt suddenly cool against the raging heat of her sex, and she gasped at the subtle thrill of it.

Moving back, B.J. slipped her panties free of her ankles. And a gasp of a different kind rose in her throat: a gasp of horror at what he did with them then. He held them up to his nose.

'Man, you smell sexy,' he said dreamily, inhaling her scent through their crotch.

Spiders of embarrassment crawled in her belly as she imagined only too well. She had become very aroused in the sex-shop, and knew her panties could not have escaped unblemished. And how long she had been wearing them since, how long she had been tied to that bed without having changed them, she had no way of knowing: but it must have been for some while and her scents on them now would doubtless be strong. And having a man breathe them in, not to mention his commenting on how sexy she smelled, was more than embarrassing; it was humiliating in the extreme.

Yet, as the fantasy kicked in, it was perversely thrilling too, as she *commanded* B.J. to hold her used underwear to his nose; transferring the humiliation from herself to him as she forced him into such demeaning contact with her most intimate bodily scents. And a wave of dark excitement surged through her loins as she watched him, enjoying his chagrin as he was forced to inhale.

At last, however, he discarded the garment, and reached instead for her skirt. There was a single clasp at the waist and he deftly snapped it undone. And then her skirt, too, was off. But for suspenders and stockings, she was now completely naked.

B.J. climbed down off the bed and stepped back, and the two men stood to regard her; greedy eyes devouring her nudity – *the eyes of acolytes adoring their goddess.* Then they, too, began to undress.

Upon her unspoken command.

* * *

'Whatever did you do to the woman in there?' said Kelly, chuckling.

McClusky was sitting in his favourite armchair. Naked. His legs were apart and Kelly was kneeling on the floor between them, serving him orally. He was hugely erect, and she was watching his face as she ran her tongue the considerable length of his penis.

She was highly impressed: she could still taste the briney essence of his first come, burning slightly at the back of her throat. Yet following climax his erection hadn't even begun to subside; he had remained hard and demanding, still in need of her mouth.

It was since he'd been down to the basement to see Alison Corsair. He hadn't been gone for long but when he'd returned to the den, the comfortable sitting room they both preferred to the formal splendour of the rest of the house, his face had been flushed with excitement. He had hardly been able to get his clothes off quickly enough, wanting Kelly to give him relief. Kelly's period had started that morning, but she enjoyed giving oral sex almost as much as she enjoyed receiving it and had been only too glad to oblige. Yet here he was in need of still more. Whatever it was he had done to the woman, it had certainly had an effect!

McClusky told her, describing how he had cut off Alison's panties; what he had done with her skirt.

'You rotten sod,' chuckled Kelly, her cheeks blushing in sympathy. 'You just left her there with her pussy on show? And her knowing that B.J. or Steve, or anyone else for that matter, could walk in at any time and see her like that?'

'I'll rig up the monitor later so you can see for yourself.'

'That's wicked, McClusky.

'Not at all,' grinned McClusky. 'Didn't you notice how horny she was feeling when we were down there earlier?'

'Horny?' Kelly's eyebrow rose in surprise.

'Yeah, don't tell me you didn't see it: it was written all

over her face. Perhaps it was because of what B.J. was up to with her before we arrived; maybe a version of the Stockholm Syndrome or something – '

'All right, so whatever the reason,' Kelly butted in. 'But I don't see how her feeling horny makes what you've just done to her any the less wicked.'

McClusky feigned a look of hurt. 'I'm letting her pussy cool off for a while, aren't I? Just doing the woman a favour, is all.'

'Oh, you liar,' challenged Kelly with a crooked grin. 'You know perfectly well that's not the effect it'll have. The very opposite, maybe.' A stab of excitement plunged through her loins as she imagined how she would have felt in the woman's place; she was almost envious. 'It would on me, anyway: turn me on something fierce, it would.'

'My kinky wee moth,' said McClusky, giving her head an affectionate pat.

Kelly kissed the clefted tip of his penis: she loved it when McClusky got kinky. But there was something else on her mind too; something that made her reflective, and for a while there was only the sound of her ministering lips on McClusky's swollen cock. Then she looked up. 'You fancy her, don't you, McClusky?' she said.

'She . . . intrigues me,' McClusky admitted. 'Yeah.'

'And you want her?'

'My dick does, yeah.'

'Then why don't you have her? She is, let's face it, there for the taking. Especially the way you've just left her.'

'Ah no,' McClusky said quickly. He reached down and stroked Kelly's hair, a tender caress. 'Partly, my wee Belfast beauty, so as not to cause you any upset. I know how you feel about that sort of thing and I would never do anything to upset you. Besides, there's a better way. A more interesting way . . . You know she's into SM – that she likes to be the dominant one?'

Kelly stopped swirling her tongue around McClusky's

lust-swollen glans, and looked up in surprise; she wondered how her man, clever as he was, could have gleaned such a personal titbit. 'No. However do you know that?'

'She had a shopping-bag with her when the lads picked her up,' McClusky explained. 'Full of penile restraints and other gadgets it makes my eyes water even to think of: made our own toy-drawer look positively innocent. I'd bet she's a real hell-cat. So it'll give me an opportunity to test that pet theory of mine, that a sexually dominant woman is really a sexually submissive woman who's never had the courage to try it; who, in essence, does unto others what deep down she'd really like done to herself.'

'You already did that, on me,' smiled Kelly, taking McClusky's penis all the way into her mouth and remembering with vivid clarity the first time McClusky had made her submit to him; the heady excitement of the Master/Slave games to which he had introduced her.

McClusky sucked in a breath as her lips closed around him. 'No, not really,' he said, his voice beginning to sound strained. 'You were never really sexually dominant, any more than you're truly submissive now.'

Kelly's lips came back up his shaft, and she looked up at him in amazement. 'What do you mean?'

'For you, just so long as it's kinky, and the kinkier it is the better, you're into it either way.'

Kelly chuckled around his cock, and mumbled what was meant to be, 'True.'

'Don't talk with your mouth full,' McClusky chided when it came out as nothing at all.

'But she, on the other hand, will make for an interesting challenge. I'm going to teach her the delights of sexual submission. Being a dominant, she'll know already the value of humiliation as a potential sexual turn-on: it'll just be a question of getting *her* to turn on to it . . .'

He paused to gasp as Kelly jabbed her tongue into the

meatus at the tip of his penis, licking away the drop of pre-seminal fluid tha thad collected there. Then, as Kelly's lips slipped back down his shaft, he managed to go on, albeit breathlessly: 'Aroused as she is – and with no way to relieve herself she can only grow more so – it shouldn't be too difficult to do. Keeping her turned on, while at the same time subjecting her to various humiliations, she'll soon come to associate one with the other; come to crave humiliation as a thrill in itself. And far from my taking her by force, she's going to beg me to fuck her before I finally do. Oh yes, she's going to beg me to subject her to the kinkiest perversions, to degradation; to the dirtiest, most demeaning . . .'

McClusky's body went suddenly rigid, and his thighs began to shake. A long groan came from deep in his being, and even Kelly was surprised by the intensity of his second orgasm; his penis throbbed and bucked in her mouth, and she almost choked on the volume of semen that suddenly flooded her throat before she managed to swallow.

And if teaching this Alison woman the delights of submission was going to affect him like this, Kelly decided, then it was a pity they had her for only a month.

The effect on Alison, of being left with her sex so profoundly exposed – so unnervingly vulnerable between her tied-open legs – was staggering.

Never had she felt more conscious, more achingly aware of her genitals, her arousal making their exposure all the more difficult to bear. Her blonde-haired pubic mound was prominent, making her pussy a scream of blatant desire, begging (it seemed) for sex with profligate boldness. And her labia, she knew, would be swollen and pouting, making them especially obvious to whoever might enter the room – the foot of the bed was facing the door and her vulva, outer lips puffing open to reveal pink inner flesh she could feel slick with her feminine juices, would be the first thing anyone would see.

It was humiliating. Utterly demeaning. And in some perverse way, it was utterly, utterly thrilling! What was it about her predicament, about McClusky with his mysterious grey eyes, about being tied to a bed in such an obscene and disquieting fashion that was so improbably, yet irrepressibly thrilling? If she were Robert, she could have understood it – to the masochist it would all have been perfect: tied up and helpless; genitals on open display; humiliated and thoroughly demeaned. It was a masochist's nirvana. But she wasn't a masochist – at least, not that she had ever known. She should be hating all this.

Should be? she thought. But she was hating it, for God's sake. Hating every moment, every second that dawdled so slowly by to become the next long minute of frustration and dread, waiting for the horror of that door to come open. Waiting for something, for anything, to happen. Yet still it excited her. And that, no matter how baffling or confounding it might be, was a fact she couldn't deny.

For even now, despite all, she had an overwhelming desire to come. Needed, desperately, to come. If only she had a hand free, she could have reached for her aching pussy and, heedless of dignity, have fingered herself to much-needed relief. If only she could close her legs, if just for a few seconds, she could squeeze her thighs together and let the pressure there trigger her climax. If only . . .

And she knew that playing 'if only' was as futile as her wanting to come, and served only to deepen her anguish.

She made herself stop, and tried to focus her thoughts elsewhere; anywhere, away from her sexual cravings. And away from her exposed genitalia.

It wasn't easy: for every breath of air that moved in the room seemed relentlessly to seek out her sex; to caress her swollen vulva with teasing, ethereal fingers, so constantly reminding her of her dreadful predicament. It made it an epic struggle to free her brain of erotic thought. But at last she began to succeed, and as the worst of her frustrated longing gradually eased, she drifted slowly to the mercy of sleep.

Belinda watched, spellbound, as the two men stripped. *Slaves denuding themselves for her visual pleasure.*

She was watching B.J. as he stripped off the last of his clothes. And when he slipped down his shorts to stand naked before her, she saw that he was massively endowed, his penis a thick ebony truncheon hanging between his legs. She almost dreaded seeing him erect, that veritable weapon engorged, cocked and ready for action. Though she knew, as surely as night follows day, that before very much longer she would.

Gulping, she switched her attention to the younger man, Steve, who was still showing signs of his earlier reticence. Not, however, that it was stopping him stripping. And as he stepped out of his briefs, she saw that his penis, unlike B.J.'s, was already beginning to harden; visibly swelling without need of physical stimulus. A cock, evidently, with none of its owner's restraint.

He might have been reticent but he wasn't shy, and as he stood by the foot of the bed, as naked as the day he was born, he was a man clearly at ease with his body.

And with some right to be too, Belinda decided, looking him over with an appreciative eye. He had a smooth, tanned torso, with a broad chest that narrowed to masculine hips, and was well-muscled without the body-builder's ugly overdevelopment. And his penis, if far from the size, even now it was fully erect, of B.J.'s awesome member, couldn't have been more beautifully sculpted, its purple head forming an attractive helmet atop a shaft that was symmetrically curved.

B.J. sat down on the foot of the bed, and grinned as he nodded at Steve. 'Doesn't waste any time, does he, your friend? I'd say he's in need of a blow-job: what d'you reckon?'

There might have been sympathy in Steve's warm, almost puppy-dog eyes as he looked down at Belinda. But if there was, it turned to apology as he sighed deeply and said, 'What the hell.'

'Attaboy,' chuckled B.J., watching him scramble onto the bed. 'Go for it.' Then, wagging a warning finger at Belinda, he said, 'And you swallow all that comes into your mouth, right?'

Straddling Belinda's chest, Steve hesitated, just for a moment, then brought the head of his cock to her lips. And Belinda opened her mouth for him. After all, she told herself, she had sucked men's penises before. That this time she had no choice was a fact it was best to forget. And with reality tucked safely away where it could do her no harm, she took her slave's penis into her mouth and began to expertly suck him, letting the scent of his musk excite her, the better to imagine he was just a regular lover with whom she was living her usual fantasy.

No sooner had she begun than she felt her legs being spread, large hands on her knees pushing them open. Then there was the feel of hot breath on her sex, making her shiver with erotic sensation. She tensed, waiting for more. And then more there was, as she felt the touch of a tongue.

Had her throat not been otherwise engaged, she would surely have cried out in delight. For the feel of B.J.'s tongue – *her slave's tongue* – sliding lubriciously along her dew-filled channel was wonderfully thrilling: her slave was accomplished indeed.

Licking slowly, his tongue moved up along one of her labia, then down the other, easing apart the delicate folds before finally snaking between them, its tip sliding directly into her now throbbing vagina to swirl deliciously inside her. She moaned softly, causing the rigid penis in her mouth to vibrate and bringing an accompanying moan from Steve.

B.J.'s lips went higher; brushed her clitoris with a delicate kiss, then clamped the sensitive button between them, sucking it into his mouth. Belinda's abdominal muscles snapped taut with the initial shock of it, and she let out a nasal moan; sucked on the penis ever more avidly as she sensed the approach of her climax.

B.J. seemed also to sense it, and his tongue began worrying her clitoris with little rapid flicks that drew climax ever closer; his lips pressing back its protective hood to keep the mass of nerve-endings helplessly exposed, at the mercy of his fluttering tongue. Belinda's thighs began to quiver, her heart thudding as orgasm gathered fast; bunching tight in her belly, the familiar spring was about to snap as she forced her slave to lick on. The penis of her other slave, the one in her mouth, was throbbing now, and seeming to swell ever further between her ministering lips: he was straining to hold himself back (so the fantasy held) while her mouth was threatening to emasculate him; to force him to come and so drain him of his masculine essence. But he wouldn't resist her for long!

The rise of her own orgasm was gathering pace. Drawing closer, and closer still; driven on by B.J.'s tongue; driven on by thrilling fantasy. And then, suddenly, she was coming, shaking in the throes of it as she tumbled in free-fall through a spinning vortex of pleasure.

She yearned to lose herself, completely and utterly, in the deluge of sensation that swept through her body. But she couldn't. For at the exact moment of her own release, perhaps triggered by watching her come, perhaps by the vibration of her ecstatic moans on his penis, she sensed the man in her mouth grow tense; heard his breathing grow uneven and heavy, and knew he was ready to come. She steeled herself, waiting for the feel of hot semen sent jetting to the back of her throat; she fancied she could taste it already, slightly salt on her tongue, and knew she would soon have its taste for real. She was wrong. For the moment before it began Steve abruptly withdrew, pulling his penis out of her mouth to spurt his ejaculate over her face.

As the first of it spattered onto her cheek, Belinda inwardly shuddered. It was humiliating. Degrading, even. She guessed Steve had withdrawn out of courtesy, a sort of perverse act of gallantry, but she might have preferred that he hadn't; that he had come in her mouth and made her swallow it as B.J. had told her she must. Rather that than the feel of it trickling down her cheek as it was, down the side of her nose, which was demeaning in the extreme.

Fantasy though once again proved her saviour. For if she were Mistress, then she must herself have suggested it; to give her slave the rare treat, which so many men seemed to enjoy, of seeing himself come over a woman's face. And where was the humiliation in being magnanimous? Anyway later – *Oh yes, good* – she would make him lick it off as the price he would pay for her generous sanction!

While these thoughts all raced through her mind, Steve's ejaculate continued to spatter: it seemed to go on for a very long time as his penis pumped on and on. But, at last, he was finished, dribbling the last of his semen onto her chin with a final grunt of effort. And wiping the tip of his now softening member off on her lips, he collapsed on the bed beside her, for now satisfied.

As Steve moved aside, however, Belinda saw B.J. was clearly not satisfied at all: kneeling between her spread thighs, his own thighs slightly apart, he was now hugely erect, his massive organ arcing up from his groin like a giant mahogany cudgel. She couldn't help but gasp at the sight of it: never had she seen a penis so big.

B.J. spoke to the younger man, his eyes aglow with overt desire.

'I've decided, Steve,' he said. 'I'm going to have her.'

Steve jerked himself up on an elbow, as if in sudden shock. 'But Kelly – ' he began.

B.J. cut him off, finishing his sentence with: 'Said nothing about us refusing to screw her if she asked us to nicely, now did she? And that's just what she's gonna do.' He looked up at Belinda. 'Ain't you, honey? You're gonna ask B.J. to put his big dong in that sweet little pussy of yours. Right?'

Belinda, somewhat mystified by the men's conversation, by Steve's apparent concern over B.J.'s announcement – *and who was this Kelly they spoke of?* – was eyeing the enormous black penis with some trepidation, wondering if it would hurt.

'Right?' B.J. pressed, when she hadn't answered. 'Come on now. Ask me nicely. Ask B.J. to fuck you.'

Belinda swallowed hard. 'Fuck me,' she whispered. Then she rallied, forcing the fantasy high in her mind: *This man's your slave*, she told herself sharply. *Believe it. Believe it, for God's sake.* And she said it again. Not a whisper this time, but more loudly; making it as much a command as she dared. She would have loved to have added, 'Slave.' But, of course, didn't.

'There,' said B.J. triumphantly. 'Now she's asked me to, how can Kelly complain?'

Steve was still frowning. 'I dunno, B.J.,' he muttered. 'I'm not sure Kelly'd see it as different.'

'Course it's different,' B.J. chuckled. 'Mind you, I ain't missing out on a bit of what you've just had: first she can come here and give me some head. Though do me a favour' – he found a cloth and threw it at Steve – 'wipe her face before she gets started, eh?'

Belinda was reminded of Steve's sperm on her face, making her skin feel tight as it dried. It was a degrading sensation, and she'd be more than glad to have it wiped off before being called upon to liberate more of the stuff from another penis.

That one a huge and mighty weapon.

* * *

In the adjoining room, Alison was again awakened by the sound of the door. She had slept only fitfully, and her eyes snapped open just as the door clicked to.

McClusky was back.

Chapter Eight

*I*n one respect, Alison was relieved it was only McClusky. He, at least, had seen already all that there was to see. All he had put on such blatant display! Had it been the young man Steve, or worse, that B.J., with his pawing hands . . . She shuddered to think.

In another respect, however, she wasn't so sure. For in truth, McClusky presented far more of an actual threat, the rules as applied to the other two men clearly not binding on him. And had he now come, Alison wondered, to do that which he hadn't done earlier? To ravish her? She didn't know, and could only wait to find out.

McClusky stood for a while with his back to the door, just looking, making Alison squirm with embarrassment as she watched his eyes settle where of course they inevitably did. It was as if they were physically touching her, and she was horrified to sense her pussy respond as if to an actual caress; her vulva twitching reflexively as he stroked them with his gaze – practically winking at the man, for God's sake! But at last he came forward into the room, shifting his eyes away, and she breathed a little more easily.

Only now did she see he was carrying a glass of water,

and she suddenly realised how thirsty she was; she pushed other concerns to the back of her mind, and hoped it was meant for her.

It apparently was: setting the glass down on a bedside table, McClusky reached to unfasten her wrist.

The cords by which she was secured to the bed had been tied to form nooses, which drew tighter the harder she struggled. But only when her wrist was released did she realise how hard on them she must have been pulling – her fingers burned as the blood rushed back to them, the circulation allowed to return.

McClusky gave her a moment to flex them, then put the glass in her hand. She drained it in one – it wasn't just thirst; her saliva was thick and cloying, with an unpleasant coppery taste, and she was glad of the water to wash it away.

McClusky took the empty glass from her, then reached again for her wrist. At first she tried to resist, straining her muscles against his in a bid to prevent his retying her hand. But he held her easily in his powerful grip, and merely waited for her strength to run out before returning her hand to the noose.

There was a straight-backed chair by the wall, and this he now drew to the side of the bed; he sat down and settled back, saying nothing of his intentions.

Indeed, all this time he had not said a word. And for a while Alison was glad: she had nothing to say to the man, and, unless he had come to tell her they were setting her free, which seemed unlikely, there was nothing he could say that she wanted to hear. This was the man who had kidnapped her, who was holding her captive. Who had removed her panties and deliberately left her in so humiliating a fashion . . . and who, despite all – or because of all? – seemed to have such an unnerving sexual effect on her!

But as the silence lengthened, she could hardly decide which was worse: talking, or having to endure this somehow unnatural quiet.

Finally the urge to speak, to break the silence, was overwhelming, and she knew she would have to say something or bust. But what? Nothing she could say would help ease her position – for it seemed pointless to issue threats, and she wouldn't plead; a tirade of outrage would serve no purpose, and making small-talk seemed ludicrous in the extreme.

There was one question on her mind, though, that it did seem reasonable to ask. 'What time is it?' she said at last.

'What does it matter?' McClusky replied with a shrug.

'Well, is it at least night or day? Is it dark or light outside?' She had no idea and, somehow, despite what McClusky might think, it did matter. It seemed to matter a lot.

But again McClusky declined to say.

Having heard Terry Waite and the others talk about their kidnap experiences in the Middle East, Alison thought she knew why.

'I suppose this is all part of your game-plan, is it?' she said. 'Disorientation?' Her tone was deliberately non-accusing, conversational. Talking about anything was better than a return to that dreadful heavy silence. Though if it helped her, too, to better understand the mind of her captor, then all to the good: it might make her captivity a little easier to deal with. 'I suppose it keeps your victims off-balance, does it?'

McClusky shrugged. 'I find it does help to keep our guests, how shall I say, subdued. Disoriented, they tend to be less of a handful, yes.'

'And abuse is a part of that too, I suppose.'

'Abuse? Ah, you mean the lads having their fun with your friend?'

'Well, yes,' Alison muttered. 'That too. But I was talking about me.'

McClusky put on a puzzled frown, as if he had no idea what she meant. 'You?'

'I'd say humiliation comes under the heading "Abuse", wouldn't you?'

'Ah.' McClusky chuckled, as if comprehension had suddenly dawned. 'You mean this?'

His hand flicked out as he spoke, and the backs of his fingers grazed lightly across her exposed vulva.

Alison jumped, the nooses tightening around her wrists and ankles as her body leapt up from the bed in a reflex, knee-jerk reaction, and she almost cried out in utter shock – his finger might have been a red-hot poker so intense was the sudden sensation of it touching her intimate flesh; so savage was the unprepared-for thrill that it caused to surge through her loins. But thrill or not, the fact he had touched her was an absolute outrage and a scream of protest rose in her throat, about to demand that he remove his hand that very instant. But as his hand remained she choked the scream back; managed, somehow, to contain it within her. For even as the words took form in her mind, it occurred to her that this might be her chance, her only chance, to attain the relief for which she was so desperately aching: he was caressing her now in earnest, and as his finger slid back and forth along the juice-slick folds of her sex, made sensual circles around the stem of her clitoris, it was edging her inexorably towards climax.

A climax that would end the misery of frustration. Oh, what relief it would be!

It was a heady hope. But at the same time it presented her with an invidious quandary: for if she *were* to come, she certainly wouldn't wish it to show. It would be embarrassing for a start. But more, she had no desire to give McClusky such satisfaction; the satisfaction of seeing it – of knowing she found him exciting, and that she had succumbed as a result of what he had done to her. No, she would need, somehow, to keep it within her; hope he would read her tension at the critical moment as being nothing more than a natural tightening of muscles in outraged response to his intimate assault; read any shudder as a shudder of disgust. It wouldn't be easy, she knew, to climax without letting it show. But she would have to risk it: if she didn't come, she would go mad with frustration.

His hand was now resting on her inner thigh, his forefinger almost absently brushing her sex. It wasn't as expedient as his more obvious caresses of a moment before, but it was still enough. Enough to make her orgasm continue to mount, gathering in her lower belly ready to burst through the dam. She focused all her attention on it. Fought to keep her thighs from trembling as her body strained in reach of it. Held her breath, her nostrils flaring in the agony of keeping herself silent. Waited. Just another few seconds would be all it would take. Another few strokes of that casually brushing finger. Just . . . one . . . more . . .

And McClusky withdrew his hand. Right at the last possible moment.

Oh no. Oh God, no! Alison could have wept with frustration, and the breath she had held in anticipation of rapture escaped from her lungs in a secret sigh of despair. It was as if he had known how very close she was, and had deliberately taken her there only to deny her the touch she needed the most; the final touch, that would have allowed her relief, the glorious release of climax. But he couldn't have known. Could he?

There was no time to dwell on it, however, for just then her thoughts were distracted by sounds from outside; from the adjacent room, she presumed. Sounds that were rising in volume, and that were now clearly discernible: they were a woman's cries of ecstasy, in the unmistakable throes of climax.

It was Belinda!

Alison knew the sound of Belinda's orgasm almost as well as she knew that of her own, and there was no doubt about it: Belinda was coming. And not only coming, but enjoying it too!

But how could she? How could she so easily have given herself, have submitted herself to those men? Had she no pride? No shame? Even if she had been at their mercy and been driven to a climax she could have done nothing to help, she could at least have endured it in a dignified silence; kept it within her just as she, Alison, would have done.

Had she, Alison, had that good fortune! And that thought made her ache all the more: knowing Belinda was coming heightening her awareness of her own deprivation.

Moreover, as the ecstatic screams rose in volume, and were joined by a man's, Alison knew they were screwing: Belinda only came as intensely or as noisily as that via actual sexual intercourse. Yet the men had been specifically instructed not to take her by force, which had to mean only one thing – she had spread her legs for them willingly. The slut!

McClusky chuckled. 'Sounds like your friend's having fun,' he said.

Alison didn't reply; fuming.

McClusky stood up and pushed back his chair. And pausing only to smooth down Alison's skirt, covering her crotch – another surprise, if this time not an unwelcome one – he left.

The sounds from the adjoining room gradually abated, dying through moans and squeals of lesser intensity to finally stop altogether. And soon there was only silence again.

Silence, and the slow passage of time.

For Belinda, the climax Alison had heard was the culmination of a three-hour session of sexual athletics. And yes, she couldn't deny it, lost in her fantasy, sexual pleasure too.

She had undergone three thrilling hours of having four hands and two tongues – *those of her slaves* – exploring every inch of her body, not a part of her left undiscovered as they each had pleasured her in their different, disparate ways: B.J. confident, assertive, aggressive; *the experienced, well-trained slave, pleasuring his mistress with consummate skill.* Steve more hesitant, sensitive, gentle; *the acolyte, learning to serve in his mistress's boudoir.* Each, in his own way, as exciting as the other, and between them they had brought her to countless orgasms, each more intense than the one before as her body had risen to higher and higher planes of carnal receptiveness.

It wasn't a one-way journey: she had sucked both men's penises several times each, and had wanked them on demand . . . *Hers!*

Steve had come three times in all – twice spending himself over her face, and a final time on her breasts; squeezing them together and taking his pleasure in the crevice thus created. While B.J., though he had been close many times, had not come at all, saving himself for the promised finale.

It might have been coerced sex, Belinda reflected, but she could not have denied that, at least in terms of physical pleasure and safe in the haven of fantasy, it had been damned good sex.

And then, at last, had come that finale: B.J. had finally taken her. *She had finally commanded her slave to mount her, to pleasure her with his magnificent phallus.*

In the event, his mammoth penis hadn't hurt her at all, as she had worried it might – he had first knelt between her thighs and spent a considerable, and considerate, time bathing its bulbous head in her sexual juices, thoroughly lubricating it before ever attempting to penetrate her. (Though whether, in truth, this was primarily for her comfort or his, Belinda wouldn't have liked to opine!) At the same time he had reached down with his hands, using his thumbs on her pubis to press the loose skin upwards and outwards, forcing her clitoris from its protective hood where his glans could slide across it, so making her juices flow all the more copiously in readiness for him. Satisfied at last, he had positioned himself carefully. And gently, but inexorably, had pushed himself forward, sliding his penis all the way into her in a single penetrative thrust; that thick ebony cudgel entering her vagina with surprisingly lubricious ease.

His huge organ had stretched her vaginal walls, but no more than was bearable, and its bulbous head had nudged at the neck of her womb, but no more than was pleasurable. And when he'd begun thrusting in earnest, his thick shaft stimulating her clitoris, his every inward push driving his glans hard against her G-spot, she had exploded in an orgasm of such massive intensity it had caused her to cry out in the throes of it. She had taken B.J. with her, and he'd thrown back his head, the veins on his muscular neck standing out like rigid cords as he was held in the grip of his own massive climax.

Whether it was to punctuate the end of the session, she didn't know. But the three were now lying sprawled on the bed, drained and exhausted. Belinda's thighs were slightly apart, and there was still a thrum vibrating between them: she fancied she could feel B.J.'s penis, even now, throbbing inside her as it had when he'd come. Mentally, there was still much to concern her – it remained the fact she was the victim of kidnap; she had no idea where she was, or for how long they intended to keep her, or even who 'they' were. But physically she was relaxed and content, no worse off for all they had done with her so far. And, she decided, as long as they continued to use her for straightforward and non-violent sex, when she could rely on fantasy to help pull her through, then she would survive the ordeal without damage.

She hoped.

Just then, the door to the room swung open and a third man came in; a man with dark, compelling eyes. *Was this the Kelly they had spoken of earlier?* wondered Belinda, instinctively snapping her legs together for want of a more modest position.

The man saw the movement and chuckled. 'I wouldn't do that if I were you,' he said. 'If I know B.J., when he's in reach of a pussy he'll want it available to him. Right, B.J.?'

B.J. and Steve had evidently been dozing, for at the sound of the man's voice they started, sat up on the bed to mumble in greeting.

'The way you like it, that, isn't it, B.J.?' the man went on. He was grinning, and evidently ribbing the man on the bed. 'A woman's legs kept spread, so you don't have the hassle of opening them.'

B.J. seemed oddly uncomfortable. 'Er, no. No, boss, it's OK,' he muttered. 'We're, er, kinda finished.'

'Oh?' The man's eyebrows rose in surprise. 'Since when did that make a difference to you?'

Surprise turned to suspicion then, and he looked at Belinda, his grin gone.

'Spread your legs,' he told her shortly. 'Open them wide.'

Belinda quailed. She was bemused by whatever was happening – something obviously was, since B.J.'s disquiet was now almost tangible – but troubled much more by the thought of spreading her legs: from where he was standing, the man would have an unnerving view of her sex.

She found an unexpected ally in the discomfited B.J. 'Er, like I said, there's really no need, boss: I mean, we're all done. Ain't we, Steve?'

Steve nodded, and opened his mouth as if to speak in support. But the man kept him silent with a withering look, and turned again to Belinda.

'I said, spread your legs,' he repeated.

Belinda swallowed hard. It would almost have been better if B.J. and Steve could have taken a leg each; spread them for her. It would have been embarrassing enough. But to have to do so herself, on this man's command, would not only be horribly embarrassing, but humiliating into the bargain. And, this time, there would be no escaping it either; there would be no finding solace in fantasy, for never in a dominant role would she conceivably put herself in such a position.

She hesitated for as long as she dared. But the man's quiet voice had been laden with menace and she knew she had better comply. Blushing furiously, she let her legs come slowly apart.

The man looked for a moment, then narrowed his eyes at B.J.

'You've had sex with her,' he said.

Belinda cringed, but there wasn't time to think what to say, for B.J. was quick to respond. 'She wanted it, boss, honest,' he sputtered. Then, to Belinda: 'Tell him. Tell him you asked me to fuck you.'

Belinda could only nod dumbly, since she could hardly deny it.

The man was still looking at B.J., not impressed. 'I'll bet,' he snorted. But after a moment he sighed. 'Oh well, I suppose there's leeway enough, just, for it not to be called rape. Though you'd be wise to say nothing to Kelly, not if you value your balls.'

So this wasn't Kelly, then, thought Belinda. Then who the hell was Kelly? A fourth man to whom she would have to submit? The number was going up all the time: *just how many of them were there, for God's sake?*

B.J. muttered something about being sure to keep it from Kelly, and the man he'd called boss looked a little placated as he turned to address Steve. 'Go and get our guest some lunch,' he told him, 'while B.J. takes her along to the bathroom so she can clean herself up. After that you can get rid of her clothes: she won't be needing them for the time she's here. But there's no need to tie her back on the bed: no reason her stay here should be any more uncomfortable than it already will be, with you two reprobates having your fun with her.'

Belinda swallowed into a dry throat. She was to be kept naked! With B.J. and Steve, at the very least, 'having their fun with her'. But at least the phrase 'her stay here' had a finite ring to it, and suggested that at some time, when that stay was over, she was to be released. At least, she hoped that's what it suggested.

'Meantime,' said the boss, 'some of us have things to do, so I'll leave you to it. But remember – you've got her for a month, so don't go wearing her out like a kid with a new toy. I'll catch you later.'

And with that he was gone.

Leaving B.J. to grin sheepishly at Steve. 'See, I told you it'd be OK.'

'Yeah, but if Kelly found out.' Steve winced; shook his hand as if cooling burned fingers. 'Ouch!'

'So who's gonna tell her, you?'

'No, but – '

'And Martin sure as hell won't. So, we've got nothing to worry about, have we? You wanna go with her now? Or can't you get it up again after three?'

'I can always get it up, you toe-rag; not me who's the one-shot wonder, is it? But you heard what the boss said, I've got to go get her some grub. And you haven't taken her to the bathroom yet, neither.'

Belinda wasn't listening: she had long since switched off. *A month!* she was thinking. She was to be held for a month. Kept naked, and at the sexual disposal of at least two men – B.J. and Steve.

So, there was some compensation, then! Just so long as the fantasy held.

Chapter Nine

Alison wished, now, she had declined the glass of water McClusky had brought to her earlier. For now she needed the bathroom.

The first stirrings of discomfort had begun some while ago, and had been growing steadily worse until now it was barely endurable; her bladder was full to bursting and she would have to relieve it soon. It didn't help that she was unable to close her legs; squeezing her thighs together might have eased the pressure a little, but she couldn't even do that.

As the discomfort had worsened, she had several times reached for the bell by her hand that McClusky had assured her would bring someone to her. But each time, she had resisted actually pressing it, deciding she would try to hold on for a while; hoping her captors would realise she would have certain natural needs – they were, after all, supposed to be experts at this heinous business of theirs – and would from time to time release her so she could avail herself of a toilet. It would have been less embarrassing for her than her having to actually ask. It was this embarrassment that had been holding her back. Well, along with the half-dread of them bringing a bed-pan to her, the ignominy of which would be awful.

However, the ignominy of wetting the bed would be a thousand times worse, and if she didn't get to a toilet soon, that was what it would come to. She could wait in hope no longer; she would have to ring the bell.

She made herself do it, and two minutes later, just as McClusky had promised, her summons was answered. It was the hateful B.J. who came, and Alison was only glad that McClusky had smoothed down her skirt on his previous visit, covering her naked crotch.

Even so, B.J. was the last of her captors she wanted to see, the thought of his hand between her legs still making her cringe. And now, minus her panties, if he were to put his hand there again . . .

Bile rose in her throat, and she swallowed it back.

'I have to use the bathroom,' she said, letting the faint embarrassment of saying it distract her from far more disquieting thoughts.

B.J.'s reaction, however, did nothing to ease her concerns. He grinned. Grinned broadly, and a glint of what might have been cruelty appeared in his gravy-brown eyes. Alison felt a vague sense of dread beginning to stir in her gut.

B.J. came forward to the foot of the bed. 'Do you now?' he said, making no effort to disguise his delight. 'And what do I get in return?'

'What do you mean?' said Alison; dread growing, becoming more clearly defined. 'I . . . I don't understand.' Though she was fearing she did.

'Well, for my taking the trouble to untie you. Taking you along to the bathroom. What's in it for me?'

So, at least there was a bathroom then: none of the indignity of a bed-pan to have to contend with. It was something. *Wait, no*, thought Alison, struck by a sudden realisation; *it wasn't just something, it was a lot*. For in the privacy of a bathroom, her hands free, she'd be able to relieve herself in more ways than one. Her heart began to pound at the thought. To come! An end, at last, to that maddening sexual ache; an end to frustration. But what would she have to do to be afforded that privilege?

'What do you want?' she said.

B.J. rubbed his chin between finger and thumb, as if to consider it. Then, 'A look at your tits,' he said at last, his handsome face looking ugly as it split in a lascivious grin.

Alison groaned inwardly. Yes, she might have known it would be something like that – more indignity; more humiliation. But it could have been worse; a great deal worse. And if he wanted to ogle her breasts there wasn't much, anyway, she could do to prevent him. She sighed in resignation.

'Oh, do what you want,' she muttered. 'I can hardly stop you, can I?'

'Ah, but no. You'll have to show them to me.' B.J. shrugged his massive shoulders. 'See, you're off limits: I'm not supposed to lay a finger. I can untie you of course, but that's about all: you'll have to unbutton your top yourself.'

Alison suddenly saw red. 'Fuck you!' she snarled. Maybe she couldn't stop him from undoing her blouse, but she'd be damned if she'd do it for him. Bare her breasts herself and be an active party to her own abasement? No way.

B.J. only chuckled. 'Well, that's the deal, honey,' he said. 'Take it or leave it. Though I think, after careful consideration, you'll take it. Don't you?'

So saying, he leaned forward over the bed; touched his fingertips lightly to Alison's abdomen. It was a less than subtle threat.

Alison winced, imagining the consequences of his applying pressure to her already tender belly; the sharp, excruciating pain. Perhaps, if it proved too much for her bursting bladder, worse.

'I . . . I thought you weren't to touch me,' she gasped, clutching for a desperate straw.

'Ah. Quite right, of course,' said B.J., lifting his hand from her distended abdomen. 'Naughty old me. Still, there's really no need, is there? Time and nature will do the same job. You'll come around sooner or later, I'd say.'

And with that he turned to leave.

Alison was struck with sudden horror. 'No, wait!' she shouted, dreading the thought of having to hold on any longer; knowing she couldn't, anyway, and that she was left with no choice but to agree to his sickening terms. 'All right, you win. I'll do as you say.'

B.J. chuckled his dirty chuckle. 'Now there's a smart lady.'

He came to the head of the bed and, one by one, he released her wrists, slackening the nooses so she could slip out her hands.

Then he stepped back, folding his arms to wait.

Alison hesitated, steeling herself for this new indignity, then quickly unbuttoned her blouse. Pulled it open and lay with her arms by her sides, her breasts naked and heaving as B.J.'s eyes fell upon them, taking in their pertness and dark areolae.

'Now give 'em a feel,' he said, unfolding his arms and cupping his hands, palms uppermost, in mime of what he required.

Alison was too weary to argue – she doubted, anyway, it would have done any good – and raised her hands to her breasts, cradling them into her palms.

B.J. watched for a while, his eyes still mocking but now beginning to hood; he licked his lower lip as he stared with growing desire.

Then this, too, wasn't enough.

'Nipples,' he told her, his voice thick and croaky. 'Let me see you pinching your nipples.'

Alison felt her blush run down to her neck, but again complied, letting her hands slide upwards to trap her nipples between fingers and thumbs; suppressed a gasp to keep secret the warm thrill that suddenly sparked through her breasts, but could do nothing to prevent her nipples erecting, betraying her erotic response.

B.J. grinned, clearly delighted to see her unbidden

arousal, and lowered a hand to his crotch; began rubbing the bulge that was just beginning to show there.

And Alison decided enough was enough.

'Look,' she said, defiantly taking her hands from her breasts. 'I've done everything you've told me to do. Now can I please go to the bathroom?'

To her considerable relief, B.J. relented – if, it appeared, reluctantly. With a heavy sigh, he moved to the foot of the bed, and while Alison rebuttoned her blouse, he busied himself with her bonds.

Free at last, Alison rolled from the bed, glad to stretch feeling back to her limbs. How long she had lain there, her arms and legs outstretched, she had no idea. But it must have been for quite a few hours; her muscles felt awkward and leaden, her legs rubbery as she struggled for balance.

'I might as well tell you,' said B.J., as he led her out of the room, 'so you can save yourself the effort if you're thinking to do anything silly, that the only way up from down here is a door at the top of those stairs.'

They were in a spacious, carpeted corridor, from which several doors led off to the right. The stairs to which B.J. referred were dead ahead, rising off to the left. The flight turned mid-way up and Alison couldn't see any door, but she had no reason to doubt it was there.

'And it's locked,' B.J. finished, as if reading her thoughts. 'It's as solid as a rock, too: no key, no way out.'

By now they had reached the fourth door along, and B.J. stopped; pushed the door open and stepped aside, allowing Alison to pass. She strode into a small but functional bathroom, complete with tub, basin, bidet, and, thank God, a lavatory. The room was clean and smelled faintly of pine, and fresh towels hung on a rail.

She turned back to the door to close it behind her, but B.J. was leaning against it, his huge shoulder propping it open.

'Do you mind?' said Alison.

B.J. grinned. 'Not at all,' he said, angling his head at the toilet. 'Go right ahead.'

A slow sinking feeling began in Alison's stomach. 'You don't mean you're going to stay there while ... while ...'

'The boss says you're not to be left alone,' B.J. shrugged. "Cept of course, when you're safely tied up.'

'But not in the bathroom for God's sake.'

Again B.J. shrugged. 'He didn't say not.'

Alison's heart sank further; not least since her hopes of at last relieving her sexual longings were now plainly dashed: with B.J. hovering there by the door, she'd be able to perform only the legitimate function for which she'd been brought there. And how embarrassing that would be, with him able to hear every sound!

Unfortunately, B.J. didn't look at all unhappy with his boss's instructions, and she knew it would be pointless to argue. She didn't, anyway, have the time.

Resigned, she crossed to the toilet and turned back to face him.

'Well, at least turn around,' she said.

B.J. only grinned, and stayed where he was.

'You're ... you're not going to *watch*?' Alison could hardly believe it, a knot tightening in the pit of her stomach as the truth of it dawned. Even thinking it reddened her cheeks. 'I refuse. I flatly refuse to go to the toilet with you standing there watching.'

'Please yourself,' said B.J. with an indifferent toss of his head, nodding back the way they had come. 'You want to go back to the room, we'll go back to the room; it's OK by me.'

'But ... but ...'

Alison was lost for words, her arguments defeated before she could voice them. She felt utterly impotent, knowing she was beaten again; that she had no way to win.

Then from out of despair reared sudden anger. 'What

are you?' she fumed. 'A pervert? It'll give you a kick, will it, watching me go to the loo?'

'Hey, honey, I ain't the only one here who gets off in unusual ways, right? As I recall, that bag you had with you when we picked you up had some real interesting stuff in it. And don't tell me the enema gear was for legitimate medical use. Seems you and me are a lot alike, lady.'

The wind was driven from Alison's sails. The bag! Oh God, yes, she had forgotten about that bag. And if B.J. had seen its contents, as he clearly had, then he must know of her proclivity for kinky sex. It was in itself a discomfiting thought, for how could she accuse B.J. of being a pervert, when, on the evidence of that bag, it was no more than she was herself!

Moreover, if, as B.J. had intimated, their sexual tastes were even remotely alike, then of course he would stand there and watch: wouldn't she have done in his place? Many were the times it had turned her on to humiliate Robert in just such a way, watching him grow scarlet down to his neck as he was forced to relieve himself in her presence. Well, she was about to find out for herself just how humiliating it was.

Cringing with embarrassment, she lifted the back of her skirt and sat down on the lavatory seat – at least she was spared the ignominy of having to take down her panties; in that one small regard McClusky had done her an unwitting favour. She closed her eyes to shut out the sight of B.J.'s sickening smirk. But could do nothing to shut out the embarrassing sound as the inevitable splashing began.

Chapter Ten

As time passed, Alison's sense of disorientation in some ways eased. There were three meals a day, and as they seemed to be brought at regular intervals she at least had some sense of time: if she dozed off, which, out of sheer ennui, she frequently did, she had only to wait until the next meal to reset her mental clock – it wasn't much, perhaps, but it was vastly better than knowing nothing at all.

The meals themselves were pleasant enough: usually brought in by Steve, there would be a light breakfast (served, she presumed, in the mornings), soup or pasta for lunch, and a nourishing supper at night; all of which she was let up to eat, allowing her to stretch feeling back to stiff muscles and to partake of the meal in relative comfort.

Other discomforts, however, remained. There were, for a start, those embarrassing trips to the bathroom. It was always B.J. who came to accompany her, and always he stood in the doorway to watch; his infernal grin making her squirm while she did what she had to do. Never was she permitted a moment of privacy. Except when her wrists and ankles were tied, and then it was almost the last thing she wanted – with so many hours spent alone, there was too much time to think. To think, and to fantasise!

Sexual longing was a constant companion. A cruel, unrelenting companion; a tormenting itch that couldn't be scratched. And that her constant daydreaming only made worse. She knew, of course, that it was crazy to fantasise, to let sexual scenarios play out in her mind, but couldn't help it – aroused as she was to begin with, and with nothing to do for so much of the time but to stare up at that featureless white ceiling, her loins aflame with unabated desire, it was impossible not to have sexual thoughts. Not least when she heard, as she frequently did, Belinda in the adjoining room, crying out in the throes of orgasm: the sounds of her ecstasy a bitter reminder of what she, Alison, couldn't attain. She could have torn out her hair with frustration. Except, had she a hand free to have been able to do so there wouldn't have been the need!

And then there was Martin McClusky.

McClusky was a frequent, if irregular visitor, who could appear at any time. He liked to talk and they would chat about anything and everything, it seemed. Including himself. Considering the circumstances, he was surprisingly open about himself and his life: a life, early on, that was as tragic as it was destined to become reprehensible. He was just sixteen, he had told her, when the troubles broke out in the North of his country. His family had been living in Belfast, then, staunch Republicans, and within less than a year it had cost him his father and two of his brothers, all lost to endemic sectarian violence. Embittered and idealistic, he had thrown in his lot with the IRA, ready to die for the Cause, an organisation which, along with other criminal methods, used kidnap as a means of financing itself: assigned to a specialist ASU, the young Martin McClusky had learned his nefarious craft from the best.

Quickly disillusioned, however, with the IRA and the unnecessary violence he had seen them perpetrate in the

105

name of Republicanism, he had soon moved on, to use all he had learned to raise funds for himself instead of for the glorious Cause.

All in all he was a fascinating man, with a fascinating, if terrible story. His lilting brogue, too, was easy to listen to, and if it was only for talk that he came Alison might well have welcomed his visits; they at least were a break from those long hours of boredom. There was, however, a price to be paid for his company: the price of further sexual frustration.

For sometimes he would unbutton her blouse, exposing her breasts while they talked. Sometimes he would uncover her crotch. Always there would be something to keep her off balance and to keep her mind constantly focused on sex. For although being exposed thus was deeply humiliating, in her aroused state – and in McClusky's presence! – this seemed only to further excite her. Which was, she had now come to realise, precisely McClusky's intention; not, as she had first supposed, to keep her disoriented, so a subdued and more malleable captive, but to arouse her for the sake of arousing her. To deliberately keep her turned on.

To what end, she couldn't guess. And what attempts she had made to discover his motives had all been met with a swift change of subject – aspects of her captivity the one topic, it seemed, he was not prepared to discuss. But if its purpose remained obscure, there could be no doubting it was a deliberate game he was playing.

It was confirmed in the way he would touch her (which he didn't always, though usually did): running his hand through her shoulder-length hair, soft, tender caresses to her breasts, her inner thighs, to her pussy. But caresses, she now knew, that were calculated only to tease; the pleasure they afforded her bitter-sweet since it only heightened her sexual tension, to leave her worse off than before. The stimulation enough to tantalise – sometimes, even, to raise her hopes, but only ever to dash them – and never to allow her the ultimate pleasure: orgasm, and the relief she so desperately craved.

Sometimes, when he left, he would leave her exposed, when she would lie in dread of B.J. or Steve coming by. So far, neither man had, but there was always that threat. A threat, just as baffling as so much else, that seemed to give her an erotic thrill!

He never left her uncovered for long, however, always returning a short while later to arrange her clothing in more decent a fashion. She could only guess that this was to prevent her from becoming accustomed to it, inured to the unnerving sensation; to make each time he left her thus as humiliating as that first. And so it was!

Though why she should find it so strangely thrilling, too, she couldn't even begin to guess, as the routine of her captivity went on.

It was on the evening of what Alison judged to be the fifth day since her capture, that this routine was suddenly broken.

Soon after supper, McClusky came to her room.

'I've run you a bath,' he told her, loosening the cords at her ankles.

Alison felt a surge of elation. A bath! Oh, a bath would be wonderful. Warm water to luxuriate in, to scrub herself clean; to scrub away the very filth of captivity. Yes, a bath would indeed be wonderful. Until she realised: she would have to strip naked to take it. In front of McClusky.

For it was too much to hope that he'd allow her to bathe in private: he would, surely, insist on remaining to watch.

But the pang of disquiet was fleeting. *So what the hell if he did want to watch?* she decided, putting it out of her mind. The thought of a bath was delightful, and she refused to let her elation be dampened by a coyness that was in any case ludicrous. For after all, she reasoned, stripping off would reveal no more of herself than

McClusky had already seen. What possible difference could it make, now, if he were to see her actually naked?

McClusky untied her hands, and she rolled from the bed.

'You can get undressed here,' he said, handing her a towelling robe.

Alison hesitated, but just for a moment. Then quickly stripped off her blouse. She put on the robe, and let her skirt and suspender belt drop to the floor from beneath it. Ready, she followed McClusky through to the bathroom.

The water was steaming hot and inviting, and with no hesitation this time, she slipped off the robe and stepped into the tub.

As she had supposed he would, McClusky remained in the bathroom. But his presence there didn't disturb her: the pleasure of bathing, of the warm, clean water, was simply too good to be spoiled by being observed. Besides, it wasn't as if McClusky's eyes were as lascivious as B.J.'s, that would by now have been making her cringe. Indeed, quite the reverse: she suddenly realised that having McClusky watching her bathe was actually rather erotic.

This was, however, a double-edged sword of course, and as the longing between her thighs suddenly flared to find a new peak, McClusky's sexy eyes on her body turning her on to distraction, it made her feel dizzy with yearning.

And it was enough to give her a sudden idea; an exciting, daring idea. One that just a few days ago would have seemed anathema, but which by now she was desperate enough to consider – *McClusky: maybe she could try to seduce him!*

Whatever the sexual game McClusky was playing with her, it seemed screwing her wasn't part of it. For despite her patent availability, there was no indication of his wishing to have sex with her. Perhaps it was in deference to Robert's 'goods'. Though given all else he had subjected her to – the sexual humiliation; the cruel, deliberate teasing – this she somehow doubted.

But whatever his reason, perhaps he could be made to forget it. If she could turn him on, really excite him, then he might be tempted. Spurred beyond his capacity to resist, and he would throw himself on her and ravish her in a mad moment of helpless, unscrupulous passion. It wouldn't have to last long – just a few seconds of unbridled thrusting would be all it would take – and she would have the relief, oh, the wonderful relief, of orgasm. An end, at last, to the misery of constant frustration.

McClusky was sitting by the side of the tub, to the front of her and just to the right, and she threw him a covert glance, wanting to be sure his eyes were still on her. Gratified to see that they were, she soaped her hands and brought them suggestively up to her breasts; she ran soapy palms over and under them, gently cupping the swelling globes and letting fingertips play over her prominent nipples. Ostensibly washing, she made her movements as sexy as she dared without betraying her secret agenda. The last thing she wanted was for McClusky to catch on, to realise she was trying to seduce him; to be aware, at all, that she wanted him. It was an integral part of her plan that he should take her 'against her will'; by physical force, even. For what she was not a willing party to, she could not be held culpable, later, when this was all over. Returning home she would, in all ways that mattered, have remained faithful to Robert.

And McClusky would never know of her sexual attraction to him, of the desperate need she'd had for his body that day: the satisfaction would be hers, not his.

Her nipples were now standing hard and erect, like small brown bullets jutting from their haloes of dark areolae. And as she continued to 'wash' them, she deliberately caught a breath in her throat, as if she were stifling a gasp of arousal, as if trying to keep secret that her lathering palms were turning her on, while at the same time her tongue flicked out over her lower lip, to signal the fact that they were. There were few things surer, she knew, to turn a man on than the sight of a woman aroused. And to a man like McClusky, she would have bet, a woman who was trying hard not to be!

And as a glance at McClusky appeared to confirm, she was right – there was an unmistakable and promising bulge rapidly growing in the front of his trousers.

Oh, my God, she thought, with a sudden new thrill; it was working. It was actually working! Just a few minutes more and he'd be helpless to resist; would succumb to the demands of his burgeoning cock, having to appease the unscrupulous monster rearing in hungry need. Would take her back to her room, where he would throw her onto the bed. Would strip himself naked. Would push her legs apart, then, and throw himself on her in a moment of uncontrolled passion, the monster nudging between her forced-open thighs. And then – oh, yes! And then he would take her. Oh yes, oh yes, oh yes!

Encouraged, she crooked her knee to raise her left thigh, knowing it would give McClusky an enticing glimpse of her sex as her legs came apart. She choked on a gasp, a genuine one this time, as warm water swirled there, and closed her eyes the better to savour the liquid caress. She let her mouth come open, her lips loose and sensual, and was aware of her breasts juddering as they rose and fell in time with her quickening breathing. She saw herself as McClusky must see her, aroused and vulnerable, and doubted any man could have resisted her then.

'Have you finished?'

McClusky's voice cut into her thoughts, and she opened her eyes. She was surprised to see he was standing; she had been so absorbed in sexual imagery she hadn't been aware of his moving.

'Ready?' He was holding the bathrobe, ready for her to step out of the tub.

Was this it? she wondered excitedly. Had she done enough? Was he hurrying her out of the bath because he couldn't wait any longer, wanted her back in the bedroom, where he could relieve the hardness that even now she could see pressing at the front of his trousers?

Her thighs were shaking as she stepped from the bath, anticipation combining with the heat of the water to make her body tingle and glow. And on legs that were weak with desire she turned to slip into the robe, expecting McClusky to hurry her as she began to pat herself dry.

Her hopes, however, quickly faded. For despite his obvious physical arousal he seemed in no hurry at all, and stood with his arms folded patiently while she continued to dry herself off; controlled boredom, if anything – but certainly not sexual excitement – showing in his steely grey eyes. And by the time he was leading her back to her room, the encouraging bulge there had been in his trousers was already a fading memory.

Sensing the battle was lost, Alison's spirits reached a new low. For if her attempted seduction had failed to sufficiently turn on McClusky, it had turned her on more than enough – to have left her aching more cruelly than ever.

Following McClusky into her room, she was distracted and didn't at first realise that her clothes had gone missing. She was still harbouring a vestige of hope – not much, but some – that McClusky would ravish her; that he would tear off her robe and take her in a frenzy of passionate need. And only when she had resigned herself to the fact that he wouldn't, that he had no such intention, and looked for her clothes to dress, did she notice them gone. Something lurched in the pit of her stomach. Was this another departure from the routine? she wondered. A disturbing departure: was she now to be kept naked?

McClusky must have sensed her concern. 'Ah, your clothes,' he said. 'Well, since you've freshened up, I

111

figured you'd want your clothes freshened up too. They've gone off to be laundered.'

Alison narrowed her eyes with suspicion. 'Then it'll be all right if I keep on the bathrobe, will it?'

She was fully expecting McClusky to come up with some excuse why she couldn't, and was more than surprised when he shrugged and said, 'Sure, if you want to. Your clothes'll be back first thing in the morning – until then, why not?' 'Now, come on. Let's have you up on the bed so I can tie you up for the night.'

By now, Alison was well used to this; inured to the inherent humiliation of being restrained, of presenting herself for the ropes. After the first couple of mealtimes, when she'd been released to eat, she had tried to reason against it; to argue that since there was no escape from the basement anyway, why did they insist on tying her up? However, argument had fallen on unlistening ears, and she knew now there was simply no point. With a long-suffering sigh she pulled the bathrobe more tightly about her, glad to have its protection, and obediently climbed onto the bed; she stretched out her arms and legs ready for McClusky to tie them.

But McClusky had other ideas. 'No, I think we'll have you in a different position tonight,' he said. 'Turn over.'

'Turn over?' Alison echoed, wondering at yet another departure from what had become the norm.

'Yes, on your front. It'll make for a change if nothing else.'

Alison feigned indifference, and careful not to allow the robe to fall open, she turned over onto her tummy; her mind working excitedly as McClusky fastened her wrists. On her stomach, she was thinking with sudden new hope, she'd be able to press her pubis down on the bed; find sufficient friction against the bedsheet to be able to trigger a climax. A poor substitute, perhaps, for having McClusky's cock do the work, but a damned sight better than nothing.

But then she felt McClusky's hands on her hips, raising them; bringing her lower body forward until her knees were supporting her weight. And her heart sank, hope yet again so cruelly crushed as she realised the consequence of what he was doing. Tying her ankles apart in the usual way, he then looped cords round her knees which he tied to the sides of the bed, a yard or so forward. This prevented her from straightening her legs, the combined forces of all six cords, working together, keeping her firmly in a semi-kneeling position.

With her pubis away from the bed!

Only inches away, but vital inches: she'd be no more able to trigger her climax in that position than when she was tied on her back! She could almost have wept in despair.

And McClusky hadn't yet finished. Rummaging beneath the mattress he produced a broad leather strap, which, Alison presumed, was affixed to the side of the bed. This he passed over the small of her back, sliding it into a buckle he conjured from under the opposite side of the mattress before cinching it tight; the pressure of it forcing her back to arch, pushing her buttocks up high. And she was struck with utter horror when the next moment McClusky flung her robe up over it, completely exposing her upthrust behind. The pressure of the strap across the base of her spine was forcing her buttocks not only up, but, she could sense with dreadful clarity, apart too, and she cringed at the thought of the sight she presented, her cheeks burning with shame: she could hardly conceive of a more lewd, humiliating and degrading position. Surely, she thought, he couldn't be meaning to leave her like that!

Though she might have been less concerned over that, had she known the full horror of what was to come . . .

McClusky came to the head of the bed where she could see him; he reached into his trouser pocket and brought out something to show her, dangling it in front of her face.

113

'Do you know what these are?' he asked.

Alison gulped, and her heart began suddenly to pound. They were Thai-beads: three marble-sized balls set along the length of a stiff plastic cord. Of course she knew what they were!

'Well?' pressed McClusky.

She could only nod, her voice lost somewhere inside her.

'Then you'll know where I'm going to put them,' he said, confirming her stricken thoughts.

It brought back her voice with a rush of dread, and she blurted tremulously: 'Oh God, no. Pl – ' She stopped herself from begging and chewed hard on her lower lip. Managing to stay calm, she said quietly, sincerely, 'But why? Why do you have to humiliate me so?'

As with all such questions though, McClusky declined to answer; only chuckled softly as he went from Alison's view. With her cheek pressed to the pillow she could see nothing behind her at all, but a moment later she felt the mattress depress with his weight; sensed him shuffle forward until he was kneeling between her spread legs. Felt his hand, then, on the cheek of her bottom, pressing firmly, spreading her buttocks still further apart.

She had always had a capacity for eidetic imagery, but never had it been more pronounced, nor so unnerving as then; seeing so vividly what McClusky must see as he brought the first of the beads to her anus.

Feeling its touch at the sensitive opening, she went instinctively to squeeze her buttocks together to prohibit the dreaded intrusion. But it was a futile attempt: her very position forbade it, and as tightly as she clenched the cheeks of her bottom the crevice between them remained wide and assailable, her anus exposed and accessible. She could do nothing to help herself as McClusky applied a gentle, but firm pressure, beginning to ease the Thai-bead inside her. She felt her sphincter resist for a moment, then suddenly give, as the bead slid into her rectum, pushing deeper as the second bead nudged, its turn to bid entry.

With dreadful awareness she felt each of the beads push into her in turn, her anus opening and closing to accept them as one by one they slid into her virgin passage, until only the rigid plastic cord was left pro-truding; this she could feel trapped by the delicate petals at the mouth of her intimate opening, tickling her there and keeping her hyper-aware of its presence. She could see it in her mind's eye as vividly as McClusky could obviously see it as he took hold of the protruding end to roll it between finger and thumb, rotating the beads inside her.

Worms of humiliation crawled in her belly, and ten-drils of arousal wormed through her loins; it was hard to discern where one finished and the other began. They were Castor and Pollux, twin sensations impossible to distinguish one from the other.

'You'll know, too,' said McClusky, continuing to rotate the beads against her sensitive rectal wall, 'that you won't be able to push them out – not without risking embarrassing consequences, anyway, which I'm sure I don't have to point out – so they'll be in for the rest of the night.'

And letting this be a thought for Alison to dwell on, he gave the beads a final twist and climbed down off the bed. He said nothing more, and the only sound was that of the door opening and closing as Alison was left alone, to wonder and worry who would be next in the room, to see the humiliating condition in which she'd been left for the night.

Wondering, more, at the perplexing dichotomy of the twin sensations conspiring to torment her with needs she couldn't assuage.

'She's close to being ready,' said McClusky, stroking his erect penis as he gazed with hooded eyes at the TV screen in the den.

Kelly was watching the monitor too: the Corsair woman was wriggling her buttocks in a lewd display, plainly conscious of the Thai-beads lodged up her bottom, her anus giving the occasional twitch around the plastic cord that was plainly visible emerging from the puckered mouth.

Though she seemed as intent, too, on trying to force her pubis down on the bed, looking for friction to bring about what it was obvious she couldn't without it.

But trying in vain, for McClusky had tied her too cleverly for that, with all but the most minimal of movement impossible; her bottom pushed helplessly up in the air, and her blonde pussy inches away from the coverlet. Inches that might have been miles for all the good the coverlet was to the hopelessly struggling woman.

Her frustration was clear to see, as her lower body continued to writhe and her pussy glistened with the liquid proof of her need, the outer lips swollen with unrelieved lust, the inner flesh clenching spasmodically in quest of a stimulus that didn't exist. It was exciting to watch. But Kelly was torn between watching the screen and watching McClusky; he was sitting naked with his thighs wide apart and stroking his penis with slow masturbatory strokes.

For his penis wasn't only erect, it was positively throbbing, as it did every time he left the woman exposed, to come back to the den to tease himself while watching her writhe on the bed with ungratified arousal, she unaware of the secret camera and struggling to achieve the climax she couldn't.

'Very close to being ready,' McClusky repeated, his voice tellingly throaty. 'She's turned on to hell: she actually tried to seduce me, you know, when I took her along for a bath just now. Oh, she tried not to make it obvious, but obvious it was – it was as plain as day.'

'Did she now?' chuckled Kelly.

Another woman might have been jealous, but not

Kelly O'Connell. Kelly didn't have an iota of jealousy in her entire being: if her man wanted to amuse himself from time to time with another woman, Alison Corsair included, that was fine by her.

'And she's turning on to humiliation too,' McClusky went on with undisguised satisfaction. 'Just as I knew she would – I've always said, haven't I, that anyone who understands humiliation from a dominant perspective, is capable of being turned on by it too. Oh yes, very soon she'll be ready. Ready to beg for more. And, the point of the exercise, ready to beg me to fuck her.'

'Oooh,' murmured Kelly. 'I'll beg you right now!'

Kelly was ready to screw – McClusky had been at his kinkiest these past few days, turned on by his 'training' of Alison Corsair and venting his lust on Kelly, making her do all sorts of unspeakable things before taking his pleasure, while her period had continued, in one of her two still-available orifices.

But her period was now over, and after almost a week of such heady excitement, her pussy denied the feel of his cock, she was dying to have it inside her: it was high time she did.

She slid down from the sofa to lie on the floor, pointing her feet to where McClusky sat watching the screen with avid intent.

'You want to see a woman writhe, McClusky?' she purred seductively. 'I can do that.'

She was wearing only panties and a skimpy black bra, and as McClusky looked over she parted her slim thighs and began writhing her hips in a sensual circular motion, running her hands down her body in a seductive caress.

McClusky smiled. 'I take it you're feeling horny,' he said.

'Mmm,' purred Kelly, her hands moving inwards over her panties, down the insides of her thighs. 'As hell.'

'Then, take off your bra and show me your breasts,' said McClusky, his own hand moving perceptibly more quickly along the length of his penis.

'Oooh, is that a command, master?'

'Do it, slave,' said McClusky.

Kelly felt the familiar tingle at the mastery in his voice, and reached up to her bra. It was front-fastening and she snapped it undone to let her breasts spill free with a jiggle. They were not large breasts, but they were full and round, with pointed nipples that rose from dark areolae. Attractive breasts, even if they would never have made page three.

'Play with them,' McClusky ordered.

She cupped the firm globes in her palms and began kneading them sexily, letting her fingers brush over her nipples to make them stand up. She continued writhing her hips in their slow sensual rhythm, and watched McClusky's eyes as McClusky watched her.

He did for a while, his eyes hooding with undisguised rapture, then said, 'Now take off your panties.'

Kelly's hands left her breasts and slid down her sides. Hooking her thumbs under the waist of her panties, she brought up her knees, her legs together, and slid the wispy garment from under her buttocks; up over her knees, then down to her ankles and off. Threw them aside and resumed her sexy gyrations, once again parting her thighs and now thrusting her pubis upwards in a lewd sexual display.

Her pussy was partially shaven, the way McClusky liked. Not completely shaved – he liked to see a V of neatly trimmed hair on her pubis – but her sex itself was totally devoid of hair, the lips smooth and giving him an enticing view of both her inner and outer vulva.

McClusky stared, the hand on his penis moving ever more rapidly, his strokes shortening and the crook of his forefinger frotting the sensitive frenum.

'Finger yourself,' he said, his eyes locked on her sex.

A tiny audible gasp rose in Kelly's throat: no matter that she had heard the command dozens of times before, it never failed to give her the same dark thrill it had given her the very first time McClusky had told her to masturbate, to play with herself while he watched. Her breathing shallow, she let a trembling middle finger slide over her trimmed bush and down between her thighs; she let it delve into the moist heat of her sex. Felt the same sense of shame she always felt when made to masturbate like this – the sense of shame that gave her such a delicious sexual thrill.

A thrill that leapt wildly when her fingertip found the stem of her clitoris, and she sensed her nostrils flare as the sudden sensation sent sparks of desire to surge through her loins; hot tendrils of need spreading up to her belly, down to the tops of her thighs.

Dizzy with erotic tension, she let a second finger combine with her first to splay either side of her clitoris, manually forcing the little nub from its surrounding hood of flesh; exposing it mercilessly while she reached in with her other hand. She brought a third finger to the exposed and helpless button, and drew her fingertip directly across the head of sensitised nerve-endings.

It was almost too much.

'Oh, McClusky,' she gasped, her orgasm gathering fast, beginning to bunch in her lower belly as her fingertip made compulsive circles around the hypersensitive button of flesh and she tried hard not to come. 'Let me stop, and come here and fuck me.'

McClusky glanced at the screen. 'No,' he said, his eyes returning to Kelly. 'No, slave, you come here and fuck me.' He slid down from his chair and lay on the floor, his eyes flicking back to the screen.

Kelly's hand left her pussy and she scrambled over to him, in as urgent need of his body as she could ever recall. His penis was iron hard and inviting, and straddling his thighs she reached for the straining shaft and prised it away from his belly; she held it upright to position its head to her aching sex, and quivered as she sank herself down. Her thighs were shaking beyond her control, and she wondered vaguely if they would continue to support her as her vagina greedily swallowed

McClusky's throbbing manhood: after almost a week it felt like a year since her pussy had been filled with hot cock, and she relished every last inch of it as his erection slid slowly inside her.

'God, I love you, McClusky,' she sighed, feeling sexual sensation through every nerve in her body, her orgasm almost upon her.

McClusky began moving his hips, meeting her stroke as she rode him with ever more fervent need. 'I love you too, Kelly,' he said. Then grinned a sly grin. 'That's why you're not going to come.'

'What?' A strange kind of excitement leapt in Kelly's belly. 'Oh, don't stop me, McClusky,' she begged. 'I'm so close: you can't stop me now.' Though a part of her wanted him to. Wanted him to make her wait for a while, to suffer the sweet torment of being held on the edge; not permitted to come.

Especially if he was going to get kinky!

'Ease yourself off me,' McClusky told her. 'And don't dare let yourself come. Me, you can finish by hand.'

Kelly's stomach lurched. 'Oh, McClusky, please no!' Making her wait was one thing while the session went on, prolonging the pleasure. But if she had to bring him to climax, to finish him by hand as he'd said, then how long would she have to wait for?

'But I'm fucking desperate, McClusky,' she wailed.

McClusky grinned. 'Yeah, I know. Now get off me.'

'Oh, you sod, McClusky. You sod, you sod, you sod.' She beat her fists on his chest – not hard, and not in anger; just out of sheer frustration – before slowly easing herself from his rigid penis. She knew McClusky was unlikely to feel kinky immediately following climax – he never did – and that he would probably leave her unsatisfied until another session later. She could only hope it wouldn't be too much later!

McClusky nodded his head at the screen. 'After all,' he said, 'why should she have all the fun, enjoying that delicious agony–ecstasy of unrelieved arousal when you, my sexy wee moth, would not? You would miss out on such exquisite sensation and have only the brief satisfaction of climax?'

'I'll suffer brief,' said Kelly quickly, urgent pleading in her glittering diamond-chip eyes.

McClusky's grin only broadened. 'Oh, but no,' he purred smoothly. 'I wouldn't hear of it. I mean, it wouldn't be fair, now would it? Not with Alison enjoying such prolonged pleasure. In fact, as she has for a while now, hasn't she? So yes, I think to even the balance a bit, I'll make you wait for some time.'

Some time had an ominous ring to it, and Kelly said warily, 'How much time is some?'

'Oh, I don't know,' shrugged McClusky. 'That'll have to be seen. But it certainly won't be before tomorrow night, that you can count on.'

'Tomorrow night!' Kelly almost choked. 'But you can't keep me waiting that long, McClusky. It'd drive me insane.'

'No, not insane,' McClusky chuckled. 'A little mad, maybe, but not insane. But wait, I haven't told you the best part yet. I'll explain while you finish me off . . .'

His legs were spread wide, with Kelly kneeling between them, and he gestured at his penis as a signal for her to begin. And Kelly furled her fingers around his hard shaft and drew it towards her, standing it upright and began to wank him in compliance with his unspoken command. It was still slick with her sexual juices, and her hand slipped easily over the tightly stretched skin as she waited for him to go on.

At last, he did. 'Yeah,' he began, 'as soon as you've satisfied me, you can go and get the love-balls. Put them inside you, where they're to stay until I decide you can come.'

Kelly stared at him with incredulous eyes. 'What, you don't mean until tomorrow night?' she squealed in horror, struggling to keep up the rhythm of her expertly frisking hand.

121

'I said tomorrow night at the soonest, remember. But yes, you've got the idea.'

'But . . . but we're going into town tomorrow.'

'Yes, so you'll be going into town with love-balls in your pussy, then won't you?'

Kelly was feeling dizzy with the perverse thrill of what she was hearing, at the thought of what McClusky proposed. The love-balls – two hollow spheres not unlike table-tennis balls – contained inside them a little of what might have been mercury, weighting them eccentrically and causing them to vibrate with the slightest bodily movement.

'But I won't be able to stop myself coming,' she protested. 'I mean, I'm already right on the verge as it is. But with love-balls inside me, and driving to and from town, for God's sake, with the vibration of the car and all . . .'

'That's your problem, not mine,' grinned McClusky. 'All I can say is, you'd better not. Or else! In fact,' – Kelly could almost see the cogs turning in her lover's brain, his thoughts getting kinkier in line with his growing arousal as her hand continued to stimulate him – 'I think you can go without knickers too. Yes, why not? That way, with nothing to help keep the love-balls in, you'll be especially aware of them as we see to our business in town.'

The tops of Kelly's thighs turned to water, her vagina twitching in anticipation of what it would have to endure. But if what he was saying was exciting her, it was no more than it was doing to McClusky himself, arousal turning his thoughts ever kinkier; the kinkier his thoughts, the more they were turning him on – an upward spiral of erotic expansion. His cock was now pulsating in Kelly's hand, preseminal dew beginning to leak from its tip; close, now, to coming.

And as Kelly continued to wank him and watch him, she was quailing at the thought of being in town with love-balls inside her, not wearing panties and having to keep her vaginal muscles tightly contracted for fear of them slipping out.

While not being allowed to let herself come!

Then she was struck by another thought, no less unnerving. 'Do I have to wear them all night? To sleep?'

'Of course,' said McClusky, burgeoning need making his voice sound husky and tense. 'I told you, you keep them in until I decide you can come.'

'But what if I come in my sleep? I couldn't help that, now could I?'

'That's always assuming you get any sleep,' grinned McClusky, a tight, rictus grin tautened by strain. The strain, Kelly knew, of him trying to hold himself back; prolonging his pleasure by delaying climax for as long as he possibly could.

Almost without thinking, she shortened her stroke on his throbbing penis; her forefinger brushing the swollen glans while her thumb worked over the frenum.

'But what if I do?' she persisted. 'What then?'

'Well,' said McClusky, 'then I'd have to think of a suitable punishment, wouldn't I? Mmmm, let's see. Oh yes, I know. You'd have to – *Ungh!*' He suddenly let out an abrupt nasal grunt, and his nostrils flared; his brow buckled as if he were in physical pain, and his eyes grew misty and dull.

Kelly knew what had happened. His mind racing with ideas for her punishment – and given his state of arousal, no doubt extremely kinky ideas too – it had all but triggered his climax.

Yet it hadn't, quite; still he had managed, if with a huge effort of will, to hold himself back. He had done so, Kelly supposed, by clearing his mind of all kinky thoughts, and she was about to press him – to insist on his telling her what her punishment would be, so forcing those thoughts back into his brain – when there was suddenly no need.

For McClusky's eyes flickered up to the monitor, where Alison's upthrust buttocks were still writhing, putting on a lewd and lascivious show. And just at that moment her anus suddenly pouted – as if, unable to bear the intrusion of the Thai-beads any longer, she were about to try to expel them. The pink petals around the puckered mouth puffed out obscenely, opening slightly as a bead appeared at the entrance, before clenching tight once again to grip the protruding plastic cord.

It was a moment of high tension, and, for McClusky, it was evidently the final irresistible straw. For at that precise moment his thighs went suddenly rigid and his abdominal muscles snapped taut; his balls lifted in their wrinkled sac, and with a shuddering groan he was coming.

Kelly was holding his cock almost upright, and a string of semen shot high in the air to splash back down on his belly; then a second spurt, and a third after that, until the contractions began at last to slow and lose force; the final, weaker ones dribbling semen onto her hand.

Kelly kept hold of him until he was finished, her hand rhythmically squeezing his pumping shaft, milking him dry. Then easing his penis to one side, she leaned forward extending her tongue. And with a myriad exciting thoughts of the twenty-four hours, perhaps longer, to come, her loins already aching with unsated desire – though loving every agonising second of it and looking forward to more – she lapped McClusky's come from his stomach.

Having it that way if she could have it no other.

Chapter Eleven

*A*lison buried her face in the pillow, in an agony she could barely endure.

Not a physical agony, for the position she was in was not especially uncomfortable. But mentally, psychologically, it was devastating: it was hard to conceive of a more degrading position – her bottom stuck ingloriously up in the air, her buttocks spread wide; her genitals and anus on open display; and with the dreadful Thai-beads lodged in her rectum, the protruding cord signalling their humiliating presence to all who would care to see. And every long minute that dawdled by with such infinite slowness was an agony of waiting; waiting for the door to open behind her.

And then, at last, open it suddenly did.

At the dreaded sound of it – knowing it would come making it no less unnerving – Alison's heart leapt to her throat; the question immediately begging: *who was it?*

She couldn't see, because even if she strained her neck, lifting her head to bring her cheek off the pillow, she still couldn't see anything beyond her shoulder. She could only wonder, quailing; knowing that someone, whoever it was, was witness to her indignity, feasting his eyes upon her most intimate places.

What appalled her further, the anonymous visitor then climbed on the bed, to kneel behind her as McClusky had knelt earlier. And as the mattress depressed between her spread knees, heightening her consciousness of the intruder's proximity, she could only pray it was McClusky again, seeing only what he had already seen.

Yet she sensed that it wasn't – McClusky had a certain presence about him, an aura that was practically tangible and that could be felt when he entered a room. And it was a presence she didn't feel now – whoever it was, it wasn't McClusky.

And then a hand touched her buttock.

Alison jumped, startled at the sudden caress; should, perhaps, have only expected it, but was taken aback when it came. Not least since, unsettling enough as the hand was itself, there was still the unanswered, and just as unsettling question – *whose hand was it?*

Not McClusky's: his she had already discounted. Then was it B.J.'s, perhaps? Again she didn't think so – B.J.'s massive paws were rough-skinned, hands accustomed to manual work, while this hand was soft, not that of a man used to physical labour. And was surely far gentler, besides, than B.J.'s could ever have been. So, if it wasn't B.J. and it wasn't McClusky, and assuming it wasn't a total stranger, then it left only one other: it had to be Steve.

The thought made Alison groan in dismay.

Steve it was who brought in her meals. And, while she ate, they had taken to engaging in light conversation – better that than an awkward silence while he waited for her to finish, to tie her back on the bed. And despite this latter part of his job (he was, after all, only following his orders), she had come to actually quite like the boy, and to look forward to their mealtime chats.

But how embarrassing those mealtimes would be from now on, now he had seen her like this!

There wasn't time to dwell on it, however, for she suddenly had a more urgent concern – the hand on her bottom was moving. The palm gliding over the taut skin of her buttock, moving inwards; fingertips entering the wide-open crevice between her trembling nates. And moving ever closer to the place where she wanted them least, discomfortingly conscious of the protruding end of the Thai-beads.

The fingers, though, impervious to the power of silent prayer, moved inexorably on, to reach the disquieting cord. They were touching it then, flicking the end of it and causing the beads to shift in her rectum. A gasp snagged in Alison's throat, the humiliating sensation of it making her squirm. Then she gasped again as humiliation transmuted, as had become its baffling capacity, to become an erotic thrill. As the beads continued to move in her bottom, stimulating the rectal wall, a thrill that was unnerving in its intensity.

Just as unnerving, as the cord moved at the delicate opening, she sensed her anus twitch in a reflex response, making her cringe as she envisaged the obscene sight it must have presented; her bottom twitching in involuntary spasm, gripping and releasing the plastic cord sticking shamingly from it. And she had to struggle to keep herself silent, telling herself over and over: *don't plead, don't plead, don't plead*, having no wish to demean herself further.

It was a struggle she almost lost when, the next moment, she sensed a tugging sensation inside her, and with a jolt of horror she felt her anus forced open as a bead was slowly pulled out; sensed Steve's watching eyes with sublime awareness, and chewed hard on her lower lip.

The bead was immediately pushed back in, but only so the indignity could be repeated when it was slowly withdrawn once again. Then again, and again after that.

Alison buried her burning face in the pillow, blonde curly hair covering her blushing cheeks, and tried to make sense of the confusion of feelings that were writhing inside her: the twin sensations – of humiliation and the direct sexual stimulus of the beads against her sensitised rectal wall – combining to dizzy her as still it went on.

Until, at last, the bead was pushed in for a final time, and as she felt Steve's fingers release the cord she breathed a silent sigh of relief. But there was no real respite, for the fingers only moved on. Moved down, reaching beneath her now towards the open groove of her sex.

Alison chewed on the pillow, awaiting their touch on her aching sex-hungry flesh; needing it more than she dreaded it.

The fingers wasted no time on finesse, and reaching her pussy they ignored the less sensitive outer lips to slide directly along the moistened channel between them, a long middle finger parting her vulva to penetrate her feminine core. Alison stifled a whimper. The finger was at once joined by a second, the two then reaching high inside her to feel for the Thai-beads lodged in the adjacent passage; massaging the sensitive membrane between the two channels. It must have been a thumb that then nudged at the end of the beads, heightening the piquant sensation, and Alison could barely breathe as she hid her gasps in the pillow.

For how long the fingers worked on her pussy, stimulating her sex-heated flesh, she couldn't have guessed. Only that it wasn't for quite long enough – enough to trigger her climax – and when the hand finally, and suddenly withdrew, it left her shaking with a desire that had found a new, almost terrible peak.

But sexual arousal was soon for the moment forgotten. For just then, as abruptly as the hand had withdrawn, and completely without warning, it delivered a sharp smack to her rump.

Alison yelped, as much out of shock as with the actual physical pain of it: it had come as such a surprise. Especially from Steve. She had read Steve to be an essentially gentle youth, not at all the sort who would want to cause anyone pain. How wrong she had been, for across the tightly stretched skin of her buttock the slap had hurt like hell; her bottom was on fire and she fancied she could feel his hand even now, its palm scalding her skin.

Dreading it coming, she braced herself for a second smack.

But there wasn't one, and the next moment the mattress bounced as Steve's weight lifted from it. The single slap must have been a parting shot, for then there was the sound of the door being opened.

Then:

'Sleep well.'

And something hit Alison in the pit of her stomach with all the force of a physical blow. For it wasn't Steve's voice at all. It was a voice with a Belfast accent: the voice of a woman!

She must have slept. She didn't remember dreaming, and had no recollection of dropping off, but she must have done.

For after the woman had left, there were a few minutes of red-faced chagrin – not since boarding school had she been sexually caressed by another woman! – and the next moment McClusky was there by her bed, setting her breakfast tray down on the table.

'Morning,' he said brightly, before moving from Alison's view.

Alison sensed his presence, was aware of his weight on the bed and knew he was there behind her, but still she jumped when she felt the touch of his hand on her bottom.

McClusky chuckled. 'My, my. We are nervous this morning, aren't we?' he teased. 'But you do want these out, don't you?'

As he spoke his fingers brushed the protruding end of the Thai-beads, and Alison squirmed as she felt them shift a little inside her. Then suddenly squealed as they were whipped from her anus in a single rapid jerk, causing her rectal muscles, her vaginal muscles – muscles she couldn't even identify – all to clench at once in sudden involuntary spasm, leaving her gasping.

Though after the initial shock of it had passed, she was grateful that at least it had been over so quickly – a slower withdrawal might have been worse; more humiliating by far. McClusky had mercifully spared her that.

She could almost have thanked him, and as he began to untie her she found herself wondering at the perversity of this; at her inapposite feelings for the man in general. For all McClusky was putting her through, she should have been ready to kill him. Yet here she was feeling grateful to him! Indeed, she could feel no animosity towards him at all. Only, maddeningly, a continuing lust for his body!

He unfastened her wrists first, then her ankles and knees; finally the strap across the small of her back, allowing her to turn over and sit up.

True to his word he had brought back her clothes, freshly laundered as promised, and after her breakfast of orange juice and cornflakes she was allowed to get dressed.

Tying her back on the bed in the more usual position, McClusky collected together the remains of her breakfast and turned to leave. He stopped by the door and turned back to face her.

'I'll be gone for the day,' he told her. 'I have some business to deal with. But I'll see you tonight; I have a special treat in mind for this evening.'

And he smiled to himself as he left.

Chapter Twelve

B.J. left rubber behind on the road as he spun the Mercedes' wheels, bulleting the car away from the lights with his foot hard down.

'Jesus-H-Christ,' muttered Steve, thrown back in the passenger seat by the sudden surge forward. 'Where the hell's the fire?'

B.J. grinned. 'In my balls: I'm feeling horny, aren't I? And out here playing errand boy ain't getting my chain pulled.'

Steve threw him a withering look. 'And in the past week you've not had enough? Jesus, B.J., since Belinda arrived you've been at it non-stop; morning, noon and night, for God's sake.'

'I don't know about for His sake,' B.J. chuckled. 'But yeah, while it's there for the taking, you take it, right?'

Steve stared vacantly out of the window. 'Don't make it right, though, does it?' he muttered.

'Oh, stop with the bleeding heart, will you?' snorted B.J. with a withering look of his own. 'I've not noticed you saying no to it.'

Steve wriggled uncomfortably into his seat. 'Yeah, so when did a standing prick have a conscience?' He lit up a Stuyvesant to plume smoke at the windscreen. 'And all right, so my prick's been standing more than it should've. It's just I find her such a helluva turn-on. One sexy lady is that: does things to me on a primordial level – I can't hardly look at her without getting a hard-on.'

'Yeah, well, doesn't take much to bring out the animal in you, then.'

'What's that supposed to mean? You saying you don't think she's sexy?'

B.J. swung the car perilously close to an Audi as they barrelled past with a coat of paint to spare.

'Course she's sexy. What woman wouldn't look sexy, kept naked like that? And us knowing she's there for the taking? Bloody obvious she's gonna look sexy, right? Though yes, I grant you, she has got a fabulous body all right.'

'So then, what?'

B.J. shrugged. 'Well, she gives it away too easy, is what.'

'Hmph! Not got much choice, has she?'

'Come off it, Steve, choice isn't the issue with her: she'd come across whether she had to or not. She loves it; no one can fake it that good.'

'Yeah, well, maybe she does and maybe she doesn't,' muttered Steve. Then sighed in resignation. 'All right, so I admit, she certainly does seem to. But suppose she does love it, what's wrong in that? Except I still say she hasn't a choice, which makes us taking advantage about as right as mugging nuns.'

'Nah, but . . .' B.J. paused to blare the horn at a wagon hogging the road. 'Will that wanker ever get out of the way?' He hung dangerously close to the wagon's bumper and went on, 'All I'm saying is, choice or not, she's just too willing by far. And where's the fun in that?'

Steve looked at him sideways, dribbling smoke. 'What? You're saying you'd prefer it if she wasn't so willing?'

'Oh yeah,' said B.J. with no hesitation, his eyes suddenly glinting. 'That's the turn-on right there: making her do what she doesn't want to do. Domination; now there's a real buzz in that.'

'What, you mean the kind of scene the boss and Kelly are into?'

B.J. chuckled. 'You been peeping through keyholes again?'

'Who has to?' Steve protested. 'It's hard not to see what those two get up to.'

'Yeah, I know,' grinned B.J. wryly. 'It's 'cos Kelly's a real exhibitionist, is why. Gets her jollies, among other things, from the risk of being seen; caught with her knickers down, and well at it in the middle of one of their sessions. It's why she so often is, by us – Martin purposely sets up scenes when he knows we're around, see, when there's a middling chance of one of us coppin' a look.' He gave the wagon-driver a middle-finger salute as the Mercedes shot by on the inside lane; swerved back out again and hit the accelerator hard.

'But no,' he went on, 'the kinda stuff they're into is just sexual play-acting. Kelly loves it when Martin does the masterful bit, with the bondage and that. But what I'm talking about is genuine domination: making someone do things they really don't want to do, not what they only pretend not to want.'

'You're sick,' muttered Steve.

'And you're a tart,' B.J. countered. 'So that's both of us with zero to our credit.'

The two fell quiet, while B.J. manoeuvred through traffic and Steve lost himself in his thoughts. The very idea of dominating women – perhaps not as McClusky did Kelly, playing harmless sexual games, but certainly subjugating them in the way B.J. was meaning – was anathema to him. The other way around, now, the concept of women dominating men, was another matter entirely. From his earliest sexual thoughts he had harboured secret fantasies of being sex-slave to a beautiful but cruel woman, who would use him to satisfy her sexual needs without necessarily satisfying his. She would instead leave him aching, aroused and ungratified, longing for her sexual favours; kept naked and at her disposal. He wouldn't have wanted it in the real world, perhaps, but during masturbation he found the fantasy immensely exciting.

But him, dominating a woman? No way.

B.J. found a clear stretch of road, careened along it, and picked up the conversation from where he'd left off: 'Like I was saying though, apart from her being a decent screw, Belinda's too willing for my kind of fun: I mean, you can't force a woman to do what she's only too glad to do, can you? And her, whatever you tell her to do she loves it, so where's the point?

'Her snotty cow of a friend. Now there's a different kettle of cod. Christ, I'd love to stick it to her.'

'Oh yeah,' said Steve with a sneer. 'And you would, would you, when the boss says she's not to be touched?'

B.J. grinned. 'As it happens, yeah. I'm gonna make her give me a blow-job.'

'You're – ' Steve was shocked almost speechless. Shook his head slowly in stunned disbelief, and recovered to say, 'You're a sandwich short of a picnic, you are. If the boss caught you at it . . .'

'Well, he won't, will he?' said B.J. evenly. 'Why d'you think I'm driving like my arse is on fire? Martin and Kelly are in town for the day. If I can just get through this sodding traffic this side of the evening rush, there'll be just enough time before they get back.'

'But you're taking a hell of a chance, aren't you? What if Martin finds out? I mean, later. Whenever.'

'What if he does?' B.J. said with a shrug. 'If I get the woman's consent to do it, how can he bitch about it? It'd be no different from when the other one asked me to fuck her, and we got away with that, right? We've been doing it ever since, and no one's said sod all about it.'

'Oh, I see, she's going to play along with it, right?' The

sneer was back in Steve's voice, his tone bristling with sarcasm. 'Well, why didn't you say? She's going to consent to sucking your dick; be as easy to manipulate as Belinda was, and be only too glad to oblige. Ha! In your dreams, maybe.

'Don't forget, B.J., she won't be scared like Belinda was: she knows she's got the boss's protection, and that you can't do anything to hurt her. She'll just tell you to sod off.'

B.J.'s grin only broadened. 'I don't think so,' he said. 'I'd say she can be persuaded to co-operate all right.'

'Oh? And like how?'

'Like this, for instance.' B.J. reached down by the side of his seat and produced a long, willowy cane.

Steve's eyes widened with shock. 'Well, now I know you've dropped out of your tree, don't I? She's not the sort to give in to mere threats, you know. I mightn't have your vast experience of women, Lothario, but even I know that. And you take it any further than threats, you put one mark on her body with that thing, and you might as well say ta-ta to your bollocks: Martin'll have 'em for ornaments.'

B.J.'s white teeth flashed as he threw the cane onto Steve's lap. 'It's not her who's down for a caning, you wally. And I won't be putting marks on anyone: it's you who'll be doing the business.'

Steve blanched, his stomach turning. 'Me? But –'

'Hold tight . . .' B.J. hit the brakes hard and skidded the car into a tight left turn, leaving the main road and speeding off along Vicarage Lane with just a few hundred yards to go.

The car straightened out of a power-wobble, and B.J. glanced over at Steve. 'Yeah, you,' he repeated. 'With Belinda. While I'm next door discussing consent with her friend. And how long d'you think she'll hold out, listening to Belinda being caned until she decides to play ball?'

He swung the car into a second left turn, onto a dirt-

135

track now, and pulled up in front of the huge iron gates that kept unwelcome visitors out of his employer's sprawling estate. He pressed the button on the remote control that would make the gates swing open, and chuckled at the look of horror that had appeared on his companion's boyish face.

Alison was immediately wary when B.J. strode into the room.

He would normally appear only in response to her summons, when she needed to visit the bathroom. Yet not since early that morning had she signalled that need, and it begged the disquieting question: what did he want?

Her sense of unease wasn't helped, either, by the oddness of his manner: he seemed agitated somehow; as if, even beyond the by now familiar bulge that was swelling in the front of his trousers – there was nothing new about that! – he was excited about something. And his ever-present grin, too, seemed strangely knowing, as if it were hiding some dark and disturbing secret.

None of it augured well, and Alison's breathing was shallow while she waited for some explanation..

She didn't have long to wait.

'You're in for a special treat this afternoon,' B.J. told her, a mischievous twinkle in his mahogany eyes. 'I'm gonna let you give me a blow-job.'

'You're going to let – ' Alison laughed without humour.

Though if it weren't such a loathsome thought, it could have almost been funny in a wry sort of way: it seemed it was her day for dubious treats, she mused, McClusky's parting words of that morning still on her mind. 'You are joking, of course.'

'No, I'm quite serious,' said B.J., keeping his grin. 'And what's more, you're going to want to do it as well.'

Now that *was* funny! 'Just why the hell would I want to?' Alison snorted.

'To prevent unnecessary suffering, of course.'

'To – ' Hairs prickled on the back of Alison's neck, instantly chary. 'But you're not supposed to touch me,' she reminded him hastily. 'Let alone hurt me.'

B.J. held up his hands in a gesture of innocence. 'I won't lay a finger,' he said. 'Honest. The only touching will be your sweet lips around my hot and throbbing dick.'

'But . . .' Alison's forehead showed her confusion. 'But you said to prevent – '

'Unnecessary suffering, yeah,' B.J. finished for her. 'But not yours. Your friend's, next door.'

'Belinda?' Something unpleasant chilled Alison's spine. 'Why, what suffering? What do you mean?'

'Well, let me explain. In there right now' – he crossed to the wall between their two rooms and jabbed his thumb at it over his shoulder – 'your friend is tied up. I won't bore you with the gory details, but suffice it to say she's extremely vulnerable. And I do mean extremely, if you take my meaning. And my mate Steve, well, he's in there too. He has this cane with him, see: a long, willowy thing, but very strong and whippy. Are you beginning to get the picture?'

He didn't wait for an answer. 'See, the way it works is this: when I rap on the wall, Steve lets fly with the cane. And I continue to rap on the wall until you decide to co-operate. It's really quite simple.'

Alison narrowed her eyes. 'You're bluffing,' she said.

'Am I? Then perhaps I should demonstrate.'

B.J. reached out a hand and gave the wall a single sharp rap with his knuckles. For a second, there was nothing. Then, suddenly, there was the sound of a *thwack*, clearly audible through the room's thin wall. And a split second later a piercing scream rent the air; a woman's scream of agony.

Alison flinched, and B.J. grinned.

'Convinced?' he said.

Alison fixed him with a piercing glare. 'You're an

animal,' she snarled vehemently. 'No, you're worse than an animal; you're filth, the worst kind of slime. But if you think I can be blackmailed, you must also be stupid.'

B.J. rapped on the wall.

Again there was the *thwack*. Again the piercing scream of agony.

'Stop it!' Alison cried. 'For God's sake stop it!'

'Me stop it?' said B.J. 'But you're the one causing it. You can stop it just' – he clicked his fingers – 'like that. Just say the word, is all. Do you see what I mean now, about her suffering being unnecessary? She's only suffering at all because you're being stubborn; you can end it whenever you want . . . Well?'

Alison chewed on her lip, her mind swirling in turmoil.

B.J.'s knuckles were poised. 'I think I should warn you before number three,' he went on, 'that Steve's been told to lay the third stroke directly into her pussy.'

'All right,' she cried. 'Stop it . . . Stop it, and I'll . . . I'll do what you want?'

'What I want?' said B.J., his grin sly. 'But it's what you want, isn't it? I mean, if not, just say so and we can carry on.'

'No!' said Alison quickly, seeing him raise his arm yet again. 'All right, so yes; it's what I want.'

'What is?'

'What . . . you said.'

B.J. scratched his head. 'I can't seem to think. You'll have to help me: what did I say now?'

Alison groaned inwardly, realising the game he was playing. He wanted to hear her say it.

She knew she had little choice. 'I . . . I want to give you a blow-job,' she muttered. 'There. Satisfied now?'

'Well, not yet,' chuckled B.J. 'But I'm going to be, aren't I, if you're going to insist on sucking me off? Course, I wouldn't want you doing anything silly, now, like being careless with your teeth. Or, God forbid, you refusing to swallow my precious gift when I come. So, I think a little reminder, huh, just to keep you behaved . . .'

And he reached for the wall once again.

In the next room, Belinda winced as she watched the cane *thwack* down on a leather bolster to send up a puff of dust, imagining how it would feel against tender human flesh; feigned a scream of pain, only glad it wasn't a genuine one.

She knew the reason for the bizarre charade – that B.J. was next door, and that her lurid screams were intended to coerce Alison into performing a sexual act with him – and was uncomfortably aware that her co-operation, in screaming on cue, made her a party to Alison's misfortune. But before B.J. had left, he had told Steve that unless Belinda were to make it convincing, then he was to forget the bolster and cane her instead. Whether she co-operated or not, therefore, it wouldn't have made any difference; the result, for Alison, would have been exactly the same.

What was more disturbing than her own complicity was Alison's continued refusal, as was apparent since the caning went on, to do as B.J. required. After all, Alison wasn't to know that this was a sham, yet had allowed Belinda – as she must have thought – to receive three vicious strokes of a cane. And for what? Just to save herself from sucking a cock; at worst, a minor indignity compared to what Belinda might have been suffering. It was typical of Alison: self, self, self!

And was especially galling since, so Belinda had now learned, it was only her friendship with Alison that had landed her in this in the first place; abducted not, as she'd first supposed, for her own sake, with a sexual motive in mind, but because she happened to have been with Alison that day. It was Robert's money the kidnappers were after and she, Belinda, had just been in the wrong place at the wrong time. Somehow it made Alison's lack of compassion, now, seem all the more hurtful.

139

But just then came the signal for the caning to stop; two knocks on the wall in rapid succession. And Belinda knew Alison must have finally ceded.

And about time, too, she thought sourly.

Steve threw down the cane as if it were carrying some noxious disease, and wiped his hand on his slacks: he clearly hadn't enjoyed his part in what had transpired.

Belinda felt almost sorry for him as she watched him sit on the bed, his expression wan and clearly glad it was over.

'How are you feeling?' McClusky asked, forcing the car through thick city traffic. 'Sexy?'

'Jesus, and then some,' Kelly replied, throwing him a sidelong look.

As close as she had been to coming the previous night, McClusky, true to his word, hadn't let her. Moreover, as soon as he had recovered from the climax she had brought him to manually, he had sent her up to the bedroom to find the love-balls. And, with a further warning not to let herself come, had watched closely to see that she didn't as she'd carefully eased them inside her. And there they'd remained ever since, driving her mad.

To the extent that, before leaving for town that morning, she had begged him, implored him, to allow her to do one or the other – to let her come or allow her to remove the maddening, self-vibratory sex-toy. But with a grin as hard as his throbbing cock he had forbidden her to do either, revelling in her enforced, unremitting arousal as he had driven them into town.

And then, worse – *better* – she'd had to retain them while they had walked from office to office, McClusky attending to his various business affairs, having to keep her vaginal muscles consistently clenched for fear, with no panties to stop them, of the balls slipping out: the potential ignominy of having them drop to the floor before one of McClusky's associates – or perhaps even worse, before some lah-de-dah secretary with her nose in the air – keeping her on absolute tenterhooks the whole of the day, never mind just highly aroused.

And by now it was almost too much to endure, as her loins ached with arousal she couldn't relieve and her head spun, dizzy with sexual tension.

But at least they were now back in the car.

Though did that really make it much easier? Not by a lot. And especially not when McClusky then spoke . . .

'Spread your legs,' he told her. 'And lift up your skirt so I can see your pussy.'

'McClusky!' Kelly squeaked. 'Not in the car!'

'Do it. Now. I want to see for myself how excited you are.'

McClusky was adamant and Kelly knew she would have to comply. Knew it would turn her on all the more!

Her eyes flicking nervously about, at the heavy traffic threading its way slowly along the busy main road, she tentatively raised her skirt, exposing her neatly trimmed bush. Then, just as tentatively, she opened her legs.

As soon as she had, McClusky reached over and slid his hand between them, stroking a finger along her honey-soaked vulva and dipping it into her sex.

'My, you are wet, too,' he observed, his tone teasing; calculated, Kelly knew, to cause her the maximum shame.

It never failed, and she choked on a gasp as embarrassment crimsoned her cheeks. Yet, together with the physical feel of his finger this only further excited her, and as tendrils of hot desire snaked through her aching loins, she murmured, 'I . . . told you . . . didn't I?' She was barely able to speak.

McClusky spanked her clitoris with the tip of his finger. 'Don't you think about coming,' he warned. 'I know that sound in your voice, and you're close.'

There was a string from the love-balls trailing from Kelly's vagina, and this he now found and gave it a gentle tug. Not enough to pull the balls out, but enough to make them vibrate and cause Kelly to shiver as she struggled to hold herself back at the very edge of climax – were she to let herself, she could have come there and then.

'Oh, God, McClusky,' she groaned, her voice husky and tremulous. 'I'm going to have to come if you keep doing that. I won't be able to help myself.'

'Oh yes you will. And you'd better. You're not to come until I tell you you can. If you're lucky, tonight, but that'll depend on Alison Corsair.'

'Oh?' Kelly looked at him in surprise. 'How so?'

McClusky grinned. 'You'll see.'

Giving the love-balls a final tug, he returned his hand to the wheel. And Kelly sighed a deep sigh of relief – if an ironic sort of relief, and not at all the kind she would have preferred – and went to smooth down her skirt.

McClusky stopped her. 'What are you doing? I don't recall saying anything about adjusting your dress.'

'But –'

'No, stay just as you are.'

'But someone's going to see,' Kelly protested, even as the very thought of it caused a fresh wave of excitement to surge through her belly, weakening the tops of her thighs.

McClusky braked as a traffic light turned as red as Kelly's cheeks.

'Only someone from a high vantage point,' he chuckled. 'Like the driver of this lorry that's about to pull up beside us.'

To Kelly's horror, the tall cab of a lorry suddenly loomed along their nearside, throwing its shadow over the car. She shot a nervous glance up at its driver – a burly, unshaven young man, with a ham of a forearm resting on his cab's open window – and squirmed in her seat, agonisingly conscious of her naked sex. The driver was looking at the road ahead, but had only to look down, Kelly knew, to have a perfect view of all she was putting on such blatant display.

She threw her eyes to the front and stared dead ahead, her knuckles white as she gripped the sides of her seat, not knowing if the driver was looking or not; not wanting – not daring – to know.

'McClusky, please,' she whispered imploringly, her thighs beginning to tremble. 'If he looks, he'll see.' She was as much excited by the thought as it filled her with horror.

McClusky chuckled again. 'Well, that's all right,' he said, leaning across to push her skirt an inch higher up. 'I doubt a hairy-arsed lorry-driver's going to be offended by the sight of your pussy. Stay just as you are: it'll give him something to tell his mates about tonight in the pub.'

And Kelly began to perspire, knowing that with McClusky in this sort of mood, she was in for a lot more torment before this session was finally over.

B.J. kicked his shorts aside and stood naked, posing for Alison with his hands on his hips. And Alison could only stare in awe at the incredible size of his penis; even semi-erect his manhood was massive, and she quailed at the thought of fellating him.

Reaching his hand to it, he gripped its base and waggled it lewdly. 'Some baby, huh?' he grinned proudly. 'Pity you're pussy's not getting it, eh? I'll bet it's never had one like this, has it, that sweet little pussy of yours? Shame, it doesn't know what it's missing.'

Alison swallowed drily, watching in dread fascination while his penis continued to grow; its purple-black shaft thickening and lengthening as it gradually grew harder, rising of its own volition.

B.J. came forward and climbed onto the bed. He knelt astride Alison's chest, and grasping his still-swelling organ in his ham of a fist he slapped it against her pursed lips, bidding entry. Alison kept a groan to herself and, resigned, she opened her mouth for him.

He still wasn't fully erect, not quite, but even so the enormous penis wasn't easy to take, the sheer volume of tumescent flesh almost too much for her mouth. She could only hope that as he achieved full erection he would just grow harder, and not any thicker; much thicker and it would put an uncomfortable strain on her jaws.

Also discomforting was that her hands were still tied: she couldn't hold him manually, to give her that bit of control as she sucked him. It made her feel unnervingly helpless as the penis pushed further into her mouth.

Nevertheless, she put negative thoughts to the back of her mind and took as much of the burgeoning shaft as she could. She began to suck, applying pressure to it with her tongue, for it would be wise, she decided, to make it good for the bastard: who knew what Belinda would suffer if she failed to pleasure him properly?

Fortunately, as the huge organ at last came fully erect its diameter didn't increase; it grew only harder and stiffer until the cock was a rigid pole of prurient maleness – forcing her jaws open wide, but not, thank God, unbearably so. And, relaxing a little, she began to fellate him in earnest; her lips and tongue combining to work in practised concert on the now throbbing tool in her mouth.

No sooner had she begun, however, than B.J. told her to stop.

This surprised her: fellatio was one of her fortes, she had always believed, with most men seeming to enjoy her technique. Yet now she had sucked him fully erect, B.J. wanted none of it, telling her instead to keep her head quite still and, rather than actively suck, just to hold his penis there in her mouth, her lips closed around it.

It didn't seem to make any sense – as this would naturally preclude her from employing her oral skills to the full, why would B.J. want her to remain passive? It made no sense at all. Until he began to thrust. And then it made all the sense in the world. For he was, it became instantly apparent, using her in the most demeaning possible way – using her mouth as he would a vagina!

It transformed an intrinsically pleasurable act, an act of giving, into something low and degrading; that was humiliating in the extreme. He was using her mouth, literally, as a masturbatory aid, a passive receptacle for his thrusting cock – it was, she realised, the ultimate fuck you!

Yet, as this comprehension sank fully home, it gave Alison that unique sense of excitement she had come, in just the past few days, to associate with sexual humiliation; a squirming something that crawled in her belly and that somehow translated to erotic arousal, stoking the furnace that burned in her loins.

A week ago she would not have believed it. Alison Corsair, sexual sadist and general bitch, turning on to being subjugated; used, as B.J. was using her, as a human sex-aid? Never, she'd have thought. Then.

But now?

Now, since the insidious awakening of Castor and Pollux, their fusing together into a single libidinous entity, she was no longer sure of her sexual self. Strange things had been happening to her since her abduction; inexplicable things. Not least in her sexual fantasies . . .

In the beginning, her unwanted but inescapable fantasies while staring up at that featureless white ceiling had all been her usual ones; those she had turned herself on to since puberty: of her dominating men, subjecting them to the cruellest sexual atrocities – in fantasy, often far more extreme than ever she would wish to enact in reality. Lately however, the scenarios playing themselves out on the silver screen of that ceiling had begun to change. Still SM-based, more and more did she picture herself in the submissive role; the one being dominated. Controlled and humiliated. By men with dark, intense, erotic eyes. Men like Martin McClusky.

In calmer moments, she had tried to analyse this

baffling reversal. And kept returning to her initial conjecture; that it was something akin to the Stockholm Syndrome. For if, regardless of what had been said at the outset, she was to be used as a sexual plaything – just as B.J. was using her now – then perhaps her subconscious mind had been preparing her for that to occur: to protect her, for if she had learned to enjoy the role, then the experience of being put into it would not be distressing. It seemed as likely a theory as any, but whatever the actual truth there was one thing for sure: the thought of sexual submission she now found strongly appealing.

B.J. was still thrusting into her mouth, now gripping the bedrail with tightened fists while his rutting grew ever more urgent, his strokes short.

Alison looked into his eyes. Eyes that were hooded with ecstasy and that were just beginning to glaze; knew his moment was close, and steeled herself for the saline fluid he was about to release into her throat.

His stroke quickened, and grew shorter still. And he threw back his head with a groan.

'Oh yeah, baby,' he moaned, the deep rumble of his voice seeming to vibrate his entire body. 'Oh God, yeah. Take it all.'

And then, suddenly, his urgent thrusting stopped. Alison felt his penis pulsating against her tongue and stared at his rigid torso in strained anticipation. A second went by, then two. Seconds laden with portent, and which caused the things that squirmed in her belly to squirm all the more. Then B.J. shuddered hugely and the first hot jet of his semen gushed into her waiting throat.

'Swallow it, baby,' he grunted breathlessly, looking down at her now, his eyes ravaged with rapture. 'Swallow it all.'

Alison could hardly do anything else, and she swallowed quickly, just as B.J.'s hips jerked and a second jet followed the first.

Then he was thrusting again: tiny, barely perceptible thrusts that made the head of his penis slide over her

146

passive tongue, stimulating his frenum to milk himself into her mouth. Alison swallowed again and again until, finally, with a second shuddering groan he was finished.

He didn't move for a while, keeping his penis in Alison's mouth until his erection began to subside. Then, with a wince as his now over-sensitised glans slipped free of her lips, he at last withdrew; breathing heavily he unstraddled her chest and climbed down off the bed.

Alison swallowed the last of his taste, and whispered. 'Thank you.' She immediately bit on her tongue.

'What's that?' said B.J. He was half-turned away from her, and obviously hadn't caught what she'd said.

Thank God! thought Alison, blushing furiously. She could hardly believe she had said it; it had just slipped out. It was like Robert saying thank you to her after some cruel degradation, just as an obedient slave should. Though with Robert she would normally have to insist – from her it had slipped out so naturally. What on earth could she have been thinking?

Just thank God he hadn't heard!

What on earth had come over her, she wondered again later when B.J. had gone. He had coerced her into fellating him. Worse, he had used her mouth in the most demeaning way possible, had made her swallow his come. And she had said thank you like a well-trained slave! She could hardly believe it.

No less confusing, the ache in her loins had found yet another new peak, and when her arousal made the pictures appear on the bedroom ceiling, they were of a man fucking her mouth just as B.J. had done. It wasn't B.J. himself – she would no more want to submit to him now than when she had first set eyes on the man. No, not him, but an anonymous man.

And then, not an anonymous man at all. But a man with dark, compelling, oh-so-erotic eyes!

Chapter Thirteen

She was still fantasising, on and off, about being orally ravished when McClusky arrived that evening. She hadn't yet had supper, so it must have been fairly early still.

He came to sit on the bed by Alison's side. 'Enjoy your day?' he asked, smiling.

'Oh, bloody marvellous, yes,' she muttered sarcastically. Though with no real rancour; it had hardly been meant as a serious question and wasn't worth ruffling her feathers about. 'Just wonderful, wasn't it.'

McClusky leaned over and touched her cheek with the tips of tender fingers. His smile was gone, and there appeared to be genuine sympathy in his mysterious grey eyes, though it was difficult to read anything in them for certain.

His voice was more readable, however, and he sounded sincere as he said, 'Yes, I know it can't be easy for you, tied up all the time – I imagine the boredom must be horrendous, huh?'

Not nearly as bad as the sexual frustration, Alison wanted to say but didn't. Though in anything but her own mind, admitting to her arousal could have made little difference – as much as she'd tried to conceal it, McClusky

148

knew only too well of her desperate sexual need. He must do, since he was largely the cause of it, with his constant and deliberate teasing. Indeed, with his very presence!

But that was a thought she preferred not to dwell on, not needing reminding, and she only nodded her head in agreement; yes, the boredom was horrendous.

'We'll have to see,' McClusky went on, 'if we can't make your stay here a little more comfortable. Perhaps not tying you down on the bed, and leaving you to move about in your room.'

Alison's spirits suddenly lifted, her heartbeat quickening at the encouraging thought: after such privation, even so limited a freedom would be welcome indeed. Though she felt, too, that perverse sense of gratitude that had fazed her before. For here she was, she realised, feeling grateful to her captor for returning only what he himself had deprived her of in the first place!

Still, she decided, be thankful for small mercies. 'Some magazines or something would help too,' she ventured.

'Whoa,' said McClusky. 'Not so fast. I only said we'd have to see, didn't I? It would of course depend . . . on you.'

Alison was about to ask what he meant, prepared to accede to almost any terms he might have in mind, when she was abruptly stopped short. For McClusky reached out and pushed up her skirt, exposing her crotch, and the question froze in her mind, forgotten, as she instantly tensed. It wasn't that it had surprised her especially; after all, it was only what she had come to expect. But still it unnerved her. It did every time.

What he did next, however, was a surprise. A shock, even.

Moving to the foot of the bed, he lay on it between her spread thighs; brought his face in close to her groin. So close she could feel his breath, warm on her intimate flesh, and her abdomen tightened in due expectation. Yet still she almost squealed with the sudden shocking

149

thrill of it when she felt the touch of his tongue. Almost, but didn't: she bit on her lip to keep herself silent and managed to contain it within her; she was still determined, whether pointless or not, to keep her arousal from showing, determined to preserve some semblance of dignity.

But it was a struggle that only grew harder. For as the tongue swept up, directly along the heated channel between her sex-swollen vulva, reaching her clitoris to swirl around its aching stem, it caused sparks of sensation to dance in her belly that brought a helpless gasp to her throat. And when McClusky closed his lips on the sensitive button and sucked it firmly into his mouth, the battle was lost; she could do nothing to prevent the low groan of rapture that finally betrayed her excitement – if there had been the remotest chance before that her arousal was secret, it was gone now.

Worse, also gone was her resolve, what little she'd had to begin with, not to be tempted into allowing the urges inside her to build towards climax. For since realising the cruel game McClusky was playing with her – that his teasing was just that, and that he had no intention of making her come – she had done her best to resist it, knowing that to follow the futile path of allowing her orgasm to gather was only a self-torture; that the closer she allowed it to come, the worse would be her frustration when the stimulus was finally withdrawn.

But resistance wasn't easy: sometimes, despite her best efforts, he would take her so very close that her hopes would soar, and she would strive for climax praying that this time he wouldn't stop at the very last moment but would, whether by design or by accident, go on to give her relief. And even though he never had, next time there was always that hope.

The hope she had now. For he had never pleasured her orally before, and this new departure gave her new promise: maybe, this time, he meant her to come. He had said, after all, he had a special treat in mind for that

150

evening: perhaps making her come was the treat he had meant.

She was certainly close. Very close. And he was rapidly taking her still closer.

His lips were clamped to the stem of her clitoris, applying a gentle suction to it that had her orgasm gathering fast. And when he began flicking the helpless nub with the tip of his tongue it was almost too much sensation to bear: red hot sparks shot through her loins, flying embers from the furnace burning within them, and her thighs shook beyond her control as the wound-up spring in her belly prepared at last to snap.

Better still, she realised, there was now no need to prevent her climax from showing. She doubted, anyway, she could even if she tried. But now her arousal was so obviously betrayed there was simply no point. No, she could let herself go, explode in the throes of it; unheeding of dignity, unmindful of spectacle, and enjoy in total abandon what was now only a moment away. Any . . . moment . . . now . . .

And McClusky lifted his head, letting her clitoris slip from his lips to beg in vain for the one last tongue-flick that would have brought merciful relief to its anguish.

Oh, God, no, screamed Alison inside her spinning head. *Not this time. For God's sake not this time!*

McClusky spoke, then; his voice soft and husky. 'You don't need to suffer like this, you know.'

Alison made the screaming voice in her head go away, to make herself listen to what McClusky was saying. *Didn't need to suffer? What did he mean?*

'All this time,' McClusky went on, 'you've been trying to pretend you're not aroused. When we both know you are; that you're aching, desperate, to come. I mean, why else would you have tried to seduce me in the bathroom yesterday?'

'I did not!' Alison inveighed, doing her best to sound indignant, her cheeks burning to know that he knew. And there was she thinking she had been so subtle!

151

'Of course you did. You were trying to seduce me but didn't want me to know it. You wanted me to take you, to have my evil way with you so you wouldn't have to admit to me what you can hardly admit to yourself: that you want me to fuck you.'

'I do not!' Alison protested again, though she knew it had sounded lame. And it wouldn't convince McClusky, especially as he seemed to know her so well; knew so exactly what was going on in her mind.

'All right, so we won't argue on that point,' said McClusky dismissively. 'But you do want to come, don't you? You want to come badly. I saw you were aroused the day you arrived here – I saw it in your eyes, even before I saw how your juices were flowing when I removed your panties, so it's no use denying it – and having had no way of relieving yourself, you've been aching to come ever since. Well, why suffer it? You have only to say, and your suffering's over.'

Alison's head was a turmoil of tumbling thoughts. *She had only to say and he would allow her to come?* Is that really what he was saying? Was wanting only that she admit her arousal, and then would give her relief? But why for God's sake? A further humiliation in making her confess to her sexual needs? Though did confessing to them matter, now it was patently obvious he already knew? And where was her dignity anyway, now, the way she had pushed her crotch into McClusky's face, seeking additional stimulus against his ministering mouth? Had writhed her hips when his mouth had withdrawn, her pussy thrusting upwards to beg for his tongue in an obscene display of salacity? Her need so desperate she no longer cared.

This last brought her thoughts around the full circle: *she had only to say and he would allow her to come!* Release, relief at last from her desperate sexual cravings.

'All right,' she blurted suddenly. 'So I want to come. There, I've said it. Satisfied now?'

'I might've been, Alison, said with less petulance.

152

Now I think begging's in order, rather than just asking. Penance for petulance, eh? Yes, that has an appropriate feel to it: you'll now have to beg me to let you come.'

'I'll do no such thing,' snapped Alison.

McClusky sighed. 'Oh well, please yourself,' – he pushed himself upright – 'I can wait if you can. After all, the month's hardly got started, has it?'

He climbed down off the bed and turned for the door.

He didn't get far. 'No, wait!' Alison exclaimed in horror. 'All right, I'm . . . I'm sorry. I'll do as you say.'

McClusky turned back to her, raised an eyebrow to say he was waiting.

Alison swallowed hard, feeling her cheeks flush all the way down to her neck. She had never had to beg a man for anything in her life, let alone for sexual favours. 'I . . . I beg,' she stammered. 'I beg you to make me come.'

McClusky sat on the foot of the bed with a smile. Was silent for a moment as if in deep thought, then held her eyes with his; said softly, 'Have you ever made love to another woman, Alison?'

Alison hesitated a little too long for her murmured denial to sound convincing, and McClusky gave her a challenging stare.

She decided she had better be strictly truthful, the stakes too high to risk McClusky's disfavour with lies he wouldn't anyway believe. 'Well, yes,' she admitted. 'Though not with a woman exactly. But a long time ago, at boarding school, the girls in the dorm . . .'

She let her voice trail away: it was something she had rarely admitted – even to Robert, who had no idea – and the memory shamed her as much as it secretly thrilled her.

'Ah,' said McClusky with a knowing look. 'Boarding school: no lads around, eh? So what was it, then? A case of lights out candles in? Mutual masturbation under the bedsheets? One girl saying, "Where's the candle?" and the other one saying, "Yes, doesn't it"?'

Alison was blushing again. 'Something like that,' she muttered, her voice a barely audible whisper.

'And how about cunnilingus?'

Alison didn't answer, only squirmed inside as the now familiar worms began to wriggle in the pit of her stomach.

'Well?' pressed McClusky. 'Did you ever lick a girl's pussy?'

The worms crawled all the faster. But finally she nodded. 'Once, yes.'

McClusky grinned and stood up.

'Don't go away,' he said. 'I'll be back.'

'Wait,' cried Alison. 'Where – '

But he was already gone.

McClusky strode into the den.

'Still feeling horny, then, Kel?'

Kelly was naked. She was sitting in McClusky's arm-chair facing the door, her arms along the arms of the chair and her legs wide apart – precisely how he had left her. And how he'd ordered her to remain in his absence: the position, not to mention the nakedness itself, helping to keep her thoughts unavoidably focused on sex, not least with the possibility, and not an unlikely one at that, of B.J. or Steve happening by. Of course she was still feeling horny!

'Christ, McClusky, I'm climbing the friggin' walls!'

'Good,' said McClusky. He went over and reached for the string of the love-balls trailing from Kelly's vagina; brought it vertical and began moving it back and forth across her exposed clitoris, enough tension in the string to make the erect nubbin of aroused flesh flip from side to side with each pass and causing Kelly to gasp with a sensation she didn't need.

He gave the string a final tug to make the balls vibrate, and said, 'Then take these out and come with me.'

Kelly had the wary, unnerved look that he so loved to see. 'Where are we going?'

'You'll see. Just do it.'

Kelly took the string that was now trailing loosely again, pulled on it gingerly, and the love-balls slipped out with a soft plop. Looking slightly relieved to be free of their maddening stimulus, she pushed herself up to her feet.

Refusing to answer her questions about where they were going or why, McClusky then led her down to the basement and along the corridor to Alison's room. And pushing open the door, he ushered Kelly inside.

Alison, with her skirt still up around her slim waist, her blonde pussy exposed, looked as embarrassed as she did delectable, thought McClusky as the two walked in. Though she appeared to be shocked, too, that his companion was naked.

Offering no explanation, he turned to Kelly. 'Untie our guest,' he told her. 'Then sit on the bed, your legs wide apart.'

'McClusky, what's going – ' Kelly began.

But McClusky silenced her with a razor-sharp look and, duly chastised, she set about doing his bidding.

When Alison's wrists and ankles were free he told her to strip, and to sit on the bed next to Kelly. She seemed somewhat awkward in Kelly's presence, he noted with some amusement; perhaps remembering her visit of the previous day, and the humiliating position in which Kelly had found her. That, or the sting on her rump from the spanking Kelly had later admitted to giving her.

And as she sat beside Kelly on the foot of the bed, adopting the same open-legged posture (without having to be told, McClusky was gratified to see!), the slight awkwardness of her manner gave her a look of almost heart-rending vulnerability – all the more delectable for that. Indeed, both women looked delightfully nervous; their wary expressions making it clear they were wondering with some angst what was about to befall them. McClusky chuckled within: telling them was going to be fun.

'Right,' he said, 'let me explain. You two ladies are both extremely aroused and both desperately aching to come. So, being united in your frustration, I'm sure you won't mind helping each other. And that's just what you're going to do, because you're going to lick each other to climax.'

Kelly blushed and swallowed hard, and Alison's mouth came open clearly about to protest.

'Either of you refuse,' McClusky said quickly, his eyes flashing between one and the other, 'and neither will be coming for a very long time.'

Alison shut her mouth again, her protest stillborn, and the two women exchanged nervous glances before quickly averting their eyes, embarrassment pinking their cheeks.

McClusky smiled, satisfied the matter was settled. 'Only there's a bit more to it than that,' he went on. 'Because actually, only one of you will be coming that way. See, it's going to be a little contest between you, with the one who does come being the loser. Of course, that's hardly an incentive to win, now is it, and like all competitions there has to be a reason to win. Or, at least, a disincentive to lose. So, as punishment, the loser will be tied up for the night; having had an orgasm, yes, but only one. And an orgasm, might I suggest, that since you'll be somewhat preoccupied, is unlikely to be the most satisfying you've ever had in your life.'

He chuckled to himself as he saw Kelly blanch: as aroused as she was, a single orgasm would barely scratch the tiniest dent in her need. 'You'd better be sure to win then, hadn't you, Kelly?' he grinned, reading her thoughts.

'And the winner gets what?' said Kelly, still looking uneasy. 'I mean, the winner still won't have come. Not only not come, but be more frustrated than ever.'

'Ah,' said McClusky. 'That's the good part. See, while the loser's tied up for the night – in the same room as the winner will be, and able only to watch and wish she'd tried harder; indeed, forced to watch so she'll know what she's missing – the winner will be spending the night with me for a night of love-making I promise she'll never forget, and as many orgasms as she could possibly wish for.'

McClusky knew he was on solid ground. Kelly, naturally, would be trying to win; desperate not to be the first to succumb and so miss out on a night of rampant sex with him. And Alison, though she had denied physically wanting him, had lied through her teeth. He had sensed her attraction to him right from the start, and it had been growing steadily since. She wanted his body all right, and with the chance to have it would be trying no less hard than Kelly would. It would make for an interesting contest!

'Any questions?' he finished.

Again the women glanced at each other, though now with something new in their eyes; seeing each other as rivals suddenly, there was a fierce determination to win.

McClusky took a coin from his pocket, flipped it, and slapped it onto the back of his hand. 'Who's going to call it?'

'Heads,' said Kelly.

'Heads it is. Do you want to be underneath or on top?'

'Underneath,' she said, with no hesitation.

'OK, then, lie down on your back with your legs apart. And you, Alison, get into position on top of her. But neither's to begin until I give the word.'

McClusky hadn't needed to spell out in what position he meant, and as Alison lay on top of Kelly she spread her thighs either side of the woman's face and brought her own face down to her crotch.

And two things struck her at once. First, her senses were filled with feminine fragrance, pungent and piquant, and evoking shaming memory of Caroline Wilburt-Jones in the sixth form dorm when she, Alison, had performed cunnilingus for the first and only time she had in her life. The girl had taken for ever to come, she recalled, but looking at Kelly's sex, inches before her eyes, she doubted the woman would be so difficult to satisfy. For her pussy was glistening with dew, her smooth, hairless vulva swollen and purpled with need; just as McClusky had said, she was clearly extremely aroused, and it couldn't, surely, take much to trigger her climax.

But nor would it take much to trigger her own, she knew. And the second thing that immediately struck her was that her position afforded McClusky an embarrassing view of her bottom. It was humiliating; the kind of humiliation she now found so thrilling, and that was turning her on even now – the last thing she needed, she thought, cursing the Gemini twins. And when Kelly's arms snaked round her thighs, her hands gripping her buttocks and forcing them wide, further exposing her anus, she realised Kelly had opted to have her on top for precisely that purpose: the embarrassment of it, as Kelly must have guessed it would, translating to erotic desire and giving Kelly a head start in the race.

And a race she, Alison, was desperate to win. As many orgasms as she could possibly wish for, McClusky had promised the winner. She would need a great many to be finally satisfied after her long deprivation, and it was an encouraging prospect. As encouraging as the alternative was daunting – the thought of being tied up for the night, forced to watch as Kelly came and came and came, forced to watch McClusky pleasuring her, sucking and fucking her to heaven and back, was one she cared not to dwell on.

'Ready, girls?' said McClusky. Then: 'Begin!'

Alison's body snapped suddenly rigid as Kelly's tongue snaked into her, swirling inside her vagina and setting sensitised nerve-endings alight. She wondered how she would possibly hold on, as she buried her face into Kelly's sex and began to lick pussy for all she was worth.

* * *

McClusky rubbed the bulge that was swelling, by now almost painfully, into the tight confines of his pants, thoroughly enjoying the erotic show.

The two women were clearly in sexual agony, writhing on the bed as they tried, in vain, to wriggle their pussies from the other girl's tongue, in search of a moment's respite from sensation they could barely endure, while keeping their own lips and tongues hard at work. Their moans and groans of sexual pleasure–angst interrupted only by their occasional grunts of effort.

But, so far, they were holding out well; neither woman had yet succumbed.

If anything, Kelly had the positional advantage. For with Alison on top, her pussy was slightly more accessible than Kelly's was, where the mattress was a little in Alison's way. And McClusky decided to redress the balance: all he needed was a kinky idea; one it would turn on Kelly to hear more than it would Alison, who, as a submissive at least, wasn't yet so depraved.

And he thought he knew just the thing. 'By the way,' he announced, 'just so you know: the loser will suffer further humiliation by being strapped to the bondage bench and being made to wear the special anal device. The one you enjoy so much, Kelly. And then, as a special treat, will lick the winner clean.'

The effect was dramatic. Almost instantly, and undoubtedly triggered by the innate kinkiness of what he'd proposed, Kelly began to shudder. A long groan, almost inaudible at first but then growing in volume, issued from somewhere deep in her being, and her face fell from between Alison's thighs as her head slumped down on the bed.

'No-o-o-o,' she wailed despairingly.

And McClusky knew she had come.

Alison's body was wracked in torment, every nerve-ending raw, alive with seething sensation. Never in her life had she been so close to climax without having actually come, and her belly was tied in a Gordian knot of writhing sexual need.

But she had won!

How, she wasn't so sure. Kelly had been licking her with consummate skill, and several times she had thought she was lost: could bear it no longer and had almost let go; allowed the wound-up spring to snap and send her plunging into defeat. But, her face slick with sweat, both her own and Kelly's, she had managed to keep licking and sucking and had somehow held on. Until, just as McClusky had said something she hadn't quite heard, Kelly's thighs clamped over her ears muffling the sound of his voice, Kelly had suddenly come, her pussy pulsing in spasm and her thighs shuddering in ecstatic release even as she groaned in despair.

And Alison had won. And, soon now, the dreadful torment would at last be over: McClusky would be giving her all the sex she could want and frustration would finally be gone.

Still trembling, she sat up on the bed just as McClusky said, 'So, it's settled. It's Kelly tied up for the night, and Alison to have all the fun.'

Kelly's cheeks puffed. 'McClusky, you're not serious,' she protested. 'I mean, you just wanted to be sure we'd put on a good show for you, right?'

'Wrong,' chuckled McClusky. 'Though I must admit you did.'

Kelly groaned, and McClusky crossed to the door; held it open.

'Right,' he said. 'Come on. We're going up to the bedroom.'

He waved the women through, but as Alison passed he put a hand on her shoulder and said, 'Oh, and by the way, from now on you'll address me as Master.'

'Yes, master,' said Alison.

It felt unnervingly natural.

Chapter Fourteen

The master bedroom was a celebration of black and gold; as modern as the bedrooms in the Corsair mansion were staid and traditional.

The ceiling was midnight black, star-lit by a grid of sunken spotlights that bathed the room in a soft yellow glow; the carpet was gold. The fitted wardrobes were expensive black ash, with gilt handles and trim. And there was a sunken jacuzzi – not in the *en suite* bathroom with its marble-tiled walls and mirrored cabinets, but there in the bedroom – the ceramic tub a gleaming jet against its gold-coloured fittings and taps. The curtains were a shiny gold satin, drawn back to reveal a sky the colour of Guinness.

The only furniture, apart from a black-upholstered seat that was standing in front of a dressing-table, was a large triple bed with a coverlet matching the curtains, and an apparatus that might have been exercise equipment in chrome and black leather, but which had another, more sinister use.

For it was to this that McClusky now directed the unfortunate Kelly, the loser of the wicked game he'd contrived.

The apparatus comprised of a padded-leather bench

161

set within a complex framework of steel-tubing and straps, and as Kelly lay down on the foot-wide bench McClusky fastened her ankles into a pair of metal-and-leather stirrups, spreading her legs wide apart. Her arms were then drawn above her head where her wrists were secured, stretching her body taut and drawing her breasts almost flat to her chest. And finally a leather strap was clinched tightly across her midriff, allowing her almost no movement at all.

'Comfy?' said McClusky, making Kelly's breast jiggle with a sharp slap to its flattened underswell.

Kelly sucked in a breath through her teeth. 'Ouch, you bastard,' she gasped.

'That should've been, "Ouch, you bastard, master",' chuckled McClusky. 'But we'll let that one go. Now, we don't want you missing the show, do we?'

As he spoke, he turned a large handle on the side of the frame and the apparatus began to tilt, raising Kelly's head while lowering her feet and stopping when she was angled at about forty-five degrees to the floor, facing the bed.

'There,' said McClusky. 'That'll give you the perfect view, to keep you reminded of all you're not getting.'

He turned to Alison then, and beckoned her closer.

'I'm very fond of my bondage bench here,' he said, proudly patting the frame. 'It's so wonderfully versatile. As you can see, Kelly is perfectly helpless and there's complete access to all her intimate places; the large hole cut out of it there allowing access to between her legs from the back as well as the front. The slave can be horizontal or vertical, or even upside down – though not so comfortable, that. And it has some interesting little attachments, too. Watch.'

There was a length of steel tubing between the two stirrups, ensuring Kelly's legs were kept wide apart, and into the centre of this, at right-angles to it, he slotted a metal rod. The rod was about a foot in length, and attached to its end was a large dildo. He then pressed a

162

button on the side of the frame, and there was the sudden soft whirr of a motor.

Alison watched, fascinated, as the rod began to extend – it was telescopic, and as it slowly unfurled, growing in length, it was inching the dildo along the bench towards Kelly's open pussy.

It took three or four seconds to reach her, then McClusky guided its rubber head between the juice-slick lips of her sex, so allowing the lengthening rod to gradually ease the dildo inside her. Kelly gasped, and gasped again, as inch after inch of it slid into her helpless vagina. The thick rubber penis must have been eight inches long, and McClusky allowed its entire length to disappear into her before pressing the button to at last stop the motor.

Kelly was writhing now, as far as her bonds would permit, shifting her hips in a circular motion as she tried to satisfy herself on the dildo. McClusky winked at Alison, a sly wink that clearly had wicked intent, and pressed a second button on the frame's mini-console – a gentle humming began as the dildo began to vibrate, and Kelly's body snapped rigid in a paroxysm of need.

'Oooh,' she moaned, squirming her pussy on the vibrating cock and clearly close to coming again.

But McClusky had other ideas about that: letting it go on for just a few seconds longer, not quite long enough for Kelly to climax, he reached back to the panel of buttons.

And Alison jumped at the abruptness of what happened then. In an instant the rod snapped back to its original length, whipping the dildo from Kelly's pussy to leave it twitching in spasm, on the verge of what it hadn't achieved, her vagina a dilated, gaping hole where the dildo had filled it the moment before.

Kelly let out a groan of despair. 'Oh God, McClusky, please . . .' she wailed.

'You must be joking,' McClusky said, a look of cruel amusement in his steely grey eyes. 'I was just demonstrating some of the bench's options, was all. Besides, it's not a dildo you want: for a girl who has difficulty controlling her urges, as you've clearly shown, I've a more appropriate attachment in mind. But first . . .'

He reached for the control console, and the motor whined as yet another button was pressed. And this time the stirrups into which Kelly's ankles were fastened began to lift, metal tubing swivelling at the sides of the frame to raise them higher and higher. Kelly's body was bent at the waist as the stirrups took her legs upwards and backwards. Further and further, rolling her back on the bench until first her bottom, then the base of her spine was lifted from the padded leather; bending her almost double and leaving her dreadfully exposed.

McClusky switched off the motor and went over to the dressing-table where he pulled open a drawer; he rummaged for a moment, then returned with a rubber butt-plug that was clearly intended for Kelly's now glaringly pregnable anus. The device was familiar to Alison: tapered to penetrate the sphincter, it then bulbed out before narrowing into a waist. This was so when the thickest part had entered the rectum – and the diameter of this one was large indeed, thought Alison with a pang of sympathy for Kelly – the sphincter would close around it, so holding it firmly in place.

McClusky held it to Alison's lips. 'Suck it,' he told her. 'It's going into Kelly's back passage, so if you're able to be magnanimous in victory you'll lubricate it well for her: as you can see, it's rather a large one.'

Alison took the thing into her mouth, not enjoying having to do so but prepared to coat it as best she could with what little saliva she had – notwithstanding her painful slap of the previous day, she bore Kelly no malice and wouldn't have wanted her to have to take the plug dry.

After a moment McClusky withdrew it, then, kneeling to the task, he carefully positioned its now glistening tip to Kelly's anus and began to push with the heel of his hand.

The tip went in easily, but as its girth began to increase Kelly suddenly squealed; began struggling and writhing desperately as McClusky continued to push. The puckered skin surrounding the intimate opening was stretched taut and almost translucent as the plug's most bulbous part entered her, then returned to normal when it was finally all the way in; her anus closing, pursing around the plug's narrow waist.

McClusky gave her rump a playful slap and winked at Alison.

'The next time you make all that fuss,' he told Kelly, 'while I'm inserting a butt-plug, I'll have you running up and down stairs for a while with it inside you.'

Kelly visibly flinched. And Alison reflected, *why had she never thought of such a delightful punishment for Robert?*

McClusky pushed the button to return Kelly to her original, if now not so comfortable, position, then said, 'And now for that little attachment I mentioned.'

Returning to the drawer in the dresser he came back with a curious device. It was a small metal arm, jointed in the middle, and to which was attached a brush-like affair made up of soft latex bristles.

'My latest toy,' he told Alison. 'Even Kelly hasn't seen it yet, let alone experienced it.'

Kelly strained her neck to see what it was, but McClusky kept it hidden as he knelt at the base of the frame.

The dildo at the end of the telescopic rod was detachable, and this he now removed. He replaced it with his new toy and let the motor extend the rod as before, stopping it as the device drew close to Kelly's crotch. He made some minor adjustments to the metal arm, positioning the brush with careful precision, then reached back for the console.

'Now, watch,' he told Alison as he pressed a button.

The arm began to rotate, taking the brush in a slow

circle within the cut-out hole of the bench. And Alison could see at once what would happen: the brush, now moving slowly away from Kelly's pussy would soon, as the circle continued, be moving towards it – where it was set close enough to caress her as it went on its way. Alison watched, spellbound, as it gradually completed the circle, waiting to see Kelly's reaction when the brush finally made contact. For Kelly, of course, could have no idea what was happening, and wouldn't be expecting the caress when it came.

And then come it did. The soft rubber bristles brushed into Kelly's sex, just above her perineum, and Kelly's lithe body jerked then began to shudder as the rotating arm took the teasing bristles right along the groove of her sex, and finally gasped as they tickled her clitoris before the arm moved them on, leaving Kelly to groan in frustration, the stimulus gone.

'That should keep her amused for the night,' chuckled McClusky, clearly delighted by Kelly's response. 'And it's set to rotate at random speed, too, so she'll never know when it's coming.'

The ache in Alison's loins flared in sympathy, as she marvelled at McClusky's cruel inventiveness. For the caress of the soft rubber bristles, coming every so often and at irregular intervals, would never be enough, surely, to induce Kelly's climax, but would be enough to keep her at a peak of arousal, achingly conscious of her own deprivation while having to watch McClusky satisfy Alison.

Alison hoped.

It was as if McClusky had just read her thoughts, for turning to face her he said, 'Right, Alison. Now the loser of your little contest has been dealt with, are you ready for the winner's reward?'

Alison's heart was suddenly racing. 'Oh, yes,' she said quickly, blushing at the enthusiasm with which she had said it but too excited to care. Then she remembered to add, 'master,' and blushed all the more.

'Go and lie on the bed, then,' McClusky told her.

She didn't need telling twice. She all but ran to the giant-sized bed and threw herself on it; lay on her back wondering excitedly how McClusky would give her the first of the many orgasms he'd promised: how he would finally douse the raging fire in her loins.

There was a console by the side of the bed that wouldn't have looked out of place in an aeroplane cockpit, and as McClusky came over he pressed one of its many buttons. A panel instantly slid back in the ceiling to reveal an enormous mirror, the size of the bed itself, and she found herself gazing up at her own naked body.

She watched McClusky leave the console and come round to the foot of the bed, climb onto it and ease open her thighs. She watched his broad back as he lay down on his stomach between them, his black hair come forward to replace her blonde bush, and saw herself jerk in muscular spasm when she felt the touch of his tongue . . .

And a moment later she could see nothing at all as her world exploded in a climax so shattering as to blot out her conscious senses entirely. She could see nothing, hear nothing, was aware of nothing, save for flashing lights in her head and wave after wave of giddying sensation that was almost too much to bear.

It might, in fact, have actually been too much to bear, for she may have passed out. She wasn't sure.

Only that, somehow, McClusky was now naked, lying on his back beside her, his body a Da Vinci study framed in the mirror above. Lean and hard, with every muscle sharply defined, it was the body of a man in the peak of physical condition. His arms were muscular, his shoulders broad. His chest was smooth and hairless, but a cordon of dark fuzz began on his rippling torso, which thickened as it ran down to his groin to provide his penis with a halo of curly black hair.

A penis that was standing hard and erect. And that was very, very enticing: he was impressively endowed, and despite having only just come she was ready again, longing for that penis inside her.

She watched his head turn on the pillow.

'Back with the living I see,' he grinned. Chuckling, he added, 'I take it you enjoyed your climax, then?'

'God, I needed it,' she said, still breathless.

She watched McClusky reach for her breast and take her nipple between finger and thumb, but didn't expect it when he squeezed, suddenly and hard. She yelped in shock.

'Number one,' said McClusky, 'you didn't say Master. And number two, you didn't answer my question: I didn't ask if you needed it, I asked did you enjoy it.'

'S-sorry, master,' she blurted, her breath shallowed by pain, then gasped with relief as McClusky released her nipple.

'Well?'

'Yes, master, I enjoyed it. Er, thank you.'

'Oh, I think you can thank me better than that,' McClusky said. 'Don't you?'

She didn't hesitate. 'Yes, master,' she said, guessing she knew what he meant.

Crawling down the bed she reached for his penis, slid her fingers beneath it and lifted it to her lips. She kissed its bulbous head and enjoyed the smell of his musk as she went to open her mouth.

But McClusky stopped her.

'You haven't asked my permission,' he said. 'I'm your master, and as such you must ask me for everything, for anything, you want. Permission to speak, permission to come – especially permission to come – permission to go to the bathroom . . . and permission to suck my cock.'

'I'm sorry, master,' she murmured, suddenly enjoying the demeaning thought, enjoying the thrill it gave her to think of herself having to beg his permission to perform even the most basic of bodily functions. She forced her thoughts to come back to the task, literally, at hand, and said throatily, 'May I suck your cock, master?'

'That's better. And yes, you may.'

'Thank you, master.'

And she took his penis into her mouth.

Sliding her lips down the rigid shaft, she took as much of its length as she could, then applied suction as she brought them slowly back up. At the top of the long, slow stroke she swirled her tongue around the bulbous glans, fluttering its tip at the frenum – which brought a small gasp to McClusky's throat and snapped his abdomen taut – then slid her lips back down him again, ready to repeat the procedure, finding a sensual rhythm as she fellated him with the skill of an Amsterdam whore.

McClusky was clearly enjoying her oral technique, just as she was enjoying applying it, but after a while, when she sensed his penis begin to pulsate, she had a disquieting thought: *what if he meant her to fellate him to climax?*

She wasn't averse to taking semen into her mouth, nor to swallowing it. Indeed, she enjoyed its taste, its texture, the feel of it in her throat. But if McClusky made her suck him to climax, then he wouldn't be able to screw her: her mouth would have drained him of his masculine need, so depriving her pussy of the feel of his cock. Yet he was making no move to stop her, and watching his testicles tightening in their wrinkled sac she knew he was close, very close, to coming.

She felt horribly impotent. It was a problem she'd never had to deal with before: as Mistress, men climaxed how and when she decided, not when they chose. Now, as a submissive, that choice was no longer hers.

As a submissive! The answer came to her in a sudden flash of new comprehension. Yes, she was now a submissive. And as a submissive she must *think* as a submissive. McClusky himself had given her the answer: whatever she wanted, he'd told her, she must ask his permission.

Letting his penis slip from her lips, she crossed mental fingers and said tentatively, 'May I stop now, master?'

McClusky raised his head to look at her. 'Why?' he said.

'I . . . I want you to fuck me.'

'Earlier, you said you didn't.'

'I know, master. I'm sorry, I . . . I lied.'

'I see. Then you'd better beg me, hadn't you, by way of penance.'

Alison swallowed hard. But she didn't balk, and it even gave her a thrill as she said, 'Yes, master. I beg you. I beg you to fuck me.'

'On your back, then. Hands behind your head, your legs wide apart. While I decide if I will or not.'

She quickly did as he said, feeling unnervingly obeisant as she adopted the required position. It was little different, perhaps, to the position she'd been in for most of that week, but now there were no cords to excuse her: now she was parting her legs willingly, offering herself for McClusky's pleasure. She prayed he wouldn't deny her, while the ache inside her only grew worse.

After a moment McClusky rolled himself onto her, his knees pushing her thighs still wider apart. Wide, wide apart, making her feel so vulnerable – so excitingly vulnerable – as he positioned the head of his cock to the mouth of her hungry vagina.

She tensed, bracing herself for the yearned-for sensation as she waited for him to thrust.

And waited.

But the thrust didn't come. He stayed just as he was, his thighs keeping hers spread wide, the head of his cock just a fraction inside her; teasing her; tormenting her.

She could have screamed. She wanted to reach down and grab hold of his penis, to manually force it inside her. But of course didn't dare, and kept her hands where McClusky had ordered them, behind her head and out of the way, her body his to do as he would with.

'Beg me again,' McClusky told her. 'Let me hear you really begging. Really meaning it.'

'Oh, I do, master,' she gasped. 'I beg, I beg, I beg.'

170

McClusky's eyes grew glassy, his breathing heavy.

And then he thrust. Hard. A single, fluid movement that drove his penis all the way into her, until his balls smacked at her rump and she almost cried out in delight.

And then did cry out, the thrill of it too much to contain, and she tightened her vaginal muscles around his thick shaft the better to savour it; gripping him tightly as he gradually withdrew ready to plunge forward again.

Kelly watched on with envious eyes. Not jealous, exactly – never that – but bloody, bloody envious; wishing it was her into whom McClusky was thrusting his glorious cock as she watched his buttocks plunge up and down.

Alison had already had an orgasm which, to judge by her shuddering response, was a thousand times more satisfying than the one to which she, Kelly, had finally and pathetically succumbed. And the lucky cow was about to be given a second!

While Kelly could only suffer, the feel of the large butt-plug in her rectum impossible to ignore, stimulating her rectal wall, and with McClusky's infernal gadget intermittently caressing her pussy, keeping her at a peak of arousal from which there was no way down.

Cursing herself for her earlier loss of control.

Alison was close to coming again.

Given the level of McClusky's arousal before he had entered her, he had managed to prolong his thrusting astonishingly well; it had driven Alison to the verge of a second climax and she was about to let herself go.

Until she remembered: she had to have permission to come. Her senses already beginning to spin, she decided dizzily she had better obtain it – in the circumstances a formality, surely, but one she had better observe before plunging over the edge.

'Can I come, master?' she gasped on a lust-shortened breath.

And couldn't believe it when McClusky said no, she absolutely must not!

Her stomach lurched. But how could she possibly stop herself? By the look in McClusky's eyes, he would be coming himself any moment: when the throbbing inside her began it would be a stimulus she would never resist.

Mercifully, however, as McClusky's eyes hooded with rapture and he quickened his thrust with the onset of climax, he grunted, 'Now ... you ... can ... come', his words timed to his stroke. And they exploded together in a mutual orgasm of almost violent force; blood pounding in Alison's temples as she rose up to heaven on a vortex of spiralling sensation.

Spent, McClusky slumped down on top of her, his breathing as heavy as the weight of his body while his orgasm gradually subsided, Alison pinned beneath him but too exhausted to care.

She stared up at his naked back, watching knotted muscles slowly unbind, saw his buttocks flinch tight as he finally withdrew. He kissed her breast, then, and rolled himself off her and left the bed with a stretch of content.

'And now a jacuzzi, I think,' he said, crossing to the sunken tub and turning on taps. 'Don't you?'

Alison was almost too exhausted to speak, but the thought of a jacuzzi was enough to invigorate her. 'Mmm, yes,' she said dreamily, climbing down off the bed and going to join him.

The tub filled quickly, and McClusky turned off the taps. He held out his hand as if to help Alison down into the water, then suddenly withdrew it.

'Ah, but wait,' he said, tapping a forefinger to his temple. 'I almost forgot. First, Kelly has a little task to perform, hasn't she?'

Alison didn't know what he meant, and it must have shown in her puzzled expression.

'The loser's additional punishment,' said McClusky. 'As I told you just before Kelly came, tonight the loser had to lick the winner clean.'

Alison recalled hearing the sound of his voice, muffled by Kelly's thighs, and realised it must have been this he'd been saying. Realised, too, that it was probably the imagined degradation of it that had precipitated Kelly's climax, and was only too glad she had missed it – it might well have triggered her own!

McClusky went over to Kelly, and, cranking the handle on the side of the frame, he returned it to its original horizontal position.

'Now, Alison, first step over the bar there . . .'

The motor whirred as he spoke, lowering the apparatus until the tubing to which Kelly's wrists were secured – the bar to which he was pointing – was about two feet off the floor, and as Alison came to the head of the frame he held her hand to help her step over it. She was now standing in the gap between Kelly's outstretched arms, looking down on her prone body.

'Right, now turn around,' McClusky instructed. 'And back up a step so you're straddling Kelly's head. Yes, that's right. In a minute you can lower yourself down on her face, so she can lick you, but for now stay just as you are. And you, Kelly, open your mouth.'

The spread of Alison's legs as she straddled the foot-wide bench automatically parted her vulva, and McClusky crouched down the better to see as a string of Alison's love juice dribbled from her pussy into Kelly's open mouth.

'Swallow it, Kelly,' he ordered, his voice thick and husky.

Alison was too fascinated not to look down, and watched Kelly obediently swallow, wondering if the sheer depravity of it turned on Kelly as much to do as it did her, Alison, to watch.

'Right, Alison,' said McClusky. 'Now you can lower yourself onto her mouth. And you, Kelly, had better lick her out properly or else.'

Alison went into a crouch, lowering herself down until the lips of her pussy met those of Kelly's mouth. The crouch put a strain on her upper thighs and wasn't easy to hold, but she was more than prepared to endure it as Kelly's tongue went to work, snaking into her sex.

It was no less physically pleasurable than it had been before, but now, not having to worry about any consequences were it to trigger a climax, she was far better able to appreciate Kelly's technique. And cunnilingus, it seemed, was a forte of hers.

At last, however, McClusky relented, and signalled for Alison to stand; he helped her step back over the bar and told her to sit on the edge of the frame, prepared for inspection. And pushing her knees apart he knelt down between them, slipped two fingers into her pussy and made her gasp when he split them apart, opening her vagina to allow him to see right inside her.

Alison blushed furiously, the indignity of it making her squirm.

'Yes, not a trace,' said McClusky at last, withdrawing his fingers to wipe them on Kelly's cheek. 'Luckily for you . . . Now, where were we? Oh yes.'

Standing, he took Alison by the hand and led her back to where the jaccuzi still steamed. The water looked hot and inviting, and at McClusky's invitation she stepped into the tub, lowering herself gingerly onto the seat. McClusky turned on the air- and water-jets, turning the water into a bubbling cauldron, and followed her in.

It was wonderfully warm and relaxing, but if Alison thought it was to be a break from the night's main event, sex, she had another think coming.

Reaching under the water McClusky pushed her thighs wide apart, and made her adjust her position on the seat until she suddenly squealed, a jet of water playing directly onto her clitoris.

McClusky smiled a knowing smile. 'Now, don't move from there,' he told her, settling back to relax.

While Alison could do anything but!

They stayed in the tub for some fifteen steamy minutes – steamy in more ways than one, with the water-jet turning Alison on to distraction! – then McClusky had had enough. Climbing out, he helped Alison out too, and they patted each other dry, McClusky taking far longer than was strictly necessary, Alison thought, with the area between her thighs; he was keen to see, it seemed, the effect the water-jet had had on her pussy.

And if she had worried when she'd been fellating him earlier, that making him come would be to forgo a screw, then she needn't have been. His powers of recovery were impressive, and when he stood up after towelling her dry he was hugely erect for a second time.

'Suck me,' he commanded her throatily, pushing her down to her knees.

The session went on for most of the night, until mackerel-cloud grew visible in a dawning sky, pinked by the sun's first rays.

But now, finally, McClusky had fallen asleep on the bed, his gentle snoring the only sound save for Kelly's occasional whimpers of agony–ecstasy each time the bristles came round to caress her. And, alone with her thoughts, Alison reflected on an incredible night of sex.

It had been an epiphany; a revelation of staggering proportion. She had always guessed that being sexually submissive must permit a certain insouciance, but never in her wildest dreams has she realised to quite what extent. To have no decisions to make – McClusky had made them all for her. To not have to control – she had been the one being controlled. To not have to worry if what she was doing was satisfying her lover as well as herself – McClusky would have soon let her know if it wasn't!

There were no responsibilities in being submissive. None. Only the need to obey, and to allow sensual pleasure to be all there was in the world. It was truly insouciant sex, and never in her life had she relinquished herself to orgasms of such stunning intensity. Exactly how many, she couldn't be certain. For some had been multiple, one triggering the next like a line of falling dominoes, while others had merged into a single sensation of such mind-numbing bliss that where one had finished and another begun hadn't always been possible to tell.

McClusky had come six times – that, she knew.

Twice he had come in her mouth, three times in her vagina. Three times when Kelly had been called upon to perform her degrading ablution. And a final time, the most thrilling of all, he had taken her from behind to bugger her to their mutual completion.

Her rectum had never accommodated a penis before – anal intercourse was an act she had never permitted, not even with her most favoured of lovers – and it had affected her on a psychological as well as a physical level: never in her life had she felt so profoundly abased as when asked to kneel to offer her anus for the sexual use of a man. Nor so profoundly thrilled.

McClusky had made her hold open the cheeks of her bottom while he had lubricated the forbidden entrance with the tip of a finger, using her own sexual juices, then had positioned himself to her. There had followed a moment of exquisite pain as the head of his penis had breached her virgin sphincter, and then pain was gone. Was gone entirely as his mighty sword had sheathed itself with synovial ease, her rectum a yielding scabbard. And when he'd begun to thrust, his vein-knotted shaft sliding lubriciously against her sensitive rectal wall, the combined physical and emotional experience was beyond her capacity to fully appreciate. All she knew was, it had blown her mind.

And now, thinking back on it all, her only regret was that she had not met a man like Martin McClusky before: she had missed out on so much, it seemed.

Kelly whimpered, the plaintive sound of it bringing Alison back to the present. And she looked up to see the soft latex bristles brushing remorselessly between Kelly's shaven vulva, stimulating tormented nerve-endings without, quite, satisfying. She felt a rush of sudden compassion, and decided to relieve Kelly's suffering. For the time being at least.

Rolling herself from the bed, she went over to the foot of the frame. And glancing back to ensure McClusky was still soundly sleeping, she tried to remember which of the buttons he had pressed to start the rotating arm; she managed to find it at the first attempt and stopped the whirr of the motor. Detaching the arm from the end of the rod, she knelt down and leaned forward, and to Kelly's clear relief she licked her to a climax it took her but seconds to reach.

Re-assembling the gadgetry, she whispered a heartfelt 'Sorry', as she set the arm in motion again, and returned to the bed wondering at what she'd just done. For a week ago, she would have enjoyed Kelly's suffering; it would have turned her on, and thoughts of ending it, of compassion and mercy, wouldn't have entered her head.

But now, her yearning to dominate, the love of sadism that had been at the core of her sexual being, seemed to have gone; to have disappeared entirely – only thoughts of sexual submission now seemed to excite her. It was, in one sense, somewhat disturbing. For how would it affect her long term, in her relationship with Robert? When this madness was over and she returned to her other, real life? Would she be able to return to her dominant self? Continue to be Mistress to Robert's Slave, able to satisfy his masochistic desires? *Would she want to?*

It was a troubling thought, and rather than allow her to think it her brain shut down; she slipped into sleep, and into a dream-world of erotic fantasy in which troubles didn't exist.

177

Chapter Fifteen

*B*elinda awoke from a dreamless sleep with an uncomfortably full bladder; she rolled out of bed to head for the bathroom, gummy-eyed and still not completely awake.

There, she used the lavatory – to her great relief – then swilled her face in cold water to help bring herself round. And, beginning to feel half human again, she left to head back.

But in the corridor she paused. She was supposed, now, to go directly back to her room: it was the proviso under which her door wasn't locked – she could avail herself of the bathroom, shower or bathe as she chose, but she wasn't to go snooping elsewhere.

And so far she hadn't. She hadn't dared: B.J. had warned her that, if she were found in breach of their trust, her door would be kept locked and the use of the bathroom would then be restricted; she'd be permitted to use it only when one of her captors was available to take her. She didn't like the sound of that, and it was enough to have kept her from breaking the rule. So far.

The urge to explore, however, had being growing steadily – perhaps, even, there was a means of escape. And with that thought in mind the temptation was suddenly too great: feeling bold, and wide awake now, she decided to risk it – if there was a way out, she intended to find it.

She looked to her right. At the end of the corridor there was a flight of steps leading up from the basement. But though she had never seen it, the door at the top was always kept locked – she had heard the key turning in it often enough to know – and there seemed little point in her trying that route; the effort would only be wasted. But perhaps there was some other way out, through one of the several doors leading off from the corridor.

There was one such door the way she was looking, the last before reaching the stairs, and she made her way to it. Carefully pushing it open, and straining her ears for any give-away sound from beyond, she peered through the widening gap.

It was a bedroom, the twin of her own: the same double bed, the bedside table and the straight-backed chair, the same fitted wardrobes built round the door. There weren't any windows, and certainly no stairs. No way out through there, she realised, pulling the door to with a click.

Turning back along the corridor she retraced her steps, passing the open door of the bathroom to stop at the next door along. She took the same caution in pushing it open, but found only another identical empty room.

There were now just two doors remaining, the one to her own room and that to the room in which Alison was being held, and her hopes of finding an easy escape route were gone. For Alison's room was sure to be the same as the others, making the locked door at the top of the stairs the only way up from the basement.

She wasn't entirely discouraged, however. For now she had found the nerve to explore, she could look in on Alison – perhaps if they put their heads together they might, between them, be able to come up with a plan for escape. Besides, she had a bone to pick with Alison Corsair!

Passing her own door to the last one along, she paused outside it to listen. What if someone were in there with her? Belinda had often heard comings and goings, and there was always that chance. She pressed her ear to the door, but there was nothing to hear but the beat of her own heart. And deciding to chance it, she pressed down on the handle and carefully opened the door . . .

And was stunned to find the room empty. Alison's skirt and blouse were there on the floor, beside a bed that had clearly been slept in, but where the hell was Alison?

There was no time to ponder, however, for just then there was the faint but now familiar sound of a key turning in a heavy lock, and Belinda ran for her room in a panic. She threw herself onto the bed, and tried to smile when Steve came in with her breakfast.

Bright morning sun dappling on the closed lids of Alison's eyes brought her gently up from a dreamful sleep, and she opened her eyes to blink.

She made no attempt to move, and it was several seconds before she realised she could. But when it had dawned on her that she wasn't tied down, she flung her arms and legs about manically, enjoying a wonderful sense of elation. She had become so used to waking from sleep to have to lie still, she had forgotten what a simple pleasure it was to be able to properly stretch.

Moreover, gone was that dreadful frustration, that empty longing between her legs that had constantly nagged her for days: her body felt content and fulfilled; her pussy requited at last. And realising she was alone in the room – the apparatus to which Kelly had been bound was now an empty, innocent-looking frame – she put a hand to herself, finding her clitoris with the tip of a finger. Not because she needed to masturbate, far from it, but simply because she could! It was wonderful having the option.

It was a brief caress, however, for after its surfeit of recent attention her clitoris was so sensitive it could hardly bear to be touched. Besides, a thought had occurred to her that was worth checking out. And withdrawing her hand, she climbed down off the bed and went to the bedroom door.

She tried the handle, but the door was locked. As were the windows, she found, when she went over to check; fitted with security locks that required a key. And from which, anyway, there was no way down even if the windows had opened.

Oh well, she thought philosophically; the chance that McClusky had been careless, and had left her a means of escape, had been remote to begin with. And she refused to allow it to sour her mood; to spoil the warm sense of well-being her night of incredible sex had left her to bask in.

The window by which she was standing looked over a large, mature garden, with beautifully manicured lawns and which, in early August, boasted a welter of summer colour. Stonecrop and gentian played on a rockery in a riot of orange and blue, and golden shrubs bordered a path that led down to a garden pond, the rippling water glinting in the late-morning sun. California lilac was in full bloom, and fuchsias bled over a wooden arch. And beyond the lawns, majestic conifers stood like silent sentinels guarding the well-tended grounds.

It all looked so peaceful, thought Alison. As tranquil as her mood, it seemed, as she continued to bask in the warm glow of physical content. And if there were going to be other nights like the last, she decided, then forget any thought of escape: the month would pass quickly enough!

Belinda sat on the bed and tried not to shake as Steve came into the room: it had been a close call and her nerves were a-dither. Had she not heard the turn of that key she would have been caught for certain in Alison's room, out of bounds, and the result of that she already knew. Thank God she had made it back to her room before Steve had come down the stairs.

Still, it had panicked her, and she couldn't prevent her ragged breathing from juddering her large breasts; a lush quivering that evidently caught Steve's eye – it showed in the flush of his cheeks, in his uncomfortable mien as he tried not to look at her, crossing the room with her tray.

Muttering a self-conscious good morning, he set the tray on the bedside table and turned to leave. But at the door he stopped, seemed to hover, then finally turned back to Belinda.

'Look, I'm sorry,' he said, tugging open his belt, his intention as plain as the growing bulge in his jeans.

Belinda was mildly surprised. Steve had not done this before. Not when alone. Until now, only with B.J. around, with the older man egging him on, had he sought to press his sexual advantage. Perhaps, it occurred to Belinda, he had misread, consciously or otherwise, the outward signs of her panic – the pink of her cheeks and neck, the trembling of her breasts, her quickened breathing – as being the symptoms of sexual arousal, and this had excited him beyond his capacity to control his considerable libido.

Better that though, she mused, than had he discovered the true reason for her apparent excitement, which would have had consequences far less appealing than a morning roll in the sack, and she gave him a forgiving smile.

'That's all right, Steve,' she said. 'The way things are, I don't suppose it can be easy, huh?'

Right, slave, she thought, switching the fantasy on; *get your kit off and let's have some fun.*

His belt undone, Steve pulled out his shirt and quickly unbuttoned it; he let it slip from his shoulders to reveal his muscular chest and reached back to the waist of his jeans.

Belinda licked her lips, watching him. She was looking forward to having Steve without B.J. around. She could well imagine that left to himself he would be a sensitive and sensual lover, to whom she would enjoy making love even without need of the fantasy. Though, she decided, she would stick with the fantasy anyway!

Steve slid down his zip, and his manhood was already a promising bulge in his shorts as his jeans came open. But it was another bulge to which Belinda's eyes were suddenly drawn. This one a much smaller bulge – the bulge of a keyring in his jeans pocket.

For on that ring must be the key to the basement door, the door at the top of the stairs; the route, the only route, of escape.

It set her mind racing as Steve came to sit on the bed, kicked off his shoes and removed his socks. And by the time he was out of his jeans and shorts she had come up with a daring plan.

Naked now, Steve reached a hand to her breast and cupped it in a warm palm, gentle fingers stroking its upswell; he brushed his thumb over her nipple and instantly made it erect. It was a pleasurable caress, but Belinda had other ideas.

Placing her own palm flat on Steve's chest, she eased him back on the bed.

'Let me pleasure you for a while,' she purred.

And pushing his thighs apart she knelt on the bed between them, furled her fingers around his erecting manhood and began to wank him with sensual strokes.

Waiting until he was fully erect, his penis throbbing hotly, she said, 'Have you ever been teased by a woman, Steve?'

'Teased?'

'Yes, I mean really teased. Played with but not permitted to come. Tantalised, until you feel your cock and balls will burst with the built-up pressure inside them.'

'Oh, Jesus,' muttered Steve throatily, his cock bucking and twitching in Belinda's hand.

And Belinda thought: *this couldn't be better*. It seemed she had struck a deep-rooted nerve.

'Well?' she pressed.

'No, never.'

She was still fondling his penis with slow masturbatory strokes, and she brought her other hand to his balls and tickled them softly.

'I have a boyfriend who likes me to tease him like that. He likes to be tied up first, so he has to lie there to let me. He says it's the most exciting thing he's ever known. And to judge by the intensity of his orgasm when I do let him come, I guess it must be.'

Steve groaned, and his cock was twitching now beyond his control: just thinking it, evidently, was driving him wild.

'Would you like me to do it for you, Steve?'

'What, the whole bit? Tying me up and that?'

'Oh, absolutely. My boyfriend says that's the best part of all. It's the helplessness, see? He knows he genuinely can't come until I choose to let him, so it makes him want to come all the more.'

'Yeah, I can see how it would,' muttered Steve, his voice thick with arousal.

Belinda crossed mental fingers. 'So then, what do you say?'

'Oh, I dunno ...' He sounded doubtful. 'I mean, letting you tie me up; I'm not sure that'd be on.'

'Well, it's up to you of course ...' Belinda lowered her head; extended her tongue and licked the length of his straining shaft, up from his balls to the sensitive web of skin at the top that made his cock jerk all the more frantically as the tip of her tongue slid over it. 'But just think: taken right to the brink, then held there. Dying to come, but can't. Able to do nothing whatsoever about it as the sensations just build and build ...'

184

A long, low groan began in Steve's belly, and he gasped breathlessly, 'Oh, go for it: why the hell not?'

'I'm sure you'll love it,' said Belinda, struggling to keep her excitement from quavering her voice. She laughed lightly. 'And I promise I won't be too cruel. So, come on then. Stretch out so I can tie you up.'

The nooses were still attached to the corners of the bed, where they'd held Belinda spreadeagled on the day she'd arrived, so it was a simple matter to render him helpless.

'Now all we need is a blindfold,' she said, satisfied he couldn't get free.

'A blindfold?'

'Yes, my boyfriend says being blindfolded let's him concentrate better on the physical sensations.'

'There's a big handkerchief in my shirt pocket,' said Steve at once. 'That ought to do it.'

Belinda slipped off the bed and knelt by his clothes; found the handkerchief in his shirt pocket ... and the keyring in the pocket of his jeans.

Leaving the keyring, which bore a single key, on the carpet, she went to the head of the bed and tied the handkerchief around Steve's head, covering his eyes.

'Listen,' she said, giving his penis a gentle pat. 'Before we get started, I'll just have to pop to the bathroom. I was about to spend a penny just as you arrived, and if I'm going to tease you I don't want to have to rush, now do I? If you know what I mean?'

'Ah, right. Yeah,' said Steve. 'You go to the bathroom.'

And retrieving the key from the carpet, Belinda ran from the room, turned right and dashed past the bathroom to take the stairs from the basement three at a time.

At the top, she paused; pressed her ear to the door to listen. Silence. Slipping the key in the lock, she turned it as quietly as the lock would allow and opened the door a crack. She listened. Still silence. Except, that was, for her heart pounding in her ears, which was thudding so loudly, she thought it must surely alert the whole house.

But that she ignored and crept out into a spacious hallway.

There were three doors leading off it. Two internal doors and, at the end of the hallway, what was seemingly the front door to the house. Beyond it, what? Did the door open directly onto the road? Or was there a garden, and then the road? It didn't matter; a road couldn't be too far away. A road to freedom.

And then she realised – she was naked. She had grown so accustomed to being naked, it hadn't occurred to her until then. She considered running downstairs for Alison's skirt and blouse – wherever Alison was, she obviously didn't need them herself – but dismissed the idea. Time might be of the essence, and if running out naked was the price to pay for freedom, then it was one she could live with.

She crept along to the door, warily eyeing the flight of stairs she now saw led up from the hallway, her ears straining for any sound from above. Still there was only the thud of her heart. A heart that fell when she tried the door only to find it was deadlocked. Not to worry, she told herself quickly, anxious to keep up her spirits, there were still two other doors. Two other possible ways out.

Turning and retracing her steps, she tried the first of the two internal doors. Cautiously pushing it open, she found herself looking into a tiny toilet. She went inside and inspected the single small window: it had a security lock and couldn't be opened. There was no escaping through that. She backed out, and turned to the second door. Silently depressing the handle, she pushed it open a crack. And heard voices.

A woman's voice: 'Jesus, McClusky, I was ready for that!'

A man's voice, replying in a soft Irish brogue, 'And when aren't you ever?' Chuckling.

No way out through there, then. At least, not yet. She decided to wait: the voices might go away.

And that was when she spotted the telephone, sitting like an answered prayer on a hallway table.

She went to it, and lifted the receiver; held it to her ear and heard the welcome purr of a dialling tone. She was about to dial 999, but caught herself short. For if she could hear voices, she realised, from beyond the door she had opened, then they would hear hers: she would first have to close it again. Easing the receiver back into its cradle, she turned to do so then stopped, and spun back to the phone: there, propped up beside it, was a bill of some sort. She snatched it up. It was a telephone bill made out to a Martin MacMahon – not McClusky, Belinda noted with interest – but much more importantly, it was, of course, addressed! It hadn't occurred to her until then that the telephone would be of no use to her – she could have contacted the police, yes, but what could she have told them? But now . . .

Just then, however, the front door rattled, and a shadow had appeared behind its stained glass: someone was coming in. She spun around, considering her options. Hiding in the toilet was too risky: whoever was coming in might be wanting the loo, and she would be trapped there. There were still voices coming from beyond the door she had opened, which left her a single option – the door back down to the basement. The telephone bill clutched in her hand, she went back the way she had come; eased the basement door to behind her and stood there to listen.

The hallway, though, was carpeted, and there were no footsteps to hear. Nothing to hear at all, until the shocking sound of a key in the lock. Belinda almost jumped out of her skin: someone was coming down to the basement!

Fortunately, as the door was already unlocked the turn of the key only locked it again, and it bought her a few precious moments. And hearing B.J. curse, 'The soft tart must have left the frigger open,' she left him to fiddle and fled back to her room.

'Sorry I was so long,' she said, struggling not to sound breathless.

'Christ, where've you been?' cried Steve, his penis like a rod of iron. 'I thought you were never coming back!'

'Oh crikey, yeah,' mumbled Belinda, slipping the key back into his pocket and secreting the telephone bill under the bed. She scrambled between his spread thighs, hoping her delay had not aroused his suspicions. 'Anyway, all good things are worth waiting for, eh?'

She took his penis in hand and began wanking him gently, watching his abdomen snap taut in reflexive response to her touch.

Steve moaned rapturously, and she breathed a sigh of relief – he clearly suspected nothing at all, and was only glad the promised activity had finally begun.

It wasn't Belinda's only cause for relief. Their captors' openness in using McClusky's name had been worrying her somewhat: would they have been so casual with such information if they really intended to set her and Alison free? But if, as now seemed the case, it wasn't his real name – some sort of nickname, perhaps? – then it answered that troubling question.

It took her but seconds to reach this conclusion. And it was all the time there was, for just then the door burst open behind her.

'You know you left the friggin' door – ' B.J. suddenly stopped. 'What the – What the frig is going on here?'

'B.J.!' grunted Steve, clearly abashed at being found as he was.

'Oh, hi, B.J.,' said Belinda, smiling sweetly as she turned to face him. 'I was telling Steve about a boyfriend of mine, who – '

'Shut it,' snapped B.J. Then, to Steve: 'Listen, you tart, don't you realise that with you tied up like that, she might've escaped? She could've lifted your key – even if you'd remembered to lock the door, which you didn't! – and had it away on her toes. You could have cocked up the whole friggin' show, you prat.'

188

'Jesus, B.J.,' moaned Steve. 'Lighten up a bit, eh? We were just messing about, was all. No one was escaping, for God's sake.'

'Yeah, well, she could have, that's all I'm saying. In future, don't be so friggin' stupid.' B.J. turned to Belinda. 'Untie him,' he told her.

And Belinda set about freeing Steve, knowing that that particular door to freedom was now firmly and permanently shut.

Kelly buttered toast to complete the breakfast-tray she was preparing for Alison.

She was feeling wonderful; bathed in the warm glow of post-orgasmic content.

After a night of agonising frustration, with McClusky's diabolical new toy intermittently stroking her pussy, her body had been screaming for climax when McClusky had woken that morning; every nerve-ending raw and begging her for a relief she couldn't provide.

Mercifully, McClusky had awoken in frisky, kinky mood. Frisky, because he'd said he wanted to screw her, and that he fancied it out in the garden – Kelly loved outdoor sex, and the thought of being screwed on the lawn, the morning dew cool on her back, had only added further fuel to the furnace that had burned in her loins. And kinky, because he'd said the butt-plug was to remain in place while he did!

Releasing her from the bondage bench, and leaving Alison sleeping, he had led her downstairs, and, walking somewhat awkwardly, she had followed him out to the garden. There, he had told her to lie on her back and to spread her legs for him.

The large plug in her rectum narrowed her vaginal canal, making it tight and sensitive, and as his penis slid into her it had caused a myriad sensations at once: as excited as she already was, she had climaxed with his very first thrust.

It was still in the ebbing throes of this that she had

spotted a curtain moving in one of the upstairs windows, and knew B.J. or Steve, or both, were secretly watching: it had instantly triggered a second climax even before the first had quite died away – knowing they were being secretly observed appealed to the exhibitionist in her, and added greatly to the thrill of it all as McClusky thrust on.

It had taken him some while to come – his cock understandably fatigued, though by no means exhausted, after his sexual marathon with Alison – and she had come a third, wonderfully satisfying time, before he had finally come with her.

No wonder, then, that she was feeling content.

The breakfast-tray ready, she looked up at McClusky.

'Will you take it up, or will I?' she asked.

'I will,' said McClusky. Suddenly grinned. 'I think I've got one last come in me before my balls are registering empty.'

'You goat of a man,' giggled Kelly. 'Are you going to keep her in the bedroom the whole time from now on?' she asked, hopefully.

But McClusky shook his head. 'No, after she's had breakfast – and after she's relieved me of that final come of mine – I'll take her back downstairs. She's safer down there: the lock on the bedroom door isn't great, and I don't want to take any unnecessary risks. Course, that's not to say she can't be a frequent visitor.'

'Brilliant,' said Kelly, her mind racing with sexual inventiveness. 'I think next time I'll be dom,' she mused.

Alison was standing by the window again, having thoroughly enjoyed the privacy of the *en suite* bathroom.

She was gazing out at the garden and missing the smell of fresh, unconditioned air, when she heard the key turning in the door behind her. Conscious of her nakedness she turned to face it, an arm across her breasts and a hand held over her crotch.

But McClusky came in with a tray, and seeing food

her nudity was instantly forgotten as she suddenly realised how ravenous she was. She hadn't eaten the previous night, brought upstairs before Steve had been in with her supper, and her tummy gave an anticipatory rumble as McClusky set the tray on the bed.

'Did you sleep well?' he enquired.

'Oh yes, wonderfully,' said Alison.

McClusky's eyebrow rose disapprovingly, and for a moment the expression perplexed her. But then she thought she knew what it meant, and added, 'Master?' her tone querying and half disbelieving.

But McClusky confirmed it. 'Of course, Master,' he told her. 'At all times.'

Alison quailed. It felt oddly discomforting to have to address him as such now, in a non-sexual situation. Last night had been different: they'd been playing a sexual game, and it was no more than Robert addressing her as Mistress during one of their sessions – it didn't mean much, it was just part of the fantasy, and once the session was over she was Alison again. This, evidently, was to be a standing arrangement, and made McClusky not just her sexual master but her master period: it was an unnerving thought.

She pushed it to the back of her mind, however; her eyes fixed hungrily on the breakfast tray as McClusky gestured to invite her to join him.

She went to sit on the bed, the tray between them, and McClusky took the top off a lightly-boiled egg with a spoon, dipped the spoon into it, and held it towards Alison's lips. Alison opened her mouth, but the more she leaned forward in reach of the spoon, the more McClusky drew it away. Her tummy rumbled uncomfortably as she wondered what cruel game he was about to play with her now.

'But you haven't begged,' McClusky explained. 'You know the rules: you have to beg me for everything you want.'

Alison swallowed hard. Begging for sexual favours

191

was one thing, as part of an SM fantasy, but to have to beg even for food was something quite different; on precisely the same plain as having to address him as Master.

Nevertheless, as the hunger pangs rumbled on she knew she would have to obey.

'I beg, master,' she muttered uneasily. 'Please may I eat?'

'Of course,' he said, letting her take the spoon in her mouth.

Leaving it between her lips, he grinned and stood up, locked the bedroom door then crossed to the bathroom.

'While you eat,' he said, 'I'm going to freshen up with a shower. Enjoy your breakfast.'

Feeling grateful that she wasn't to beg for each mouthful, Alison tucked in with relish, clearing the tray in a few minutes.

She had been finished for some while before McClusky emerged. He was naked, and his skin was pinked by long exposure to scalding water. He was also partly erect, and clearly had sex in mind.

Well, that was fine by her, thought Alison, eyeing his lean, hard body and sensing a *frisson* tingle her loins. Until she remembered the acute tenderness of her clitoris, and then she flinched.

McClusky sat on the edge of the bed.

'Down here and suck me,' he commanded, spreading his legs apart.

'Yes, master,' said Alison, relieved her clitoris was to be evidently spared: a blow-job she would gladly give him.

She slid from the bed to kneel on the floor between his parted thighs. Lifted his semi-flaccid organ, and drew back his foreskin as she leaned in towards it, brushed its tip with her lips in a delicate kiss, then extended her tongue. Licking the purple helmet, she raised her free hand to his testicles and began to carefully knead. His penis hardened a little, but not by a lot.

She took its head all the way into her mouth, and slid her lips down its shaft, then applied a gentle suction as she came slowly back up. She paused to press her tongue against the sensitive frenum, before sucking him back into her mouth, trying for a sensual rhythm.

It began to have an effect, and his penis, no doubt jaded by so many orgasms last night, at last began to swell, his shaft stiffening and allowing her lips to be more effective as they continued to glide up and down it: the sensual rhythm was achieved.

She encircled his balls with finger and thumb and applied a firm downward pressure; not sufficient to cause any pain, but enough to pull on his cock and erect it still further. And finally it was fully erect, the shaft hard and throbbing, the head a large smooth bulb in her mouth.

She fellated him for several minutes, then for several minutes more, but despite her skilful technique there was no sign at all of his coming. Her jaws and tongue were beginning to ache, and her knees were beginning to hurt. And then she had an idea.

Letting his penis slip from her lips, she looked up into his sex-strained face, his eyes reflecting his effort.

'Master,' she said. 'Would you do it the way B.J. did? He – '

'B.J.?' McClusky looked surprised.

'Yes, master. He made me keep my head still while he literally fucked my mouth.' Recalling it, a *frisson* of perverse excitement ran the length of her spine. If the humiliation of it had given her an erotic thrill with the hateful B.J., then what would it do with McClusky? More importantly, though, it would allow him to find his own rhythm, and so may help him to come.

But McClusky was still looking surprised. 'When was this?'

'Yesterday, master,' Alison told him.

'Did he now?' He had clearly not known, and looked disapproving. But then appeared to dismiss it. 'Fucking your mouth, eh?' he murmured huskily. 'Yes, it's an interesting thought.'

He stood up. 'Lie up on the bed, then, and bring your head to the edge here.'

Alison did as he said. Or thought she had.

'No, further,' McClusky told her. 'Let your head hang right over the side.'

Alison shuffled herself backwards, her throat arching as her head tilted back. And still standing, McClusky bent his knees into a half crouch, then gripped his penis to guide it into Alison's mouth as he leaned forward over the bed.

It wasn't quite what she'd had in mind, and she was worried that it might be uncomfortable. But when McClusky then told her to spread her legs, she at least understood his reasoning – in that position, he now had the added stimulus of her parted thighs to look at; if he wished, could reach forward and finger her pussy. (*Ouch!*) Moreover, as he began moving his lips in simulation of intercourse, fucking her mouth with short but rapid strokes, it brought the most sensitive part of his penis to where it would best be stimulated, his frenum sliding over her tongue.

Even so, it still took time. And it wasn't until he began spanking her breasts – not viciously hard, and not really painfully, but enough to make them jiggle and grow hot – that he finally achieved his climax, grunting with effort as his penis released a few drops of semen into her mouth. In the event, she was thankful it was no more than that, for although her head-back position wasn't as uncomfortable as she had worried it might be, it did make it difficult to swallow.

Having come, his penis began to soften at once and he took it out of her mouth. And as Alison sat up on the bed, rubbing the strain from her neck, she saw the once-proud organ was now limp and lifeless, dangling ingloriously between McClusky's thighs as he went over to rummage in a familiar drawer.

When he came back he had with him a handful of leather and a long length of chain. He sat on the edge of the bed. 'Come and stand here, Alison,' he told her. 'With your back to me.'

Alison jumped down off the bed and stood where he'd told her.

'Good. Now put your arms behind your back. OK, good.'

He passed what she assumed was a leather strap around both of her arms, above her elbows, and cinched it tight. She gasped: it wasn't that it hurt especially, but the backward pull on her shoulders thrust her breasts, still reddened from the slaps they'd received, unnervingly forward, as if she were proffering them for a further spanking; it made them feel dreadfully vulnerable.

Next, he fastened a leather collar around her neck: it was stiff and broad and prevented her from lowering her chin, and apart from anything else it made her breasts feel even more vulnerable than they already had.

Attaching the chain to a metal D-ring set in the collar, he said, 'This is just until we've got you downstairs, safely back under lock and key. We can't have you running off on the way, now can we?'

Alison's heart sank: she had dared to hope she might be allowed to remain in that comfortable bedroom, with its windows and view of the garden. With its jacuzzi. And with its private, *en suite* bathroom!

'I . . . I won't be tied up again, will I?' At least that would be something.

'Not if you observe the rules, no,' said McClusky, standing up and giving the chain a tug to urge her along. He unlocked the bedroom door and led her through it. 'I think we can dispense with keeping you tied up from now on. Once you're safely down in the basement, I'll take off the bondage and you'll be free to move around in your room. You'll find magazines and things in the

195

cupboards, which should help to relieve the boredom a little.'

He was pulling Alison along by the chain, and Alison was finding it difficult to walk: with the collar keeping her head held up, she couldn't look down to see where she was treading, and the stairs especially were awkward to manage. And if she were to trip, she knew with her arms tied behind her there would be nothing to help break her fall.

McClusky might have excused the bondage by maintaining it was to prevent her from trying to escape. But Alison knew it was primarily for McClusky's sexual amusement; her very helplessness turning him on as she stumbled along behind him: her vulnerable, forward thrust breasts, her high-held head, being attached to a chain like a dog on a lead – a chain that he controlled – all of it giving him sadistic enjoyment.

But at least they were now almost there – they had reached the bottom of the basement stairs, with just the length of the corridor to go. And then, once in her room, the bondage would be removed as McClusky had promised, and she would be left untied. Provided she observed the rules, she remembered.

What were the rules?

She asked.

'First and foremost,' McClusky told her, 'that you stay in your room. You can use the bathroom, of course – there's always hot water and clean towels, and you'll find shampoo and the like – but you must then come directly back to your room . . . Talking of which, here we are.'

He pushed open the door and led her inside. Alison was thinking, thank God, no more of those embarrassing trips to the bathroom with B.J. for company! It seemed almost like heaven against how it had been.

McClusky unfastened the collar and freed her arms.

'Oh yes, just one other thing,' he said. 'You're not to

masturbate. You're not to give yourself sexual relief of any kind: after all, how can you come if your master's not here to give you permission?'

And so saying, he left.

Chapter Sixteen

*T*he following morning Alison was in high spirits.

After breakfast she had spent the best part of an hour luxuriating in a hot bath. Her morning bath had always been a favourite indulgence; one which, in real life – that oddly detached *other* life beyond her life here – she would never have forgone for the world. But she hadn't realised just how much she had missed them: it had been wonderful.

There had been only one problem. Aroused when McClusky had taken his pleasure in her mouth the previous day, it had never really abated, and with the warm water swirling between her legs, and the sensual feel of soapy palms on her breasts, the urge to masturbate had been barely resistible. And she had almost succumbed: after all, despite McClusky's rule that she mustn't, how could he ever know? However, resist it she had. And wasn't even sure why. Except that she felt a strange but powerful compulsion to remain submissive to her 'Master', obeying his command even when he wasn't there to enforce it. Indeed, especially when he wasn't there to enforce it, when to obey was a true test of her new-found sexual submissiveness.

And so, though the gnawing urge had remained, she

had refrained from touching herself any more than was strictly necessary to wash.

Apart from that, though, the bath had been a delight. Moreover, as well as the magazines McClusky had promised she would find in the cupboards, there had been some basic necessities; these had included a hair-dryer, and she had been able to wash her hair. And now, as she came out of the bathroom, one towel knotted above her breasts and a second one turbanning her head, she felt cleaner and fresher than she had in an age. It not occurring to her to do anything other, she tripped directly back to her room.

There was a mirror on the inside of the open cupboard door, and she sat down before it; studied her face in the glass. Even without make-up she was very attractive, with good skin and an excellent bone structure, and the face that looked back at her wasn't displeasing. Never-theless, having found some basic cosmetics in one of the cupboard drawers – not her own brands, but they would do well enough – she decided to give herself a complete make-over. Unwinding the towel from her head, she shook out her hair and reached for the dryer.

Some half an hour later, having dried and styled her curly, blonde hair – as best she could, with the basic equipment to hand – and her face made up, she felt forty feet tall and bazooka-proof. Slipping into her skirt and blouse, she searched for a magazine that would comple-ment her good mood.

That was when the door opened, and McClusky and B.J. came in.

On seeing B.J., Alison's heart fell. She had dared to hope, now it was no longer necessary for him to accompany her to the bathroom, that she would never have to see him again. She was only glad they weren't two minutes earlier, and she had dressed before they'd arrived.

Though McClusky could change that with a snap of his fingers, she realised, if that was what he wished. And her heart fell further as the thought suddenly occurred: was it sex for which they had come? Would she now be required to sexually serve the rest of the household, starting with B.J.?

However, something about the men's demeanour suggested this wasn't a visit with a sexual motive. B.J. was looking puzzled and McClusky's unreadable eyes were dull, and something was clearly amiss. *But what?* wondered Alison, suddenly curious.

B.J. wrinkled his brow into a questioning frown and addressed McClusky. 'What's this all about, boss?'

'You'll see,' said McClusky. Then, to Alison: 'You said B.J. paid you a visit the day before yesterday?'

Alison nodded, and B.J. shuffled his feet looking slightly uncomfortable.

'And that he had you suck his cock?'

'Yes,' said Alison. 'He – '

'She wanted to, boss,' B.J. cut in. 'Honest. She told me she did; said it in those very words.' His eyes flashed to Alison. 'Didn't you? You actually said it, right, that you wanted to do it?'

'Yes, but – '

'There, you see! She says so herself.'

Though she had no idea what this was about, Alison refused to be cowed; she intended to have her full say whether B.J. liked it or not. 'But Steve was whipping Belinda,' she continued undaunted. 'I did it only so he would stop.'

McClusky flashed B.J. a thunderous look, and B.J.'s cheeks puffed as he said quickly, 'He never was, boss. Who, Steve? That soft tart? You must be joking. In fact, why don't you go see for yourself? I mean, whipping leaves marks, right? And I'll bet you won't find a mark on her body.'

McClusky looked back to Alison, cocking an eyebrow for some explanation.

An explanation she didn't have. 'But . . . but . . .'

'Not a single mark,' B.J. came in, a smirk beginning to

200

curl his lips as he pressed his advantage home. 'Besides, you can ask her if you don't believe me. Yeah, that's it: c'mon, let's go ask her right now.'

There was doubt showing in McClusky's eyes, and Alison almost choked. It was somehow important that McClusky believed her.

'But I didn't want to do it,' she blurted. 'Not like he's trying to say. But Steve was whipping Belinda, and . . .'

She let her voice peter out, upset and confused. But there had to be marks to prove it: as severely as Steve had been caning her, it must have left bruising. Yet B.J. seemed so sure of himself, encouraging McClusky as he was to go in and see her. And even if there weren't any marks, why would Belinda lie and say it had never happened? It didn't make any sense. And the way it was, it looked as if she, Alison, was making it up; that she had actually wanted to fellate the horrible man.

B.J. was still exhorting McClusky to leave, to check with Belinda himself. 'Come on, boss, we can go in and see her.'

McClusky seemed ready to dismiss the whole thing.

But then suddenly narrowed his eyes. 'Just a minute,' he said. He turned to Alison. 'Did you actually see your friend being whipped?'

'Well, no,' said Alison. 'I mean, they were in the next room. But I could hear – '

And then it dawned. Belinda hadn't been caned at all: she had been conned; duped into dancing to B.J.'s tune. Duped into sucking his cock.

And McClusky had uncovered the truth. 'So,' he said, turning back to B.J., 'you fixed it up to sound like Belinda was being whipped; so Alison would think she was.'

B.J. grinned a sheepish grin. 'She might've got that impression, yeah. But hey, no one got hurt: it was only a bit of harmless persuasion.'

'It was blackmail; coercion of the very worst kind, you rat. And after I'd told you Alison was not to be touched – given you a direct order to that effect.'

The smirk had gone from B.J.'s face. 'Yeah, but, I mean, no big deal, huh? I mean, it was only a blow-job, right?'

'A blow-job too many, B.J. I let you get away with screwing Belinda, with your dubious "she asked me to", but you're not getting away with the same trick twice.' McClusky turned away and went to sit on the bed. 'Strip,' he said.

Alison's fingers were already working at buttons before she realised the order was not meant for her, but for B.J.

And B.J. was a beached whale with a harpoon in his gut, his cheeks puffing in mortal spasm.

'Wh – What are you talking about, boss?'

'You've a choice,' McClusky told him. 'You can walk out of here now, and not come back. Or you can do as I say.'

'And if I walk?' B.J. looked defiant. 'What about my cut of the deal?'

'If you go, you're gone – I'll give your hundred grand to Children in Need, so I will. I'm sure they'd be very grateful for your generous donation. Or else, you strip.'

B.J. suddenly grinned. 'You're kidding me, right? This is a joke; a wind-up.'

McClusky's face didn't change. 'I'm deadly serious.'

The grin wiped itself from B.J.'s face as quickly as it had appeared. 'All right, so I strip. So what then?'

'I'm going to teach you a lesson, that's what. To teach you I'm not to be screwed with; that when I give you an order I expect it obeyed – in its spirit as well as in substance. What's more, I'm going to let Alison teach you that lesson, so she can even the score.'

If B.J. could have paled, he undoubtedly would have.

'But this isn't fair,' he complained. 'I mean, why just me? Steve had a hand in it too.'

'Yes, and if I know Steve, a hand he would've despised. Come off it, B.J., we both know you bullied

202

him into it. Now, either get out and don't come back, or strip. The choice is yours.'

For a moment B.J.'s mouth worked without making sound. Then he gave a shrug that tried to look nonchalant, but which failed, and began to undress.

When he was naked McClusky had him stand for a while, shamed and humiliated, then turned to Alison.

'Right,' he said. 'He's all yours. Take your revenge however you like.'

Alison could hardly believe it; that McClusky had actually meant it. But it was too good an opportunity to miss.

'I can do anything?' she asked, feeling breathless.

'Well, short of tearing his balls off. If he's going to be working for me still, I don't want him maimed; he's no use to me as a cripple. But yes, within reason, do whatever you like. And anything you want him to do, he'll do . . . Right, B.J.?'

B.J. swallowed a tacit yes, looking ill.

'There's nothing I'd want him to do for me,' said Alison. 'And only one thing I'd have the slightest interest in doing to him.'

'Then, go for it,' chuckled McClusky.

Alison took the still-damp towel from the back of the chair where she'd left it, and threw it at B.J.'s feet.

'Spread that on the floor and lie on it,' she told him.

'What the – ' B.J. began.

McClusky stopped him. 'Just do it,' he snapped.

B.J. hesitated, then finally did as Alison had said.

Alison went to stand over him, planting a foot either side of his head. Lifting her skirt to her hips, she looked down at his face.

'You like watching a woman pee, don't you, B.J.?' She bent her knees a little, into a slight squat. 'Well, is this a good enough view for you?'

And revenge was indeed sweet as B.J., with his share of the ransom money at stake, could only stare up in horror as Alison bore down and the golden stream began.

Chapter Seventeen

*T*wo days later Alison was sitting on her bed, a pillow propping her upright and browsing idly through a copy of *Hello* magazine, when the door to her room swung slowly open.

She looked up, to see a head appear around it. Belinda's head.

'Bel!' she cried.

'Shhh!' warned Belinda, creeping all the way in and leaving the door ajar; an ear cocked for the sound of a key in a lock. 'I'm not supposed to be in here. I'm supposed to stay in my room.'

'Yes, same here, or I'd have looked in on you.'

'Yeah, well,' Belinda said sourly, 'maybe some of us think enough of our friends to be less concerned for ourselves.'

'What's that supposed to mean?' challenged Alison, responding to the accusation in Belinda's tone.

'You. Letting that caning go on as you did, when you could've stopped it before it began.'

'But it wasn't for real,' Alison protested.

'Ah, you might know that now,' snorted Belinda. 'But you didn't then, did you? Not at the time.'

Alison looked at her hands, needing to look anywhere

but into Belinda's narrowed eyes; feeling guilty that she couldn't deny it.

'And you'd've let me suffer it for what?' Belindafjwent on. 'Just to save yourself from sucking a guy's dick!'

There followed a lengthening silence – Alison studying a cuticle and feeling uncomfortable, Belinda's annoyance tangible where it hung on the air between them – until, finally, Alison took a deep breath and looked up. 'All I can say is I'm sorry,' she said. Shook her head slowly as she went on, 'You know, the crazy thing, the ironic thing, is if it happened now I wouldn't be nearly so reticent.'

'Oh?' Belinda looked surprised. 'You make it sound like something's changed.'

'Something has,' Alison told her. 'Me. I've changed. You're not going to believe this, Bel, but I've suddenly become sexually submissive.'

'Y – ' If Belinda was surprised a moment ago, she was positively shocked now. 'You, Alison Corsair, submissive? Well, I've heard it all now.'

'It's true,' said Alison. 'I just don't feel dominant any more; all my fantasies are of being submissive. Since meeting Martin McClusky – '

'The guy with intense grey eyes?' Belinda interjected. 'Yes, I saw him the day we were brought here.'

'What . . .' – it was Alison's turn for surprise – 'and you haven't since?'

Belinda shook her head. 'No. The other two, B.J. and Steve, I've seen plenty of them. But not McClusky, no.'

Alison felt strangely elated: so McClusky had chosen her, and her alone, as his love-slave. She had vaguely supposed he had his way with all his female 'guests'. But not so, it seemed: she, alone, was special.

Belinda was still shaking her head in amazement. 'Who'd ever have thought it, eh? Alison Corsair wanting to be dominated.'

'Oh, but it's so wonderfully exhilarating, Bel,' said Alison, bringing herself back down to earth. 'Until you've experienced the sheer insouciance of sexual submission, having only to do what you're told to do and – ' She stopped and bit on her lip. 'Oh, I'm sorry, Bel. I suppose you have, haven't you, having to submit to B.J. and Steve?'

Belinda tapped her temple. 'Not in here, I haven't.'

'Oh?'

'Not at all. See, I've been fantasising myself into a dominant role, so whatever they do – in here – they're doing it on my command: I'm the mistress and they're my slaves. It's actually a hell of a turn-on.'

'Oh, but how can it be, Bel? I mean, with Steve, maybe; I could understand that. But with B.J.? Having that great ox pawing your body.' Alison shuddered. She hadn't seen B.J. since the bizarre episode of two days before, but she knew he was still around. For after the salutary lesson she had given him, McClusky had decided it was punishment enough and had considered the matter closed. She shuddered again. 'Ugh! How can fantasy possibly cope with that?'

Belinda grinned. 'Oh, it's not so difficult. After all, I've been doing it all my life, haven't I, imagining my lovers are Slaves. The mind's a poweful thing, and it wouldn't much matter who it was; B.J., Quasimodo, whoever. Anyway, they only ever want more or less straight-forward sex: they never get kinky or force me to do anything I wouldn't want to do with a guy, so like I said, it's a terrific turn-on.' She grinned. 'The one aspect of all this that I'm actually rather enjoying.'

'Yes, I've heard you enjoying it often enough,' said Alison with a wry grin of her own. 'Though, for me, it's the kinky part that's best.' She told Belinda about her night in McClusky's bedroom, about the humiliations and how those humiliations had been such a turn-on. Turning herself on again as she went into detail, she finished with; 'And McClusky himself! Jesus, Bel, I just can't resist him. It's those erotic eyes of his. And the way he's so wonderfully masterful; so in control. It turns me on like hell. It's turning me on now, just thinking about it.'

Belinda chuckled. 'You have got it bad, haven't you? You really have turned submissive ... Hey, but look, I didn't risk coming in here so we could turn each other on with our different sexual experiences: we've got to get our heads together, and come up with a plan of escape.'

'Escape?' But for those fleeting thoughts of an unlocked door the morning she had awoken in McClusky's bedroom, the idea of escape hadn't entered Alison's head. She wasn't sure she would want to!

'Of course,' said Belinda. 'We've got to think of some way to get out of here. I nearly made it once, by tricking Steve into letting me tie him up. I got the key and everything, but there was too much going on upstairs at the time, and I had to back off. And unfortunately it blew the idea; the same trick won't work again. No, we need some other plan.'

'But why risk it?' said Alison. 'Robert's paying the ransom: it's just a question of us sitting it out till he does. And a million's only a small drop in the Corsair coffers; Robert'll hardly miss it. So why try to escape, and risk getting caught, for the sake of a bit of money?'

'For the – I don't believe I'm hearing this,' said Belinda. 'It isn't about money, Alison. We're being held captive, for God's sake, deprived of our freedom – I have no intention of "sitting it out", as you say, for a day longer than I absolutely must. If there's a way to escape, then I intend to find it.'

'But what if we're caught, Bel? Have you thought of the consequences? I mean, at least as we are we're reasonably comfortable. But it could be a lot worse. Believe me, I know – I spent the first few days tied to this bed.'

'And I spent them naked,' Belinda snapped. 'Unlike some, who it seems are allowed the privilege of clothes. And I'm still naked; kept naked, the sexual plaything of two men.'

207

'But you're enjoying the sex,' argued Alison. 'You've just said so yourself.'

'That's hardly the point, is it?'

Alison sighed. 'No, I suppose. And I guess you're right; if there is a way out of here, we ought really to be trying to find it.'

'That's more like it,' said Belinda. 'Now, listen, you put your thinking head on and I'll do the same; I'll come back tomorrow so we can compare notes. Between the two of us, surely to God we can come up with some sort of plan. Look, I'd best be getting back to my room. Until tomorrow then, eh?'

'OK, love, take care.'

McClusky switched off the monitor in the den, and smiled as he turned to Kelly.

'I think that warrants a punishment session, don't you? How about we set if up for tonight?'

Kelly pressed her fingertips to the front of her skirt, savouring the warm tingle that suddenly washed through her loins.

'I think tonight would be grand.'

The matter was settled.

Later that afternoon, McClusky looked in on Alison.

'Kelly and I are planning to have some fun this evening,' he told her. 'And you're invited.'

Alison wondered if the invitation was optional. She doubted it, but thought even if it was she would have accepted: an evening being sexually satisfied by McClusky and/or Kelly seemed infinitely more appealing than reading endless magazines in her room.

'Thank you, master,' she said.

'One of us will come down for you later,' he told her. Oh, and by the way, Kelly wants to be the dominant one today. So it's to be Mistress Kelly tonight, right?'

'Yes, master.'

And he left.

Leaving Alison to tremble with anticipation, wondering what it would be like to sexually submit to a woman.

An hour or so after supper, 'Mistress' Kelly arrived, looking stunning. She was wearing a mini-dress in soft black leather that clung to her figure like a second skin. The skirt was short and tight, hugging her shapely thighs. The bodice was strapless, nestling her breasts in a quarter-cup bra, silver zips running beneath it making it apparent that this was detachable. Her outfit was completed by thigh-length black leather boots with very high heels, and she looked every inch the dominatrix.

'Stand up, slave,' she said to Alison.

'Yes, mistress,' said Alison at once, shuffling down off the bed to stand before her; her head held high and her arms behind her, her legs a little apart.

'Good,' said Kelly, smiling. Evidently impressed by Alison's immediate servility, her willingness to adopt so submissive a stance without having to be told.

Reaching for the buttons of Alison's blouse, she deftly plucked them undone, pulled the blouse from the waist of her skirt and pushed it open, exposing her breasts.

Alison swallowed drily, and held her position. Though Kelly had seen her breasts before, having them exposed like this – while Kelly was dressed, especially – felt subtly humiliating. And very, very exciting.

Kelly brought her fingertips up to them and stroked their underswell softly. Then in a sudden and unexpected movement, she clamped their nipples between finger and thumbs and squeezed. Squeezed hard, and Alison gasped as Kelly lifted, bringing her up on her toes.

Her nipples were on fire and the urge to reach up, to push Kelly's hands away, was compelling. But she didn't, and kept her arms as they were until Kelly at last relented.

'Good,' Kelly smiled again, releasing her vice-like grip.

Alison sank down on her heels with a sigh. But the

sudden release was almost as painful as the initial assault, and she winced as the blood rushed back into the delicate buds, making them burn even hotter. Again the urge to reach her hands to them, to rub the fire away, was strong. Again she resisted.

'Did that hurt?' said Kelly.

'Yes, mistress,' gasped Alison in a sibilant whisper, still wincing.

Kelly ran the back of her fingers across the burning buds, flicking them gently, gradually drawing the heat from them with their tender knowing touch.

'But they feel good now, don't they?' she said.

'Oh, yes, mistress,' breathed Alison. And so they did. As the searing heat became a warm glow it transmuted to erotic sensation, her nipples tingling with sensual desire.

Kelly had brought a small bag with her, and this she now tipped out on the floor.

'Turn around, slave,' she commanded.

She did so, and Kelly slipped Alison's blouse off her shoulders and let it drop to the floor. She pulled Alison's arms behind her and strapped them just as McClusky had done, thrusting forward her breasts as the strap was cinched tight. Next, she unfastened Alison's skirt, let it follow her blouse and told Alison to kick it aside.

'All right, now face me again.'

Alison turned around once again, and Kelly stood to regard her.

'Yes,' she purred. 'Quite lovely. So submissive. So available.'

Reaching again for Alison's breasts, she cupped the now trembling mounds in her palms and began kneading them gently. Kept it up for a minute, then, while one hand continued to knead, the other traced a sensuous path down Alison's body; down her side to her hip, then across and in, reaching the pubis.

Stroking the flaxen hair at her crotch, Kelly said:

210

'Mmm, I think we might shave this. Then you'd really be naked, wouldn't you, slave?'

'Yes, mistress,' murmured Alison huskily, blushing at even the thought of being rendered so utterly naked.

'But not tonight. Tonight we have other pleasures in store for your pussy.'

Sliding her finger between Alison's slightly opened thighs, she slipped it into her sex.

'Mmm, we are wet, aren't we, slave?'

'Yes, mistress,' squeaked Alison, gasping at the sudden caress.

'Excited, eh?'

'Oh, yes, mistress.'

'Good.' Withdrawing her finger, Kelly stooped, picked up a pair of rubber panties she had brought in the bag and held them for Alison to see. 'Your arousal will help these go on more easily,' she said.

Alison's heart rose in her throat and began suddenly to thud. For the panties had two internal appendages, she saw: a large penis-shaped one, and a smaller one the size of a small cigar. Their purpose was obvious.

Kneeling down, Kelly smeared the rear appendage with KY gell and held the panties for Alison to step into.

Pulling them up Alison's legs, she paused to position the head of the dildo to the entrance of her vagina and slid it inside her an inch. Then it was the turn of the anal rod. This was a little more difficult, but after a moment or two of intimate, and for Alison embarrassing fiddling, it, too, found its place and began to slide in. With both appendages thus positioned, Kelly pulled the panties all the way up; finally pressing front and back to ensure the intrusions were fully home.

They were! The rubber penis seemed to fill Alison's vagina entirely. And the rod in her rectum felt huge, making her feel as if she needed a bowel movement. Yet the sensation of being so overly full was surprisingly erotic, and only turned her on all the more.

Next came a leather collar, which Kelly fastened

around Alison's neck. This collar wasn't as broad as the one McClusky had put on her, and was even quite comfortable to wear; the leather was soft, and it was more like a fashionable choker than a restraint device.

But, as Alison was to discover, it wasn't intended as a means of restraint, to take a leash, as the other one had. It wasn't needed, for Kelly had her own means of fulfilling this purpose . . .

Stooping again to the tipped-out bag, she retrieved a length of slender gold chain and reached for Alison's breast. At the end of the chain was a tiny gold ring that was clearly intended for Alison's nipple. The ring was fashioned like a miniature handcuff, and snapped around the base of the tender bud with an audible click. Ignoring Alison's intake of breath, Kelly then leaned in and took the nipple into her mouth, sucking it to engorge the flesh around the ring, so ensuring it couldn't slip off.

Alison's other nipple was then similarly ensnared, leaving the foot-long chain to dangle between them. And finally, attaching a further gold chain to this, Kelly announced they were ready to go. She led the way, pulling Alison along by her breasts.

Walking was awkward: movement made the lubricated rod mack in and out of her bottom, interacting with the penis lodged in her vagina to sensitise the delicate membrane trapped between the two rubber bungs. Moreover, the penile dildo was of diabolical design: there was a hard rubber nub at its base that pressed onto her clitoris, stimulating the sensitive button with every step she took.

Stairs were the worse (the best!) and there were many of them: the stairs up from the basement, then the two flights up to the bedroom. By the time they reached there, Alison thighs were trembling with arousal and the inside of the rubber panties was awash with her sexual juices.

Kelly pushed open the door and led her inside. And Alison's legs almost buckled as they turned to sudden jelly. For they were all there: McClusky, Steve, B.J. . . . and Belinda.

Hyper-aware of her own discomfiture in the presence of B.J. and Steve – of the brazen thrust of her naked breasts, the humiliation of being led along by her nipples, of the rubber panties with their wicked appendages – it took a few moments for the scene to sink in. Belinda was tied into a chair, facing the door. A chair that hadn't been there before, and so must have been brought in for the purpose. Her legs were draped over its upholstered arms and could hardly have been spread any wider, her ankles tied to its feet. And her hands were down by her crotch where her fingers were holding her labia open, displaying herself in the lewdest possible fashion. She was blushing furiously, and knowing of her inhibition about having a man's eyes on her sex, Alison could guess how she felt, for before they had turned at the sound of the door, all three men had been facing her, gazing directly into her wide open pussy.

'Ah,' said McClusky on seeing Alison. 'Come join the party.'

Kelly unhooked the lead from the chain between Alison's nipples and pushed her towards the men.

'Let me explain,' said McClusky, his grey eyes dark. 'This is a punishment party. It's what happens to our guests when they talk of escape. As Belinda did earlier . . . didn't she, Alison?'

Alison gulped. 'H-how . . . how would I know, er, master?' (She cringed at addressing him so in front of the others, but did it anyway, thinking it wise.)

'Because she was in your room, of course,' said McClusky. 'And it was you to whom she was speaking.'

'I – ' Alison clammed up. She didn't want to deny it, and lie: there might be a high price to pay. Yet she had no wish to incriminate Belinda. Besides, hadn't she, eventually, voiced her complicity? To speak up would be to incriminate herself.

McClusky chuckled. 'There's no need to confirm or

deny it,' he said. 'She's already been tried and convicted – somewhat summarily, I'll grant – and her sentence decided. This is a part of it. See, we've noticed how coy she is about anyone seeing her pussy: she obviously has some kind of hang-up about it. Well, I have a hang-up about my guests trying to escape, so it's a fitting punishment, wouldn't you say, having to hold her pussy open like that, for all to see? And B.J., why don't you show Alison what we were doing just before she arrived?'

'Sure, boss.'

B.J. grinned a sadistic grin as he reached a hand to Belinda's crotch, slipped two fingers into her vagina, and split them apart.

'There,' said McClusky. 'Now we can all see right up inside her.'

Belinda visibly squirmed, a tiny whimper escaping her lips.

'As I said though,' McClusky went on, 'this is only a part of her punishment. For the main event she's been sentenced to six strokes of the whip.' He held out his hand. 'Steve?'

Steve, with apparent reluctance, passed him a whip.

And seeing it, Alison felt a little less angst on Belinda's behalf. For it was, at least, a sauna-whip; eight or nine strands of soft leather about a foot and a half in length, attached to a handle shaped like a phallus. She had one like it at home, and it wasn't too severe: she had laid it across Robert's buttocks with all the strength she could muster, to cause nothing more than a reddening of skin. Across his genitals it was more effective; the leather strands snapping around his testicles could be painful enough.

'Of course, Alison,' McClusky went on, 'since you yourself were not entirely blameless in this serious matter, you're to be punished too. Open your mouth.'

It took Alison by surprise.

'My . . . my mouth?' she echoed inanely.

214

'Yes, your mouth,' McClusky repeated, as if he were addressing an obtuse child. 'Open your mouth.'

Alison hesitated, then slowly obeyed. And McClusky pushed the whip's phallic handle between her parted lips, let go of it and left her to hold it.

'Your punishment,' he said, 'is to do the whipping. Six strokes, directly into her pussy.'

If her mouth had been free, she might have cried out in protest: it was simply too cruel of McClusky to make her do the whipping. Once, it would have delighted her, given her a sadistic thrill to have whipped a woman's pussy. But not now. And not Belinda's. Now, to have to be the instrument of her best friend's suffering was entirely anathema; a punishment indeed.

But her mouth wasn't free, it was holding the whip, and she could only plead with her eyes.

A plea McClusky ignored.

'And we've every reason to believe,' he said, while Kelly unfastened her arms, 'that you know how to handle a whip. So, think on this – any stroke we deem to be delivered with insufficient accuracy or strength, B.J. will only repeat. And will then deliver likewise on you. That, of course, also applies should you refuse to do it at all: that's up to you. But' – he suddenly chuckled – 'after the other day, I don't think B.J. is likely to be in a generous mood, do you?'

Alison quailed, taking his point.

McClusky moved B.J. aside to crouch down in front of Belinda. He reached under her buttocks and pulled her forward, until her lower back was pressed to the edge of the seat and her pussy was stranded in air, where it looked, and must have felt thought Alison, dreadfully vulnerable. Belinda's hands were then taken above and behind her, and tied to the back of the chair.

'Right,' said McClusky. 'Begin.'

Alison took the whip from her mouth to feel its weight in her hand, and stepped forward, her eyes begging

Belinda's forgiveness as she measured her for the stroke. She raised her arm.

And Kelly held it, stopping her.

'Wait a minute, McClusky,' she said. 'She might scream.'

McClusky frowned. 'So?'

'Neighbours,' said Kelly.

'What neighbours? There's none close enough by to hear.'

'Still, I think we should gag her.' Kelly was adamant.

'All right,' McClusky sighed long-sufferingly, prepared to indulge her. 'Steve, in that drawer over there –'

'No need,' said Kelly quickly, instead pointing Steve towards the bathroom. 'Get a piece of sticking plaster from the medicine box.'

And as Steve set off for the bathroom, she reached under her skirt, slipped her thumbs under the waist of her panties and stripped them down her legs.

'These'll do grand, so they will,' she said, slipping them off her feet.

She turned them inside out. 'Oh dear,' she crooned, her eyes holding Belinda's. 'I'm very excited, and I'm afraid I've rather moistened them.'

'You little vixen,' chuckled McClusky, realising Kelly's game. 'So that's why you wanted her gagged.'

'McClusky,' she pouted. 'As if.'

Stepping forward, she reached a hand to Belinda's helpless crotch; grabbed a handful of pubic hair, and said: 'Open your mouth.'

Whether in actual pain, or in anticipation of threatened pain, Alison couldn't be sure, but Belinda didn't hesitate. And Kelly stuffed in her panties, being sure to press their dampened gusset to Belinda's tongue where she'd be sure to taste it most keenly. And as Steve returned with the sticking plaster, she took it from him and taped it firmly over her lips.

Stepping aside, she said to Alison: 'Now you can begin.'

Alison again raised her arm, and mouthing 'I'm sorry' to Belinda, she was about to snap down with the whip when again she was stopped, this time by McClusky himself.

He grinned. 'No, you don't have to do it,' he chuckled, taking the whip from her hand. 'I just wanted to be sure you would: that you'd obey without question.'

He told Steve to untie Belinda, and B.J. was suddenly a bear with a toothache. 'What? She's not gonna get pussy-whipped after all?' he complained. 'This was all a charade?'

Even Kelly looked surprised at Belinda's reprieve, while Steve looked distinctly relieved as he set about untying her hands.

McClusky cured B.J.'s toothache with 'I thought you liked charades' and a look that would have soured cream. He went on, 'But no, I think they've both learned their lessons. Belinda especially. Wouldn't you say so, Belinda?'

Belinda's eyes were wide with pleading, and she gave her head a frantic nod.

McClusky reached down to finger her pussy. 'And there'll be no more talk of escape?'

Belinda shook her head, just as vigorously.

'Then, I think you've been punished enough. Though do be warned' – his finger came out of Belinda's vagina to make her wince as it brushed threateningly over her clitoris – 'next time you won't get away so lightly, and this truly will feel the kiss of the whip.'

He turned to Steve. 'When you've finished untying her,' he said, 'you can take her back to her room. And B.J., you get rid of this chair. And then I suggest you get rid of yourself – you'd be wise to make yourself scarce around me for a day or two; give me a chance to forget what an arsehole you are.'

B.J. opened his mouth as if to protest, but evidently

thought better of it. And as Steve helped Belinda up to her feet, B.J. picked up the chair in his massive arms as if it weighed nothing at all, and the three of them left together.

'Right,' said McClusky, briskly rubbing his hands. 'That's the punishment over with; now it's time for the pleasure. How do you want to begin, Kel?'

Kelly turned Alison to face her, and stood to regard her. At the thought of whipping Belinda Alison's arousal had abated somewhat. But it quickly began to grow again as the eyes of the other woman roved salaciously over her body, moving slowly downwards, taking in the collar around her neck, her pert naked breasts with the chain adorning her nipples, the tight rubber panties.

'I think with these,' said Kelly.

And taking a step closer, she hooked her thumbs into the waist of the rubber briefs and began taking them down. The air on Alison's buttocks and belly was suddenly cool, her skin slick with sweat where the rubber had prevented it breathing.

Letting the panties come inside out, Kelly left them around the tops of Alison's thighs with the dildo and rod still inside her, and knelt down in front of her. Leaning in, she brushed her nose into Alison's bush, and inhaled deeply.

'Mmmm,' she murmured. 'You smell hot and sexy.'

Alison cringed with embarrassment: she could imagine only too well.

'And how wet you are too,' Kelly went on with a purr. She ran a finger around the protruding shaft of the dildo. 'And not only with sweat, either. Look McClusky,' she said, holding up a glistening finger. 'She's fairly gushing with love-juice.'

Again Alison cringed. But worse was to come: Kelly then put her finger to Alison's lips.

'Suck it,' she said.

Worms of humiliation crawled in Alison's tummy as she took Kelly's finger into her mouth, forced to clean it of her sexual juices. Humiliation that had its now familiar effect, and caused a *frisson* of arousal to tease her already sex-heated loins.

Kelly finally withdrew her finger and returned her hand to the dildo in Alison's pussy; she gripped its base and began working the phallus inside her vagina. Being connected, the slippery rod in her rectum macked too, and it felt to Alison as if her entire lower body was alive with sensation. A familiar gathering began in her belly and her thighs felt heavy and full, and as the two appendages continued to work she knew she was close to coming.

But just as her body rose towards climax Kelly suddenly pushed the panties down to her knees, causing the dildo and rod to slip out together in a single rapid movement and bringing a muffled squeal to her throat.

'Take them off,' Kelly ordered, her amused smile telling Alison she knew perfectly well how close she had been.

Alison stepped shakily out of the panties, to stand naked but for the slim leather collar around her neck, and trembling with sexual need; her breasts rose and fell with her quickened breathing, and her loins were aflame with desire.

Kelly stood up. 'Over here,' she said, allowing Alison no time to recover and leading her to where the bondage frame lay in ominous wait. 'Lie down on the bench,' she ordered. 'Your feet in the stirrups.'

Alison gulped at the thought of being put on the frame. Having seen Kelly on it she could well imagine how it must feel; the helplessness of being so utterly bound, her legs spread wide above the hole in the bench that would make her available from both front and back.

Nevertheless, as she sat down at the centre of the padded leather bench, a part of her yearned for it, and swinging her legs round, parting them widely to put her feet into the leather stirrups, it caused a dark thrill to sing through her senses.

Kelly fastened her ankles into the leather cuffs, securing them with tiny gold padlocks, then drew her arms above her to cuff her wrists to the frame. She was stretched unnervingly, but not uncomfortably, taut.

McClusky came over then, and standing either side of the bench, the two began to caress her – McClusky stroking her neck, her throat, her breasts; his touch light and sensual; Kelly, her fingers no less sensual, caressing her inner thighs, her groin, occasionally touching her vulva – four hands driving her wild as they teased her with consummate skill; not letting her come, but once again, taking her right to the edge. Holding her there, on an excruciating knife-edge between agony and ecstasy, her senses swimming in an endless ocean of erotic sensation.

And then, at last, there was the sound of McClusky's voice; it floating to her like driftwood on the swirling tide of her mind: 'I think it's time,' he said.

Alison's heart almost stopped. *Time*, she thought, hardly daring to let herself hope. Did he mean time to let her come? Oh God, yes, please let it be what he meant.

She sensed Kelly's hands leave her body then, and her closed eyes snapped open as she strained her neck to see what the woman was doing.

Kelly had moved to the foot of the bench, and Alison caught a glimpse of the dildo attachment before McClusky's hand came to her forehead, easing her head back down on the bench. Listening to Kelly slotting the gadgetry into position, she thought excitedly: *yes, they were going to use the dildo*. They would extend it inside her and turn on the vibrator, and let it explode her to climax.

The next moment there was the whirr of the motor, and she could envisage the rod slowly extending, edging the dildo inexorably towards her open pussy. McClusky's hand left her brow to guide its head to her

220

glistening entrance, and she gasped as the large rubber penis began to slide into her.

Higher and higher it went, deeper and deeper, inch by gradual inch. Seemingly without end, until the head of it nudged gently at the neck of her womb and the whirr of the motor stopped.

She waited for the vibrator to hum: tense and ready.

But it didn't.

Instead, McClusky cranked the handle on the side of the frame, tilting it until she was upright.

Then he looked into her eyes. 'We have to leave you for a while,' he said. 'But remember, you're not to come: you haven't been given permission to, have you?'

A long low groan of frustration came up from Alison's belly, her eyes going to Kelly's eyes to implore, to plead for a woman's compassion.

But Kelly's eyes only glittered like diamonds as McClusky said, 'If you come, it'll be the last orgasm you'll have while you're here.'

And with those as his parting words, he and Kelly left.

Leaving Alison in an agony of need, impaled on the rubber penis, the dildo all she would need to trigger her climax, yet not daring to move for fear that it might.

But it was tempting. Oh, so very tempting!

Kelly and McClusky were arguing playfully as the two walked into the den.

'She will, you know,' said Kelly.

'And I say she won't,' McClusky maintained.

'Then if you're so sure, what are you prepared to bet?'

'Whatever you like.'

'Anything? Anything at all?' Kelly's mind began to race, a myriad kinky thoughts flashing at once through her brain.

'More to the point,' said McClusky, narrowing his eyes, 'what would you be prepared to bet?'

Kelly's tummy did sudden somersaults, knowing immediately what he was thinking. For some months now McClusky had been gently badgering her to have her labia pierced, to wear a silver ring through each of the lips. But though she couldn't deny it had a certain kinky appeal, the thought of the actual piercing was enough to send a chill down her spine. And she had so far flatly refused.

'Not fair, McClusky,' she said, wagging a finger. 'I know what you'd want me to bet.'

'Well, if you're so sure you're right, why not? After all, you won't be the one paying up, you'll be the one collecting. So what do you have to lose? Course, if you're not so sure as you're trying to make out, well . . .'

He let his words hang.

'Damn you, McClusky,' said Kelly. He was pushing her buttons, she knew. She could seldom resist rising to the bait when he goaded her like that, and McClusky knew it.

But don't be tempted, she told herself firmly. Not on this one, whatever you do.

'I'm perfectly sure,' she said. 'But I don't have to make silly bets to prove it, do I?' She wished, now, she hadn't started this. For even to her it sounded a lame excuse not to take the bet on.

'Course not,' said McClusky. 'But then, you'd have to say that, wouldn't you? . . . if you were chicken.'

'I am not chicken, McClusky!'

'No?'

Kelly bit on her lip. The thought of gambling for such a high stake was actually quite thrilling.

But totally out of the question.

'No, I'm not. But what about you, huh? I mean, you haven't even said what you're prepared to put up, have you? Just what, exactly, is "anything" supposed to mean?'

'Precisely that,' said McClusky. 'Name it.'

Kelly chewed so hard on her lip that it hurt, struggling not to consider it; to find a way out, and not to rise to the bait. Finally she had an idea.

'All right,' she said. 'Here's the deal. If I lose, I have my labia pierced. If you lose, you not only have your foreskin pierced, but you let me put a padlock through it as well. And I have the only key, so you can only ever get an erection when I let you, when I take the padlock off to allow you to.'

'Done,' said McClusky.

Kelly's knees almost buckled. She hadn't for a moment expected him to agree, and had suggested it only as a way for her to save face – she could then have turned the tables and hectored McClusky for being chicken.

But now the bet was actually on.

'Oh, Jesus,' she breathed, both excited and appalled by what she'd agreed.

McClusky chuckled, and switched the monitor on.

The screen brightened to show Belinda sitting on the bed in her room; her naked body still trembling after her humiliation of earlier. But it wasn't this they had come to watch.

McClusky hit a button on the monitor's keyboard, and the screen blanked for a moment as the cameras were switched. Brightened again to the scene in the bedroom, and there was Alison's naked body in place of Belinda's; spreadeagled and impaled on the dildo.

Kelly glanced at the clock on the mantel. It was precisely seven minutes since they'd left her alone. If she endured fifty-three minutes more without letting herself come, then Kelly would have lost the bet.

Kelly shivered.

On the other hand, she thought, the woman would surely never endure the full hour. Or even close to it – they had taken her right to the verge before they had left, and believing herself to be alone, unobserved, the temptation to writhe herself to relief on the dildo would be one she would surely never resist. McClusky's command that she mustn't come in his absence counting for nothing.

And then, thought Kelly excitedly, the bet would be won.

And wouldn't McClusky be sorry!

Alison's body was wracked with need, every nerve-end alive with sensation. Tendrils of lust seared her lower belly and upper thighs, making them quiver with un-abated desire. And with every quiver, with every slight movement of any kind, came the feel of the dildo inside her, reminding her of its so-tempting presence.

As if she had needed reminding!

Every second that passed was an agonising dilemma: the temptation to writhe herself onto the dildo, if just for a moment, was almost unbearable; to take a moment's pleasure from its friction against yearning vaginal walls. But to then have to stop? To leave herself aching even more than she already was for a brief moment of heightened sensation?

And that was assuming she *could* stop; that once having begun, she would then have the will-power to stop short of climax – to become still once again. Having to keep perfectly still was already a mind-numbing torment, without her making it worse.

Yet, the dilemma remained. A dilemma that grew into a greater dilemma with the further passage of time. For the need to come, the need for relief, grew almost too dreadful to bear. *And how could McClusky know if she did*, she thought, with ever more desperate reasoning. When he and Kelly returned, she could always put on an act: pretend to be suffering the agony–ecstasy they would be expecting and wanting to see. Indeed it wouldn't be much of an act – it would take more than a single orgasm to even begin to satisfy the cravings seething within her. So, if McClusky would never know, then why continue to torture herself? Why not let herself come?

Except McClusky was her Master and he had told her she mustn't! And she wanted so much to be truly in his thrall: obedient to him in or out of his physical presence.

Even so, it wasn't easy. And several times she almost succumbed. But each time she managed to hold herself back, deciding to wait just a few minutes longer in the hope of McClusky and Kelly returning.

Then they might be merciful and relieve her at last. She prayed!

Kelly was watching the clock with ever more anxious eyes. There were just three minutes to go and she was beginning to panic. She was going to lose; she just knew it.

No, she told herself sharply; don't be defeatist. Three minutes was three minutes: there was still time enough.

McClusky was meantime enjoying himself. He had stripped naked and was lazily stroking his penis while his free hand played over the keyboard, remotely adjusting the camera.

'Just look at that face,' he murmured, staring intently at the screen as he made the camera zoom in on Alison's face. 'Have you ever seen such desperate sexual need? Look at her eyes; almost in tears with frustration, liquid pools of agony–ecstasy.'

Kelly gulped as the clock's hand ticked off another minute – two to go, and counting – and glanced at the screen. Alison was rolling her head from side to side, and was clearly engaged in a desperate inner struggle.

'Come, you bitch,' she breathed inaudibly. 'For Christ's sake let yourself go.'

She, Kelly, would have done!

The camera pulled back to take in the whole picture, then zoomed in again. This time on Alison's pussy.

For the most part there was practically no movement at all, Alison keeping her lower body remarkably, almost unnaturally, still. But periodically her pussy would twitch, clenching the dildo in an involuntary muscular spasm, and then her thighs would visibly quiver and her belly judder until she brought herself under control.

Damn, Kelly would curse to herself each time she did;

225

each time convinced that this had been it – the one contraction that wouldn't stop, but would go on to become the uncontrollable spasm of climax.

But so far it hadn't. And the clock ticked on another minute; just sixty seconds to go.

But Alison had no way of knowing that, Kelly told herself, desperately clutching at ever more tenuous straws. She had no way of knowing the tape was in sight, and could come at any moment.

She didn't. And as the last second ticked inexorably away, McClusky thumped on the table in triumph.

'There,' he said, delighted. 'What did I tell you? Now there's a true slave.' He threw Kelly a sidelong look. 'Not like someone I know,' he chuckled.

'Yeah, well,' muttered Kelly, abashed.

For he had once put her through the same ordeal, soon after installing the hidden cameras. And before she had known he had done so! Despite his order not to, she had come three times during the hour he had left her: she hadn't been able to help herself, and was the reason she had been so certain Alison would fail.

'So,' said McClusky, beaming. 'I'll make an appointment for you with Jacob. Don't worry, he's medically trained and won't make a botch of it.'

Kelly's pussy flinched in dread anticipation, and she groaned.

McClusky grinned. 'Hey, look on the bright side. I reckon Alison's done you a favour.'

'Oh yeah?' said Kelly sourly. 'And just how d'you work that out, then?'

'Well, think of all the kinky possibilities it'll open up once you're wearing the rings. I could pass cords through them, then round the tops of your thighs; tying them off to hold your labia open. Take you out in public like that, with your pussy-lips held wide apart. No one would know, of course. Except you and me. Though we'd know only too well, wouldn't we?' McClusky's hand was moving less lazily now, stroking his penis with growing fervency as the cogs in his mind turned on. 'Or I could hang weights from them before taking you out: you'd feel the pull on your lips whenever you moved, the weights between your thighs when you sit. Or . . .'

His eyes began to glaze and lose focus. As did Kelly's, imagining herself as McClusky was saying. And even the thought was enough, as she shuddered hugely and came.

Alison sighed with relief when the door finally opened and McClusky and Kelly came in. They were both looking flushed, Alison noticed and, guessing it was the glow of sexual fulfilment, she could only pray it wouldn't have jaded them, which might mean her own relief would be longer in coming.

There was, too, something dark and unreadable in Kelly's glittering eyes, and McClusky was looking amused about something. And none of it augured well.

But she needn't have worried. For approaching the frame, Kelly at once reached down to the panel of controls; pressed a button, and Alison's body instantly snapped taut as the dildo in her pussy began to vibrate. Sensation flowed through her like flood-water over a breached dam, and her eyes flashed imploringly at McClusky.

McClusky smiled. 'Yes, you can come,' he said.

'Oh thank you, master,' she gasped on a rush of air, just as her body exploded in climax. Would have done anyway, without his permission – there would have been no way to stop it – but was all the sweeter for being condoned. At least she could enjoy her orgasm without the worry of punishment to follow.

And enjoy it she did, as conscious awareness ceased to exist and all there was was sensation.

The next she knew, McClusky and Kelly were helping her down from the frame, the last throes of her orgasm finally dying away. She was led to the bed where she was told to lie on her back. The ceiling panel was already withdrawn to reveal the overhead mirror, and she watched herself stretch out in languid content.

Not that there was time to relax.

'My turn for a come,' said Kelly, climbing up on the bed.

She hitched up her short leather skirt and knelt astride Alison's head, facing her feet.

'Lick me, slave,' she commanded.

Kelly was leaning forward, and as Alison extended her tongue to obey her command, she had an excellent view in the mirror above: looking up, looking down on Kelly's leather-clad back, the cleft between her wide-spread buttocks revealing her own forehead and eyes. And as her tongue found Kelly's pussy, she saw McClusky, naked now, step up on the bed to stand before Kelly and present his penis for Kelly to suck. She saw Kelly reach up a hand to it and guide it into her mouth, and watched it swiftly grow to full and impressive erection.

Kelly's pussy responded to its throbbing promise, twitching in spasm as its soft flesh crushed down onto Alison's mouth.

Kelly let the penis slip from her lips. 'Fuck me, McClusky,' she exhorted throatily. 'I need your cock, and I need it now.'

McClusky seemed only too pleased to oblige. Coming behind her he dropped to his knees by Alison's head, taking his penis in hand. Kelly arched her back and pushed up her buttocks expectantly, making Alison strain to keep her tongue to its task, and McClusky came forward; he positioned the bulging head of his cock to Kelly's pussy and made her gasp as he drove himself into her, his pendulous balls dangling inches from Alison's eyes as he buried himself to the root.

Kelly pushed Alison's thighs apart, and as McClusky began to thrust she lowered her face to Alison's crotch.

Alison grunted nasally as Kelly's tongue found her

228

clitoris, and struggled to keep her own tongue busy licking the length of McClusky's penis as it slid in and out of Kelly's sex in a steady, sensual rhythm. The tastes and smells and even the sounds of sex pervaded her senses and was driving her wild with desire.

The three bodies writhed together in a Gordian knot of erotic embrace, each pleasuring the other as tongues licked and fingers probed and McClusky's penis thrust on; muscles tensing, breathing shallowing, as each grew close to climax.

Until, with a guttural groan, McClusky snatched his cock from Kelly's pussy and drove it into Alison's mouth. And as it erupted, blasting his hot seed into Alison's throat, they all came together in a triple climax that left them shaking and panting as their bodies gradually unwound – first unwinding internally, and only then from each other.

McClusky was first to recover, as he seemed to be always.

Kelly was sprawled face down on the bed, her skirt still up round her waist, and Alison watched in the mirror as he patted her bare rump.

'Why don't you have our slave run the jacuzzi?' he said, 'while I go get us a bottle of champers.'

'Oooh, lovely bubbly,' enthused Kelly, rolling over and sitting up. And as McClusky left the room, she gave Alison's nipple a sharp tweak between finger and thumb, and said, 'You heard, slave. Go and run the jacuzzi.'

Alison was still dreamy in the wake of climax, floating high on cotton-wool clouds of content, but the sudden fire in her nipple brought her swiftly back down to earth.

'Yes, mistress,' she yelped, twisting her breast from Kelly's grip as she rolled herself from the bed.

But Kelly called her back. 'Just a minute,' she said.

While Alison stood by the bed, Kelly knelt up and sucked each of her nipples in turn, ensuring the flesh was fully engorged, then took the slender gold chain that was dangling between them and clipped it to the collar around Alison's neck. The chain was of such a length that it pulled on her nipples, uptilting her breasts: it wasn't painful especially, but nor could it be ignored, the tension on her nipples making them tingle.

And it must have been aesthetically pleasing, because Kelly smiled at her handiwork and said, 'Right, now off you go.'

Alison went to the jacuzzi and turned on the taps. She was in the process of turning them off again, the tub full, when McClusky returned with the promised bottle. And, Alison was grateful to see, three glasses: she could have died for a glass of champagne.

Seeing Alison's upchained breasts, he smiled at Kelly. 'Nice touch,' he approved, busying himself with the bottle.

Setting the glasses down on the dresser, he popped the cork with a flourish, and filling the glasses he handed one to Kelly, sipped from his own, and made Alison beg for the third.

'Right,' he said, addressing Alison. 'Get into the tub – you know how to sit.'

Alison stepped into the bubbling cauldron and gingerly lowered herself onto the seat; she found a water-jet and gave a little gasp as it played directly onto her clitoris.

Kelly stripped off and followed her in. 'These water-jets are really something, aren't they?' she said, reaching between Alison's legs to ensure she was properly seated, with her thighs wide apart, and where the jet of water would keep her constantly stimulated.

She was, and Kelly smiled. 'Can't have you relaxing, now, can we? A good slave should always be aching for sex. Isn't that right, McClusky?'

McClusky stepped into the tub and reached for Kelly's breast and caressed it with a gentle squeeze. 'A good slave, and a good slave-mistress,' he said. 'Come on, we can't have you missing out on the fun; over a jet yourself.'

The water was hot and refreshing, the champagne chilled and dry, and with the water-jet playing onto her pussy, the constant tingle of her chained nipples, it wasn't long before Alison was craving for relief once again, in need of more sex.

Fortunately, Kelly was obviously of similar mind. 'Can you get it up again yet, McClusky?' she said.

McClusky stood up, brandishing his erect cock like a weapon.

'You utter satyr of a man,' said Kelly with a happy smile.

She reached a hand to his penis, and climbing out of the tub she encouraged McClusky to follow her with a none-too-gentle tug.

The session set to resume.

Once again, it went on until dawn, with McClusky and Kelly pleasuring themselves in and on Alison's body in every imaginable way; using her as their sexual play-thing, their sex-slave, but, in terms of raw pleasure giving as much as they took.

And having to submit to not only McClusky but to the wicked Kelly too, it all added up to a session even more thrilling than the last. Indeed, to the most exciting night of sex Alison had ever known.

Chapter Eighteen

*T*he days came and went. The stultifying routine of breakfast, lunch and supper, and the ennui of reading endless magazines in between was relieved, for Alison, in small ways by bathing and washing her hair. And in a big way by intermittent sessions of sexual depravity.

Belinda was faring less well. Following her talk of escape, her room was kept locked, and she wasn't allowed from it even to visit the bathroom: she now had the ignominy of a chamber pot with which to contend. Moreover, the sex she'd enjoyed – the only aspect of her imprisonment it had been possible to enjoy – now occurred less often: B.J. was keeping a low profile, it seemed, to keep out of McClusky's way, and Steve wasn't the sort, at least until his libido boiled over, to take sexual advantage of a vulnerable woman. And so, without even the sex to help break the monotony, Belinda's days were a nightmare of unrelieved boredom.

Alison, who occasionally dared to exchange a few words with her, whispering through her locked door, could only sympathise. At least she, Alison, got to spend every second night or so out of her room, in McClusky's comfortable bedroom, enjoying the jacuzzi and sipping champagne. And indulging in thrilling SM.

Sessions for which she had come to yearn. And not only as an escape from boredom!

Kelly, who had just acquired two silver rings through her labia, was sometimes dominant, sometimes submissive, always she wanted it kinky. And for Alison, always the Slave, they continued to be the most exciting sessions of sex she had ever experienced.

It was now three days since the last one, however – indeed, three days since she had seen McClusky at all – and she longed for the next.

She was sitting in front of the mirror drying her hair, and wondering when it would be, when the door opened behind her and McClusky at last appeared.

Was it to be tonight, then? she wondered with sudden excitement.

She turned to face him, quivering with anticipation.

'I've got some good news for you,' he told her, his expression ambivalent as he sat on the edge of the bed.

'Oh? What's that, master?'

McClusky smiled, kindly and warmly. 'No need for that any more,' he said. 'You're going home.'

The news hit her like a physical blow. 'What?' she gasped. 'When? I mean, how?' She knew she had long since lost track of the days, but the month couldn't possibly be up.

'It seems your husband's in a hurry to get you back,' McClusky explained. 'And who ever would blame him? Anyway, he's managed to come up with the money ahead of time: the ransom's been paid.'

'So . . . so when will you be letting us go?'

'This afternoon, just as soon as B.J. gets back with the van.'

'I see,' muttered Alison.

She hardly knew what to think: she was stunned and confused. She wanted to go home, of course: wanted to have back her freedom, her dignity. For this to be over. Yet . . .

Yet a part of her didn't – some dark part deep inside

her that wished to continue as McClusky's slave; to continue to enjoy sessions of depraved, yes, but wonderfully insouciant sex. The kind of sex that wasn't available to her back in the real world. A few moments before she had been hoping for one of those sessions tonight: now she'd been told there would never be one again. She could almost have cried.

McClusky was looking at her, his mysterious grey eyes for once readable – they were showing genuine sorrow.

His voice was soft and tender. 'I'm going to miss you, Alison,' he said.

'I . . .'

She didn't say it. She wanted to tell him she would miss him too. But with freedom imminent, this life over and a return to her old one – a return to Robert – it seemed hardly appropriate. Instead she said nothing.

McClusky's eyes instantly became secret again, shielding his inner feelings. And he only smiled and stood up.

'You'll have a couple of hours to wait at the most,' he said. 'Try to be patient.'

And then he was gone.

Belinda was sitting on the edge of her bed when Steve arrived with her clothes.

She knew she was being released: he had told her earlier when he'd brought in her lunch. And in the meantime, in case there was no opportunity to do so later, she had recovered the telephone bill she had found. Tearing off the address, the part that mattered, she had rolled it up and secreted it on her person in the only feasible place, stuffing the rest back under the mattress where she had hidden it all along.

Now, once they were free, the police could be led to their captors.

Steve gave her the clothes, substituting a man's T-shirt – presumably one of his own – for the top B.J. had ruined, and she quickly dressed.

* * *

In the room next door, McClusky stood before Alison. He had a length of cord in his hand.

'I'm sorry about having to tie you,' he said with a hint of irony, moving behind her and taking hold of her hands, drawing them back, 'but you have to be restrained somehow.'

He tied her wrists together. Not, Alison noted, her upper arms, as had hitherto been his practice when taking her from her room. There was no pull on her shoulders making her breasts thrust forward, vulnerable, and pleasing to the dominant's eye: this wasn't bondage, but restraint for the sake of restraint. She felt a twinge of what was almost dismay.

He slipped a blindfold over her eyes, and then she was being led out. Along the corridor, and up the now familiar stairs. Along the landing, but not, this time, up the stairs to his room, but through an external door.

Outside it was warm, and the air smelled fresh and sweet, redolent with summer scents; honeysuckle and newly mown grass. She inhaled deeply, realising how much she had missed them. But they were scents that were in stark contrast to those in the back of the van into which she was summarily bundled, which stank of oily rags.

She was aware of another smell; a feminine smell.

'Is that you, Bel?' she whispered.

'Yeah. What's happening?'

'If you know we're being released, then you know as much as me.'

The rear of the van slammed shut, and the engine started up. And then they were moving.

There followed a twenty-minute drive, by the feel of it along country lanes – there was none of the stop and start of traffic lights along a main road, and the way they were thrown about in the back of the van, there were many twists and turns. Finally, there were the bumps and lurches of some sort of track before the van was jerked to a halt.

The rear door slid open with a metallic squeal, then strong hands were helping them out.

Alison sniffed the air. There was the earthy smell of a farm. And a few moments later they found themselves lying on dry straw in what was evidently some sort of a barn.

McClusky spoke.

'There's no point in you screaming,' he said. 'You're miles from anywhere and there's no one to hear – this farm has been derelict for years. You can try to struggle yourselves free, I suppose, but there's really no point: your husband, Alison, will be told where to find you – he's waiting for our call right now – and unless he's driving a donkey and cart he'll be here in less than an hour.

'Meantime, of course, we'll be long gone. So, ladies, what can I say? I'll be seeing you, eh? Not.'

A few moments later there was the sound of the van bumping off down the track. Then silence.

'You OK?' said Belinda.

'I guess,' muttered Alison.

'So, that's it then. It's over.'

'Yeah,' said Alison. Fearing her troubles were only about to begin.

Chapter Nineteen

'God, I can hardly believe I'm home,' said Alison, striding into the lounge.

She flopped down on a sofa, and inhaled deeply. The Corsair mansion, like most houses of character, had its own distinct smell, and Alison filled her lungs with it – it was like greeting an old friend. It was less than two hours since McClusky had dumped them in the disused barn, but it already felt like a million years ago: a part of that surreal, other life she had lived for the past few weeks.

Robert sat beside her and slid an arm round her shoulder, and Belinda sat in the armchair opposite, the other side of the expensive onyx coffee table that had been a wedding gift from Robert's mother – and which Alison had always detested.

Tina looked into the room as they all settled down. 'Welcome home, madam,' she said cheerily, flashing white teeth at Belinda in a smile of greeting.

'Thank you,' said Alison. Then she fixed the young maid with a mock-stern look. 'Do we have a bottle on ice?'

'But of course, madam.'

'Then why the hell are we sitting here dying of thirst? Go and fetch it, for goodness' sake!'

'Yes, madam,' Tina chuckled, quickly hurrying off.

'Bastards,' said Robert.

Robert had cried tears of relief when he'd picked the two women up, just thankful to see Alison was safe. But relief had now turned to anger. 'We'll call the police right away,' he announced.

Alison shrugged. 'To what purpose?' she sighed, having to think about it souring her mood.

'What on earth do you mean?' snorted Robert. 'To report a kidnap, of course. And the rest . . .'

That sexual humiliation had taken place had come out in the car, during the hour's drive home. Though not the full story: Alison had said nothing of the curious relationship she had forged with McClusky and Kelly. And neither woman had admitted enjoying the sex thrust upon them – some things were best left unsaid.

'I couldn't involve the police before, for fear of your lives, but now you're home and safe there's nothing to stop me.'

'And tell them what?' said Alison.

'Well, the facts as they stand.'

'But we don't have any facts. None that would help, at least.'

'No, but still. The police will still have to know. And anyway, now you're safe what harm can it do?'

'What harm?' cried Alison. 'I'll tell you what harm: the media would have a field day with it, that's what. Think about it – ' She drew a hand through the air describing a headline. '"Millionaire's wife in kidnap ordeal: RANSOM AND SEX DEMANDED. Our names all over the place, bandied across the media for the cheap titillation of the drooling masses. No thanks.'

Tina came in with a bottle of Krug, three glasses tinkling on a silver tray. She bent slightly to set them down on the table, and Alison caught a fleeting glimpse of the curve of her buttock below the short hem of her skirt: she appreciated the girl's long legs, her uniform's lack of panties, in a way she hadn't before . . . with

Sapphic desire! Her experiences with Kelly had re-awakened old interests it seemed.

'Thank you, Tina,' she muttered, a little fazed by the thought. 'That'll be all.'

She recovered as the maid withdrew and her eyes came back to the bottle. 'Are you going to do the honours, Bobbums? Right now I could die for a glass of champagne.'

Robert picked up the bottle and vented frustration on the foil of the cap, tearing it to shreds as Alison went on, 'I mean, if it would serve some purpose – if it would lead to the kidnappers being caught, brought to book – then fine, I'd be happy to go public. But not for nothing, for God's sake.'

Robert popped the cork, filled the three glasses and set the bottle down with a bang. 'But they can't be allowed to just get away with it,' he growled.

'But they have got away with it, haven't they?' Alison argued. 'That's what I'm saying. If we went to the police, what could we tell them? We have no idea where we were – that it's a twenty-minute drive from where we were found tells them nothing useful at all. And other than that, what do we have? Four names: McClusky, Kelly, B.J. and Steve. Huh! What are the police going to do? Look them up in the telephone book? No, accept it' – she picked up her glass and swigged champagne – 'they're home and dry. And quite frankly, since that's the case, all I want now is to forget all about it and get on with the rest of my life . . . What say you, Bel?'

Belinda was fidgeting nervously and had a far-away look in her eyes.

'You OK, Bel?' said Alison, concerned.

'What? Oh, yeah, er, fine,' muttered Belinda. 'But I, er, I do need to go to the bathroom.'

She pushed to her feet and left the room, her champagne still untouched.

Watching her go, Alison lowered her voice to a whisper. 'Listen, Robert, she had it rougher than I did,' she said, without explaining it further. 'So if she seems a bit strange, well . . .'

Robert drew her close and hugged her to him. 'An experience like you two have had? It'll take you both a little while to get over it, I'd say,' he said, tenderly.

His eyes were as distant as Belinda's had been the moment before.

Robert had said nothing to Alison of the video tapes he had received that morning, prior to his paying the ransom – video tapes of his wife being made love to by another man; by a woman. And nor would he: the tapes had been carefully edited, and the man and woman could not be identified; they would be of no help to the police. Alison's face, on the other hand, had been clear to see – a face contorted in sexual ecstasy.

Watching the tapes through had been, for Robert, like a kick in the stomach. It was close to the ultimate humiliation to have one's wife ravished by another man, helpless to stop it. For one's wife to enjoy it *was* the ultimate humiliation.

To his shame, however, this very humiliation had touched a masochistic nerve, and he had watched the last of the tapes with an invidious erection: a disgraceful excitement he knew would show through if he were to raise the matter with Alison. And in the end he had destroyed the tapes, vowing never to reveal what he'd seen.

Of more lasting concern, though, was that on the video evidence Alison was not merely enjoying all that was done to her, but was positively revelling in her sexual submission: never had he seen her so highly aroused.

In one scene, especially, standing with her hands clasped behind her neck, her shoulders pulled back and her legs wide apart – the classic position of sexual subservience – her breasts had been heavy and full, swollen with need; her nipples like tiny bullets so engorged was the flesh as she had begged her 'Master' to pleasure her. She had begged with poignant sincerity, while her thighs had trembled and her pussy had twitched, yearning for further attention. And when she had come, the man's hand working between her legs – from behind, to favour the camera – the intensity of her orgasm was clearly staggering, like nothing Robert had seen her experience in her more usual dominant role. Like nothing, he knew, that could be experienced unless given the insouciance of total sexual surrender.

It worried him. Had Alison now learned the potential of the submissive role? Would she now yearn to submit, and no longer to dominate? Would the perfect balance of the sexual relationship they had once enjoyed – the perfect balance of dominant and submissive, of Mistress and Slave – have now been destroyed just as surely as he had destroyed those telling tapes, for good?

He didn't know, and only time would tell.

In the bathroom Belinda retrieved the address she had smuggled from McClusky's house. McMahon's house, she reminded herself as she unrolled the paper and re-read the address, her mind in turmoil.

The sensible course, she knew, was to give the address to Robert. Well, to dry it off first, then to give it to Robert! Let him go to the police with it, when they could lay siege to the house and round up the gang.

But another, more daring plan had come into her head. A plan so daring it was dizzying even to think of, but which, if she could pull it off, would kill several birds with a single apposite stone, one of them being equally dizzying to think of.

But it was a plan, surely, that was simply too danger-ous to try; that she was crazy to even consider. And, she decided, she would do the sensible thing and hand the address over to Robert.

Flushing the toilet, she came out of the bathroom. The door to the lounge was straight ahead. The back stairs of the house were off to her left. She looked from one to the other in an agony of indecision: the door led to the safer, more sensible course; the stairs to the putting in progress of the crazy, yet potentially estimable plan.

She dithered. The door or the stairs. Which would it be?

Which?

Fuck it, she thought, the decision made. Racing for the stairs, she took them two at a time and dashed into the upstairs sitting-room, the one next to the playroom. Her steps silent on the deep-piled carpet, she made for the display cabinet standing next to the fireplace; she slid back its catch and gingerly lifted its lid. There, amongst Robert's collection of guns, was the silver Derringer that Alison had told her was always kept loaded – Robert insisted on it for Alison's protection because he was so often away.

Taking the gun from the case, she checked it. Belinda wasn't an expert on guns, but she had once been a member of Braybridge gun-club to be close to the shooting team captain, a veritable hunk of a man, and she knew enough to see it was loaded; the safety catch on, but otherwise ready to fire. And slipping it into the waist of her skirt beneath Steve's baggy T-shirt, she ran back downstairs.

'I think I'd better be going,' she said, trying not to sound breathless as she returned to the lounge. 'I want to get home and bathe; make myself feel human again.'

'Are you sure you're OK to drive, Bel?' said Alison, her expression concerned. 'Only you look a bit flushed, you know.'

'I could always drive you,' offered Robert.

'No, I'll be fine, really. Is the Mini still where I left it?'

'Of course,' said Robert. 'Though I took out the keys and locked it; even out here in the country so-called joy-riders are a pain in the proverbial. Hold on a sec and I'll get them for you.'

'Thanks,' said Belinda. Then, to Alison: 'Look, I'm

sorry to dash off like this. And after you've opened champagne, and all.'

Alison held up her hand. 'No, that's fine, love. I understand. You go on home and have a good bath, followed by a good long rest. And I'll see you when I see you, eh?'

Robert returned with Belinda's keys, and she thanked him on her way out.

Chapter Twenty

The following day, Belinda was sitting in the small sitting-room of her one-bedroomed flat, fingering the gun on the table before her and gathering her nerve while she waited for night to fall.

That afternoon she had bought a map, and had found the address she now knew by heart: she had carried out a cautious, but reasonably thorough reconnaissance. The house was a large modern building set in an acre of land, and though it had a tall perimeter wall, it was a wall she was confident of climbing. Through the wrought-iron gates at its entrance she had spotted a burglar alarm, but this was unlikely to be switched on while they were there in the house. And if they weren't in the house there wasn't much point in her entering; she would have to wait for another night.

She hoped she wouldn't have to, though. For she was now dressed in black jeans and a black roll-neck sweater, and as she stood up to tuck the gun into the waist of her jeans, looking out at the gathering dusk, she was as ready now as she ever would be.

An hour later she was crouched behind bushes, and for the past fifteen minutes had been watching the house.

McClusky and Kelly were in a downstairs room, and appeared to be watching TV. She wasn't to know it, but had they been watching the monitor instead they might well have seen her – there was a hidden security camera aimed directly at her position!

In the bliss of ignorance, she continued to watch.

She had seen Steve pass by the window of one of the bedrooms but hadn't yet seen B.J., and she wanted to know where each of them was before making her move on the house.

Just then there was a sudden noise behind her, and she almost cried out in shock. She spun round with the gun and peered through the gloom, the Derringer aimed. Something scurried through a pile of dry leaves, and she let out a juddering breath as she turned away from a foraging rat and looked back to the house relieved. A breath she abruptly caught. For there was B.J., standing at the window in the same room as McClusky and Kelly, and looking directly at her!

She froze. It seemed impossible that he hadn't seen her, yet if he had he gave no outward sign of it. And finally he turned from the window and walked away.

Belinda remembered to breathe again, and heaved in several deep gulps of air. She steadied the shake of her body, and thought: right, this is it.

A breeze whispered through the trees above, making moonlight dapple on the manicured lawn as she crossed the grass in a running crouch; she reached the house and flattened herself to the wall, sidling along it until she came to a door. She had seen an open window at the other side of the house, but if the door wasn't locked it would be an easier way in.

She tried the handle with fingers crossed, and the door fell open with a metallic snick.

Trying to remember how Cagney and Lacey did it, she brought the gun to the ready and crept inside. She was in a kitchen.

She paused to listen to nothing, then silently crossed

the linoleum floor. The kitchen door was standing ajar, and she carefully peered around it. There was another door along the wall to the right, and if her assumption of the house's layout was correct, this was to the sitting-room that all but Steve were in.

Keeping her back to the wall, the gun at the ready, she edged towards the door; she breathed deeply and counted to three. It was now or never.

She pressed down on the doorhandle until she heard a soft click then shoved on the door and hurtled inside, the gun held in front of her in a two-handed grip. Three heads spun to face her, three pairs of eyes widening in shock. McClusky and Kelly were on a settee, B.J. was standing. She shifted the gun from one to the other.

'Move and you won't again,' she said.

McClusky was the first to recover. He held up his hands in a calming gesture.

'Now, come on,' he said, his voice even. 'You don't want to do anything silly. You don't want to make anyone dead.'

Belinda dropped the gun to his groin. 'Or worse.'

McClusky didn't flinch. 'No,' he said soothingly, almost hypnotically. 'You don't want to hurt anyone. Sure you're angry – and that's understandable – but you don't want to see anyone hurt.'

He was coming slowly off the settee, a hand held out for the gun.

'We can talk about this but give me the gun, eh? Let's put it away. You don't want to be using a gun, now.'

Belinda snapped the Derringer an inch to the side and fired. There was a loud report, and a hole was drilled in the leather of the settee, puffing its innards into the air.

It was enough. McClusky threw himself back on the sofa, looking shaken as he stared at the still-smoking hole.

'And I ought to warn you, I'm an excellent shot,' said Belinda, backing to the door and pushing it to with her heel. The shot was bound to bring Steve at a run, and she wanted to be in position behind it.

Sure enough, five seconds later the door barged open and Steve ran in.

'What the – '

Belinda banged the door shut behind him, and he spun on his heel to stare into the Derringer's barrel; his mouth working without forming words.

Belinda gestured with the gun.

'Back up,' she said, keeping a weather eye on the others.

As Steve stepped back from her, out of threatening range, she risked taking one hand from the gun and reached to the back pocket of her jeans, pulling out a handful of cords.

'Stand up,' she told McClusky and Kelly. 'Turn around, and put your hands together behind you.' She threw the cords at Steve. 'Tie their wrists,' she ordered.

When he had finished, she gestured with the gun for him to back off again, and checked the knots he had tied. He seemed to have tied them well and she was satisfied they would hold.

'Sit down,' she said. Then, to Steve. 'Now B.J.'

B.J. glowered in warning as Steve came towards him, but Belinda blew a hole in the ceiling above his head, showering him with plaster, which seemed to take the edge off his attitude.

'Not the same as the others, though,' she said. 'Tie his hands in front.' She waited until he had, then added, 'Now tie them up to the curtain rod.'

Steve had to stand up on the window-sill to accomplish the task, but when he had finished B.J.'s arms were stretched high above him. He was all but up on his toes, and since the curtain rod looked good and robust he was well and truly secured.

'Good,' said Belinda. Then directed Steve back to Kelly. 'Push up her skirt,' she said. 'Let's see if she's wearing any knickers tonight.'

She wasn't.

'Pity,' pouted Belinda, though she took a certain satisfaction from Kelly's flinch as Steve exposed her crotch. 'They make such an effective gag, don't they, Kelly?' As you were about to have found out for yourself. Still, never mind.' She turned to McClusky. 'You, get down on the floor.'

McClusky slid down from the sofa to sit on the floor, and Belinda pointed the Derringer at Kelly's groin.

'Spread your legs,' she said. 'And you, Steve, tie them apart. Tie them to the legs of the sofa.'

Kelly squirmed, but with an eye on the gun she quickly parted her thighs.

'Pretty adornments,' Belinda observed, seeing the rings through Kelly's shaven labia. They gave her an idea.

Waiting until Steve had tied her ankles to the legs of the sofa, she told McClusky to kneel between Kelly's legs, facing her. She then had Steve tie a thin cord round his neck, pass it through the rings, and draw it tight before tying it off.

'That should prevent any sudden movement,' chuckled Belinda.

The cord drew McClusky's chin into Kelly's crotch and, with his hands tied behind him, it left him kneeling in an awkward position; a position that would soon become extremely uncomfortable to hold. Yet, unless he wanted to cause Kelly a great deal of pain, hold it he'd better.

Leaving McClusky to struggle, she went over to B.J. She held the gun to his temple while she unzipped his fly and, reaching into his trousers, she pulled his penis and testicles out through the gap.

'What's the matter, B.J.?' she mocked. 'No hard-on tonight? Doesn't seem so keen to rise, does it, when you're the one being abused? Come on, get it up for me or I'll shoot the useless thing off.'

She watched him struggle in vain for a while, his

massive penis twitching but doing no more, then reached a hand to it; she massaged the soft flesh until it at last began to harden.

'Come on,' she urged, slapping the stiffening shaft from side to side. 'Get it all the way up.'

It took a few moments, but at last his penis stood fully erect, leaving his testicles dangling, unprotected and vulnerable, beneath the now throbbing organ. And remembering the cruel glint there had been in his eyes when he had humiliated her on the day of her punishment, opening her sex for all to see, she gave his balls a sharp rap with the backs of her fingers; watched his mouth form a silent zero of sudden pain and enjoyed the sweet taste of revenge.

It might have been fun to do more, but time was marching on. There was a telephone on a corner-unit close by the windows, and this she now went to. She lifted the receiver and dialled 999.

'Police,' she said.

There was a moment or two of dead static, then the connection was made.

'Two women,' she began, 'Alison Corsair and Belinda Chessington, were recently kidnapped. They were held captive for almost a month by a man named Martin McMahon, alias Martin McClusky. He and his gang are now at the following address' – she recited it, no longer needing to read it – 'and are awaiting, ah, collection . . .

'My name? It doesn't matter. Their Nemesis, let's say . . .

'Confirmation? Yes, of course. I understand – I take it you've heard of Robert Corsair of WonderMart fame? Good, well, contact him: he can confirm what I'm telling you; Alison Corsair is his wife.

'Oh, just one other thing. One of the gang is a woman . . .' – she glanced over at B.J., with his genitals on display – 'so you'll need to send a couple of WPCs along too.'

She broke the connection and replaced the receiver,

chuckling at B.J.'s chagrined expression. Then she heard Kelly give a sharp yelp of pain and looked over to see McClusky settling back to his awkward position, having tried to relieve the strain on his thighs.

'Yes, you're going to have to keep very still, aren't you?' She grinned. Then she turned to Steve, waving the gun from him to the door. 'You, out,' she told him.

She followed him through to the kitchen, and closing the door with her back, said, 'Now strip.'

With a wary eye on the gun, Steve quickly stripped and stood naked before her.

'Right,' she said. 'You have a choice. You can go back in there, and be tied up with the others to await the police. Or . . .'

She took a sheet of paper from the pocket of her jeans, and handed it to him. 'Read that.'

Steve read it. Two typed paragraphs, with a dotted line at the bottom.

'A confession,' muttered Steve, looking bemused.

'Exactly. A full statement confessing your part in everything that went on here. With your signature on it, when it's lodged with my bank, it will be my guarantee.'

She handed him a second typed sheet.

'I'll save you the bother of reading it for now,' she said. 'It's a Contract of Slavery. It says the signatory agrees, for a period of one year, to serve as my unconditional slave. Of course, that largely means my sex-slave. Sign it, and you agree to obey my every command without question, no matter how degrading or unsavoury it might be; to accept whatever punishments I might choose to inflict on you, whether it be physical pain or by way of humiliation of some sort. And, of course, irrespective of whether or not you deserve it: it may be for no more than my personal amusement and pleasure.'

There was shock in Steve's eyes. But his penis was beginning to harden, betraying a certain excitement. Belinda smiled to herself. She had thought she had struck

250

a nerve the day she had tied him up and teased him while he was helpless to stop it. Now she knew it for sure: to one degree or another, Steve was masochistically inclined. And though he was clearly shocked by what she proposed, the thought of it was turning him on.

Though whether he would enjoy the reality of the regime she envisaged was another question, and a sadistic *frisson* made her loins suddenly ache.

'It's that or go to prison with the others,' she said. 'But it's only fair to warn you, this is not a soft option. If you choose to serve as my slave, I won't be an easy Mistress. You will keep me sexually satisfied at all times, and howsoever I choose, but your own gratification will be strictly limited; with masturbation absolutely forbidden – except, of course, upon my command – and coming only when I permit you to come.

'So, think carefully before you decide: if merely seeing me naked was sufficient to drive you crazy – enough to persuade you to ignore your conscience, and lose control out of sheer desperation – then imagine being my slave. Especially as even the thought of it is having such an effect.' Steve was now fully erect, his penis arcing up from his groin to stand almost flat to his belly. She pointed to it with the gun. 'And you'll be permitted one of those only when I want you to have one. So imagine: constantly serving my sexual needs, yet punished if you get an erection without my permission to do so. Subjected, daily, to sexual use and abuse, yet seldom permitted relief. It would be, for much of the time, a living nightmare. And I would fully intend to see that it was. But the choice is up to you.'

Steve was quiet for a while, then at last swallowed hard. 'For a year, you said. And then I'd be free to go.'

'One year from today I'll tear up your confession, and you can do whatever you like.'

'It's not much of a choice, then, is it? It's that, or seven or eight years inside.'

251

'Not much choice, no,' said Belinda. 'But it's more choice than I had during the time I was here.'

Steve looked abashed, and finally sighed. 'OK,' he muttered. 'I'll sign.'

He found a pen in a kitchen drawer, signed both papers and handed them back.

'Right,' said Belinda. 'We'd better get going. The police will be checking things out before they respond, but they won't take for ever. Do you have the key to the gates? There's no point in us climbing walls we don't have to.' She suddenly chuckled. 'You'll be doing enough of that as it is!'

'They're remote-controlled,' Steve told her, wincing at her remark. 'The box is in the car.'

'OK, we'll pick it up on the way. Leave your clothes: you won't be needing them.' She pointed the gun. 'And I'll keep this trained on you until I get your confession safely into the bank. Go on, lead the way.'

Five minutes later, with Steve rolled up in a naked ball in the well of the passenger seat, Belinda pulled the Mini off the grass verge on which she had parked and barrelled off down the lane.

Just as a convoy of police cars shot by in the opposite direction, sirens whining.

Chapter Twenty-one

'More tea, madam?'

'No thank you, Tina,' said Alison. 'If I have any more tea, I'll turn into one of those little Tetley men who advertise the stuff on the telly.'

She had been up all night drinking tea; she had a lot on her mind.

For one thing, Norman Wadsworth had telephoned at about ten the previous evening. Wadsworth belonged to the same Masonic lodge as Robert . . . and was Chief of Police in Braybridge. He'd wanted to know if there was any truth in a report that Alison had been kidnapped, along with another woman. It seemed the police had received an anonymous phone call to this effect, and Wadsworth had intercepted the paperwork ready to do what he could to keep it hushed up if this was what Robert wanted – a local reporter was already sniffing around, he'd warned.

Of course, Robert had been forced to admit it was true, but had been more concerned about where the tip-off had come from and what had been said than about muzzling the nosey newshound. However, there was little more Wadsworth had been able to tell him, and it was all a great mystery still.

Not, though, that this was the principal cause of Alison's lack of sleep, intriguing as it was. But it was a far more worrying concern that had kept her awake all night.

'In fact, Tina,' she said. 'You can take the pot away, too: I don't even want to look at the stuff.'

'Yes, madam.'

The maid was about to pick the tray up when there was a sudden hammering at the back door; loud enough, almost, to rattle the leaded windows.

'What the –' Alison began.

Tina went to see who it was, and a moment later Belinda charged in, flushed and excited.

'The telly,' she cried, waving a finger at the TV in the corner. 'Turn on the telly. The one o'clock news. I've just heard it on the radio on the way over here.'

'Heard what?' said Alison, pointing the remote control with little interest. 'The only news I'm bothered about is that the police have had some sort of a tip-off: they know about –'

'Shhh!' hissed Belinda. 'This is it.'

'. . . acting on an anonymous tip-off,' the silver-haired announcer was saying, 'police last night arrested the McMahon gang, believed to be responsible for at least a dozen ransom-related kidnaps in as many years . . .'

Alison looked at Belinda. 'Jesus, that's a coincidence – that's what I was trying to tell you, they –'

'Shhh!' said Belinda again. 'Look.'

Alison looked back to the TV. The screen had switched to a city street, outside the sort of pretentious building that could only have been a courthouse. It was hackneyed newsreel footage: two men being led up steps with blankets over their heads.

'Arriving at court today,' said the voice-over, 'Martin McMahon, a one-time member of the IRA, and alleged gang-member Beresford James were . . .'

Alison's mouth dropped open, and she pointed inanely at the TV. 'It's . . . It's . . .'

It was B.J. she recognised first. The blanket couldn't disguise his huge size, and the hand that was holding it over his head was as black as polished ebony. B.J. – Beresford James.

And the other man she now saw was McClusky, not McMahon as was being announced.

The screen switched back to the newsreader. 'A third member of the gang, Kelly Patricia O'Connell, is to appear in court later today, charged with aiding and abetting abduction. And now for today's weather . . .'

Alison switched it off, shaking her head in wonder.

'So who the hell tipped them off?' she said.

'Me!' squealed Belinda.

'You?' Alison's mouth was open again. 'But . . . but how?'

'You remember I told you I almost escaped that time? Well, what I forgot to tell you was that I found a telephone bill with the address on it of where we were being held. So, last night I went back there – I, er, borrowed a bit of back-up, I'm afraid . . .' She produced the Derringer from her jacket pocket and laid it on the table. 'I didn't ask, because I knew you'd try and stop me. Anyway, so I went over there. I tied them all up at gun-point, and called the police; told them the story and got the hell out.'

'My God,' said Alison, in awe at Belinda's nerve. 'But you're right; we wouldn't have let you go on such a hair-brained escapade. What on earth possessed you to go there yourself? I mean, gun or no gun, it was horribly risky. Why didn't you just go straight to the police?'

'Ah, well, that's the best bit. Did you notice there was no mention of Steve on the news?'

'Now you mention it, yes. I take it he wasn't there?'

'Ah, but he was,' said Belinda.

And Alison listened in mute fascination as Belinda told her about the deal they had struck; the signed confession that was now in Belinda's bank; the Contract of Slavery. She finished with: 'He's tied up in my wardrobe right now, with a pair of my dirty knickers stuffed in his mouth and a carriage clock tied to his balls. Awaiting my pleasure.'

'You devil, you,' muttered Alison. Admiring her friend's ingenuity in acquiring a slave for a year, though discomfitingly aware that the image she'd conjured – of a man tied up in a wardrobe, suffering pain and discomfort as he awaited a woman's pleasure – didn't give her the thrill it once would have done.

And the realisation turned her mood sour, as thoughts of her troubles returned.

It must have shown.

'You're not mad at me, are you?' said Belinda, her expression suddenly concerned. 'I mean, I know it'll all have to go public now, with a trial and all that, but – '

Alison shook her head. 'No, as I said the other day, I don't mind that so long as it serves a purpose. And now of course it will.'

'Then is it McClusky?' Belinda persisted. 'That he's been caught? I mean, I know you two had something between you.'

'Something special, yes,' said Alison truthfully. 'But based purely and solely on lust. Certainly not love – no, he deserves all he gets as far as I'm concerned. I hope he goes down for a very long time. No, it's not that at all.'

'Then what is it? I know something's the matter, Ali. So are you going to tell me or what?'

Alison stared at her hands. She muttered at last, 'I'm worried about Robert and me.'

'You and Robert?' Belinda's eyebrows rose in surprise. 'But why? You two are great.'

'But how great will we stay if the sex isn't great?' railed Alison. 'And right now, it isn't; I can't see it ever being great again. Look, we had a session last night – or at least I tried to – but I just couldn't get to feel dominant. I didn't enjoy it at all. I mean, you know the turn-on I used to get from teasing, the thrill it would give me to make a man wait. Not last night: I let him come after a quarter of an hour, just glad it was over.

'Robert tried not to show it, but I could tell he was as disappointed as hell. And who could blame him – it was hardly much of a session, was it? And the first for him in almost a month. I put my lack of interest down to my being tired; worn out by the trauma of what we've been through, you know? And he seemed to accept that, wonderful man that he is, and didn't complain. But I can't use that as an excuse for ever, can I?'

'Maybe you won't have to,' ventured Belinda. 'Maybe it wasn't an excuse, but actually the truth: that the trauma really did get to you. And when it wears off you'll be back as you were.'

'Ach! It's not something I'll get over like a dose of the 'flu, Bel. I've changed, for God's sake, and I'm terrified our marriage won't survive the new me. Now I've tasted SM as a submissive, I can't get enough of it. It's my every fantasy, my every sexual thought.'

'It wouldn't necessarily stop you from dominating Robert though, would it?' said Belinda, always the pragmatist. 'I mean, you still could.'

'Oh, yes, I could go through the physical motions all right: dominate him for his sake. And if I thought I could get away with it, I'd be quite willing to do that. But he'd be bound to see my heart wasn't in it, like last night, and where's the thrill for anyone in that? And even if I could convincingly fake it, which I doubt, what would I do for my own needs?'

'I could always dominate you,' suggested Belinda, her eyes suddenly twinkling. 'I mean, you and Robert together; satisfy the needs of you both. That's if it'd turn you on to submit to a woman, of course?'

Alison played with the thought, remembering the thrill of submitting to Kelly. 'That's not a problem,' she said, with growing interest.

'And anyway,' Belinda went on, 'it wouldn't much matter. Because if I was dominating you both together, I

could have Robert dominate you as part of his submission to me – make him put on an SM sex-show for
his Mistress's entertainment. With some suitable punishment if I judged him to be less than inventive. You'd
then be submitting to a man as well as a woman.

'I could have you reverse roles, too, and make you
dominate him. That way you could maybe enjoy it again,
because although you'd be dominating, you'd still be
submitting – to me, and having to do it on my
command.'

Picturing the potential scenario Alison felt a familiar
stirring, a warm moistening between her thighs beginning to spread upwards into her lower belly: dominating
Robert on Belinda's command, knowing she must, or
incur some punishment herself, might indeed be enough
to put her heart back in it. And reversing roles to be
dominated by Robert would certainly be thrilling. If
Robert could rise to the challenge, and with the threat of
a whipping – or no whipping! – as his incentive, there
should be no problem there. Belinda might indeed have
come up with the answer.

But then troubled thoughts came swamping back as
she recognised the practical limitations of such an
arrangement. For even if it could work, it could only be
an occasional session at best. Especially now Belinda had
a slave of her own, with whom, naturally, she would
want to spend time. No, it might make for an occasional
exciting departure, but it was hardly the abiding solution
she needed.

She shook her head. 'Thanks for offering, Bel. And yes,
I'm sure it'd be great from time to time; let's do it. But
you know Robert and me: SM is an integral part of our
lifestyle – or at least it was – with some of our sessions
lasting all day. Sometimes even longer. To be really
worthwhile, you'd have to practically move in with us!'

'Then why not look to someone who already has?' said
Belinda. 'If not me as your Mistress, why not Tina?'

'Tina?'

258

'Yes. You've talked about getting her more involved in your scene; maybe this is the perfect way. You're always saying what a minx she is; why not see if that's true? And since she lives here, who could be handier?'

Yes, thought Alison with sudden excitement. Tina! Why not? The girl had seen enough of her, Alison, dominating Robert to have a good understanding of what SM was about. And she was hardly short on confidence. Perhaps with a little tutoring she could become the ideal Mistress to control the sort of scenario Belinda had put in mind. If she could be persuaded to give it a try.

'You know, Belinda,' she said. 'You're brilliant.'

'Well, I don't know about brilliant,' said Belinda modestly. 'But if I've given you some food for thought, that's great. And talking of food for thought, I've got a few thoughts of my own – I'd best be off: there's a little something – or a big something! – waiting for me in a certain wardrobe at home.'

'Yes, and listen, Bel, you know what you've got there, don't you?' said Alison, suddenly more appreciative of Belinda's good fortune now her own problem had found at least a potential solution. 'You've got a slave as a lover, as opposed to a lover as a slave. And that's a whole different thing.'

'Oh? How so?'

'Well, think about it. In a normal SM relationship, you have your partner's limits to respect. At least, you do if you want him to play along the next time. Not so with Steve, though: he's a real slave. You can do with him just as you wish, be as extreme as you like, and there's not a thing he can do about it. He has no choice but to play along whenever you want.'

Belinda rubbed her chin, excitement pinking her cheeks. 'I hadn't actually thought about it,' she said. 'But yes, you're right. I can do absolutely anything I like to him, can't I?' She dropped a hand to the front of her

259

skirt; pressed fingertips to her pubic mound, beginning to tremble. 'Oh, God, yes.'

Alison chuckled. 'Christ, a month ago I'd have pulled my own eye-teeth to have a situation like that: it's a sadist's dream.'

'And one I can't wait to start living,' said Belinda, pushing herself to her feet.

Later that afternoon, after much rehearsing of what she would say, Alison called Tina into the lounge, her fingers crossed hard.

'Listen, Tina,' she began, 'I have a proposition to put to you.'

She waved the maid into a chair, and Tina sat down.

'As you know,' she went on, 'the master and I have unusual sexual tastes, and are into sado-masochism.'

Tina nodded and didn't blush.

'Well, I've been very impressed with your acceptance of all the things you've seen going on in this house – nothing seems to have shocked you. And for a while now I've been wondering if you might be interested in joining in more fully with what we get up to.' She studied Tina's face for a sign of reaction; she saw what might have been a gleam appear in the girl's eye and went on encouraged. 'The thing is,' she said, deciding to put all her cards on the table, 'the timing would now be perfect. You see, I've recently lost the urge to dominate. I needn't go into the reasons, but lately I'm feeling sexually submissive. Which, as you can imagine, makes life a bit difficult: with the master and I both submissive, who is there to dominate?

'Now, if we were in the control of a third party, we could be made to dominate each other, and – '

'And you want me to be that third party,' said Tina.

'Well, precisely,' said Alison, taken a little aback by Tina's forthrightness but glad she had gathered the point. 'What do you think?'

260

Tina was silent for a moment, then shook her head. 'I don't think I could, madam.'

'Oh, but I'm sure you could, Tina,' Alison protested. 'I mean, you've seen how an SM session works; the way a Mistress acts with a Slave. And to a large extent, acting is just what it is; it would just be a question of you carrying the part, as it were, and with a bit of tutoring – '

Tina was shaking her head again. 'No, that's not what I mean. I mean, yes, I'm sure I could carry the part as you say – I'm sure I could do that quite well in fact; that isn't the problem.'

'Well, is it money?' said Alison hopefully. 'I mean, obviously you would have a considerable pay increase to take full account of your, ah, additional duties – '

Once again Tina stopped her. 'No, madam. That'd be very generous, of course, but it isn't the money.'

'Oh?'

'The thing is, madam . . . If I can speak frankly?'

'Of course.'

'Then frankly, what you're asking just isn't on.'

'Well, I know it's a bit unusual, yes, but – '

'No, that isn't it,' said Tina. 'The thing is, you'd be wanting me to assume the role of Mistress, and in that role to make you and the master dominate each other, yes?'

'That would be the gist of it, yes,' Alison agreed.

'But you see, for me to be involved to that extent, and no further, would be awful. It would be so frustrating I just couldn't do it.'

'Ah,' said Alison as the penny dropped. It was Tina's hots for Robert – the very attraction she had once counted on to persuade the girl into taking a more active part in their sessions – that was now the problem. For given her lust for his body, if she were to be Mistress to him it would of course be frustrating for her in the extreme if she couldn't have him and take full advantage of her dominant role.

261

The solution, though, was a little disturbing: it would mean her, Alison, sharing her husband with another woman. And not just as she had with Belinda – on a very occasional basis, and then very much under her own control – but sharing him on a more or less permanent footing.

Still, she decided, the pros of such an arrangement would more than outweigh the cons.

'But what if you weren't restricted?' she said. 'Not only having us dominate each other, but dominating the master in your own right; have him satisfy your needs as well as mine?'

The gleam was instantly back in Tina's eye. 'You mean ... I could have him make love to me?' she said, suddenly breathless.

'Of course. As Mistress to him, you could have him do whatever you wished.'

'And ...' For the first time Tina blushed, and she averted her eyes shyly.

'Go on,' Alison pressed. 'And what?'

'And yourself, madam?' Tina was blushing furiously now. 'Could I have you make love to me, too?'

Excitement suddenly surged through Alison's loins. Just submitting to the girl's commands would have been thrilling enough, submitting to Robert with her looking on, but if Tina were AC/DC into the bargain, then that would be an unexpected and wonderful bonus.

She all but blushed herself. 'You'd be my Mistress,' she murmured throatily. 'I'd have to do whatever you said.'

'Then I'd be in total control?' Tina went on. 'Of you both? With your full authority to do whatever I wished? Could be cruel if I wanted, and punish you however I pleased?'

Jesus! thought Alison, *she's even more of a minx than I thought!*

'Well, within our limits at least, yes,' she said. 'As you know, we have the word "Mercy" as a sort of safety valve if anything's genuinely going too far. That would need to be respected of course.'

'Oh yes, I realise that, madam,' said Tina. 'But given that one limitation?'

'Absolutely. Total control.'

Tina was quiet for a moment, cogitative. Then she said, 'And who would instigate the sessions we have?'

Alison considered this, and it was an excellent point – Tina was remarkably percipient for a girl of her years. For if she were to have full authority as Mistress, then she would also need the authority to instigate sessions. One of the reasons the Mistress/Slave fantasy lived so convincingly for Alison and Robert was that it was one of their rules that she could insist on a session whenever she chose – even when Robert wasn't necessarily feeling submissive. It made her dominance over him as real as could be.

'Let's say,' she began at last, 'that we'll compromise here. If we – that is the master and I – are in the mood for a session, then we'll let you know. And as your employers we would naturally expect you to earn your salary. However, you may yourself instigate a session whenever you wish: you have only to say the word "Slave".' A *frisson* of excitement ran down her spine at the thought of ceding such unnerving control. And Robert would take some convincing, she knew. But if they were to play this game, she'd decided, then they might as well play it for real. 'How does that sound?'

'And I could do that at any time, with either of you?'

'Of course.'

Again Tina fell quiet.

And after a few moments Alison prompted her. 'Well, what do you say?'

Tina looked up. 'I say, "Slave".'

Alison laughed.

Tina didn't.

'I said "Slave",' she repeated, her expression stern.

'Stand up. There, with your hands behind your head and your legs apart.'

Alison was taken aback. But having just made the rules she could hardly go back on them at the first time of asking, and with a tremble of anticipation she pushed to her feet and stood as Tina had said.

Tina stood up and came towards her. 'The master's due home early today, isn't he, madam?'

'Yes,' said Alison. 'But, ah, I don't think "madam" is appropriate, do you? I think when you're Mistress it had better be Alison.'

'Or just Slave, eh?' grinned Tina. 'But back to the master – er, to Robert. I'll bet after almost a month without, apart from that very brief episode last night, he'll be ready for a full-blown session, wouldn't you say?'

'I would, yes. But I haven't spoken to him yet about out new arrangement: he doesn't know anything about it yet.'

'Doesn't matter,' said Tina.

And nor does it, thought Alison, shrugging it off. She could always, for now, put Robert under her own command; order him to go along with it and do as Tina told him. They could discuss Tina's full Mistress-ship later.

'What time, exactly, is Robert due home?' said Tina.

Alison glanced at the clock on the mantel. 'In about ten minutes,' she said. Then gasped as Tina reached forward, pushed up her skirt to her hips and slid a hand between her parted thighs – the caress so blatant it caught her off guard.

'Then it doesn't give us much time, does it?' said Tina. 'To get you ready for him. Although,' she added, running a finger along Alison's sex through the thin silk of her panties, 'it doesn't feel as if you need much getting ready. You're very hot and damp down here, aren't you?'

Alison blushed, and Tina repeated, 'Aren't you?' when she hadn't immediately answered.

Alison's blush grew deeper. 'Yes, mistress,' she muttered.

With a smile of knowing amusement, Tina withdrew her hand. 'Right, slave,' she said. 'Now strip, down to your oh-so-wet knickers. I'll be back in a minute.'

And as Alison began to undress, Tina ran from the room.

When she returned a minute or so later she was carrying a handful of clothes, which she dropped at Alison's feet. Alison was now naked but for her brief silk panties, her clothes thrown over the arm of a chair, and Tina pointed at the ones she had brought.

'Put them on,' she ordered.

There was a tight, shiny red top, a short black skirt, a suspender-belt and a pair of black fish-net stockings. A pair of open-toed sling-back shoes in black patent leather were a size too small, but Alison managed, just, to squeeze them onto her feet.

Finally, there was a cheap belt in shiny red plastic, but when Alison went to put it on, Tina stopped her. Stepping forward she rolled up the skirt at the waist, making it shorter still and revealing a large expanse of creamy white thigh above the tops of the stockings.

'There,' she said. 'Now you can put on the belt.' And when Alison had done so, she stood back to regard her. She smiled and said, 'And now the lady's a tramp.'

Alison almost felt it, too, knowing she looked like a Dock Road tart and wondering vaguely what Tina was doing with such a sluttish outfit in her wardrobe.

Her thoughts were soon interrupted when Tina said, 'Hands back on your head, slave. Legs wide apart,' and Castor and Pollux joined forces to turn her lower belly into a quivering mass of eroticized jelly.

Tina then came behind her, and once again reached a hand between her now trembling thighs; she gathered the crotch of Alison's panties into a silken thong and ran it into the groove of her sex, leaving her outer labia protruding each side.

265

'And now,' she said, 'we wait.'

Alison was facing the door, and two minutes later she presented a bizarre sight when Robert walked into the room.

Seeing her standing in the classic stance of sexual submission, hands behind her head, her shoulders pulled back to thrust out her breasts, their nipples poking at the cheap red top, her legs wide apart and her skirt short enough to be revealing her exposed labia, his mouth dropped open in shock.

But before he could speak, Tina said, 'Slave!' adding bemusement to the look of startled surprise on his face.

'What?' he muttered distractedly.

'I said "Slave",' said Tina, facing him square on. 'You know the word. It's the one that makes you my slave until I release you with the word Free.'

'What on earth are you babbling about, girl?' His eyes returned to Alison. 'Will you please explain to me what the hell is going on here; why you're standing like that; dressed in those . . . things.'

'I should've thought it was obvious, Bobbums.' Alison grinned. 'I'm Tina's slave. And now she's said Slave to you, you are too.'

'You . . . She . . . *What*? But this is preposterous,' Robert blustered. 'No, Alison, you're going too far now. You can do as you like, but if you think I'm going to have Tina as Mistress, then you can just think again.'

Alison decided it was time to say Slave herself; to put Robert under her domination when he would then have to do as she said. And if that was to submit to Tina, then submit to Tina he must. She opened her mouth to give the command.

But Tina stopped her. 'Do you have permission to speak, slave?'

'Er, no, mistress. But – '

'Then, don't.' Her eyes were still holding Robert's. 'I suggest you do as I say, Robert. You see, I still have a certain Polaroid of you . . . Yes, I can see by your face

266

you'd forgotten about that. But I'm sure you won't have forgotten the extremely degrading position you were in at the time it was taken; very embarrassing for you, eh, if the photo were to fall into the wrong hands.' She tutted and gave a slow shake of her head. 'Pillar of the local community into sordid sex games? Very embarrassing, I'd say.'

Robert had turned pale, and Alison couldn't help but chuckle. Well, the crafty imp, she thought; she didn't need Alison's help at all in putting Robert under her thumb. She had done it all by herself.

'I think you'd better do as she says, Robert,' she gurgled. 'Don't you?' Remembering she shouldn't be speaking she added, 'Oh, sorry, mistress,' when Tina flashed her a look.

Tina turned back to Robert. 'Now, slave, are you going to do as I say?'

Robert shuffled his feet and didn't speak, seemingly lost for words; his air of defeat almost tangible.

'I'll take your silence as a tacit yes,' said Tina, pressing her advantage home. 'So, go on up to the playroom and strip naked. I'll be up to you shortly.'

Robert looked to Alison, as if hoping for some sort of reprieve, but saw only a glint of amusement in Alison's eyes and knew, with her connivance to back Tina up, he had little choice but to do as the girl said. His cheeks glowing scarlet, he meekly left the room.

'Oh, well done, Tina ... er, mistress,' said Alison, genuinely impressed by the maid's composure and the way she had handled Robert's recalcitrance. Tutoring? she thought wryly. She would hardly need much of that; she seemed to have things well enough in control as it was.

Tina waited a minute, giving Robert enough time to undress, then telling Alison to stay as she was she followed him up to the playroom.

Some ten minutes later she was back, to find Alison just as she'd left her.

'Right,' she said, reaching a hand between Alison's legs to caress her exposed vulva. 'He's tied up on the bed and can now wait for a while. While you, slave, can go fetch a bottle of Krug.'

And as Alison enthused, 'Oh, yes, mistress,' and headed for the kitchen all but tasting the sparkling nectar already, Tina added, 'One glass will suffice, by the way. You won't be needing one!'

Tina pushed open the playroom door and ushered Alison in.

Robert was naked and tied on the bed, just as Tina had said. He was not, though, in the expected spread-eagle position: his wrists were tied to the bed-rail all right, but his ankles weren't bound to the foot of the bed. Instead, his heels were drawn up to his buttocks, with cords lashing his ankles to his upper thighs to keep his legs bent double, and with his knees tied almost flat to the bed splaying them wide apart.

And once again Alison admired Tina's style. For no position could have left a man more humiliatingly exposed, his engorged genitals on more obscene and open display. Moreover, there was a large cushion pushed under his buttocks, making his lower body still more accessible, and making visible the end of a vibrator that was protruding from his anus. It was only a small, slim vibrator, one of the smallest in Alison's collection, but still, its very presence – the presence of anything lodged in his rectum – would be enough to have Robert squirming inside. And there was no doubt it was a combination of all these factors that was responsible for his massive erection.

Alison smiled to herself. For his erection was a sure sign that, whether he liked it or not, having Tina as Mistress was very much turning him on; it augured well for the future.

Tina climbed up on the foot of the bed and reached for Robert's testicles; she gripped them firmly and made

Robert grunt when she bore down on them to bring his penis upright away from his belly.

She turned to Alison. 'Come here and suck him,' she said.

Alison went to the bed and sat down on the edge; she leaned over to take Robert's penis into her mouth. Robert moaned softly at the feel of her lips on his shaft, at the heat of her tongue on his swollen glans as it found the most sensitive parts of his cock.

Tina let her go on for a while, then pushed her away.

'That'll be enough,' she said. 'Now you've made him nice and slick for me, I want to feel him inside me. But fetch the ball-beater – I don't want him coming while I fuck him; you're to see that he doesn't.'

Alison went over to one of the drawers, pulled it open and found the ball-beater amongst a variety of items for genital torture she had collected over the years – though the ball-beater, simple that it was, was as effective as any. A small ball of hard rubber on the end of a six-inch stick, it looked not unlike one of Kojak's lollipops. But its innocent look was deceptive, for it could cause exquisite pain with the minimum of effort.

Returning to the bed with it, she found Tina almost ready. She was kneeling astride Robert's torso and was in the process of shuffling backwards, sliding her heels beneath his thighs to inch herself into position.

'Get onto the bed behind me, slave,' she told Alison, hitching her skirt to her waist. 'And hold his cock for me so I can lower myself onto it. As soon as I have, you're to start on his balls – not viciously hard, but hard enough to prevent him from coming.'

Alison followed Tina's instructions, holding Robert's cock and watching in envy as the girl's pussy slowly engulfed it; there was something poignant – a subtlety Tina had clearly not missed – in a wife having to guide her husband's penis, by her own hand, into the sex of another woman!

Yet the innate humiliation of it served only to further

excite her, and as Tina began to ride him, she thought: *Who loves ya, baby*, and flicked the beater at Robert's balls, ready to keep him from coming and so allow the girl to enjoy her husband for as long a time as she wished. Heard Robert grunt in sudden pain and watched his testicles jerk in their sac, trying to protect themselves by withdrawing into his body, but in vain, as Alison settled into an erratic rhythm.

Downstairs, she had looked on in longing while Tina had sipped champagne, dying for a glass herself. But it was as nothing compared with the longing she felt now, watching Tina, with equal relish, enjoying Robert's body. She wasn't feeling the thrill she once would have felt at causing Robert pain, but there was plenty to excite her besides: the sight of Robert's long penis glistening each time Tina's pussy rode up its shaft and the sound of Tina's moans of pleasure and Robert's of pleasure-pain. She revelled in the ache of her own deprivation.

At last, however, Tina's thighs began to tremble, and her ecstatic moans grew louder. And Alison beat Robert's balls with a little more strength, knowing Tina was about to come: knowing he would need the additional pain to keep him preoccupied when her vagina contracted, clenching his shaft in orgasmic spasm.

It wasn't a moment too soon. For Tina suddenly bore down, grinding herself frantically onto Robert's cock. She arched her spine and threw back her head, and her body went suddenly rigid. And with a long sibilant hiss of release, she came. Robert didn't.

After a while Tina recovered and lifted herself carefully from Robert's penis, it springing free to slap at his belly with a wet smack, hard and ungratified. Swinging round, she reached down between Robert's legs and brought a muffled grunt to his throat as she slipped the vibrator out of his bottom.

'That's for being a good Slave and not coming,' she said, discarding the plastic toy, then turned to Alison.

'You untie his legs, while I take care of his wrists – it's time he was put to more active use.'

A minute later Robert was free, wincing as he straightened his legs; he looked unsure about whether or not he should close them, and in the end left them apart, his swollen genitals on humiliating display.

Tina smiled. 'Right decision, slave,' she purred.

But she didn't leave him to lie there for long. Sitting on the edge of the bed, she said, 'Come here and stand in front of me, now.' Then, to Alison, 'And you stand up, too. Just there.'

Alison rolled off the bed and stood where Tina was pointing. She watched Robert stand nervously before his new Mistress, his penis still glistening with her sexual juices.

Tina reached a hand to it, stroking its shaft while she spoke. 'Now, slave,' she began. 'In a moment you're going to screw Alison. Except she isn't Alison, is she? Look at her; how she's dressed. She's a tramp, a slut, a twopenny tart. So, you're going to treat her as such: ravish her as a cheap slut deserves.'

Alison swallowed hard and felt a blush go down to her neck. Even in fantasy, playing the game they were, it felt oddly humiliating to be described in such terms.

'You're going to take her by force,' Tina was saying, still fondling Robert's penis. 'To pleasure yourself in her body, and use her as the cheap whore she is. Just what you do with her is up to you, and you can even come if you want to. But, on that point, be warned: it won't be the end of the session. Not by a long way: I'm feeling very horny tonight, and it'll take a long session before I'll be fully satisfied. More than that, though, I'm feeling extremely kinky too. So if you find it distasteful to have to do kinky things in the wake of orgasm, then you'd better bear that in mind, hadn't you? Don't say you weren't warned.

'Oh, and just one other thing: if you fail to treat the slut with anything less than utter contempt, you'll be very sorry indeed. It amuses me to think of an up-market woman reduced to common tart; it's a favourite fantasy of mine, so you'd better make it look real. Or else.'

Alison began to tremble, aching with anticipation and erotic tension. Robert treating her with contempt? That would be different. As Slave, naturally, he had always to treat her with the utmost respect. But even during ordinary, non-SM sex he was only ever the tenderest, most respectful of lovers. And the thought of him being otherwise was strangely thrilling. Apart from whatever else, it would be like having sex with a perfect stranger!

If this was a foretaste of things to come, she mused, then having Tina in charge of their sessions, ordering Robert to dominate her, was going to be more exciting, it seemed, than she had even imagined.

Tina gave Robert's penis a none-too-gentle slap, making it sway in a bobbing arc, and said, 'Right, slave, begin.'

Even expecting it, Robert's assault took Alison aback.

'Come here, whore,' he snapped, reaching out and grabbing her shoulder.

He spun her to face him and forced her down on her knees.

'Suck my cock,' he told her, thrusting his penis into her face.

Alison took it into her mouth, smelling and tasting Tina's sex.

'Suck it clean, you whore,' said Robert, his hands entwined in her hair and giving her no other choice.

'Oh good,' said Tina. 'Yes, I like that. Suck it clean, you whore. Yes, very good.' She was clearly enjoying the show.

And Robert was certainly playing the part, thought Alison, as the thrill of it surged through her loins. She had sucked his penis hundreds of times, but never before had it felt humiliating. Yet this, forced to suck the penis of this man she didn't know – this total stranger – even if it hadn't been coated with Tina's feminine juices, felt humiliating in the extreme. Degrading, even. And very, very exciting!

The next moment, however, Robert had pulled his penis out of her mouth and was hauling her up to her feet, throwing her, face down, on the bed; was rucking her skirt up, and forcing her legs apart, kneeling between them to keep them apart. He tore the silk of her panties as he ripped them from her without the bother of taking them down, and his knees forced her thighs still wider apart as his weight came forward above her; wide, wide apart. And then his hand was between her legs, guiding the head of his penis. Guiding it not to where she expected it to, but to her anus!

'Robert!' she squealed, struggling as she felt the swollen knob butt her rear opening. 'What are you doing?'

Robert knew anal intercourse was about her one and only taboo, that it was something she never permitted. He couldn't have known she had recently afforded that privilege to another man and had thoroughly enjoyed the experience. But that man wasn't her husband, whom she would have to face when the session was over and they were Alison and Robert once more; back in the real world!

She threw a hand behind her, trying to push him away, trying to reach for her bottom to prevent the forbidden intrusion. But Robert grabbed her wrist in his powerful grip and held it to the small of her back, his weight there keeping her lower body pinned down to the bed and making her struggles useless. Her other arm was trapped beneath her, and as she felt the head of his penis beginning to prod, there was nothing she could do but blush. And hope he wouldn't stop now!

She heard Robert say, 'Keep still, you whore.'

Then Tina's voice, high with excitement: 'Yes, that's it; give it the slut in the arse,' egging him on.

Alison squirmed, just as Robert lunged forward.

There was a sharp flash of pain as the head of his cock breached her sphincter, then only the feel of it sliding inside her; filling her rectum with throbbing heat. And with bated breath she waited for the thrusting to start.

But it didn't start: having driven himself in to the hilt, Robert was suddenly still. Perfectly still. And sensing his tension Alison knew why. For it was the tension she could always feel in him when he was right on the edge of orgasm, and she knew he was engaged in a desperate struggle: so excited by entering her forbidden passage – a passage he believed to be virgin – it had taken him right to the brink. And he was trying hard not to move until the crisis had passed, when he could begin to thrust without making himself come.

For if he came he would then have to face the continuing session, and whatever kinkiness Tina might have in mind, without the protection of his sexual need, his masochism at a low ebb.

Well, Alison decided, that was his problem not hers; she wanted his onslaught now. And clenching her inner muscles, she gripped and released his straining shaft three times in rapid succession, pumping him into submission.

Three times was enough. For Robert let out a long wailing groan, the groan of defeat, and unable to help himself he began suddenly to thrust; short, urgent, frenetic thrusts that almost instantly triggered his climax. The throb of it triggered her own, and they came together in a mutual orgasm that left her still shaking when Robert collapsed on her back, both of them panting and drained.

Robert didn't move for a while, but finally withdrew his softening member and rolled from Alison's back.

Alison went to move too, intending to roll over and sit up, but Tina stopped her.

'Stay just as you are, slave,' she commanded. 'And you, Robert; don't think you can relax. You have a job to do now. Sit up.'

Alison felt Tina lean over and spread the cheeks of her

bottom; she cringed as she felt a dribble of semen trickle across her perineum.

'Look,' said Tina to Robert. Then after a moment: 'Well? What are you waiting for, slave? I shouldn't need to tell you what you have to do now: it's what a slave's tongue's for. Do it.'

Alison heard Robert groan. But as she felt his face come down to her bottom, felt him begin tonguing her ravaged anus, a surge of excitement tingled her spine. For if Robert would submit to Tina now, immediately following climax when his brain wasn't ruled by his cock – and in such a dreadful and testing manner, too – then the new arrangement, with Tina as Mistress, was going to be an undoubted success.

Her problem had found a permanent, and very exciting, solution.

Chapter Twenty-two

*B*elinda was sitting in a comfortable armchair, scribbling furiously into an A4 pad. Her feet were up on a tabouret, and Steve was kneeling beside it – sucking her toes while she worked.

Life for both women had changed considerably in the wake of their kidnap six months before, but the episode's greatest impact, by far, had been on Belinda's. No longer was she a penniless writer struggling to sell her work: it was now in great demand. For although the trial had been relatively short – the case against the McMahon gang had been too overwhelming to have given them much to defend – it had kept her in the public eye for long enough to have won her a certain celebrity. And it had done her bank account no harm at all: as well as the huge sum the tabloids had paid for her story, and her earnings from articles that the glossies were now screaming out for, a well-known publisher had advanced her a five-figure sum for the novel she was currently writing – *The Wrong Place, The Wrong Time*.

And with the coming of financial success, life was materially more comfortable. Long gone was her tiny one-bedroomed flat, and home for Belinda was now a roomy cottage set in an acre of woodland; a gleaming

Renault had replaced her battered Mini and her chest-nut colt, Captain, grazed in a nearby field. Changes indeed.

Though none more welcome than having Steve as her slave.

For one thing, having a slave had been extremely useful in getting her new home into shape. There had been an Indian summer that year and she had put him to work in the garden, which had been somewhat overgrown. The cottage's seclusion had meant she could have him work naked, and she had spent many a pleasant afternoon sunning herself on the lawn, sipping iced tea while ogling his tanned, muscular body, bathed in sweat as he toiled. Sweating not least when he'd cut back the several patches of nettles that had grown high along the borders!

And nor had she made the work easy for him. Even now she could smile, thinking back, to watching him mowing the lawn with lengths of elastic noosed round his testicles, these tied off to his feet – the elastic long enough, just, to allow him to stand, but only by putting a painful strain on his balls. It had been fun to watch his dilemma; one minute following the mower in an ungainly crouch, keeping the elastic slack, the next forced to straighten when the strain on his thighs grew too much to bear, only to then wince as the elastic stretched tight to pull sharply down on his balls; each step behind the mower a lesson in testicular pain. His look of relief when the lawn was finished was plain to see ... unless she made him do it again because the stripes were not running in a direction that pleased her!

With the decline of the weather she had moved him indoors where she'd had him redecorating the cottage throughout. Again she had not made the work easy – he was there to pay for his wrongdoing and she fully intended to see that he did – and at the risk of his producing less than perfect results (after all, she could

277

always have him redo a job if it failed to come up to her high expectations), she could usually think of some bizarre or painful impediment to make his efforts all the more interesting to watch.

Aside from his suffering though, and her pleasure in watching it, the practical benefit was that the cottage had soon been restored to its one-time best. And with a slave to do all the work, at a fraction of what it would otherwise have cost.

As slave, however, he wasn't only a cheap source of labour, there to do chores: he was first and foremost her sex-slave – there for her sexual pleasure and the gratification of her sadistic desires.

And in this regard, they had fallen into a daily routine. Each morning, after waking her with breakfast in bed, he would report to the bathroom to wait for her, when his day would begin with an enema. Ordinarily this would be a no-fuss affair, administered as a clinical wash-out simply to allow the more hygienic use throughout the day of the vibrators and dildos that were a regular part of his 'training'.

But woe betide him if he had displeased her in some way, for then his morning enema would not be so simple. To administer a punishment enema she would roll his legs back over his head, making him support his hips with his hands, and run into him two litres of warm, soapy water, which he would then have to retain at her pleasure whilst holding the awkward, and potentially disastrous, position. If she was feeling merciful she would insert a butt-plug to help him. If she wasn't, she wouldn't! And would instead watch amused as his look of dread would gradually worsen – watch his thighs begin to tremble with the onset of internal discomfort; his face contort with horror lest his sphincter should fail him as the cramps grew worse – before finally relenting and letting him up on the toilet. Privacy, of course, was a privilege denied – privacy of any kind, ever – and even following a normal enema the red of his face as he expelled the water, with her standing there watching, would never fail to delight her.

The routine would then vary from day to day, depending on what household jobs would need to be done, how kinky Belinda was feeling, or how horny. Or, often the most pressing consideration, how far behind she was with the book. For having to write placed a necessary, if irksome demand on her time, restricting her pursuance of pleasure. Though even at her busiest Steve's torment, as befitted a slave, was unremitting. There were many ways of seeing to this when time was at a premium, but one of the more amusing of these was the nettle game . . .

Using ring-bolts she'd had set in her study wall, Steve would be tied in an upright spreadeagle position and aroused to full erection. A freshly cut nettle, attached to an adjustable wire, would then be placed in such a way that as his erection began to subside it would bring his penis into eventual and inevitable contact. Belinda had come up with the idea after reading how the ancient Romans had used urtrification, or stinging with nettles, as a cure for impotence. And it was certainly an effective stimulant, for each time Steve's softening cock drooped onto the nettle it would jerk with the sting and instantly re-erect. And thus he could suffer for as long as she left him with the minimum of effort from her, his torment – unrelieved arousal punctuated by a jolt of sudden pain whenever it began to abate – continuing unchecked while she got on with her writing.

And an erect penis, kept hard and yearning, was an inspiring sight whenever she glanced up from her work!

Toe-sucking, of course, was another means of effortless domination: keeping her slave thoroughly subjugated, reminded of his lowly position, while for her it was intrinsically pleasant without being overly distracting.

Though after an hour, now, it was distracting enough, and finishing a chapter she laid her pad aside beginning to feel pleasantly sexy, the feel of his tongue swirling between her toes erotically stimulating.

That was when the telephone rang.

She reached for the receiver and said, 'Yes?' dreamily into the mouthpiece.

'Hi, Bel, it's me.'

'Alison, hi. How are you doing?'

'Just fine. You?'

'Never better. The book's coming along pretty well, really, given the distractions; I'd say I'm just about on schedule for once.'

Alison chuckled. 'I take it by distractions you mean Steve?'

'What else? Keeping him naked the whole time does have its disadvantages, I'm afraid: it's just so tempting to keep putting the book aside and using his gorgeous body as an excuse not to work. In fact, that's just what I'd done when you rang.'

'Why, what have you got him doing? Something exciting?'

'Oh, he's just sucking my toes at the moment. But it's beginning to turn me on, yes. And I was just thinking I could do with his tongue somewhere else.' Her tone became wry. 'For the umpteenth time today, I might add.'

'Lucky you.'

'Oh crikey, yeah. I'm not complaining. Doesn't get books written though, does it? ... Anyway, how's your own love-life? Still going well with Tina as Mistress?'

'I'll say. God, she's a bitch. Worse than I ever was as a dominant, I'll swear.'

Belinda's ears pricked up. 'Oh?' she said, always keen to hear about another dominant's methods. 'Why, what's she been up to?'

'Well, for one thing, at the end of our last session she sucked Robert off, then, without swallowing, she French-kissed him; made him take the lot, the poor dear. I mean, you know how Robert is about swallowing his own come – that's why I used only to threaten it. But Tina?

280

Jesus, not a qualm. And making him take it from her own mouth too; something decidedly kinky about that.'

'Mmmm,' mused Belinda; yes, there was. Sudden arousal flared in her loins at the thought of it – and of doing just that with Steve the next time she allowed him to come. 'Yes, I like that,' she said.

She snapped her fingers for Steve's attention, and lifting her foot from the tabouret she draped her leg over the arm of the chair. She hitched her skirt to just below her crotch, and beckoned Steve to come forward, urgently needing his tongue.

'Tell me more,' she said, and couldn't help the catch in her voice as Steve's tongue found her clitoris.

Alison chuckled. 'Do I get three guesses?'

'You don't need them,' grinned Belinda, knowing she had sounded like Jane Birkin towards the end of 'Je T'aime'. 'Now come on, tell me more. What else is Tina getting up to these days?'

'Well, instead of me telling you, Bel, why don't you come see for yourself? That's why I'm ringing: it's ages since we've had a session together, and I was wondering if you'd fancy bringing Steve over on Saturday night.'

'Oh, excellent, yes,' Belinda enthused. They'd had several joint sessions over the months, with herself and Tina dominating the other three, and they had all been a great success. Especially as the Corsairs' playroom now sported a new piece of equipment: an extremely versatile bondage bench that Robert, with the aid of a funny handshake and a generous donation to the Police Widows' Fund, had acquired from a certain black-and-gold bedroom!

Besides, given their history, there was something uniquely sweet in dominating Alison Corsair! 'Yes, that'd be great. What time?'

'Eight?'

'We'll see you at eight then. Burma.'

'Burma?'

'Yes. Didn't you ever write it on love notes with SWALK and the rest? Burma – Be Undressed And Ready My Angel.'

Alison chuckled. 'Is that an order, mistress?'

'Unless Mistress Tina has a better idea.'

'Yes, mistress,' said Alison, still chuckling when she hung up the phone.

Belinda put down the receiver, and felt rather than heard the little whimper of pain that escaped from Steve's lips; she knew the excitement of servicing her was causing his cock to respond – it always did – and that locked into the chastity ring as it was, arousal was a painful experience.

She smiled to herself as she pushed his head from between her thighs. 'Come and stand here, slave, where I can look at you.'

Steve stood up and came to the side of her chair, and she regarded his penis with a slow shake of her head.

'When will you ever learn, eh?' she taunted. 'You know it only hurts when you let your cock begin to get hard like that.'

His penis was partially erect but prevented from hardening further by the tight metal ring encircling its base; this was held in place by slender chains that passed round his balls to be locked at the front of his scrotum with a miniature padlock. Apart from being aesthetically pleasing it was a supremely effective chastity device, for the metal ring had tiny studs on its inner surface that bit painfully into the cock's shaft at the first sign of hardening. It obviated vigilance in ensuring he didn't masturbate, since any attempt to do so would result in unbearable agony long before he could possibly reach climax; assuming he could climax anyway with a cock that physically couldn't erect.

The device was a boon. For before she'd acquired it, it had been necessary to tie him to his bed at night when the temptation to masturbate, after a day of stimulation without relief, might have been too much for him to

282

resist. So her own sleep wasn't disturbed if he needed to urinate during the night, it had meant taping a plastic tube in place on his penis, running down to a bucket by the side of the bed. Now such crudities were a thing of the past, for the device could only be removed with a key she kept on a gold chain round her neck, and while it permitted him normal bathroom functions, his sexual relief was entirely in her control.

'Anyway, I've some good news for you,' she said, reaching a hand to his penis.

Steve winced as she lifted his cock on her forefinger, stimulating the sensitive frenum.

'Yes, that was Alison on the phone just now. And she's invited us over for a session on Saturday ... with Mistress Tina. You like Mistress Tina, don't you, slave? She turns you on, doesn't she?'

She drew his foreskin back and forth while she spoke, her touch light and sensual. And Steve gave out an agonised grunt as his penis responded, trying to erect despite the cruel metal ring.

'You didn't answer me, slave,' Belinda persisted. 'I said, Mistress Tina turns you on, doesn't she?'

'Yes, mistress,' gasped Steve, his thighs beginning to shake as the pain grew worse.

'Yes,' Belinda purred, her voice soft and husky. 'She's pretty, isn't she? And about your own age, too. Can you picture her now, dressed in one of those sexy outfits of hers, her breasts all but showing?'

Steve's groans became constant, and he seemed to be trying to shrink his groin from her teasing fingers without actually daring to move.

'And she gets kinky with you, doesn't she?' Belinda went on. 'Which turns you on all the more. And she's going to do all sorts of things to you on Saturday night ...'

She paused to let his imagination run wild, then continued, 'But not only kinky things. Other things too ...' – she gave his penis a squeeze – 'like sucking this for

283

you. Or making Slave Alison suck it. Or even, who knows, Slave Robert . . .'

She chuckled at the look of sudden horror that swept over Steve's face, and went quickly on, 'You know, she might even want to fuck you. That'd be a treat for you, wouldn't it? Unless I forgot the key to your padlock, of course. Oh dear, what a shame that'd be; her wanting your dick and you not able to give it her. But I'm not very likely to do that. So just think, eh, fucking Mistress Tina . . .'

It was too much for Steve. 'Oh, mistress, don't. Please, I beg you: it's hurting like hell. Please stop.'

His hands were hovering by his sides, as if he were daring himself to push Belinda's away. But Belinda flashed him a warning look and watched him keep them still; she kept up her sensual teasing, sliding his foreskin back and forth.

'Oh please, mistress,' he gasped. 'No more, I beg you.'

'What?' said Belinda, her expression innocent. 'I'm only toying with your cock. And after all, it is mine to do as I like with, isn't it?'

'Yes . . . mistress . . .' grunted Steve.

'Yes, so stop with the whining, then.'

But she had already decided he had suffered enough. Besides, she was hankering to see his magnificent cock as it should be; hard and throbbing and yearning for sex. And leaning forward she slipped the key on her neck-chain into the tiny gold padlock, drew the metal ring from his penis with considerable care and resumed her sensual fondling. It was five days since she had last let him come – five days of erotic stimulation of one sort or another; five days of serving her sexually, both orally and with his cock; five days of near-constant arousal – and within just a few seconds he was standing fully erect, his swollen organ seeming ready to burst.

She began to wank him in earnest, running her hand the length of his shaft. 'Do you want to come, slave?' she said.

Instant hope appeared in Steve's eyes. 'Oh yes, mistress,' he gasped. 'Very much, mistress.'

'Then I think I should let you.' She quickened her hand, watching Steve's body swell with relief as he tensed in anticipation of climax – before she released his penis and gave it a sharp slap, adding, 'On Saturday.'

She chuckled at Steve's devastation, at his utter dismay, having deliberately allowed him to mistake what she'd meant; to build up his hopes only to so thoroughly dash them.

She was more than merely amused, however: the cruelty of what she had done had touched a sadistic nerve, causing arousal to flare in her loins and reminding her of her own need to come. 'And now,' she said, 'you're not coming, but I sure as hell need to; time to finish what you began. Tongue, slave.'

She settled herself comfortably while Steve went to kneel between her spread thighs, watching him lean forward, extending his tongue.

As he began she switched her eyes to the wall, where a picture frame held pride of place above an antique open fireplace. It was her favourite wall-decoration – a framed and mounted telephone bill!

'God, McClusky,' she breathed. 'Do I owe you, or what?'

She felt Steve's tongue sweep her into the amorphous arms of ecstasy, and heard herself whisper, 'Oh crikey, yeah,' in reply.

Visit the Black Lace website at
www.blacklace-books.co.uk

LOOK OUT FOR THE ALL-NEW BLACK LACE BOOKS – AVAILABLE NOW!

All books priced £7.99 in the UK. Please note publication dates apply to the UK only. For other territories, please contact your retailer.

CAT SCRATCH FEVER
Sophie Mouette
ISBN 0 352 34021 5

Creditors breathing down her neck. Crazy board members. A make-or-break benefit that's far behind schedule. Felicia DuBois, development coordinator at the Southern California Cat Sanctuary, has problems – including a bad case of the empty-bed blues. Then sexy Gabe Sullivan walks into the Sanctuary and sets her body tingling. Felicia's tempted to dive into bed with him . . . except it could mean she'd be sleeping with the enemy. Gabe's from the Zoological Association, a watchdog organisation that could decide to close the cash-strapped cat facility. Soon Gabe and Felicia are acting like cats in heat, but someone's sabotaging the benefit. Could it be Gabe? Or maybe it's the bad-boy volunteer, the delicious caterer, or the board member with a penchant for leather? Throw in a handsome veterinarian and a pixieish female animal handler who likes handling Felicia, and everyone ought to be purring. But if Felicia can't find the saboteur, the Sanctuary's future will be as endangered as the felines it houses.

Coming in April

ENTERTAINING MR STONE
Portia da Costa
ISBN O 352 34029 O

When reforming bad girl Maria Lewis takes a drone job in local
government back in her home town, the quiet life she was looking for is
quickly disrupted by the enigmatic presence of her boss, Borough
Director, Robert Stone. A dangerous and unlikely object of lust, Stone
touches something deep in Maria's sensual psyche and attunes her to
the erotic underworld that parallels life in the dusty offices of Borough
Hall. But the charismatic Mr Stone isn't the only one interested in Maria
– knowing lesbian Mel and cute young techno geek Greg both have
designs on the newcomer, as does Human Resources Manager William
Youngblood, who wants to prize the Borough's latest employee away
from the arch-rival for whom he has ambiguous feelings.

DANGEROUS CONSEQUENCES
Pamela Rochford
ISBN O 352 33185 2

When Rachel Kemp is in danger of losing her job at a London university,
visiting academic Luke Holloway takes her for a sybaritic weekend in the
country to cheer her up. Her encounters with Luke and his enigmatic
friend Max open up a world of sensual possibilities and she is even
offered a new job editing a sexually explicit Victorian diary. Life is
looking good until Rachel returns to London, and, accused of smuggling
papers out of the country, is sacked on the spot. In the meantime, Luke
disappears and Rachel is left wondering about the connection between
these elusive academics, their friends and the missing papers. When she
tries to clear her name, she discovers her actions have dangerous – and
highly erotic – consequences.

Black Lace Booklist

Information is correct at time of printing. To avoid disappointment, check availability before ordering. Go to www.blacklace-books.co.uk. All books are priced £6.99 unless another price is given.

BLACK LACE BOOKS WITH A CONTEMPORARY SETTING

☐ ON THE EDGE Laura Hamilton	ISBN 0 352 33534 3	£5.99
☐ THE TRANSFORMATION Natasha Rostova	ISBN 0 352 33311 1	
☐ SIN.NET Helena Ravenscroft	ISBN 0 352 33598 X	
☐ TWO WEEKS IN TANGIER Annabel Lee	ISBN 0 352 33599 8	
☐ SYMPHONY X Jasmine Stone	ISBN 0 352 33629 3	
☐ A SECRET PLACE Ella Broussard	ISBN 0 352 33307 3	
☐ GOING TOO FAR Laura Hamilton	ISBN 0 352 33657 9	
☐ RELEASE ME Suki Cunningham	ISBN 0 352 33671 4	
☐ SLAVE TO SUCCESS Kimberley Raines	ISBN 0 352 33687 0	
☐ SHADOWPLAY Portia Da Costa	ISBN 0 352 33313 8	
☐ ARIA APASSIONATA Julie Hastings	ISBN 0 352 33056 2	
☐ A MULTITUDE OF SINS Kit Mason	ISBN 0 352 33737 0	
☐ COMING ROUND THE MOUNTAIN Tabitha Flyte	ISBN 0 352 33873 3	
☐ FEMININE WILES Karina Moore	ISBN 0 352 33235 2	
☐ MIXED SIGNALS Anna Clare	ISBN 0 352 33889 X	
☐ BLACK LIPSTICK KISSES Monica Belle	ISBN 0 352 33885 7	
☐ GOING DEEP Kimberly Dean	ISBN 0 352 33876 8	
☐ PACKING HEAT Karina Moore	ISBN 0 352 33356 1	
☐ MIXED DOUBLES Zoe le Verdier	ISBN 0 352 33312 X	
☐ UP TO NO GOOD Karen S. Smith	ISBN 0 352 33589 0	
☐ CLUB CRÈME Primula Bond	ISBN 0 352 33907 1	
☐ BONDED Fleur Reynolds	ISBN 0 352 33192 5	
☐ SWITCHING HANDS Alaine Hood	ISBN 0 352 33896 2	
☐ EDEN'S FLESH Robyn Russell	ISBN 0 352 33923 3	
☐ PEEP SHOW Mathilde Madden	ISBN 0 352 33924 1	£7.99
☐ RISKY BUSINESS Lisette Allen	ISBN 0 352 33280 8	£7.99
☐ CAMPAIGN HEAT Gabrielle Marcola	ISBN 0 352 33941 1	£7.99
☐ MS BEHAVIOUR Mini Lee	ISBN 0 352 33962 4	£7.99

BLACK LACE NON-FICTION

To find out the latest information about Black Lace titles, check out the website: www.blacklace-books.co.uk or send for a booklist with complete synopses by writing to:

Black Lace Booklist, Virgin Books Ltd
Thames Wharf Studios
Rainville Road
London W6 9HA

Please include an SAE of decent size. Please note only British stamps are valid.

Our privacy policy
We will not disclose information you supply us to any other parties. We will not disclose any information which identifies you personally to any person without your express consent.

From time to time we may send out information about Black Lace books and special offers. Please tick here if you do not wish to receive Black Lace information. ❑